D1491783

10 r

SALLY

Freya North holds a Masters Degree in History of Art from the Courtauld Institute. She has worked for the National Art Collections Fund as well as for a commercial sculpture garden and has freelanced as a picture researcher. *Sally* is her first novel.

FREYA NORTH

Sally

HEINEMANN : LONDON

First published in Great Britain 1996
by William Heinemann
an imprint of Reed International Books Ltd
Michelin House, 81 Fulham Road, London SW3 6RB
and Auckland, Melbourne, Singapore and Toronto

Lines for 'Wish You Were Here'
Lyrics by Roger Waters
© 1975 Pink Floyd Music Publishers Limited

A CIP catalogue record for this title
is available from the British Library
ISBN 0 434 00388 3

Sally is a work of fiction. Any resemblance
to actual events or persons, living or dead,
is entirely coincidental.

Typeset by Deltatype Ltd in Melior 11.5pt
Printed and bound in Great Britain
by Clays Ltd, St Ives plc

For BJP

PROLOGUE

*S*he lay there, in a small heaven of sorts.

This is the definitive rampant fling.

She grinned widely, partly because her clitoris was being rubbed, partly because she suddenly envisaged her actions set down in type, immortalized, in a racy best-seller. *I could sell these details to Jackie Collins*, she thought, as her right nipple was being nibbled and her left was being kneaded. *This kind of thing is right up her street.*

Yes, nibbled nipples had a certain titillating ring to it (titillating, oh very droll), but would also look good on the printed page. In her mind's eye, she inverted the 'b' and played with the 'p':

bb

pp

ni*bb*led

ni*pp*les

and thought that Jackie C would really rather like them. So, while he left her nipples to traverse her body, she penned a few thoughts.

Dear Ms Collins, this is what happened. No, this is what's

1

happening: I'm lying on my back with my legs wrapped around the back of a most glorious superstud, his 'throbbing manhood', his 'enormous dick', his 'stupendous cock' is surging into me. My neck is thrown back and is being licked greedily. This man on top of me has the physique of a Rodin sculpture, Ms Collins, a Rodin sculpture with an insatiable sexual appetite.

I am grabbing on to a pair of buttocks so firm, so exquisitely honed, that it is only their warmth and a slight fuzz of hair which persuade me they are real and not perfectly hewn marble. We've been going at it, this fast-motion super-bonking, for the best part of two hours, so you see real people really can keep it up (literally).

Hello hello, I am now being flipped over and I am on top, in the driving seat. I am grinding down on him, now I am lifting myself off. Plunge, lunge, down I go again. I think I'll sit upright and throw my head back alluringly – just in case he can see me through those eyes glazed with near-fulfilled desire. He is surging, make that 'pumping'. He is abandoned to the sensation. And do you know what? I am doing this, I am making him feel this way. He is putty in my hands, but he is hard as a rock inside. A 'rock-cock' – now there's a jaunty little phrase for you, Ms C. Oh, up he sits, a moment's tenderness too. Kisses are slower, more lip, less tongue. He's actually rather nice, sweet and gentle, but tonight I want wild and rampant. So, here I go, pushing him down, covering him again. Forget in-out, I'm rotating fluidly and what a pelvis I have! Ten years of ballet had its merits after all. Our legs are so entwined, so taut, that cramp threatens in my left thigh, but a potentially mammoth orgasm is very much on the horizon. Here it comes. Here I come. More more more.

Yes.

Jesus.

Oh!

Pure bestseller material, that'll be me. I'll give your

*previous heroines a run for their money. I'm coming to your
rescue, Jackie. Oh!*

As the regular throbs racked her body, her brain (which
was really quite a good one, having gained a First from
Bristol University) was working energetically too.

*On second thoughts, Ms Collins will not have this, not for
a while at least. No, this will be for me, this shall become
my secret, my own touchstone. When I am either a) an aged
spinster* (she was 25 – the official age, she'd recently read,
for spinsterhood to commence) *or b) a good little house-
wife, cooking and breeding superlatively, then shall I
derive much pleasure recounting to myself (be it in a
rocking-chair or at a school play), the time I was an
outrageous vamp, a shameless slapper, an utterly
debauched nympho.*

She came to her conclusion as he came to his. He started
to pant raspingly and called out 'Oh my God, oh goddo
goddo Goh' with enormous conviction. She felt rather
proud of herself.

*No, Mister Man, it's 'goddess' actually, oh your goddess.
For that is what I shall be. That is who I am for today, and
for the times when I shall again allow you to experience
such delicious sex with me.*

Inadvertently, she gave out a little sigh, one of satisfaction, intellectual rather than physical. It was answered by a
sucking kiss from the man whom she straddled. She
smiled. He smiled. She smiled again, with ulterior
motives. He smiled back, oblivious but ensnared.

*Ho ho! So my secret is safe. Look at you, smugly grinning,
proud as punch, purely because you think you've taken me
to heaven and back. Which you have. But who was it who
was in control? I shall strive hard to keep it that way, and I
shall strive to keep it hard. I shall not fall in love with this
man. I shall not day-dream wistfully of babies and scones
baking in an Aga. Nor must you fall in love with me, only
lust and long for me until you positively ache. Even if you*

3

marry and live in blissful domesticity, you will frequently think of me and surge inside on remembering the joy and liberation of sex with me.

I must, she decided, *become an enigma. Remain one. To everyone, henceforth.* A wave of absolute exhilaration coursed through her. *This is it; this is not a search for self but the creation of it. I shall play and I shall act and I shall have much fun. I shall be the conductor. The baton is in my hand and the balls are in my caught.*

She rushed to the bathroom with Handel's 'Hallelujah Chorus' careering around her head. Predictably, the orgasm had sent urgent messages to her bladder and, sitting in the silence of her bathroom, she contemplated the release of pee versus an orgasm on the pleasure scale. Today, peeing came second. She checked it was really her in the mirror.

Gracious Good Lord! It is me! Sally Lomax, what on earth have you just done?

I've just had rampant sex.

She smiled hugely, winked, said 'Go for it, girl' out loud, and flushed the toilet with triumphant force. The phone had begun to ring. Sally gave herself another beaming smile and then sauntered, positively swaggered, to answer it. It was her mother, officious as ever, voice shrill, no time for a greeting.

'Darling I've been ringing for hours, I thought you'd be busy marking essays?'

'No, I had to be elsewhere, something far more pressing,' Sally said truthfully.

'What?'

Oh, you know how it is, Mum. When there's six foot of beefcake in your bed, more handsome and brawny than in your most incorrigible dreams, great hands, a wonderful mouth and a dick to die for; obviously marking a ten-year old's 'What I did over half term' rather pales into insignificance.

4

Taking a sharp bite on her tongue, Sally, however, did not speak her mind. My, how she would have relished the ensuing stunned silence of matriarchal disbelief. How she would have loved to have breezed straight on with mundane enquiries about the health of the cat and the younger sisters (in that order). Today, though, decorum won. The ravaged Rodin was diplomatically replaced by an old friend who would have been quite compliant had she known the circumstances (she was, in fact, holidaying in Tunisia).

'Daph is a little low, so I've been with her.'

'Darling, you did remember Aunt Martha's seventieth?'

Sally had forgotten.

'Is blasphemy really necessary? I suggest you phone her right this minute.'

So she did. Sally, sweet Sally; the prettiest of the nieces, the dutiful, good-natured Sally, chatted to Aunt Martha for a full and enjoyable ten minutes. She was careful not to mention her late uncle, and remembered to ask if the cold was causing the dreaded arthritis.

'Arthur Ritus comes to us all in old age, it's to be expected, I'm not one to complain . . .' But she was and she did. Sally ummed, ahhed and tutted at the apposite moments and Aunt Martha, as she hung up the phone, took down the silver-framed photo of her husband and declared to it that Sally was a gem and would make a treasure of a wife.

Sally gazed at the replaced handset.

Do I feel guilty? Should I? For what? For forgetting Aunt Martha's birthday? For lying to my mother? Or for having performed a carnal act of such outrageous proportions? Guilt, show me thy face! I'll give you three seconds!

Right then, off I go, back to my boudoir, quick-change into my doppelgänger, the temptress, the vixen, the wicked lusting girl. Woman! Hardly a lady, hardly a girl. Today I am suddenly the sort of person I thought I was not and yet today I really feel like Me. Pure and simple, this is who I am.

5

She entered her room and any purity simply vanished. She flew on top of the knackered male form and kissed it outrageously with a scheming and very lively tongue.

ONE

*S*uch a lovely girl, what an angel, isn't she wonderful, such a good girl. Sally Lomax was adorable and adored. She was extremely polite, tirelessly friendly, always amiable and genteel. She was chatty and respectful to the elderly and a much-loved teacher of youngsters. She kept herself trim, never let the ends of her hair split and always folded clothes away at the end of a day. She cooked well, cleaned well, and although she could not knit, she made enviable things on her sewing machine. When in her car, a spotless if noisy six-year-old Mini Cooper, she was courteous and never lost her temper, never overtook on the inside and slowed down well in advance of pedestrian crossings – even on a deserted Sunday. Just in case.

When Sally was a child, she was angelic in physique and character. Skin as smooth and opalescent as her prettiest Bakelite doll, features and figure doll-like too, her demeanour open and engaging. Sally at six was altogether flawless, faultless. It was as much a pleasure for her parents to invite ageing relatives for tea, as it was for them to venture out of retirement bungalows to be sung to and danced for. At tea-time, Sally never stretched over, never ate with her mouth open, and always asked if she could have some more with a 'please'. At her birthday parties she never snatched her guests' presents and was always keen for the entertainer not to show her any favouritism. But Sally was simply everyone's favourite.

At twenty-five, her skin is still flawless and, though we would be hard-pressed to call the Sally we've just met *angelic*, it took very little hard pressing for the Rodin to deem the ways and wiles of her body thoroughly heavenly.

Well, where do we find Sally today? It is the day after the Big Bonk. She is spending Sunday afternoon by herself, in the one-bedroom flat she rents in Highgate. He had stayed for breakfast-cum-lunch and had thus deprived Sally of her sacred hour with the *Observer*, so she is reading it now. Her routine is out of sync, she really should be ironing. It will wait a week. Today Sally is not flustered by such a thing, today she is enjoying aloneness. Today she enjoys the self-condoned liberation from the previously self-imposed Sunday schedule. She is very proud of herself and finds she frequently bursts into an ecstatic smile.

What does it mean, this smile, what does it mean?
Her answer is defiant.

I feel wonderful. It was good. It was a good thing to do.
She laughs at the paradox. In the clear light of a November day, and looked at objectively, she had indeed committed a wanton act of slack morals and shameful lust which, justifiably, could be categorized by most as Bad. Yet Sally feels good and can see nothing to be ashamed of. She feels elated, happy and downright proud.

My flesh might be ravaged, my mind sullied, but Gracious Good Lord do they feel the better for it!
Sally knows what she wants, and what she must do.
It'll be a swift and easy transition, and it must start,

quite simply, with a change to my wardrobe. I shall do Ms Collins proud and move with one fell swoop from Laura Ashley to Whistles, from Marks and Sparks undies to none whatsoever. Hampstead here I come, cheque book at the ready.

Should I be ironing?

No.

I should be buying clothes that are Dry Clean Only.

TWO

Sunday in Hampstead, silver winter sun making everybody look beautiful. The Barbour Brigade are out walking retrievers who have never retrieved in the countryside because the Heath suffices. The Young Trendies are here in force, hanging out, hanging about, sipping cappuccino at the pavement café, queuing for crêpes, looking around all the while to catch sight of their reflection whilst spying out anyone good-looking to look good for.

There is a young woman who weaves in and around these two species. She is smiling; it is a smile of energy and ease and it is infectious. She seems simultaneously absorbed in her own world yet aware of, and enjoying, her surroundings. And the shopping, by the looks of the two bags she swings. She is of average height, of slight build and her hair is a nothing-special brown, mid-length with a kink that is natural and nice. Her skin glows and there is a sheen to her very good cheekbones, a becoming blush to her cheeks, an endearing rosiness to the edge of her chin and the end of her nose. Her hazel eyes glint and dance. Her lips, naturally full, are soft red – Sally always uses lip balm during the winter months. And, though her legs would not see her to a Levi jeans commercial, her walk is a sexy, assertive stride. As a package, she looks very pleasingly put together. She is not stunning but she is radiant and heads turn.

Sally jigs past a boutique, one selling excessively expensive accessories. Two strides later (and unknowingly witnessed by at least three envious Hampstead Darlings), our erstwhile ballerina performs a fluid halt, heel-spin, about-turn, and floats effortlessly into the shop. Inside, the opulent aroma of fine leather envelops her, the hand of a skilled interior decorator is much in evidence and her senses are solicited at once. The rag-rolled walls in *Homes-and-Gardens* hues of ecru and taupe, and the polished wood floor covered here and there by a jaded kelim, provide a splendid setting for pieces of old furniture over which cashmere throws and finely woven woollen shawls are nonchalantly draped. Belts hang from a fabulously gnarled piece of driftwood; from leather trunks, suitcases and holdalls, a carefully spewed selection of socks and silk camisoles accost the eye. But Sally, who thinks the current fashion and hefty prices for bashed, blemished, artistically distressed leather goods somewhat daft, has made a beeline for the old Welsh dresser where the hats are displayed.

She has never worn a hat but she is trying them on with the jaunty confidence of one who would not entertain going out without one. The black felt cloche suits her well but makes her look too cutesy, the trilby is too butch and the beret too *ordinaire*. She looks stunning in the claret bowler but feels best in the black velvet. It is soft, floppy but beautifully cut. It hugs her skull and the brim, up at the front, falls gently around her face and drapes elegantly at the back. She looks at herself in the mirror and the shop assistant, usually pushy, looks on too. She makes no attempt to goad her customer; she watches, slightly jealous, from a discreet distance. Sally is intrigued to find that the shape of the hat accentuates

11

her bone structure and appears to lengthen her neck; under the black velvet, her eyes turn from hazelnuts into freshly shelled conkers.

I look really rather good, sort of alluring, feminine and vampish all at the same time.

It takes Sally but an instant to decide the hat must be hers; costing, though it does, a day's pay.

At the Tea Pot Shoppe, Carlos was clearing the mountain of froth-stained cups from one of the outside tables, pocketing a mound of gratuitously small change left as a gratuity. It was nearing the end of his first month in England, he was tired and slightly homesick. It was a thankless job for a nuclear physics graduate, and the tips were lower than he'd been led to believe. Then he saw her, caught in profile as she started to cross the road, a pretty face framed perfectly by a sumptuous black hat. Suddenly, life in this strange country of offish Barbours and oafish Trendies had a plus to it. This, Carlos realized with a great deal of excitement, was his first glimpse of an English Rose. He gawped transfixed; watching the cars slither and toot while she danced and laughed her way between them. There is a zebra crossing a hundred yards ahead but today Sally prefers to jay-walk. *Bella, bella!* The hat, the face, the rosiness – and here she is, ordering a cappuccino and a Danish pastry.

Sally graciously accepted the compliments of the waiter. Soon she was deftly scooping up the chocolate-dusted froth and thinking of nothing in particular as it fluffed into nothingness on her tongue. The pastry was absolutely heavenly and she even closed her eyes as the first mouthful revealed to her tastebuds apple, *crème patissière* and the lightest of pastry. By the second sip and third mouthful, Sally was happily recalling the details of her decadent afternoon. A coffee-brown lambs-wool blazer; two silk shirts, one olive, one cream; a pair of exorbitant expensive designer jeans; and a short (was it too short?) black devoré velvet skirt.

When on earth am I going to wear that?

You will.

She had indulged in garments of the finest fabrics, and at the most exorbitant prices. The whole experience had been so pleasurable, the looking, the touching, the trying on; the decision-making so effortless. Finally, it had been a joy and well worth the money to watch her acquisitions being coddled in tissue paper and then handed to her so reverently.

As she pressed a determined fork against the last flakes of Danish, she pondered for a moment; common sense versus decadence. Sally, you must understand, had spent her rainy-day money. Frequently she put a little aside 'for a rainy day', not really knowing when that would be. But it was definitely today and common sense had a place neither in her scheme of things nor her purse.

Today, she told herself as the brisk November breeze reddened her nose and chin a little more, *today it is pouring.*

Despite the pavements being dry and no umbrella in sight, Sally decided that it was the rainiest day in ages and the spending of pounds amassed from hard-saved pennies was utterly justified. These purchases, after all, were an *investment*. She turned to look for her waiter, and in doing so felt a whisper of velvet against her cheek. Its caress felt wonderful and, as the waiter was nowhere to be seen, she kept her head still a moment longer.

Over her second cappuccino, Sally indulged in recalling, moment by moment, thrust by thrust, the athletics of the previous night, and if one can feel light-headed between the legs, then that was how Sally was feeling.

Never have I been worshipped like that, never have I been so aware of my body, what it can do, how it can feel, how it can make another feel.

Perhaps it was because she had consciously watched,

13

analyzed even, a man totally absorbed in her, so hungry for her, that her own physical awareness had been heightened. The sex seemed so much more fulfilling, the orgasm so exquisite. New. Sitting there, in Hampstead, with the light growing thin, a November navy replacing the afternoon silver, Sally decided to recast herself as a fly on the wall of her replay and ran the whole sequence again, this time as a series of film stills. Vivid in her mind's eye was the interlocking of two bodies, the various formations and patterns, firm flesh, the spaces in between; Rodin's marble; Henry Moore's bronze.

Carlos found himself unable to resist. The English Rose, smiling carefree out loud, was compelling, magnetic. He was helpless in the face of her. As his luck would have it, she turned to him with that very smile as he presented the bill to her. With his very best English, he let go:

'Señorita, your smile, it makes my day. Is so very beautiful. In you I see the English Rosa. If I was Shake His Speare, I write a play for you. You are foods for my 'eart and a vision for my eyes. Is so very lovely. I am breaking open for your smile of pretty innocence.'

Hand pressed with conviction against his heart, he kissed up at the sky as if imploring the gods to grant his wish. Sally was flattered to the hilt. Cocking her head, she gave him the smile to make his day, a wink too, and a tip which far exceeded her previously uniform ten per cent.

Not quite, thought Sally as she strolled away home, *but thank you anyway.* She threw back her head and grinned hugely at the near-dark sky. *Actually, the smile that has made your day is not that of an innocent English Rose, but is rather the glow of a well-laid woman.*

THREE

'*F*oxy Lady!'

Jimi Hendrix's chocolate voice, the aggressive twang and slice of his guitar, rings out and reverberates off the walls. The music is loud and frantic. It adds action and life to the room.

There is little furniture but what there is has, undoubtedly, the British Design Council seal of approval. The run of the floorboards, interrupted only occasionally by a piece of carefully chosen, intelligently placed furniture, leads the eye to the fireplace above which an Alexander Calder gouache explodes colour and shape on to the intensely white wall. The low coffee table is a sleek construction in burnished steel and tinted glass. It supports a matt black vase stuffed with emphatically upright tulips; white, waxy but real. On a diagonal to the table's edge is a copy of Warhol's *Diaries*. Along one wall stands an ash and glass cabinet. Understated and stunning, the carpentry is exquisite. It is filled with books meticulously organized into a personal library system. Pride of place is given to the leather-bound volumes: Shakespeare, Donne, Fielding, the *Complete Oxford Dictionary*, the *Dictionary of Quotations*. On the shelf above

15

are art books, epic tomes and sumptuous catalogues: Mantegna, Vermeer, Cézanne and Poussin. The shelves below carry novels, all hardback, all standing proud in alphabetical order: Bellow, Heller, Kafka, Marquez, Nabokov, Pasternak, Seth.

On one side of the fireplace, a fabulous Conran standard lamp stands to attention while on the other side is the CD system, a veritable piece of sculpture in itself; wafer-thin, subtle Scandinavian lines, matt black, obviously. On custom-built shelves (oak and chrome) are enough CDs to open a shop. They are categorized, of course; the concise rock section alphabetically, the comprehensive classical section chronologically: Monteverdi, Bach, Mozart, Beethoven, Brahms, Mahler, Schoenberg, Bartok, Tippett. And yet it is Mr Hendrix who somewhat anomalously fills this unnervingly chic room in Notting Hill with sound.

Can you guess where we are? It is still the day of the Big B. and, a few miles away, Sally has just arrived home, where she is presently dancing Giselle in the devoré skirt and nothing else. Physically, she may be some distance from Jimi and the Calder and the tulips; however, the memory of her is very much here, clear and current in the mind of this flat's occupant, evoked by Mr Hendrix's beast of chase. It is time for the Rodin to assume his true identity.

Would Richard Stonehill please stand up?

Look there! Against the long sash window, framed movie-like by imperceptibly breezing muslin drapes. That's him, resting his brow against his outstretched arm against the window. Turn around – oh, just look! Six foot two and-a-bit, perfectly carved and gorgeously chiselled. Now this *is* the stuff of Levi jeans commercials. Hair the colour of the sand at Rosilli Bay where his childhood was spent, Richard's skin boasts the health, vitality and natural tan of someone who lived long in the care and goodness of Welsh sea air. His eyes are the most extraordinary dark violet, his teeth are very good, his hands could be those of a concert pianist, he is fiendishly good-looking and he smells delicious – a fine mixture of freshly laundered clothes, scrubbed skin and Calvin Klein scent.

Eyes closed, long and lithe legs stretched out, arms relaxed, Richard Stonehill slithers into his black leather recliner, and converses with Jimi.

'I'm too exhausted to get up and scream, Mr Hendrix,' he apologises, but finds ample energy to sing that he too has wasted precious time; that he has therefore made up his mind to make this foxy lady his, all his.

Bay-beh!

Jimi, it appears is singing about Sally. Or someone just like her. But Richard has never met anyone who comes remotely near her. He sincerely hopes that this vixen will have her sport with him a while longer.

A wry smile creeps from one side of his mouth to the other. He opens his eyes and shakes his head. What does he shake in it? Disbelief? But it did happen, his pleasantly tired body is proof, and so are the images which constantly assault his memory. Does he shake it in amusement? But the night with Sally was more than just fun. His gaze rests upon *Julius Caesar*, third volume into the run of Shakespeare. Richard sees its title and suddenly Sally, in her naked glory, appears before him too. Caesar. *Seize her.*

Seize who? Who on earth is this woman? This Sally Lomax? The classic friend of a friend of a friend whom he met less than twenty-four hours ago at the party of a friend of a friend. How come he had not met, even heard of her before? Fate. It must have been. At 11 o'clock the previous evening, Fate had pushed them both on to the balcony at that dull party in Barnes. Fate had allowed conversation to flow, flattery and flirtations to be accepted, and Sally to be without a ride back into London. Fate took them past an all-night bagel bakery and Fate uncovered a shared passion for the smoked salmon-cream cheese variety. Fate filled Richard's car with laughter and sexual chemistry. If Fate took him to Highgate, where he'd never even thought of going before, where was it to take him from here?

As quickly as the vision came, Sally now disappeared from the cabinet and the complete works of Shakespeare stared back at Richard in their leather-bound splendour. Hendrix was now proclaiming that an angel had come down from heaven yesterday, staying just long enough to rescue him.

Richard, who did not feel rescued so much as released, rose and sauntered to the bathroom, a tiler's delight in damson, citron and *bleu di bleu* majolica ceramic. His bladder was full and he stood expectant for the blissful moment of release. Nothing happened. Puzzled, he glanced down. It looked like it always did and felt like it should. Eyes tightly closed, he tried again. Nothing. Slight pain but nothing.

Come on, mate, syphon the python, have a slash, take a leak.

Nothing. He fiddled a bit, gave a little squeeze, a little pull, a slight twist, a gentle shake. Nothing. He turned the tap on to a drizzle.

But I'm bursting.

Bursting. Immediately his mind flashed up an image of the night before, a clear picture and a vivid sensation at the same time. There is Sally's nipple brushing the corner of his mouth; he sees himself thrusting into her, pump, spurt, release.

Stop it, I've got to piss.

Richard looked down and his penis, as erect and straining as his perfect tulips, leered up at him lasciviously. No peeing for the time being. He ached in his lower back and his groin and decided to sit awhile instead. Chin resting on a fist, elbow balanced on a knee; he is Rodin's Thinker to a 't'. Catching sight of himself in the mirror, he took a long, hard stare.

I am thirty-five and have had a mind-blowing sexual encounter. I do not know the girl, though carnally I know her inside out. And today I cannot pee. Look at me, blond, handsome – very – virile, manly, hunky, horny. Suave, debonair, sophisticated. In control – of my life, of my mind, of my work.

But not of my dick.

Who is this woman? This Sally Lomax? She is a teacher, she is twenty-five, she lives by herself in urban cottagey style amongst pine dressers, floral table cloths, Lloyd-Loom chairs and a patchwork eiderdown. Shabby chic, everything fresh, clean and bright. Objectively, she is not even that beautiful, not really my type. So what has she done to me? My tackle has never ached before, nor my gut felt so hollow, my mind so distracted. What have I done? What has been done to me? Why can't I pee? When will I see her again? Jeez, will I see her again?

The horror and accompanying adrenalin at the thought of never seeing Sally again opened the sluice gates of the Stonehill bladder. Richard had just enough time to release the Thinker's pose so that the torrent hit the bowl and not the double weave, thick-pile carpet.

FOUR

'*D*id you see Miss Lomax in assembly? Did you see what she was wearing? You can see her *knees*! And she has make-up on. Definitely mascara and lipstick.'

'My mum says that a woman should never go out without lipstick on.'

'But Miss Lomax is a teacher!'

'My mum says it's tarty to put make-up on unless it's a special occasion.'

'Yes, but Miss Lomax is a *teacher*.'

Gossip was always an integral part of Monday morning school but rarely were the teachers its main topic. On a Thursday or a Friday maybe, but Monday was usually dedicated to the football scores, shopping trips and birthday parties of the weekend just past. That Monday morning, in the all-too-short ten minutes between assembly and first lesson, Miss Lomax was the exclusive subject for discussion.

Class Five were stupefied, traumatized and desperately excited. Scandal, they believed, was about to shake the school. Of what it was they were as yet unsure. To an extent it was irrelevant, the truth may not be nearly so exciting as wild conjecture. Was she going somewhere after school? If so, where? To dinner? To the opera, the theatre? To court? Was she about to get engaged? Was she leading a double life as a model as well as a teacher? (To a ten-year-old, anyone taller or older, anyone in high heels or even just a trace of lipstick, was very glamorous indeed.) Maybe she was going to elope – please, no, that would mean a new teacher and Miss Lomax was irreplaceable. Miss Lomax warranted compliments usually paid to footballers, pop stars and ponies; she was the business, the bestest, brill, fab.

'Who do you think she's going to elope with?'

'Maybe they'll be catching a train to Gretna Green straight after school!'

'Quick, who passes King's Cross Station on their way home?'

Suddenly the classroom reverberated with the age-old sound of desks creaking, chairs being scraped into forward-facing position and a few nervous, last-minute giggles and whispers. Teacher had arrived. There she was, resplendent in a tight skirt and loose, silky blouse. Miss Lomax stood before them, feet slightly apart, hands on hips.

'Hi.'

Thirty champion chatterboxes were stunned into a unified hush.

Hi?

Hi?

What's 'Hi'?

Hey, maybe she's on drugs!

Miss Lomax perched herself in a perfect serpentine on the edge of her table, black Lycra-clad legs plaited around each other.

Maybe she's drunk!

'Today I thought we'd do something different. I read your "What I did over half term" stories and I'm not particularly interested in what you did this weekend. It

21

seems that you all tend to do the same old things anyway, and your writing is rather boring. You lot don't seem to have much imagination. With the exception of Rajiv, who seems to have a little too much because every weekend he apparently saves family or friends from fire, flood or sinking ship.'

Twenty-nine children laughed. Miss Lomax smiled gently at Rajiv and cocked her head as if to say, Don't take it to heart.

'Shush. Thank you. No, today I thought we could talk about our best daydreams, our favourite fantasies. Now who will start? Rajiv? Okay. And easy on the fires, floods or drowning baby cousins. Fire away, fire away.'

Rajiv began his story. His fantasy was to be all by himself, away from his family and friends, in a spacecraft made for one, operated by one. He would leave Earth, head for the stars, alight on one and discover living aliens. He would stay and befriend this new people, introduce them to such concepts as clothing empires and hotel chains and fast-food outlets. He would become their undisputed, much-loved leader, an intergalactic Richard Branson.

Marsha, who had a soft spot for Rajiv, explained that she aimed to become a fireman-woman, so that she could help Rajiv in his brave adventures. They could be a team – firefighting heroes but also husband and wife with six children. Rajiv buried his head in his hands, wishing his spacecraft could be ready that afternoon. Miss Lomax succeeded – but only just – in suppressing potentially uncontrollable giggles. Rajiv, however, quickly succumbed to a tell-tale redness which travelled all over his face and burnt right through to his ears. A roar of 'Ugghh' and a spatter of laughter erupted. Marsha stared straight at him and at Miss Lomax alternately, imploring, 'But it's true, it's true.'

Law and order was easily re-established, the class was keen to listen and tell. Ambitions were mooted: to win the Grand National on a small Welsh pony; to become a very famous actress and appear on *This Is Your Life*; to take England to victory as the top goal scorer in the next World Cup ('Come on now, Andrew, be slightly realistic', 'Well, maybe the World Cup after next'); to be the Queen's favourite chef. The children were loose, stimulated and creative. They produced some of their best work that day without realizing it was work at all. Miss Lomax felt proud. She was having fun.

'Yes, Alice? Tell you my fantasy or daydream?' The bell for break clanged. *Saved by the bell*, *ho ho*, thought Sally. Yet for once none of the children moved. Pen lids were left off pens, books lay threateningly open. Thirty pairs of inquisitive eyes said that break did not matter, they wanted Miss Lomax's dreams.

'My dream?'

Yes, Miss, your dream.

'Maybe next time, it's break-time.'

We don't want our break, we want your fantasy!

There was no escape, she could not punish them for showing such enthusiasm for her lesson. She could not disappoint them by merely taking theirs and not giving them hers.

'Okay, okay. In a nutshell, I would like to live in Tuscany – that's in Italy, here on the map. In a beautiful stone villa set amidst flowers and cypress trees, with its own pool and near a perfect little village. I'd like a devilishly good-looking Italian husband who is a pasta wizard, a batch of beautiful babies and a satisfying job teaching perfectly behaved, diligent (look it up in the dictionary) pupils.'

Sally only sort-of lied. It had certainly been her fantasy right up until last week, but that was before Richard Stonehill and her current fantasies, which would most certainly earn her a dismissal and severely disturb the fresh, absorbent minds of her young charges. The Tuscan Idyll would have to suffice.

'Now scram!' Thirty pairs of androgynous legs scrammed. Out, out into the playground to munch chocolate, elaborate further on their stories and to discuss whether or not they believed Miss Lomax. The majority (all except Paula-Teacher's-Pet-Thomson) did not.

As she headed towards the staff-room, Miss Lomax talked silently to the satchels and gym shoes which lined the walls.

My fantasy? Best daydream? If it's come true, or is coming true, is it still valid? I want the memory of me, the feel of me, my taste, my smell, my touch, to stay with Richard Stonehill for the rest of his life. The knowledge that it has done so will give me the pleasure and strength never to let myself feel small and worthless. Actually, maybe that's all a little too metaphysical. Let's start again. On a physical level. My fantasy is to have the most delicious, wicked, life-enhancing affair with this Adonis, this Richard 'call me Conan' Stonehill.

'Hullo, Sal!' (*Don't call me that.*) Mr Bernard – John – (Head of Maths), greeted Miss Lomax – Sally (great at giving head).

'You certainly look radiant today. Don't tell me Class Five had done their homework? All of them? I've a double period with them after break, so help me God. Might you be free for a drink this evening? No? A shame, a great pity. Some other time, perhaps, maybe?'

Miss Lomax, who had never talked much more than shop with Bernard, was a little taken aback.

It's not the short skirt, is it? She hastily persuaded herself it must be her aura instead.

Miss Lomax made coffee in a mug bearing the school's emblem and maxim, *In Loco Parentis*, and sauntered over to where Miss Lewis – Diana – (teacher of Art and Craft) sat. They were close friends and allies in the field of staff-room politics. Diana, the dictionary definition of a wacky art teacher, was always bowled over by the small happenings and vagaries of life. Indeed, great interest and pure enthusiasm were expressed for practically everything and everyone around her. Her exaggerated inflection assisted the expression of such fascinations. To her great amusement, this rendered her a willing sitting duck for many a playground impersonation. She had an absolute field day with Sally that break-time.

'Look at you! You look *fab*-u-lous. Who is he?'

'Huh?'

'Sa-*lly*!'

But all Diana had for a reply was Sally taking a non-committal gulp at her coffee.

'Okay then, Miss Sexy Sal.' (*Don't call me that*!) 'What did you do over the weekend? Apart from *plun*-der your bank account?'

'Actually, that was about it. Just a quiet weekend, a bit of sewing, finishing a novel, generally pottering about. You know, one of *those* weekends.'

I do know 'those weekends', thought Diana, *and you most certainly did not have one! You're fibbing to me, but you have your reasons. Only tell me soon, Sally, Sexy Sal, do!*

FIVE

'*H*e's late today, isn't he? Most unusual. Did he have a meeting? Check for me, will you? I don't think I could stand these butterflies all day!'

'No, Sandra, no meeting for him. Maybe he's sick? Or maybe he's eloped!'

'Stop it, Mary, that's not fair.'

'But you've been working here over two years and you get the same courteous "Good Morning, Good Evening, Merry Christmas" as the rest of us. You know he'll only ever be married to his work. He's probably a lousy lover anyway. No one female ever rings for him. You never know, maybe women aren't his *thing* anyway.'

'Oh, shut it. Let me have my hopes and fantasies. It's all right for you, with your mortgage and your steady Steve and your ... oh my God, he's coming! Oh my Gordon Flipping Bennett. Keep cool and sophis, San. Hello, Mr Stonehill!'

'Good morning, Sandra. Morning, Mary.'

Morning, morning. Mourning.

Sandra's gaze followed him down the corridor. Mary watched her closely. Smitten. Sandra absorbed every detail, storing it for later, for the arduous journey that she would make, always made, seatless and depressed, back to High Barnet.

I love that navy suit, I love the way he walks. His hair lifts slightly with each stride, the trousers outline his calf muscles with every step. Why was he late? How can I find out? Please, please, please not a woman in his life. Pretty please a gas leak or something. One day, me, please. One day, me. Or, for one day, me. All I ask.

0181 348 6523. No answer. Of course not, Sally's at school. But does she have an answering machine? Richard wonders, hanging on. Obviously not. But does she go home for lunch? he wonders two hours later as he re-dials. Obviously not. Does school end at 3.30 nowadays? No, apparently it does not.

Richard has done little work. As the working day nears a close, his drawing board remains irritatingly bare. He just could not seem to settle down to concentrate on the plan for the quasi-Georgian building commissioned by the Americans. Instead, he doodles and a Play School house stares back, with a chimney, a door, and windows; one, two, three, four. You never know the Americans, they might like it. He twirls around in his swivel chair; his jacket is off, his shirt sleeves rolled up to the elbow revealing beautifully tanned forearms brushed with a down of flaxen hairs. He clasps his hands behind his head and places his left foot on his right knee. Fine ankles can be discerned beneath Ralph Lauren socks. Out of the window he sees the river, a pleasure boat, captivated tourists on board, the guide changing her microphone from hand to hand as she points to the left, to the right. On the opposite bank, a crane performs its slow-motion task. Up river, Waterloo Bridge straddles south and north banks. Matisse is showing at the Hayward Gallery, he read the review in yesterday's paper. Maybe Sally would like to go? Maybe Titian at the Royal Academy is more her thing? Something to find out. 0181

27

348 6523. Was that dialled correctly? 0181 348 6523. She's his first 0181 girl.

638 5454. 'Bob Woods, please . . . Bob? Hey! Fancy a *sesh* at the gym? Great. In an hour? Fine.'

Keeping at a constant 80 r.p.m., Bob and Richard tackle the simulated hill programme on the *Lifecycle*. They've broken the twenty-minute, red-face barrier and are working through into the serious sweat zone. Speech comes in staccato gasps, whole sentences interspersed with long pauses. However, having worked out together for many years, Bob and Richard have brought such conversation to a fine art, barely comprehensible to those uninitiated but utterly intelligible between these two.

'So, you and Sally Lomax left together and then what?'

'What do you know about her?'

'Not a lot. Friend of a friend of Catherine. Met her once before, about six months ago. So, you left and *then* what?'

'Does Catherine know her?'

'And then WHAT?'

'What?'

They pedalled on, then pedalled down, then stopped. Both leant forward and dropped their heads on to folded arms and huffed in unison for a few moments.

'*Stairmaster?*'

'After you, I'll work on my abs.'

Delts, quads, glutes, abs. Half an hour later, they met up over the bicep curls, heaving their limbs, exhaling and grimacing in such perfect time as to make any synchronized swimming corps envious. They were, unknowingly, the centre of attention, the brawniest there, the handsomest. Admiring women, in fluorescent, up-the-bum all-in-ones, strutted their well-toned stuff in the hope that they might be seen and even achieve a date. Less brawny blokes were suddenly inspired to work harder, to up the level on the *Lifecycle*, to increase their weights by 10 Ks. Today, like any other day past or to come, Bob and

Richard were unaware of their audience. To them, the gym was less a place to see and be seen as it was their sanctuary where they could dissolve the pressures of work or relationships and simply enjoy their easy friendship which spanned well over a decade. And keep their bodies in peak condition too, of course.

Over the gush of the shower, the waft of shampoo-conditioner and the clatter of lockers, Bob picked up where Richard had left off.

'Have you phoned her?'

'Who?'

'Who-my-arse!'

'Sort of.'

'*Sort of*! What's "sort of"? How can you *sort of* ring a person? Either you have or you have not. She was either there or she was not. She either said: "Yes, I'd love to", or she said "No" and thanked you for calling. Enough "sort of". Did you?'

'Yes.'

'Yes?'

'Yes.'

'And? And?'

'No reply.'

'Try again?'

'No reply.'

'*Will* you try again?'

'What do you know about her?'

'Ri-*chard*! She's a friend of a friend of Catherine's. I met her once before. I am sure – in fact, there can be no question about it – she'll be sitting in all evening willing the phone to ring with your dulcet tones offering dinner *chez Ricardo*. So, stop skirting the issue. You left together and then what?'

'I took her home. Fancy a drink? My shout.'

Bob watched his friend as he dressed and preened.

Good Lord, he's gone! A goner! Not that he knows it yet. Goodbye, Old Mister Pump-and-Dump, Sir Love 'Em

29

and Leave 'Em. Or rather Lord Leave 'Em Before You
Fallinlovewith 'Em. I don't believe it!

Bob felt a wave of fondness and happiness for his pal
so he slapped his back and squeezed his delts.

'Your shout. Just a swift half, mind. Promised Catherine that we'd go to the flicks.'

Their swift half turned into a leisurely two-pinter. Bob
decided not to pry further. This one needed nurturing.
Instead, they indulged in a trip down Memory Lane,
recalling wild times shared at college, remembering, try
for try, every rugby game that they'd played together,
remarking on how far they had both come since moving
to London to make their respective marks on the world of
Law and Architecture. Bob talked about Catherine, their
next holiday to Northern Portugal, the extension to the
house, the current discord over the baby issue – her
desire, his reluctance. ('But me, a dad? I mean, I'm not
old enough! I've got a dad of my own still! Catherine's
broody though, very. I've even checked her Pill packets
recently to make sure she's not forgetting accidentally-
on-purpose.')

Richard was simultaneously envious of Bob's security,
his constant and loving relationship, and yet also thankful that he had no one but himself to think of. Poor old
Bob, soon to be dragged off to a schmaltzy American
weepy that he'd never go to see out of choice. But there
again, didn't he seem to beam with affection when, on
the way to the pub, he'd made a detour to buy tissues and
wine gums?

'Hey, look at the time! I've got fifteen minutes to get to
Leicester Square! Great to see you, Richie.' (*Don't call me
that.*) 'Still on for squash on Sunday morning? Great. You
going to call her? You *are* going to call her! Must dash.
Later!'

'Later! Love to Catherine. Don't sob too hard!'

Bob left the pub backwards, making a telephone

gesture as he did so. Richard raised his pint and smiled. A minute or two later he left it, half-full, and caught a cab home to Notting Hill.

0181 348 6523.
   'Hullo?'
   'Sally! Richard here.'
   'Hu-*low*!'
   'How are you?'
   'Well! Yes! You?'
   'Mmm!'
   A pause verging on embarrassing silence.
   'Sally, would you like to have dinner with me? Friday night? At mine?'
   'That would be nice. Why, yes. Thank you. Address? Time? Lovely!'
   'Friday, then.' *And wear those lovely little knickers.*
   'Friday.' *And make sure the sheets are fresh.*

SIX

With the mock-Georgian folly taking good form on the drawing-board, Richard felt justified, for the first time in his working career, in packing up at lunch-time and taking the afternoon off.

Goodbye Sandra, goodbye Mary. Goodbye, Mr Stonehill. Goodbye navy suit and calf muscles. Sandra plunged herself into a chasm of pessimism rescued only by a chocolate éclair tactfully provided by Mary. No, Mary, he's far too fit ever to need a doctor. It can only mean a woman.

What a delight, thought Richard, *to shop at Sainsbury's on a weekday afternoon.* What a revelation it was that a supermarket could look like that. No obstacle course of trollies and baskets, plenty of everything left, no people-snake at the check-out. *No men*, realized Richard.

As he trollied his way to the cereals, he thought what a mercy it was that he was unmarried. He pondered how it was that shopping for groceries became such a trial for the married man. On your soap box, Richard, away you go.

Take any ordinary Saturday – tomorrow for instance –

they'll be here in force, frantic and bewildered, chained to The List. It says baked beans so Married Man stops by the baked beans, and regards them. Look at the list, look at the produce, look at the list. Move on a couple of paces, walk backwards knocking over a child before finally plucking two tins of said beans. Place them carefully in the trolley but manage somehow to bruise the avocados in the process. Wipe brow, unscrunch List and go in search of Free-range Eggs. Buy Farm Fresh instead – they're cheaper after all. Little does M.M. realize that they will ultimately work out twice as dear when Wife sees them, bins them and hollers: 'FREE-RANGE!' Don't they know that there's a reason for lard, crinkle cut chips, white sliced bread and bumper-pack beer not to be on The List?

Richard Stonehill, I think you will find that a packet of SuperNoodles lurks behind that box of lo-fat, lo-salt, sugar free lite-bran (organic) which you have strategically positioned in your trolley.

It is at the check-out, Richard rued whilst searching for an eco-friendly bleach, *where M.M. comes most unstuck. You can see them gaze in wonder at the well-spaced items processing along on the conveyor belt of the female shopper* (or that of Mr Stonehill). *The contents of M.M.'s trolley are in a veritable profiterole pile as they head towards the black looks of the check-out assistant. M.M. wonders how women know instinctively how to pack – is it passed down from Mother to Daughter?*

More to the point, why on earth does M.M. insist on packing eggs and pastry cases, watercress and tomatoes first; soap powder, bottles and tins last? What happens to men when they marry? Richard pondered as he sashayed past the beverages and preserves (choosing Broken Orange Pekoe and Damson Extra respectively). *Do these married men – erstwhile bachelors after all – lose all notion, every shred of common sense as to what constitutes a well-stocked larder? Why and how does this innate and irrational fear of supermarkets suddenly develop?*

Is there a cure?

Divorce?

Richard was relieved, on that decadent afternoon, that this sub-species was busy elsewhere (probably making important decisions at business, running the city, organizing the country, designing buildings, ministering law, order, justice and peace) so that he could cruise the aisles without incident or irritation. Deftly he swooped and plucked and picked as he breezed along. Under his expertise, his trolley behaved impeccably. Gone were those forever-spinning wheels; it became some kind of miniature hovercraft. Such was his skill and grace at handling corners, the elegant stops and effortless starts, the two of them became the Torvill and Dean of Sainsbury's. Packed to perfection – frozen goods in one bag, bottles, tins and tubes in a box, fresh produce in another bag – Richard headed home.

It never occurred to him that Married Man is the beast he is because he thinks not only for himself. He has responsibilities to others. Commitment. After all, Richard has had fifteen years to bring his shopping – content and technique – to a fine art for he has bought and thought only for himself. He has been his own man. And nobody else's.

The few special ingredients, those which would make his meal for Sally a veritable and memorable feast, were brought from Gambini's, the specialist Italian delicatessen that was, by a useful turn of Fate, Richard's corner shop. Now here was a place he would browse and deliberate at leisure. *Pappardelle* or *Orecchiette* or *Gigli del Gargano*? *Ciabatta* or *Focaccia*? Stuffed olives or those marinating happily in thyme-flavoured cold-pressed extra virgin olive oil? The shop was cramped, the smell almost overpowering as cheese mingled with

34

salami and olives jostled for olfactory recognition against garlic-drenched sauces. From floor to ceiling, the Gambinis had packed the shelves tight with the necessities for maintaining Italian culinary standards in England. All the regions of Italy were represented under this one roof in Notting Hill. From Umbria, Tuscany, Sicily and Pugilia was extra virgin olive oil spanning the spectrum from pale gold to deep khaki. Small pots of *Pesto Genovese* rubbed shoulders with little jars of capers from Lipari. Jams of wild chestnut and wild fig jostled for space next to jars of chocolate hazelnut cream, and packets of *Cantucci* biscuits were balanced precariously against a tower of boxed *Panforte*.

Richard was caught, quite compliantly, in the Gambinis' web of luxury and tantalizing variety. When it came to vinegar there was Chianti, Balsamic, peach or plum to choose from. Impossibly fat olives vied for attention, gleaming up at him from their bowls of marinades. Although the *porcini secchi* seemed somewhat *ordinaire* next to dry morels from Tibet and Fairy Ring *Champignons*, Richard bought some anyway and Sardinian Saffron proved to be a must-have, despite its imaginative price tag (in fact, *because* of its price tag).

Signora Gambini, known to the select few (Richard amongst them) as Rosa, watched as he smelt, felt and tasted his way through her wares. His shopping list was at once forgotten as his eyes, nose and mouth traversed the shop. His eyes lingered over the chargrilled baby onions in olive oil, the wild mountain goat pâté and the grilled polenta but his nose pulled him away and positioned him in front of the cheeses where the *Taleggio*, with its peach rind striated with powder grey, solicited him uncompromisingly. The *Torta al Limone* proved even harder to resist, glinting up at him wickedly with its creamy golden heart dusted delightfully with icing sugar, the whole encased by crisp, caramel-coloured pastry.

35

'Someone special for dinner, Signor?' cooed Rosa. 'I give to you my special menu, guaranteed to win her heart. With it, I captured Germano and for forty-three years he is with me.'

Rosa was a clever lady. Her suggestions, made shyly, were each concluded with a question mark. Consequently, Richard bought exactly what she planned he should, but believed himself to have conceived the entire selection. With his wallet pleasurably empty and his bags satisfyingly full, he bade Rosa farewell and promised to tell her how the meal went. With plump arms folded triumphantly across a magnificent bosom encased by straining floral polyester, she sent him on his way with a 'Ciao' and a conspiratorial wink.

Back at his flat, Richard took the shopping into the kitchen, simultaneously undoing his tie and unbuttoning his shirt. He draped his tie (Hermès) around the bedroom door handle, his shirt (Thomas Pink) he bundled into the washing machine from whose drum stared the crumpled faces of four other white, worn-once shirts (Turbull & Asser, Hilditch & Key, Hawes & Curtis, Lewin). His suit (Hugo Boss) was given a good shake, placed over a thick wooden hanger and hung in the far left section of the wardrobe where it joined a regiment of other finely tailored suits (David Rose, Yves Saint Laurent, Armani – Giorgio, not Emporio). Socks (Ralph Lauren – we already know that) and boxer shorts (Calvin Klein – we would have guessed) were put in the laundry basket (Richard never mixes his washes). Shoes (Church's?) (Yes) were shoe-treed and placed at the foot of the cupboard. They will of course be polished before they are next worn.

Naked, Richard was heading for the shower when he stopped and philosophized. *No, cook first, then clean, then shower.*

He jumped into jogging pants and a faded polo shirt (both Timberland) and selected the music for the afternoon's industry. He'd cook to Mendelssohn's Italian, he'd clean to the Scottish, then relax and await Sally with Brahms. *Più animato*, Richard joined the strings of the first movement and skittered around his kitchen, gathering utensils and food stuffs and placing them in rational order according to the menu.

Richard, you could have been a Michelin-starred chef. Just look at you with your Sabatiers, how fast you chop, so evenly and accurately. Why don't the onions make your eyes water, why do you not subconsciously lick a finger and find it coated with garlic? How can you cook so exquisitely without using every utensil in your kitchen? Why is there no mess on the floor? You remember to preheat the oven, you wash up as you go, you do not splash tomato juice on your shirt, no bits of parsley wedge themselves under your nails. There really is no need for you to wear an apron but you look dinky in one anyway. All is cooked to perfection, you needn't taste it but you do, with a special spoon for the very purpose because you wouldn't dream of using the spoon with which you stirred the sauce (*à la* Marco Pierre White) and with which you were compelled to conduct the fourth movement *saltarello*. Talking of salt, you even know intuitively what constitutes a definitive pinch.

Finito.

The perfect four hours left for the flavours to mellow and the pungent fumes in the kitchen to subside into provocative wafts.

On with the second task. Cleaning. No *Shake 'n' Vac* short cuts for Richard. He glides around the sitting-room, eyes constantly searching out invisible dust, ears tuned to the oboe, serene above the crowded strings of the opening of the Scottish Symphony. Dust first, plump the cushions, straighten the tulips. Hoover. Spick and span.

Bedroom. Change the sheets, open the window. Hoover. Next.

Bathroom. Clean the bath, the sink; disinfect the toilet,

37

change the pot pourri; wash the tiles and the mirror, rinse well. Buff up. Hoover. Done. Next?

Body. 'Go running' is next on the Stonehill Schedule. Put on Nikes, put the wine in the fridge, look once round the flat, feel pleased, proud and at ease. Off you go.

Richard's daily run took him four miles and twenty-six minutes. Usually he thought of nothing, and thinking of nothing ensured he was relaxed and psychologically out of the office by the time he returned. Today, however, his mind was running faster than his feet.

Say she doesn't turn up? Say she's a vegetarian? Say my mother rings? Say Bob and Catherine pop round? Shit, did I turn the gas off? Have I got any condoms at home? Shall I buy Beaumes de Venise too? Yes, definitely. But I'd better buy that now so it can chill thoroughly. Wait, work this through. Get home, check condoms . . . no, check gas first. Then condoms. Shower? No, buy the pudding wine, then shower, then phone Mother. Other way round. Let's just get home.

Sprint, Richard, sprint!

Home, James. You didn't spare the horses today: 23 minutes 34 seconds. Not bad, not bad.

The gas was, of course, off.

Half an hour later, with condoms and wine bought and placed in bedside table and fridge respectively, Mother was phoned, the table laid, the sauce checked and fresh purple basil scattered through it. At last, Richard can start the final, crucial lap. Preening.

Hands on hips, upper lip sucked in by lower, wardrobe doors thrown open, he peruses his clothes. He touches nothing, just looks and assesses. Navy cotton chinos, brown suede belt, shirt striped thickly in blue and thinly in peppermint, white boxers, navy socks and navy nubuck loafers.

Navy, navy, navy, do you think that's too conservative?

38

No, Richard, you look wonderful in navy. Anyway, if you want to be pedantic, there's a subtle but effective difference between the French Navy of your shoes and the true navy of your trousers. If you're not happy, why not wear the shirt striped with olive and pink?

I'll go for the olive and pink.

In the tiler's delight bathroom, Richard showers. It is his routine to take it moderately hot and to finish off with a prolonged blast of freezing cold which, he assures himself, is invigorating and good for the circulation. Old habits die hard and this one stemmed from eight not always easy years at boarding school.

With a towel wrapped effortlessly around his trunk and another draped nonchalantly over his shoulder, Richard gives himself a close shave. To a fly on the wall, or on a majolica tile, the scene has all the features of a classic after-shave advert, bar the transatlantic voice-over drawl proclaiming: *'L'Homme, one hundred per cent.'* But this is Notting Hill and our Richard, towel now slipping irretrievably, is standing with eyes watering from the healthy smart of his one-hundred-per-cent manly after-shave. A few strange and not desperately appealing physiognomic contortions aid recovery but his towel still lies, somewhat comically, about his feet. No need and no time to rescue it and save his style. There is pressing work to be done involving a comb, an agile wrist and a damp mop of light-magnetic, sand-coloured hair. Comb it this way, then that. Run through a little mousse, comb again then lightly shake through with your fingertips. Result: the perfect, tousled look.

Get dressed, Richard, Sally will arrive in the hour. No, there's another job; out with the nail clippers and emery board, ensure that fingers and toes are neat and tidy. They are, they always are. Step into your boxers, slip on your trousers, pull on your shirt and slide into your loafers. You're ready, you're gorgeous. Now just lounge about, reinstate Mr Mendelssohn where your run so rudely cut him off, relax and await the arrival of Ms Lomax.

Miss Lomax was late back from school. An emergency meeting had been held to determine whether to expel or merely suspend an eleven-year-old boy for smoking in the girls' toilets. Sally suggested doing neither but making him smoke the entire packet. In front of his friends. However, the boy was suspended and sent home directly, with his packet of cigarettes. After school the teachers gathered to formulate the Monday morning assembly on the evils of smoking. It's bad for your health, very expensive and *not clever at all.*

But she's home now and is perturbed to find that she does not have time for her customary Friday evening bath, her *luxuriate.* Instead, a quick shower must suffice.

The Lomax legs are shaved and two stray hairs are tweezed from the bridge of her nose. Sally gives her hair an energetic brush and thanks the stars that she'd washed it the previous evening. She swirls a soft brush around a pot of bronze balls of rouge and carelessly but effectively whispers it over her cheeks and eyes. And cleavage, why not! After a quick spritz of *Ysatis*, she deftly flosses her teeth. Into the bedroom she goes, humming absent-mindedly 'The Lord Is My Shepherd', that morning's hymn. It's black velvet skirt time. She teams it with the olive silk shirt and black suede pumps with just the right height of heel to give her unremarkable legs an elegant send-off. Under it all, her little white cotton broderie anglaise knickers, for good luck.

Sally, you won't need it.

Before leaving the flat, she stops for a prolonged glance in the mirror and gives herself a slightly bashful smile.

Off you go, you old slapper! Shall I seduce him in between hors d'oeuvres and main course? Or before?

That's something for you to ponder on the Highgate–Notting Hill drive. Off you go, Sally.

Adjusting the choke, smoothing non-existent wrinkles from her skirt, Sally mirrored, signalled and manoeuvred – and then reversed straight back into the space she had just vacated. She unclipped her seatbelt and walked briskly back to her flat. She stopped in the sitting-room and gazed at the telephone which was ringing pleadingly. Beaming an ecstatic smile at it, she marched assertively into the bathroom. Giving her reflection a conniving wink, Sally plucked her toothbrush from the beaker and slipped it into her bag.

SEVEN

As soon as Sally entered Richard's flat, it was she who was seduced. And not by Richard. It was the smell of cooking: a mellow base of tomato and something she couldn't put her finger on, laced with top notes of garlic and basil. She realized how ravenous she was. For food. For sex too, but for food first and foremost. She'd passed on the shepherd's pie offered for lunch that day at school and had had to make do with a floury Cox's and a rubbery chunk of cheddar.

Sally was surprised that she wasn't in the least nervous. Richard, however, was. Unseen, and feeling queasy with excitement, he had watched Sally drive up and down the street looking for a parking place. He had gone straight to the kitchen and kept his hands motionless under the cold tap – sweaty palms would not be a turn on and were most unStonehill.

And here they are now, together again less than a week since their first meeting. How do they look to each other? How do they feel? Knowing full well how memory can often play havoc with reality and turn reptiles into royalty, Sally is relieved that Richard is just as good-looking and suave as she remembered. Richard is thrilled, his flat seems instantly infused with energy and light and his palms remain cool and dry. He thinks she looks scrumptious and has to fight back an impulse to scoop her up and twirl her around.

Nonchalant 'Hi's were followed with the briefest of pecks on the cheek. Richard led Sally through and lowered the volume of the Brahms. While he fixed her the obligatory drink ('Spritzer will be lovely, thanks'), she perused his books – just as Richard had at Sally's. She was amused that many of her dog-eared paperbacks were duplicated in here in pristine hardback. She wondered if he really *enjoyed* Nietzsche and what his favourite Shakespeare was.

'Seize her,' Richard murmured.

'I like the History Plays too,' Sally agreed.

Mentally, she catalogued all she saw and it all seemed to add up to the man she thought and hoped Richard was. Tulips in November, how decadent. A gleaming kitchen, ten out of ten. Leather recliner, lose five points. Cream sofa piled high with cushions, five points restored.

'Can I use your bathroom?'

'Sure, through there.'

Full marks for hygiene, bonus marks for the thickness of the towels, an overall gold star for taste. She flushed the loo just to make it seem that her trip to the bathroom had been for a purpose other than a snoop. Coming back into the lounge she had a furtive glance into the bedroom – it seemed quiet, airy and muted. Good.

'Sally, let's eat.'

For Sally, this meal was to be a sounding board for her scheme. All week, in the privacy of her flat and with a mirror propped close as the harshest of critics, she had practised a new technique on a variety of foods. Food, she had decided, was not so much to be eaten to be digested, as eaten to seduce. Hitherto she had merely cut asparagus into spearable, bite-sized chunks, now she could devour them whole with slow, sensual appeal. Although she had never really got to grips with the taste or method of oysters, she could now sip and gulp them with the alluring grace of a film star. To her relief, neither was on the menu tonight – anyway, asparagus had a strange effect on her bladder and she simply did not like those slithering detritus feeders, full stop.

Richard had prepared a meal that was as chic and delicious as it was simple. He had laid the table with a fine white damask cloth, dark red linen napkins, and cutlery and glass that shone proud. He'd toyed with the idea of a candle and a rose but was instantly repelled at the corniness of it (they would have had minus marks from Sally anyway). Instead, he dimmed the lights just slightly and, at Sally's request, replaced Brahms with Van the Man. *'My Brown-eyed Girl' indeed*, thought Richard.

He brought out the *Prosciutto S. Daniele* which he had rolled around *grissini*.

Shall I lick at it and suck at it suggestively?

Hold off a while, Sally. You don't want to be too obvious.

Ultimately, it was far too delicious to do anything to but eat and enjoy.

Richard stared at her, held her gaze for a groin-stirring moment and then dropped his eyes to her mouth.

Just look at that crumb nestling in the corner of her lips. A peony mouth, just like Hardy's Tess. Don't realize it's there, Sally, let me linger on it a while longer. I have to have that crumb, your mouth.

He leant forward, driven by the desire to lick the crumb, but Sally's tongue beat him by a split second. He'd lost the crumb but was awarded a tantalizing taste of her tongue tip. Her eyes spoke of the wry smile her lips wore but which he could not see, so close was he to her face. Unfortunately, it was not a pose he could hold comfortably indefinitely, propped as he was on his elbows and precariously close to the jug of vinaigrette. He sat back and saw how Sally's wry smile was not confined to her lips but covered her whole face. It raised her cheekbones, it caused delicate lines around her eyes, it dimpled her chin just very slightly.

I want to suck your chin.

'Delicious.'

Giving himself a dignified minute in which to let his erection melt away, he rose to fetch the next dish. A warm salad of rocket and baby spinach with roasted red peppers and individual goat cheeses. Richard offered to dress it for Sally. She watched him whisk the vinaigrette and liked the way that such a simple task was possible only with great effort from the ligaments and tendons of his wrist – she wanted to place a finger over them lightly as they twitched and sprang. She thought how lovely Richard's wrist was, slender and tanned and sporting a most beautiful watch (Cartier). She had never paid attention to a wrist before.

Sally ate delicately, folding the leaves securely over her fork and cutting each slither of pepper into careful pieces. She could not risk splash-back tonight – for the sake of both Richard's libido and her new silk shirt.

Richard finished before Sally. He watched. She stared back, eating all the while.

The skill of it! Every forkful placed perfectly in the centre of your perfect mouth without looking! Can I kiss you yet? When?

The plate was now bare but there was still a film of vinaigrette left. It was such a beautiful dressing, why shouldn't Sally run her finger round her plate? After all, *waste not, want not.* And, after all, it stirred Richard's groin again, not that Sally was aware of it.

The main course consisted of a bed of *pappardelle* woven throughout with *porcini* and chicken, and suffused with garlic, basil, sage and the ubiquitous olive oil.

45

That it was extra virgin and cold pressed goes without saying, we know Richard now. Sally had never had *porcini* before and was at first baffled as to whether they were meat or vegetable, so savoury was the taste, so firm the texture.

I must buy some of these.

Sally, they cost Richard twelve pounds.

The whole was a perfect partnership and created a lovely warm aromatic cloud in the mouth.

Thank God we're both having garlic, thought Sally, anticipating post-dinner sport. The pasta, broader than *tagliatelle*, was much more fork-friendly, preventing dribbles of sauce to the chin, or stray pieces hanging regrettably from the corner of the mouth (much to the chagrin of Richard's tongue).

The olive oil gave Sally's lips a gloss, too tantalizing for Richard to sit and merely observe. The vinaigrette jug was now off the table, the bread basket was on the floor. The scene had set itself for Richard; there was space for him to lean across, there were the sides of the table to hold for stability. Assertively he swiped Sally's mouth with his tongue. Her lips tasted of dressing, her mouth of Sally. Richard's tongue tasted of passion. Sally was buzzing between her legs, her bosom was heaving cinematically. She was ready to leave the meal for a banquet of sex.

No. Wait. Not yet. Keep it going, keep him just there. Let him stay a while hovering on the brink of being crazed and senseless with desire. Pull away. Smile as sweetly as you can and take a coy sip of that lovely Bardolino.

'Cheese?' Richard croaked.

'Please,' Sally purred.

Just two cheeses, complementing each other and the food that had gone before and that was to follow; the oozing, subtle *Taleggio* and spicier *Pecorino* accompanied by further slithers of Rosa Gambini's *ciabatta*, flatter yet with so much more spring and taste than the dull supermarket counterfeits. Richard had cleverly judged the servings and though they were both thoroughly satisfied, an all-important space still existed in their stomachs.

Undoubtedly, the *pièce de résistance* was the pudding. *Tiramisù*, of course. Another first for Sally. Richard had bought a complete dish from Rosa, just under a foot square, and Sally was soon fantasizing about diving into the centre of it and eating her way to the surface. Remembering his first taste of *tiramisù*, that it was not merely a delicious flavour but a sensation, an unforgettable experience too, Richard decided to halt his spoon midway to his portion so he could observe Sally's reaction.

As she spooned into it, she thought how beautiful it looked. The dark matt brown of the cocoa powder, the soft ivory of the *marscapone*, the glistening sponge, speckled through with espresso coffee.

I think I'm probably going to enjoy this very much. It could be dangerous!

As the spoon neared her mouth, a wisp of scent seduced her nose. Coffee-booze-chocolate. She looked across at Richard, waiting in anticipation. She smiled, giving a fleeting twitch of eyebrow. Still holding his gaze, she slowly pushed the loaded spoon into her mouth. It was like a trigger, a chemical reaction: her eyes snapped shut and simultaneously Richard grinned broadly. The first thing to accost her was the bitterness of the cocoa, thick and dry against the roof of her mouth. In an instant, the cool fluff of *marscapone* filtered through, wetting the powder which metamorphosed into a subtle and heavenly chocolaty sludge. The texture and taste were heady and incomparable. Then the marsala and rum, sodden in the sponge, broke through and created a warmth that trickled down into her chest. Finally, a kick from the espresso forced her eyes open and her head to shake slowly in astonishment. It was the signal for Richard to

47

have his spoonful. For Sally, *tiramisù* was more than a 'pick me up', she was literally stoned on the stuff.

An orgasm versus a first taste of tiramisù. *A tough choice if ever there was one! Both, please!*

Later, Sally, later. There's still one more thing for you to try.

After Sally's second helping (Richard was delighted – he could not abide the Abstemious Woman), he poured her a full and very chilled glass of Beaumes de Venise. Again he watched. First Sally cleaned her teeth with her tongue, searching for any hidden cocoa. Somewhat dismayed, she found nothing. She raised the glass, now aesthetically bloomed with condensation, and took note of the golden blush colour and the sweet, floral smell. Bouquet, Sally, bouquet. She took a sip. It was liquid silk. It was cold, clean and exquisite. If ambrosia is *tiramisù*, and she suspected it very probably was, then Beaumes de Venise was nectar. The food, the drink of the gods.

Sally's eyes wore a glazed expression. She looked across to Richard who looked soft and mellow under the wine and the dimmed lights. She was having a thoroughly good time. Never had she been so overwhelmed by such different taste sensations. Never had she simply enjoyed food so much. Now she knew for sure that aphrodisiacs existed.

Clever boy, Richard, you've seduced her with food, she's now ready, waiting and willing for part two of the evening's schedule. Physical pleasure.

Up you get, walk across and stand behind her chair. Scoop her hair up into a pony tail, tilt her head back slightly. Release her hair and let your hands fall on to her neck. It's delicate, you notice how vulnerable it feels, encircled entirely by your overlapping hands. Venture down and let your finger tips rest on her collar bone. Stroke that soft dip at her throat. Take one hand away and palm back the hair from her forehead. Gaze into those eyes, keep the gaze and move your other hand from her neck down across the silk of her shirt. You are between her breasts now. Find her left breast, cup it, press it, squeeze it. Let your hand lie soft, feeling her pip-like nipple in your palm. The touch of silk, the warmth and firmness of the flesh beneath.

Pull her to her feet and grasp her close to you. Keep the one hand holding her neck, put the other into the small of her back and pull her tightly against you. Press yourself against her; feel yourself hard, straining. Move your leg across and push her legs slightly apart. Now she too has something to push against. Lower your hand and feel her buttocks tense, you remember perfectly what they look like.

A gorgeous peach of an arse.

To feel its curve under velvet is as alluring as a breast under silk. But flesh itself is better. Her flesh is what you want.

Kiss her. Don't open your mouth, just press your lips against hers. Her tongue fleets at your lips. You respond. As the kisses become longer and deeper, you both push and grind your groins against each other. You feel like eating her. Nibbling at her lips does not suffice. Push her mouth open wide, as wide as it will go and probe as deep as you can. Feel her search back. Feel her run her tongue over the inside of your teeth. Bite her. Feel her simultaneously flinch yet move even closer and more insistently against you. Bite her again and feel her bite back. You are aware that her hand is starting to travel down. Away from your earlobe, down, down.

Lower, Sally, lower. Find me hard, rub your hand against me. Trace the shape of me. No don't take your hand away. Don't pull away from my lips. I want you. Where have you gone?

The CD had long stopped but the silence was loaded. Richard and Sally stood there, panting, mouths reddened, feet apart, a foot apart. Sally reached out and pulled Richard towards her by grasping the front of his trousers. Again they ate-kissed. Again they separated. Again at her instigation. He stepped towards her and she stepped back. He stepped towards her and again she retreated. The two were tangoing. Then he was ready. He took two steps forward to her one back and had her again, close to him, squeezing her waist with one arm, the other enmeshed in her hair. She gasped as her hair snagged around his fingers. She tried to tug away but he simply tightened his grip. To hear her breath, rasping, sent him into a fast frenzy of desire. He held her at arms' length as she tried to approach. Now he pushed her away.

Once more they stared, like matador and bull. Slowly he came to her and slid his hand up her skirt. It was tight but she helped by standing on her tiptoes. He wriggled upwards, effortlessly, to bullseye position. Sally lowered her heels back down. He could feel how moist she was under her panties and, with his thumb and third finger, tweaked and pressed superlatively.

Spot on, Richard.

Still they stared relentlessly into each other's eyes while Richard's skilful fingers set to work.

Look at her face, glazed eyes as if she does not see me though she looks right at me. Let me rub you right there. Let me go a little further. Look at your eyelids flicker. Look at your head tilt slightly back exposing your neck which I must graze with my teeth. Let me undo your blouse.

Deftly, Richard unbuttoned just enough of Sally's blouse to expose an exquisite breast. He ceased movement with his other hand though Sally pushed herself against it eagerly.

Look at me, Richard. Never have you desired a woman so much as you yearn for me this very moment. Feel me, move your hand from my arm but don't leave my gaze. Feel the breast that you've released from its shield of

olive silk. Feel it. Yes, just like that. Increase the pressure.
Again. Oh.

Richard introduced his finger tips and twisted Sally's nipple gently. He felt her move against his other hand and he made his fingers there come suddenly alive. Probing, twisting, rubbing. He looked at Sally's face. Her head was now involuntarily thrown backwards and to one side; it enticed him to suck at her neck, to fondle her breast firmly, to increase the speed of his fingers below. He felt her rocking her pelvis faster and faster. A surge of moistness. She let out a noise midway between a yelp and a gasp and brought her head back straight, once again meeting his eye directly. They stared into each other as they both felt the pulsations ebb away and stop. After a moment's stillness, Richard probed again, stroking with dexterous mastery. The throbs returned, less defined but certainly there. Sally's face had begun to soften. Her eyelids closed more frequently and for longer. Her head dropped slightly. To both of them, her body seemed to be melting.

Richard drew Sally towards him and cradled her carefully, holding her still and steady and close for minutes. Her head was buried against his chest, her shoulders were slumped, her exposed breast was now blushed, the nipple soft and puffy. She stayed against him feeling safe with the smell of him; sweat and pheromones filling her nose, his taste still in her mouth. He kissed the top of her head. She looked up and kissed him on his lips while he kept them motionless. With a hand on her shoulder and another around her waist, he led her to his bedroom and, on the bed with the fresh, crisp linen, he made slow and languid love to her.

EIGHT

Was it a chip in the paintwork or was it a spider?

Sally had been staring at the small, dark mark on the ceiling, trying to make up her mind. In that state of reverie, when eyes are young and focusing is lazy, she had been sure, alternately, that it was the one and then the other. Now that her eyes were awake and functioning she decided that it must be a mark or a dent.

And then it moved.

It was a spider. The intimate peace of the situation had been disrupted. Sally was now aware of other movements and noises. The blind breezed forward every now and then. The duvet curved up and fell down peacefully with her breathing. She could hear the clock, digital but audible; phit, phit, phit. For every three phits came one long, hushed, oblivious breath from Richard. A distant thrush sang to the morning while an occasional car hummed by. Under it all she could decipher the fridge adjusting its thermostat.

She lay on her back with Richard's arm lolling on top of the quilt over her stomach. She checked for the spider and found him a little further along the ceiling, playing dents again.

If I woke now, and saw him, I'd probably presume again that he was a dent. I wonder if he times his sorties according to phits? Sally grinned at her early-morning dedication to pointless ponderings, her commitment to theorizing over nothing particular. Shyly, she looked across at Richard. Asleep and safe and soundless. She wondered what time it was and reckoned round about 7.30. But then knowing the exact time suddenly assumed great importance so she tuned into the phitting and travelled her eyes up over Richard to locate the clock. 7.45. She smiled. And then smiled again, not knowing why.

He's awfully good-looking. I have chosen well.

But over and above the surge she felt on gazing at him, was a softness and warmth inside for him.

Stop it, stop it. Sally, stop.

And yet she found herself not recalling, thrust by thrust, the athletics of the previous night, but simply looking at him in the here and now. Asleep. Lovely. She felt compelled to reach out and delicately stroke away the flop of hair meandering over his eye and the bridge of his nose. Then she lingered and, with her fingertips, traced his eyebrows and the soft dips in the corners of his eyes. A careful fingertip brushed away an endearing pip of sleepydust. Again she found herself smiling and felt that same softness and warmth within.

No, Sally, no. Stop it. No. Impossible. Not after a week. Not ever.

The spider was on the move again and scuttled across and over to where the cupboards met the ceiling. The crack was plenty big enough and it disappeared from view.

Well, if the spider can snoop then so can I.

She left the bedroom noiselessly and went through to the lounge and over to the kitchen.

You can tell a lot about a person by what he keeps in the fridge.

You can tell a lot about a person by what they eat for breakfast, and with the fridge door still open, Sally ate *tiramisù* straight from the dish. Crouching on her heels, she noted that the milk was semi-skimmed and the eggs were free-range. There were peppers of every conceivable colour, flat-leaf parsley in a small tumbler of water, live yoghurts, slices of meat in Harrod's cellophane and a punnet of raspberries.

In November!

Having had enough *tiramisù* (for now), Sally opened a limed oak cupboard and catalogued the fine oils and vinegar, the packet of *porcini* which looked withered, rather sorry and somewhat inedible in their dried state. Much to her amusement and relief, right at the back she spied a large bottle of HP Sauce. She smiled and opened the next cupboard and examined the china. Villeroy and Boch.

That'll do.

Over in the lounge, she went to the bookcase to handle those sumptuous leather volumes. She ran her hand along the ash, very smooth and surprisingly warm. With a tentative fingertip, she felt the embossed spines and read the titles to herself. She took down *Julius Caesar* and ran it over her cheek. She fanned the pages and inhaled deeply. Then she touched the spine with her tongue tip and was miles away in another small heaven of her own when peace was shattered by the post.

He gets The National Geographic, *what luxury!*

Leaving the rest of the post with the *Guardian* on the doormat, Sally curled up on the leather recliner and lost herself in the social behaviour of the humpback whale, and went on a fascinating trip through Alaska by husky.

And that was how Richard found her when he surfaced half an hour later.

'Morning, Sal.'

'Morning, Richie.'

'Breakfast?'

'Mmm.'

'In bed?'

'And why not!'

How civilized: warm croissants, freshly juiced oranges, a good pot of Earl Grey and the morning paper.

'This is my favourite part of Saturday's *Guardian*, the Questionnaire,' revealed Sally, and they laughed out loud at Alan Bennett's disclosures. Richard grabbed a spoon and turned it into a microphone.

'Sally Lomax, twenty-five, teacher, *National Geographic* reader, *tiramisù* demolisher and sex-goddess, what is your idea of perfect happiness?' He thrust the spoon at her.

Delighted, Sally sparked back: 'A beautiful stone farmhouse in Tuscany and a dark swarthy male to go with it.'

Actually, Saturday morning, breakfast in bed, the paper and you would do nicely. But you shan't know that.

'With which historical figure do you most identify?'

'Lady Godiva.'

'Which living person do you most admire?'

'Aunt Celia. She's seventy and has the strength of an ox and the courage of Samson.'

'What vehicles do you own?'

'Strong pair of legs.'

'And a Mini Cooper. What is your greatest extravagance?'

'Danish pastries.'

'And *tiramisù* for breakfast?'

Sally blushed.

'Sal, you're blushing! What objects do you always carry with you?'

'Donor card, paracetamol, rape alarm, pocket hankies, emery board, safety pins, stamps, address book.'

'Am I in it?'

'No.'

'What makes you most depressed?'

'Child abuse. Oh, and synthetic cream.'

'What do you most dislike about your appearance?'

'I rather like it!'

'Sally!' Richard chastized.

'Okay, my bikini line hair,' Sally confided.

'What is your most unappealing habit?'

'I don't have any.'

'Sally!' Richard warned again.

'Oh, God. Okay, I fart in the bath.' They fell about laughing and Richard admitted quite happily that he did too.

'What would you like for your next birthday?'

'An answerphone. No, a weekend in Boston.'

'When is your birthday?'

'Next year. May the nineteenth.'

'What is your favourite word?'

'Funicular.'

'You *what*?'

'It's a lovely word to say. Try it.'

'Fu-nic-u-lar. Hmm. What is your favourite journey?'

'The road to Oban, the boat to Mull; to Aunt Celia's.'

'Who are your favourite musicians?'

'Genesis, Van the Man, Dylan.'

'Anyone told you it's now the 1990s? Who are your favourite writers?'

'Alice Thomas Ellis and Jane Austen.' *Oh, and Ms Collins.*

'What or who is the greatest love of your life?'

She panicked momentarily and looked at him blankly. 'Myself?' she ventured. He seemed pleased with that.

'Which living person do you most despise?'

'Despise? I don't care much for Myra Hindley or Peter Sutcliffe.'

'What do you consider the most overrated virtue?'

'Chasteness. Decorum.' Richard raised his eyebrows at the intensity of her proclamation.

'What is your greatest regret?'

'Not being good enough to go to ballet school.'

'Ballet?'

'Ten years of it.'

'That explains your hyper-mobility then! When and where were you happiest?'

'Childhood holidays at Aunt Celia's in Mull.'

'What single thing would improve the quality of your life?'

'A farmhouse in Tuscany.'

'And the dark, swarthy man?'

'Him too.'

'What would your motto be?'

'Don't look before you leap.'

'How would you like to die?'

'When I'm ready.'

'How would you like to be remembered?'

'With desire and longing and a twinkle in the eye.'

'Thank you, Ms Lomax,' said Richard, pouring her another cup of Earl Grey and stirring it with the microphone, 'that was intriguing!'

And necessary, my love. 'But there's one more question,' he asked lasciviously, 'how do you like it best?'

Sally smirked. 'Milk, no sugar?' she ventured.

Richard raised his eyebrows in a that-won't-do fashion.

'I'll show you later. First, there's the small but pressing issue of your answers, Richard Stonehill.'

'And then you'll show me?'

'Then I'll show you.'

NINE

'*R*ichard Stonehill, thirty-five, architect, new-age man and all round good-looker, what is your idea of perfect happiness?'

'Yachting in Australia.' *You, Sal.*

'Ever done it?'

'Yes, I have.'

'What is your greatest fear?'

'Multiple sclerosis.'

'With which historical figure do you most identify?'

'Byron.'

'How pretentious! Which living person do you most admire?'

'Bob.'

'Bob-and-Catherine Bob?'

'Yes.'

'What vehicles do you own?'

'An Alfa Romeo Spyder and a Cannondale mountain bike.'

'What is your greatest extravagance?'

'Silk ties and olive oil that's as expensive as the former.'

'What objects do you always carry with you?'

'Why, my little black book of course.'

'Am I in your little black book?'

'You are in my little black book.'

'What makes you most depressed?'

'Housing estates. Oh, and nylon.'

'Hear hear. What do you most dislike about your appearance?'

'My legs.'

'Your legs?'

'Too skinny.'

Richard, they're gorgeous, unquestionably masculine, you vain old thing.

'What is your most unappealing habit?'

'*Moi? Rien!*'

'Ri-*chard!*'

'Okay, I pick my nose, fart and belch.'

'Big deal.'

'Simultaneously. In the bath.'

'Gracious Good Lord. What would you most like for your next birthday present?'

'You. Wrapped up in brown paper and red ribbons.'

'When is your birthday?'

'June the second.'

'I'll see what I can do. What is your favourite word?'

'Telecommunication,' proclaimed Richard. 'Well, it *sounds* nice, doesn't it?' Sally raised an eyebrow. 'Oh, all right then – copulation.'

'Later. What or who is the greatest love of your life?'

'My mummy!'

Laughter erupted and Sally tickled Richard into saying 'Architecture' and finally admitting 'Food'.

'Oops, watch that cup! What do you consider the most overrated virtue?'

'Etiquette.'

'What is your greatest regret?'

'That my father and I did not get along.'

'It's never too late for a reconciliation.'

'He's dead.'

'Oh. Poor Richie. Mine died when I was fifteen. When and where were you happiest?'

'Finishing the London marathon three years ago.'

'What single thing would improve the quality of your life?'

'A housekeeper-cum-therapist-cum-masseuse-cum-sex-goddess. Want the job? Seven-fifty an hour?'

'Ten? Done! Which talent would you most like to have?'

'Telepathy.'

'What would your motto be?'

'*Bien faire ce que j'ai à faire.*' Sally nodded, earnestly hoping to veil the fact that she had not the faintest idea what that meant.

'How would you like to be remembered?'

'As Sally Lomax's favourite lay!' *As Sally Lomax's favourite.*

'Thank you, Richard Stonehill, for your co-operation and honesty. Would you like your reward now or after lunch?'

'What do you think?'

Richard and Sally explored each other's bodies with a new inquisitiveness and a new depth. A new tenderness, too. Richard found how Sally's personality shone through; her breasts spoke of it, her fuzzy bikini line proclaimed it. She spent a long time caressing his legs, with hands, lips and eyes, showing him that they drove her wild. She whispered 'telecommunication' as she chewed and licked his ear lobes. He hummed Genesis and sang 'Turn It On Again' after she came. She came again. She felt more fulfilled than she had with any other man, not that there had been that many. Now they both wanted to give, not merely to take. To give and to receive, to linger and to lap it up.

What is it that I am feeling? thought Sally as she

showered, alone, in Richard's bathroom. *What is it?* she wondered, as she swathed herself in Richard's thick, burgundy towelling robe. *What is it that feels so, well, nice?* she asked herself as she padded across the bedroom to gaze out of the window at nothing in particular.

They lunched and munched together, snuggled deep in Richard's voluminous sofa; *du pain, du vin, du Boursin.* Later, they browsed and tinkered at Portobello Market. He bought her two pounds of Cox's Orange Pippins, she bought him half a pound of pear drops which tasted of white paper bag, just like they had in childhood, just as they should. The weather was as crisp as the apples, their noses were reddened and noisy, their fingers chilled. They thawed out at the Gate Cinema and were warmed by coffee, carrot cake and a Louis Malle matinée.

On her way home she stopped at a chemist. And bought a new toothbrush. She had not forgotten to take hers home, nor had she planned to leave it. She did not leave it accidentally-on-purpose, nor had she connived with herself in the bathroom mirror. She had done no grinning at the toothbrush. It was in the same beaker as Richard's but they were not touching. His was an angle-poised, hard bristle; hers was small-headed and soft. She had left it merely because it had looked just fine in the beaker with Richard's. Richard was not madly excited to find it there later, but certainly he was happy that it was there. That night, alone but not lonely in their respective beds, they did not think of each other but of themselves. Friday nights and Saturday mornings were to become an institution, not that they knew it then. If waves of contentment can travel, then the vibes from Highgate and those from Notting Hill would have met, crashed and fallen to earth somewhere around Regents Park. Which is precisely where, three days later, Sally and Richard next met.

TEN

With the future of the Zoo uncertain, schools all over London chose it over Hatfield House or Madame Tussaud's for their annual school outings.

With the future of the Zoo uncertain, a team of architects was consulted over proposals for a building dedicated to research and conservation of endangered species. The idea was to promote the Zoo as a foundation, a trust dedicated to understanding and preserving and improving the future for threatened wildlife. It was to lose its image of merely housing bored tigers and sloping-shouldered eagles in cracked concrete. The hope was, that if seen as environmentally aware and ecologically sympathetic, funding from all sectors would be more readily available. In theory alone, the proposal had been met with great enthusiasm from the public and the government had given it a quiet nod or two already.

The Zoological Society, placed as it is in the outer circle of the Park, affords a sweeping vista. Especially from the wide window from which Richard gazed, plastic beaker of instant coffee in hand, waiting for the first, crucial meeting with his potential clients. He watched nostalgically as a human crocodile of ten-year-olds made its haphazard approach to the main gates, sections of its vertebrae frequently slipping out of alignment. He remembered well the joy of walking hand in hand with a best friend, the despair of having to hold hands tightly with an enemy, the humiliation of holding hands with the most unpopular boy in the class. The crocodile's nose was black and red, because those were the only colours Diana Lewis wore. Its body was a multicoloured jumble of school children in mufti. Its navy tail caught and captured Richard's attention.

The tail of the crocodile was Sally Lomax.

'Good morning, Mr Stonehill, we are sorry to have kept you waiting. Shall we start?'

But I want to see the crocodile!

'Mr Stonehill?'

I don't want to be in this stuffy building, I want to find the crocodile and watch its tail swish.

'Gentlemen, lady, this is Richard Stonehill from Mendle-Brooke Associates.'

'Good morning,' said Richard somewhat reluctantly, as he took the head of the table and began unravelling the roll of drawings, crocodiles still foremost in his mind. However, as soon as his design unfurled itself, Richard was totally focused. His personality, his gifted presentation and the skill of the design itself kept his audience rapt. An hour and a half shot by. Had they had the money there and then, they would have pressed cash into his hand and given him *carte blanche* to start immediately. Reality, however, would impose a minimum two-year wait.

'I think I'll just have a wander,' Richard informed his hosts as everybody shook hands. 'It's the crocodiles that fascinate me.'

The children were having a lovely time, especially Marsha and Rajiv who were still holding hands long after the crocodile had disintegrated. Sharp, sweet wafts of dung and straw were filtered by the chill air and were pleasing to the nose. The bellow of the camel was impersonated very well by Marcus who was offered a ride by the keeper. Squeals of delight filled the air as the dromedary lunged and lurched itself up. The children's zoo proved very popular too; little hands gently petted even littler furries and packed lunches were shared illicitly with the bleating, pleading, pocket-nuzzling deer and goats.

Around Miss Lewis, a band of keen young artists had gathered to sketch the elephants.

It was cold, cold, but clear. Everyone was in a thoroughly good mood.

'Oh, children, the light's just *per*fect! *Sim*ply perfect. I've brought charcoal and 4B pencils and some waxy crayons. Who wants what?' The waxy crayons were the first to be snapped up followed sharply by the charcoal. The pencils were the last to go because Miss Lewis forbade erasers – 'Work *through* your mistakes, make your errors a part of your de*sign*' was her oft-chanted dictum. Experience had taught Class Five that any child caught smuggling a rubber would have it ceremoniously confiscated and, worse, would have to contend with Miss Lewis's inconsolable hurt.

With not much more than an ear or tusk completed, the children began to complain of cold toes and numb fingers. Miss Lewis had overcome that problem by investing in a pair of red mittens, the tips of which could be folded back to reveal black, fingerless gloves. She sat on the bench surrounded by the hastily dumped materials of her protégés (off to see the *yeuch! spi*ders and *urgh! beet*les) and breathed in the coarse, sweet smell of elephant. Wielding a 4B as a conductor might his baton, she began to draw fervently, making any mistake a committed part of the overall design.

Sally, who had just finished a quick chat with the polar

bear (he had winked at her, slowly and wisely), contemplated the scamper and flurry of her class, released from the greyness of school and its buildings. She felt a little sad, imagining how the animals too would kick up their heels and squeal with delight if they were turned out into pastures new, let alone to their native habitats. She thought it cruel how the children teased the rhino for being so ugly, the way they grimaced and growled at the motionless lion, chattered and jumped around in front of the chimps and tapped on the glass of the aquarium to see if the fish would budge or the clam slam shut. She walked past the birds of prey and couldn't associate the moth-eaten raptors with those she remembered from her childhood holidays, soaring in majestic abandon over the hills near Aunt Celia's.

Miss Lewis had a hushed audience about her. All over her scarf (black) and her jumper (red) were chunks and furls of wood and lead: 'Never use a sharpener, gives a *gha*stly line. Scalpel. That's the answer. *Su*per edge. Absolutely not, Marcus, only I can use it. *Horribly* sharp. Trust me.' The children were wowed into silence by the skill with which Miss Lewis brandished her 4B, the verisimilitude of her drawing. The keeper recognized the sage old face immediately as Bertha. Richard Stonehill had glanced at the picture, greatly impressed. But he looked more intently at what had been the nose of the crocodile; he wondered what her name was and how well she knew Sally. Bertha, with unarguable dignity and grace, nevertheless answered the call of nature with an extremely ripe-smelling and resounding thud. The keeper didn't smell it at all any more but the children shrieked with delight and bolted away, proclaiming 'Poo! Poo!' for the uninformed. Distracted, Miss Lewis looked up momentarily, caught Richard's eyes, smiled fleetingly and returned her undivided attention to Bertha who was, she decided, the most beautiful creature she had ever seen. Richard wandered off in search of a sandwich.

Sally wandered over to Diana.

'Lunch?'

'Mmm? Nyet. Iniminit.' Sally wandered off in search of a sandwich.

Every corner Richard turned, every enclosure he went to see, he felt sure he would finally come across Sally. His adrenal glands were in overdrive and he had demolished the sandwich in seconds without tasting it. Now it sat in his throat in a stodgy lump and felt as if it further protruded his Adam's apple. Swallow as he might, he could not shift it an inch lower nor soften it at all. A drink was a possible solution.

The kiosk was a round structure with only one serving hatch. As Sally bought her cheese and pickle sandwich and carton of Ribena and walked away anticlockwise, Richard came from the other direction and exited clockwise. But there was no Chaplinesque crash and they each remained oblivious to the tantalizing proximity of the other. Sally had already disappeared behind the pandas and was wondering what bamboo tasted like.

Richard went to the reptile house to look at the crocodiles.

Are those Sally's kids?

'What time did Miss Lomax say we were to meet at the penguins?'

Yes, they are.

'Two o'clock. Ten minutes' time.'

The penguins, two o'clock, nine minutes' time. As he stared at the crocodile, it flickered its eye shut, opened it again and stared back at Richard. He found it rather disconcerting and decided to arrive early at the penguins to ensure the best possible view. As he approached he could see Sally from the back, a posse of children surrounding her. They held her hands and all hopped from foot to foot – whether this was a bid to keep warm or an imitation of the penguins was not altogether clear.

They seem to like her, she's probably their favourite

teacher. Lenient, no doubt, but commanding respect and obedience.

Richard was puzzled at just how nervous he was, hands clammy and the sandwich had reappeared to pester his Adam's apple. The contents of the butterfly house had taken residence deep in his stomach and the sawdust of the possums' cage appeared to be in his mouth. As he approached he could hear her voice.

'Ooh, wouldn't you love to take one home with you?' she cooed to her entourage. Richard was within a couple of yards of her. He could now see just how enthralled she was by her flippered friends. Up she was on tiptoes, bouncing, as she marvelled at their clumsy acrobatics.

She's quite wonderful. Enchanting.

He walked past and around the penguin pool and took position on the opposite side. He stared at Sally but Sally was rapt. And anyway, Richard was the last person she was expecting to see at London Zoo on a Tuesday lunchtime.

The penguins seemed to like their enclosure. Richard did too. A hilly maze of steps and slopes in blue and white, just like the Arctic, surrounding a generous pool of cold water. He would make few changes to it. Perhaps a bridge. Deepen the pool. A few hidey-holes in the sides. New surfacing. The penguins never seemed to tire of running up and down and around in a complicated and irrational route to the water into which they joyfully tumbled. Natural entertainers, the bigger their audience, the more comic their antics. An audience *and* feeding time was the best possible combination; clapping and laughter encouraged them to catch their fish in the most elaborate fashion. And there was a fair-sized audience at two o'clock. But Richard saw only Sally. And he soaked up what he saw.

She watched one penguin in particular, slightly smaller than the others, his tuxedo glossy, his shirt snowy, his walk pompous and assertive. A fish had been thrown into the centre of the pool and two penguins, positioned on a ridge above it, looked at the water and shifted from leg to leg. Sally's pal hurried along the ridge and barged into one who crashed into the other. Both fell in while he stood, shifting from side to side, proudly smacking himself with his flippers. He then belly-flopped into the water and surfaced almost immediately with the fish while his two comrades splashed about, thoroughly disoriented. Sally was thrilled and clapped energetically while jumping up and down on the spot, cheering. She had her hands splayed and ridged, bashing them together enthusiastically, her smile wide, her jaws well apart, her lips forced back to reveal every tooth in her mouth.

And then she saw Richard.

And she brought her hands together in one final clap. Her mouth was still open but the corners had dropped. She stood paralysed with her hands still rigid, as if in prayer. Richard beamed a broad grin in her direction. The penguins were satiated and dozed on their stomachs, heads and legs suspended. Richard waved his roll of drawings at Sally, Diana saw him and then turned to Sally who was still praying. *Ah ha!* she thought. *Here is the reason for the swagger, the new wardrobe, the infuriating evasiveness, The Glow. Introduce me, Sal – oops, Sally. Do!*

Richard had begun to stroll around the pool. Sally remained transfixed by the space he left. Though rosy and alive, her face spoke a glimmer of slow panic too. Diana saw this and acted upon it immediately.

'Okay, kids, one last look at the creepy crawlies and then back to the coach,' she more or less ordered, and though she was desperately intrigued by Sally's stunned immobility, she tore herself away and went off in search of tarantulas and stag beetles. Sally remained motionless, her pose and poise reminiscent of church sculpture. She did not, however, feel her exterior stillness within. She was lurching and churning, not knowing what to make of the situation.

I hadn't planned this. I don't quite know what to do. What shall I do? Think. He should not have seen me like this. Soft. Penguins. Clapping. That won't do. Think.

Richard was very near.

'Wait!' Sally suddenly cried after Diana. But Richard was there and Diana was not. He was unaware of Sally's sudden crisis.

'Hello, Sal!'

'Hello, Richard. I must dash.'

'Call me.'

The coach was a zoo in itself. Rubbery spiders careered through the air, jelly snakes and sugary polar bears littered the floor. The children were now chimps, charged with manic chattering, climbing all over the seats. Diana, still mittened, wasn't that bothered about enforcing order and silence. She was more concerned and extremely inquisitive about Sally's defiant silence. She nudged her with her elbow. Sally turned slowly towards her.

'Well?'

'Well what?'

'Who was that gorgeous man thing?'

'Someone I sort of know.'

The women looked at each other. Sally wanted to look away but found the pull of Diana's enquiring eyes too strong, too comforting. Still Diana searched Sally's face. Sally felt safe and she also felt strong. She broke into a broad, conspiratorial smile. The camaraderie between the two women was intense, almost tangible. Knowing full well that she could trust Diana implicitly, Sally felt euphoric and, in hushed tones, she told Diana why.

'I've been terribly naughty, Di.'

'Oh, *do* tell!' implored Diana, grasping Sally's knee with mittened zeal but trying not to sound too keen. So

Sally gave Diana an uncensored account in glorious Technicolor replete with close-ups. Though no detail of the action was neglected, she did, however, omit the underlying motive. There was no insinuation that this unbridled lust was driven by a carefully conceived plan. What Sally wanted was an approval of sorts, a 'God, I wish I'd done that'. Diana did not disappoint her there.

'This is the stuff of an airport groin-grinder! A veritable Jackie Collins bonk-buster. Wow!'

Sally was delighted. She did not expose the psychological bent of the situation, for not only did she fear the inevitable 'It'll only end in tears, someone's bound to get hurt', but fundamentally she wanted the fact that it was a calculated project kept all to herself.

Diana was quite exhausted when they arrived back at school.

When Sally arrived home she felt strangely depleted and a little anxious.

But I didn't want him to see me like that. What can he think? Surely a true femme fatale wouldn't go potty for penguins? She wouldn't clap and squeal like a child. I don't want to break the spell. I wonder if I have. He probably thought me quite sweet. I don't want to be sweet, I want to be scandalous. He's probably contemplating my merits as child-bearer and biscuit-baker this very moment. I must remedy the situation, reassert myself as a veritable vamp, a tough cookie, a steel butterfly. But how?

'Hello, Richard?'

'Sal! Enjoy the Zoo?'

'Very much.'

'Pop over?'

'Now? Ten-thirty?' Sally was in her red nightshirt (a present from Diana), fluffy green bed socks, an old tatty cotton scarf in her hair. 'Sure,' she purred, already scrambling out of her night clothes. She slipped on a black skirt and polo neck and declared to the African Violet that all was not lost. She hovered at her front door and then returned to her bedroom where she derobed and then dived back into her nightshirt. She drew the line at the socks and scarf, dabbed on a little perfume and slipped on her pumps. She covered up with her long trench coat, partly as protection against the drizzle, partly because what was underneath was for Richard alone.

It felt exciting to be going out when normally she would have been going to bed. But she also felt old and bemused, remembering how University nights would not yet have started. The roads were fairly empty and the traffic lights were on her side. She enjoyed hearing the fizzy whish made by wheels on the wet tarmac, seeing the sparkling orange flecks on the road cast by the street lights. It took less than twenty minutes, without breaking the speed limit or jumping amber lights, for Sally to arrive and park in Notting Hill where the bars were still throbbing and the bright young things would be enjoying *tapas* for a good while yet.

The lift in Richard's building was old and cumbersome. The door had to be opened, the grille coaxed back then cranked closed, the floor selected with an assertive press and then an infuriating delay tolerated until the instructions registered. In the chug between ground and first floors, Sally had an idea. As first floor came and went, she unbuckled and unbuttoned her coat. By the time the lift was approaching the second floor, she had her nightshirt over her head. The lift stopped and so did Sally's heart. But nothing happened and no one was there. Was the machinery trying to tell her something? It juddered on up and, for a delicious few seconds between the second and third floors, Sally stood completely naked.

The young lady who got out of the lift on the fourth floor smiled sweetly at the pizza delivery boy who got in. He watched her saunter down the hall and thought how well her long mac suited her. Sally's knickers were still in the lift but he presumed them to be a handkerchief and, having recently recovered from a cold, he kept a clear distance. (They were discovered by the porter the next morning who sincerely hoped that nothing untoward had happened. In twenty-seven years he had never once had a pair of knickers lurking in his lift. Handkerchiefs and scarves maybe. Knickers, no. Mr Stonehill from Flat C tutted with him and said it was a disgrace.)

Richard answered the door, enveloped in his towelling robe. He kissed Sally on the cheek and before he had a chance to ask her more about the school trip, about her job, her colleague the elephant lover – all of which he was keen to know – Sally had pulled him towards her and nearly suffocated him with the deepest kiss imaginable. Her carrier bag fell to the floor and Richard's penis soared skyward, pressing somewhat uncomfortably against the buckle on Sally's coat.

Let's undo that for starters.

Go on, Richard, unbelt me, unbuckle me, unbutton me, see what you can find. Richard had the belt off immediately and, still enmeshed in her kiss, he began to fumble with the buttons which were big but sat tight in their button holes.

I'm enjoying this! thought Sally.

I'm enjoying this! thought Richard.

When Richard had all the buttons undone, he slipped his hands under the lapels to push the coat away. Sally's soft shoulders greeted him. *What has she got on?* he wondered, images of black lacy basques and cream, silky camisoles assaulting his mind while he glued his mouth to Sally's and shut his eyes with the pressure of pleasure.

What has she got on? Nothing? Nothing! Goddo!

Sally felt the muscles of Richard's lips break into a smile. She pulled her head back to look at him and he looked at her, naked, glorious and right there in his apartment. She raised her eyebrows in a cheeky quiver

72

and he tutted before grabbing her towards him and planting a scorching kiss on her right breast.

They made love, there and then, by the door which was still ajar. Sally later had to take her mac to the dry cleaners. When she left at 7 a.m. Richard pressed a little paper bag into her hand before sending her to school with a kiss on the forehead, a nip on the lips and a smack on her bottom. In her rush to race home, shower, dress appropriately for a teacher and make it to assembly, Sally forgot about the packet until morning break. Sitting on the toilet, she unscrunched the bag and saw it had *London Zoo* and a tiger design emblazoned on the front. Out of it she tipped a small keyring. In the shape of a penguin.

ELEVEN

When can love begin? And can you fight it? When does love begin and when should it? But can you fight it?

Richard fell in love with Sally that morning at the Zoo. In a moment. He was as sure as his walk that he was in love with Sally Lomax. He felt peaceful and content about it. And happy. Secure. He didn't bother to pontificate on what love is or should be, whether it was possible or realistic to feel love and know it after just a few meetings, meetings in which physical desire had, after all, played a dominant part. Sally had never stopped to think whether she might fall in love with Richard, too busy was she making sure that he didn't fall in love with her but was instead subsumed by lust for her. Richard certainly lusted after her, but now he lusted out of love. Sally was blind to that love, she judged her happiness and success solely on the rigidity, endurance and explosion of his penis. Consequently, she completely neglected any exploration of her own subconscious, devoting all energy to new and invariably more outrageous seduction situations.

But, Sally, you are so lovable, togged up in your old

Swan Lake tutu and turning up at Richard's a mere two hours after you had left one Sunday night. Who could not love a girl who pulls her man into the ladies' toilets to give him a blow job after an overlong Belgian film? Or guides his hand under her skirt beneath the table of a dinner party so he can discover she has on no panties? And Sally, your eyes are artless and provide a short cut into your soul; Richard has gazed at them, beyond them, often. Your smile is so full and real and alluring. He sees your face, Sally, in ecstatic rapture as you climax under him, on top of him, on his hand, on his mouth. He watches you and he feels he could burst with desire.

But he watches you when you do not know it. He observes you as you watch the News and he sees your face crease in anguish for war victims, for beached whales, for families of the murdered, for the women who were raped. And he gazes at you for hours while you sleep, he watches while you stare out of windows at nothing in particular. What he sees, he loves. Laughing at penguins. 'Gracious Good Lord'. He sees the tears film over your eyes at the close of a play, the end of a film, as you finish a novel. Richard watches you all the while, but you don't know it. Richard is in love with you but you don't see it. You will, you will. And then how will you feel?

Richard wanted to sing his joy from the roof-tops, to swing from the steeple and proclaim it, to climb trees and laud it. Instead, he informed Bob quite casually over their customary post-workout swift half.

'Where are you spending Christmas? Want to come for lunch? We're also having a New Year's Eve bash, can't decide whether to have a theme or not. You know, come as a painting, come as a film. I could just see you as a Degas ballerina!'

'I am in love with Sally Lomax.'

'And he just said it, no prompting?'

'He just came right out with it, I hadn't even mentioned her.'

Bob had ensured that it had indeed been a true and very swift half indeed and not the usual excuse for a two-pinter. He could not wait to tell Catherine. It really was ground-breaking news. It really was the most extraordinary occurrence.

Richard is in love. Gracious, old Richie boy in love and declaring it. No more 'she's all right's, now it's 'she's the one'. He's found her! At long bloody last, he's found her. And he seems so sure. And he seems, well, just so bloody happy! And I knew it, I knew it, didn't I? I could see it a mile and a half off and now he can see it too and he's as happy as fucking Larry.

Outwardly, Catherine was delighted. Secretly she was just a little dismayed. It had been nice to have Richard generally unattached, to know that she was perhaps the most important woman in his life. She loved it that he spent much of his time with them, being charming, good-looking – and hers, in a way. For as long as she had known him, he had never been short of female attention. He had always brought them over to Catherine and Bob's for Catherine to dissect later over a lengthy phone call. And when such liaisons inevitably came to grief, he had always enjoyed a healthy *post mortem* with her. They exchanged *Vogue* for *GQ*. They often lunched together and shopped together – Richard provided the perfect mannequin for Catherine to outfit her shop-shy husband. For Catherine, Richard was the older brother she never had, and for whom she would gladly swap her younger one (whose passions were fired almost solely by motor-bikes). Now Richard was in love and intuition told her it very well might be The One. Sally Lomax she liked though she was but a friend of a friend's. Catherine was inquisitive to see if Richard-in-Love differed in any fundamental way from the Richard she knew and adored.

'Let's have them to dinner. No, how about Sunday lunch? This Sunday. Go on, Bob, phone. Phone now!'

And so the four of them lunched together on Sunday, and on other Sundays. They all dined at Richard's too, and went to the theatre, and walked on Kenwood, and went to exhibitions at the Serpentine. They decided together that the New Year's Eve party would be a masked ball. Sally conspired with Catherine to make their outfits on her sewing machine and, with inordinate pleasure, they refused to help the men in any way with theirs. The women became more than the partners of their partners, they became friends. Catherine was delighted that Richard was just the same only more so, more animated, more charming, happier than ever she had known him. Bob liked Sally but rarely spoke to her one to one. Sally didn't really notice Bob, Richard was her project, he was not. The more time the four of them spent together, the more Richard spoke to Bob in private about Sally. But he never told Sally. He never said the 'L' word to her though he used it frequently with Bob. The word was never empty but always saturated with conviction.

Sally called him Richie, and to him Sally was Sal. Bob and Catherine never tired of shooting each other knowing smiles and conspiratorially raised eyebrows when these diminutives, forbidden to all others, were used. Catherine tried using it once with Richard but his wince was sharp. Richard would remain Richie to Sally alone.

Diana too was let into their cocoon. Or rather they into her black and red one. Evenings of macro-biotic food, ambient music and good grass became almost a weekly institution in the run-up to Christmas. Invariably it was a Monday night, serving as a boost for the architect and two teachers for the week ahead. Richard and Sally would lie sprawled on the black, sagging couch, watching Diana gesticulating vividly from the depths of the voluminous

77

red bean-bag, listening with mirth to her many tales – some true, some surely not, who cared? They would wend a weary way home to Sally's, make love lazily and then embrace a stoned slumber, to awake amazingly refreshed and energetic to continue their working weeks.

Sally grew fonder of Diana and loved to hear her describing Richard, admiring his statuesque body, his composed but agreeable person. '*Mar*vellous teeth and *beau*tiful nails, prerequistes you know, pre*req*uisites.' Sally often granted Diana an insight into their sex life – something Richard never gave Bob. The women would sit in a corner of the drab staff-room and fill it with colourful laughter. Sally loved to see Diana reel back in awe and delight. It made her feel proud. Sometimes Sally's account was deliciously bawdy, sometimes downright scientific. Mostly, she recalled their couplings so eloquently and with such passion that Diana's eyes watered and she was rendered anomalously speechless. Occasionally, she even suggested little bed-time tricks and Sally could not wait to tell her the effect they had had. These were the machinations of Diana's increasingly warped imagination – she had not tried them out. She wouldn't dare. Anyway, on whom? The live yoghurt was completely unsuccessful, the raw cake mixture downright messy, but the carefully proportioned mix of orange juice and just a little olive oil (extra virgin, cold-pressed) was a gem of Diana's for which Sally became eternally grateful.

But Sally never mentioned the 'L' word. Sally didn't know anything about it. 'L' for what? Yet Diana, gifted with some intrinsic insight, could see it. She quietly made notes of their body language, the way that Sally so comfortably welded to Richard on the sofa. She observed how attentive Sally became when Richard was speaking, how she laughed more strongly if Richard laughed, how she watched him and not Diana when the other two spoke. And Diana saw how Sally would touch Richard somewhere, anywhere, if he got up. And how she'd slip her hand around the top of his thigh as he led her out at the end of an evening, his arm about her waist. And Diana felt Sally glower when, on one occasion, she called her Sal. Richard witnessed this and his head buzzed.

Though the pair of them now shared themselves with their trusted friends, they spent much time locked into each other. They walked and they talked, they sat together in communicative silence; they enjoyed each other's company as normal couples do. The Heath or Holland Park were favourite stamping grounds. Sometimes they visited briefly just to feed the ducks; at other times they marched round these urban swathes of green, lost and deep in intimate conversation. When Richard spoke of his late father, of his childhood, Sally brimmed with tenderness and support. When he talked of his work, she concentrated hard. Now when she was out and about she didn't restrict her sight to eye-level but conscientiously looked up and around and noted pediments and architraves, Corinthian capitals and original window glass in the most unlikely of buildings. Sally talked, too, but carefully. Richard understood her childhood to have been happy, her previous relationships to have been few, fairly short-term and unsuccessful.

'Why unsuccessful? In what way? Have you been hurt?'
'I have never been in love.'

Her love was her work, he decided, for on that subject she became animated and spoke so descriptively about her pupils, past and present, that Richard formed a clear picture of each. She spoke with great fondness of her friends, who were few but to whom she was devoted though they lived as far afield as Ireland and South Africa. She talked of her passion for ballet and what she deemed to be her failure – weak knees. She danced for him on Hampstead Heath in her wellingtons, quickly, lightly, and, he believed, perfectly.

But such walks, talks and insights always finished with

passionate love-making, more often than not at Sally's instigation. For Richard, this sealed such days, for Sally it was a necessity. Just in case.

Just in case he loses sight of what I am, the extraordinary lover I must be.

You mean, just in case this mere rampant fling should dare to transmute into something quite other.

And hasn't it?

Their love-making was as exciting and as satisfying as it had ever been. The physical peaks that they reached were a revelation, and an exquisite one. But a spiritual element crept in, silently, unannounced and uninvited. It was inevitable. And it was welcome. They looked at each other more while they were making love. They were able to penetrate deeper. And though Sally did not necessarily look at and into Richard with love, she did look at him as Sally, as herself. And he saw that. She liked to gaze at him. She wasn't entirely sure why.

Maybe my funny old shyness has gone.

Maybe, Sally, maybe. But perhaps there's something else you ought to consider. When you're ready.

TWELVE

*O*n New Year's Eve, when Richard told Sally that he loved her, her world fell apart. It crashed about her feet in a deluge of shattered hopes and splintered desires. Ruined ambition lay smattered about her.

'Merry Christmas, Miss Lomax!'

'Merry Christmas, everyone. Now remember, the coach leaves for Paris from school at five in the morning on January the fourth. Remember too that we will be away for five days so bring enough underwear and any medication. And I want you all to prepare a piece on one figure of French History – painter, King or Emperor, whoever. Oh, and no hand-held computer games.'

'Mi-iss!'

'*Is* that understood?' she bellowed. Grudgingly, it was understood. The girls placed Miss Lomax's presents in front of her with a smile, some with a kiss, and skipped merrily out of the classroom and into their Christmas holidays. Most of the boys shuffled up to the desk and reluctantly dumped their gifts, furiously avoiding eye-contact, before swaggering to the door and defiantly beeping into life their electronic games.

'Oh, Diana!'

'My, what a pile of goodies you've amassed! Now, have yourself a *won*derful Christmas and make sure you take snaps of your outfit for the Thingies' masked ball. Call me before Paris – I must have *all* the intricacies of the Stonehill-saga before you go! Oh! I read something about cold macaroni cheese and the libido but I can't remember if you *eat* it or *use* it. I'll be sure to let you know! Merry Christmas! Mmwah! Mmwah!' With a pair of vivid scarlet lip marks on either cheek, Sally gathered her things together and left school for Christmas.

Christmas was Christmas. Sally being Sally did not overeat nor did she drink too much. She bought thoughtful presents for her family and sent charity cards to everyone she knew, including Bob and Catherine with a PS: 'Outfit-making, Highgate, 27th'. She bought Richard two truffles and a pasta dish; he gave her a vibrator. Momentarily she was taken aback but quickly asserted a knowing smirk for him.

But his doesn't look like that at all. And what an odd colour.

She tried it in private but the noise was like a shaver and its mechanical quivers reminded her of her car starting; giggles quashed any glimmer of sexual connotation and Sally's first and last vibrator was banished to the back of her socks drawer. She went to Lincoln where she was a priceless mother's help. Richard spent a dutiful Christmas Eve with his mother and then returned to London and shared Christmas and Boxing Days with Bob and Catherine.

He thought about Sally and he missed her. He was surprised that he missed her but inwardly it pleased him.

You can only miss what you know, and like.

Love.

Sally, surrounded and swamped by the mundanities and trivialities of her mother's Lincoln set, the sagas of her sisters' lives and the monotony of being good and courteous, longed for Richard.

For sex, she persuaded herself.

On Boxing Day evening, their coming together, in every sense of the word, was urgent and passionate. It was delicious, like a favourite food not tasted for many months.

Sally was pleased, Richard had exchanged his customary 'Omigod o goddos' for 'Oh Sally, oh Sal, oSallio'. But she sent him home to his own bed that night, relishing her power and his disappointment, and really quite looking forward to playing seamstress with Catherine the next morning.

'And I also found this piece with black sequins. How's Richard?'

'Oh, fine, fine.'

Fingers picked at buttons, the bobbin hurtled merrily, the needle pumped incessantly. Eyes were cast down, scrutinizing, measuring; the atmosphere was one of committed and creative labour. There was, however, space enough to chatter and to allow the occasional dip into one of the many end-of-term chocolate boxes.

'Yuk, strawberry fondant!'

'Pass it over then, I'll swap you a caramel. Bob thinks he may just don his goggles. Any idea what Richard's planning?'

'Nope.'

'Everything all right between you two?'

'Yes, why?'

'Oh, nothing really. I don't know, it's just whenever I bring him into the conversation, you never really linger.'

'That's because I'm a doer, not a talker!'

'So what do you do?'

'Bonk superlatively.'

'Good gracious! Sally Lomax, was that you?'

''Fraid so!'

But that was all that Catherine was given. She tried, she pried, but Sally smiled sweetly and kept her secrets tucked into her thimble.

'I've done something bad, Sally. Can I tell you? In confidence?' Sally laid down the feathers and tipped the diamanté bits back into their little pot. She was flattered.

'Of course you can.'

'I've stopped taking the Pill. Bob doesn't know. I take one out of the packet each night and I tip it down the sink.'

'But why?'

'Why? Because I want to have a baby, thickie.'

'Yes, yes, but why mustn't Bob know?'

'Because he feels too young to be a father and he says I'm too young to be a mother. But, you know, I feel ready . . . I don't know, *ripe*. Nougat? I think there comes a time when you just have to look inward and see how old or ready you *feel*. Not go by all this media bullshit dictating that couples ought now to breed only well into their thirties when they have a combined salary of "X". I'm not even that gooey or broody. Quite simply, I feel it is the right time to get pregnant. I looked inward, and that's what I saw.'

Sally sucked on the nougat thoughtfully. She was quite stunned by Catherine's frankness but was moved too by her wisdom. A closeness and warmth and camaraderie now existed between the two women. Sally had heard that elusive click, the bonding that ties women together as soul friends. She had it with Diana and with Daph. Not with her mother, nor Aunt Martha. But with Aunt Celia, yes. And now Catherine too. After that, they rarely talked about their menfolk but about themselves, about women they knew and others they admired, about vices they had and virtues they longed for. It made for a great working atmosphere and by the end of the afternoon, feathers and sequins and brocade and frogging had been coaxed into masks of supreme beauty and formidable workmanship. Catherine had also been afforded snippets of Sally.

'So after James at Bristol Uni, there was . . . ?'

'Jim.'

'Not one and the same?'

'No! But funnily enough, after Jim came Jamie.'

'You obviously go for Jims.'

'Actually, I prefer Dicks.'

'What was wrong with Jim?'

'Jim was okay, but boring. He used the "L" word halfway through our first date. And then frequently thereafter. He was a fair bit older than me and kept saying how I needed someone to watch over me and take care of me and pamper me. Meaning him. Thank you but no thank you. I sent him packing.'

'Ooh, you're a cruel woman! How?'

'He told me he loved me and I said "But I don't love you" and he said "But you will, you know, you will" and I said "I won't, you know, I won't". That didn't work so I told him, without beating about the metaphorical bush, that I found him physically unappetizing. But in truth, the greatest turn-off had been to declare his undying love.'

'And that worked?'

'Obviously – enter Jamie.'

'Jamie.'

'Scottish, a cab driver.'

'Is that how you met? In the back of his cab?'

'Well, yes, actually.'

'But did you ever do it in the back of his cab?'

'No.'

'Have you with Richard?'

'Yes.'

'In your car or his?'

'Mine.'

'In a *Mini*? Wait up, I've got to work this one out?'

'Well, I'll ramble on about Jamie while you do. Jamie was such fun at first, always cracking jokes in his glorious accent and bringing me little treats. He was dark and swarthy but gentle too. At first.' Sally trailed off and Catherine observed her turn to her sewing with a near-desperate application. She waited and as she waited she could see the pain.

'Sally?'

'Mmm?'

'Talk to me.' Sally laid down the feathers and bows and sighed. It was as if the memory had worn her out and aged her visibly. She looked Catherine in the eye and was comforted by a smile of sympathy and support. She focused at some point over Catherine's shoulder and her eyes glazed, her speech became dull and flat.

'Jamie had a temper. He broke my crockery and he smashed my nose. Here, feel.'

Sally guided Catherine's forefinger over the bridge of her nose. They felt the bump and dent together and Catherine allowed her finger to linger, letting it stroke Sally in a gentle whisper of comfort. Sally allowed her eyes to close under Catherine's touch while she worked hard to shut the memory back out.

On opening her eyes, the matter was closed. And would remain so. Catherine knew Sally had taken her into her confidence and that in itself had been a difficult and generous decision. She was grateful and flattered. It felt good to have a part of Sally that Bob and Richard didn't have. Catherine felt her first wave of love for Sally and was half-tempted to embrace her fully. Instinctively, however, she knew that her job was to lessen the load and lighten the atmosphere.

'James, Jim, Scumbag and now Richard. And I think you've scored at last there, Ms Lomax.'

'Yes, Richard. Richard is – ' Sally paused, fiddling with a line of red sequins before concluding ' – nice.'

*

Bob, meanwhile, plundered the impeccably dressed Christmas tree and strung his booty in glorious abandon over his old diving mask.

Richard went to the local toyshop and bought a Lone Ranger mask. And then he went to Dunn and Co. and bought an extremely expensive Stetson.

'Sal?'
   'Hey, Richie!'
'So you didn't need me to thread your needles?'
'No, I just about managed.'
'Will you come?'
'I beg your pardon?'
'Over? Now?'
'But I'm in bed!'
'Hasn't stopped you in the past.'
'But I'm tired!'
'Ditto.'
'Beaumes de Venise?'
'It's in the fridge.'
'I'm there!'
''Bye.'
''Bye.'
'Sal? Sally?'
'Yes?'
'Nothing.'

THIRTEEN

*R*ichard had his hand full of buttock.

'I'll pick you up, shall I, eightish?'

'No you shan't! We are to arrive separately!'

'Why?'

'Because, if you take me, then it won't be a surprise. And you'll recognize me which defeats the purpose of a masked ball utterly. And anyway, because I say so.'

'Ooh, but say I don't? Say I mistake another for you?'

'I'll give you a little sign.'

'A little sign, and what will that be?' Sally ran her finger tip lightly and temptingly up Richard's fly. He let go of her buttock. With one arm he pulled her towards him; with the other cinched around her waist he kept her there, and sewed a kiss deep into her mouth. Her eyes smiled lasciviously at him. He let her go and watched her dress, craning for a last look at the two tiny dimples at the base of her back before they were swallowed away by denim.

The best thing, thought Sally, *about sex in the afternoon is that it sends you on your way with a spring in your step and a euphoric energy to tide you through the rest of the day.*

She had always loved New Year's Eve day and as she sauntered along Highgate High Street the shopkeepers to whom she usually smiled were now given a big wave.

'Happy New Year, Miss Lomax!'

'Happy New Year, Joe!'

'Off dancing tonight, love?'

'Certainly am!'

'Dancing and Romancing?'

'You bet!'

'See ya next year, love!'

'It'll be a good one, Joe!'

On a whim, Sally went to the newsagent and bought a packet of ten cigarettes, low-tar and mentholated. 'Oh, yes, and a box of matches, please. Happy New Year.' She then went to the bookshop, old, musty, magnetic, and browsed the minutes away into three-quarters of an hour before selecting two recently reviewed, highly acclaimed novels. 'You'll enjoy those, Happy New Year.' Her final stop was at the French *patisserie* where she ummed, ahhed and crooned and then chose a strawberry tartlet, gloriously red and glazed to glistening perfection. '*Année!*'

Back in her flat, Sally placed the books, in the bag, on the mantelpiece. She tapped them, deciding not to peek at all until she was on French soil. She then went into her kitchen and took out a cake fork and tea plate on to which she slid the tartlet. Kettle boiled, Earl Grey brewed and poured into a matching tea-cup and saucer, she retired into the lounge and settled down to a few minutes of luxury. Such times had to be conducted in silence. No television or radio, no rustling of magazines, no pencil in one hand hovering over a crossword. It had to be just Sally, her cake and her cuppa. Too soon, though, there was not even a crumb left despite a hopeful dabbing finger searching every inch of the plate, just in case. She

89

burped quietly under her breath and sat a while longer, looking, as always, at nothing in particular. She enjoyed the friendly silence of her own company, she liked her little flat, and was content just to sit and look around her, itemizing her possessions, checking on her paintwork and scanning her heaving bookcase, smiling and nodding at favourite volumes as they came into view.

Well, this is no good, just sitting here like a lazy lemon. There's work to be done, a party to prepare for, a man to wow! Come on, let's have a fag, Sal!

Sally smoked self-consciously as she pottered from room to room. Every now and then she darted back to the kitchen to flick ash into the sink.

Disgusting habit, but what can one do when one does not possess an ash-tray?

The cigarette gave her a slight head-rush which she thought amusing, and she giggled out loud as she went into the bathroom to check how she looked, fag in hand, fag in mouth. Could she talk like that? No. She tried blowing smoke rings but couldn't. She checked how she looked sucking on the butt in side profile and again from the front. She watched herself inhale and exhale. Inhale and exhale.

Lordy, I feel dizzy!

She exhaled and smiled, watching the smoke whisper over her teeth and veil her face.

Nope! Smoking does not suit me at all. So I shan't.

With that, she threw the butt down the toilet and retrieved the packet from the lounge, took it outside and dumped it ceremoniously in the dustbin.

Sally ran a bath. Deep. She tweezed stray eyebrows and scrutinized her face for anything to squeeze. Nothing. She soaked for a while but found she was not in a luxuriating frame of mind so she shaved her legs and her armpits, showered off freezing cold (she'd learnt it from Richard) and then swooped her bath sheet around her. Getting dry was such a bore so she took the phone into her room and called Diana. Who wasn't in. So she called Richard, who was.

'I've got nothing on.'

'Neither have I.'

'See you later.'

'Alligator.'

'Crocodile.'

Time to get ready, body is dry and silk-soft, hair likewise. What a lovely little dress you've bought, Sally.

I know, I couldn't resist it. It's from that shop that I've only ever drooled in front of. I should'nt've. But I just had to. I want to knock him for six tonight.

But you have already done so, you know.

Mmm, I want to make sure.

It's black crêpe, isn't it? Completely straight, two little darts giving it a perfect line. It's just above your knee, just right. Sleeveless though, mightn't you be chilly?

No, not once I'm at the party. Look, do you see how cleverly the zip is hidden at the back? It feels heavenly on.

It suits you, fits beautifully.

Look, little Dupion court shoes too!

Perfect. What knickers have you chosen?

At first, I wasn't going to wear any at all. But it is December. I know Richard goes wild for those little white cottony ones but I've never had black silk panties so I bought some. I'll make sure he likes them.

Let us see your mask, Sally.

Just look at my mask! I know it's bad to brag but I'm terribly pleased with it. See how it fits snugly over the bridge of my nose? And then dips down over the tops of my cheeks? Catherine's is more elaborate but I decided against any wild flourishes. I just studded the edges alternately with silver sequins and little pearls, then I attached the soft downy black feathers over the brow. I wanted to look swan-like, or cat-like, or something. But it fits well, doesn't it? It's awful when a mask is lop-sided, or reveals more of one eye than the other.

It fits, Sally. Perfectly.

Actually, it's rather nice to wear. You can sort of hide behind it. It's as if I can see out but they can't see in.

Go on, one last check in front of the mirror, then you'd best be on your way.

I hope I arrive after Richard. I've never really been in a situation where I can make my big entrance. It is my prerogative after all!

Check your flat, Sally, the gas, the plugs, the windows. Close the curtains, the doors. Double lock. Outside lights on. Off you go, off to the Ball, Sally Lomax. Have the most wonderful night. And Happy New Year.

See the Mini chortle down the road, heading for West London and a night of festive celebration. See its precious load: a young woman, decked out in her finery. She looks almost beautiful. Not classically, not even that classy, but there is something about her that is enchanting and rather lovely. She smiles and she is excited, anticipating an evening of fun and frolics. The lights turn orange but tonight our usually pedantic driver throws caution to the wind and accelerates through, a rush of adrenalin adding to her fizzy mood. Does she not seem happy, her fine mask coddled in tissue on the seat beside her? She is happy and she tells herself so out loud. You can see her mouth it as she drums on the dash-board: *I am happy, I'm really happy.*

So one year is on its way out and the next is tangibly near. What does it hold in store? Sally has no idea. If she's at the metaphorical steering wheel, as she intends to be, she believes she'll journey through it safely and soundly.

But what if someone else takes the wheel, uninvited? Sally hasn't thought of that. And if there is someone else

there, where will they take her? And will she let herself
be taken?

Just now, however, it is Sally's New Year's Eve and she
is looking forward to it very, very much.

FOURTEEN

'*B*ob! It's completely wonky. Up on the left, up on the left!'

'Stop flapping, would you? Is that better?'

'Up on the bloody left!'

'There.'

'Now the streamers, now the streamers!'

'Where?'

'Door frames, door frames!'

'Leave me to it, you old bag! Go and get yourself ready and then lie down for half an hour.'

Catherine obeyed. Their parties were always a success, but if she didn't fret and if certain things weren't left to the last minute it could surely be a bad omen.

I must try and calm down. I really must. Just in case.

Catherine's period should have come the previous morning so she was hoping and praying, silently and desperately.

If I am, then I must keep calm. Just in case.

She lay down on their bed and wondered if the faint nausea was due to pregnancy and not pre-party nerves. Bob woke her half an hour later and she had no recollection of falling asleep. Deeply too. His usual kiss on the nose had been ineffectual, a good shake was required. She clambered into her rich violet silk two-piece and gave him a twirl. He marvelled at her elegant beauty. Dark and sinuous like a willowy, giant anemone. Bob put on a loud Hawaiian shirt and a pair of garish Bermuda shorts. The ensemble clashed violently.

He looks quite revolting, marvelled Catherine, *but he looks the part!*

Catherine breezed around, placing bowls of nuts and nibbles on every available surface. Bob stuck himself at her dressing-table mirror and wrestled with his diving goggles, trying to find a way to make them fit snugly without forcing his lips and cheeks into a rubbery and uncomfortable contortion.

Well, I'll just have to suffer for my art until all the guests have seen it on, then I'll tip it up on to my head. But that bauble clonks me in the eye, so I'll just adjust it – slightly. There.

'Catherine! Where's the string?' She appeared with the errant string and a piping hot canapé, a dazzling smile beaming from a cloud of purple-blue silk. Delicious.

'You are a treasure, darling. Belle of the ball.'

'And that's a hell of a bauble clonking your eye, Bob. Here, let me help.'

The beauty of a fancy dress party, although everybody initially moans wondering where they'll find the time and inspiration to make their costume, is that enormous effort is inevitably made by all and such parties have great atmosphere before the doorbell is even sounded. Bob and Catherine's parties were talked about for years: The Bad Taste Party for Bob's big three-o, The Flowers and Flares Party on their third wedding anniversary, Catherine's Sinners and Saints Party; all went down in the annals of record-breaking party history. And now the New Year's Masked Ball. They had transformed the ground floor of their home into a magical grotto. Black net, sprinkled with glittery stars, had been draped over and across all the ceilings. The long wall of the living-room was covered entirely with silver foil, the other walls adorned with burgundy crêpe-paper bows and swathes of steel-grey shiny material (Sally knew of the shop, £2 a metre).

The hallway leading in had been turned into an avenue of six-foot weeping figs (hired for the night). In the kitchen, reams of dark red velvet swagged the doorway and masked the cupboards that were not to be opened. The long, rustic beech-wood trestle table was covered with a starched white sheet and adorned around the edges with black crêpe-paper rosettes. On it, a glutton's wildest fantasy met the eye. Bowls of new potato salad, sprigged through with wisps of dill; an enormous shallow dish heaped with leaves of ruccola, radicchio and oak-leaf lettuce, coloured exquisitely with borage flowers and dressed to perfection with Bob's famous vinaigrette. In between sat two mounds of Catherine's home-baked herbed bread but the eye was drawn compulsively to the centrepiece, a twelve-and-a-half-pound wild Scotch salmon lying pink-peach and fat on a bed of transparent-thin cucumber slithers. The fridge hid from view the two Pavlovas, one raspberry, one strawberry, both a foot high. The oven warmed the canapés, Catherine's forte. Mouthfuls of ecstasy; puff, filo and shortcrust pastries enveloping creative fillings of spinach (fresh), chicken (spiced) and mushrooms (wild), all treated to proportionately extravagant doses of cream, fresh herbs and the ubiquitous garlic.

('Bit anti-social, darling?'
'Bob! You know everyone'll eat 'em!')

The guests arrived in a flurry and whirl of cloaks, coats and good cheer. At the doorstep bursts of laughter, coos of admiration and peals of excited chatter as the masks met. Oddly, or perhaps not so oddly, the men for the most part went for the wildly eccentric and humorous, while the women opted for demurely bejewelled intricacy and opulent glamour. There were two Batmen and two stocking-headed bank robbers. Marilyn Monroe arrived with Margaret Thatcher. And while the bought masks were entertaining, those that were home-made were infinitely more impressive and deceptive. All manner of objects had been coaxed and teased into face-concealing devices. Friends with children had studied their comics, made fact-finding trips to Hamleys and plundered the dressing-up boxes. And nearly everyone admitted to having watched the odd *Blue Peter* programme hoping for ingenious ways to transform a cereal packet, a yoghurt pot and polystyrene egg cartons into the mask of their dreams (with a little help from double-sided sticky tape and that globby white glue).

Andy Dalken had taken it one step further. A partner of Bob's, at work he was famous for his waste-paper, paper-clip and used biro sculptures. For the party, he had taken a cereal packet, two sizes of yoghurt pot and a host of cardboard tubes from toilet and kitchen rolls, constructed them into a towering and intricate head-dress and sprayed them evenly with gold and silver paint. But he had also strategically added fairy lights and propellers. For the first half-hour he hardly spoke but flashed, whirred and twinkled when spoken to. Robert Tobias, an old rugby chum of Bob and Richard's, wheezed his way through the party, intimidating and unrecognizable behind a Second World War gas mask. Douglas Christian (also an old First Fifteener) arrived masked beyond recognition, delectably coiffured by a foot-high, Marie Antoinette wig, his face powdered white, his lips painted into a pert and very scarlet rosebud. Only his jeans and trade-mark tennis pumps gave him away. Alex Daniels, Catherine's errant younger brother, turned up on his motorbike in an enormous glitter-gold crash helmet and a slinky black cat-suit adorned by a Groucho Marx jock-strap.

'Masked Balls, Cath, Masked Balls.'

'*Marx*ed Balls, Alex, Marxed Balls!'

Richard arrived and looked gorgeous, like a grown-up little boy in his Lone Ranger outfit.

'Catherine, is that Richard S.? I haven't seen him for years. What a dish! I'm feeling exceptionally frivolous tonight, might just get my net out.'

'No hope, I'm afraid. He's well and truly spoken for.'

'You're joking! Richard? Never! Who by?'

'Sally Lomax. Oh, funny! Look, that's her just arrived, over there with Bob.' The women watched her, one with fondness and pride, the other with inquisitiveness laced with envy. Catherine swished over to her.

'Sally! Magnificent!'

'Happy New Year, Catherine! The mask looks brilliant – mind you, I don't think we could have dreamt up Bob's in a million years, it's a masterpiece!'

'Richard's here, or somewhere!'

'Mmm, is he?'

'Douglas, tell me about your move then. Manchester, isn't it?' Richard had found Douglas whom he had not seen for many moons.

'No, Sheffield. I'm looking forward to it. Fed up with the Old Smoke. Jane's already found a house. And a job. And she's pregnant! Bob was saying that, er, you've found yourself a, um, partner?'

'Mmm. She'll be coming later. You'll like her. She's very natural. And absolutely beautiful.'

'She the one, then?'

'The one? Where? Oh, *the one*! Ha! Oh! Hmm.' Richard fiddled with his waistcoat and fumbled with his words.

She is *the one*, thought Douglas.

'Playing any rugger?'

'No, not for years. I run a fair bit, and thrash Bob at squash.'

'Do you remember that last season at college? Invincible or what! If BJ hadn't been injured in the semis, we'd've won the lot without a doubt. Boy, could he *kick*! You and I, what a second row we made. Wow, look there!'

They looked and watched her move, catlike and languid, over to the table to swoop up a glass of champagne. Her black cocktail dress whispered against her, revealing now and again a curve or line of the body beneath. It ended just above the knee; shapely calves and dainty ankles delineated by the sheerest of stockings. Her arms were bare and slender, and every time she moved her head, her neck was kissed by locks of glossy hair. Her face was pretty – the parts which the mask did not hide. The darkness of the mask itself, the richness of its decoration, accentuated the milky softness of her skin. Her lips shone red, full and defined under the puffs of black feathers which adorned her brow. Richard oozed with pride.

'That, Douglas, is Sally.'

Douglas watched as Richard sauntered over, unnoticed, behind her. He watched as Richard encircled his arms around her waist, one hand resting gently on her stomach, the other grasping her wrist. He saw her tilt her head back and Richard make sweeping kisses from behind her ear down her neck, feathers touching his hair, his Stetson casting aesthetic shadows over their faces. Douglas watched as Sally turned her body towards Richard, so lithe and balletic so that he could keep his face buried in her neck as she turned. Douglas felt his mouth dry and his groin stir as Sally wrapped her arms around Richard's neck, held his face in her hands, slipped one hand through his hair, the other over his ear, and drew him close so she could kiss him deeply. They remained like that, glued and tongue-tied, for minutes. Then Sally laughed; Douglas could hear it above the music, melodic, excited. He saw her twang Richard's mask and then he saw Richard lift hers, place his thumbs just below her eyes, return the mask and then kiss her. Sally grasped Richard close with all the strength in her body; they were pressed against each other and folded into one another. Douglas watched, mesmerized, turned on. Envious.

'You recognized me!' Sally pouted.

'It could only have been!' Richard replied.

Had Bob and Catherine owned a chandelier, it would have been swung from. But the party was swinging regardless. The dancing was lively, the chatter was animated. The food was excellent and plentiful, the drink flowed extravagantly. Everybody mixed and mingled. Sally was enjoying herself thoroughly. She was charming and she was charmed by Bob and Catherine's friends. It was wonderful to catch sight of Richard in earnest conversation over the other side of the room. To catch his eye. To watch him unnoticed. To brush against him, accidentally on purpose. They found each other in the corridor, they shared a mound of Pavlova. He sucked the cream from her chin, she held her glass for him to sip from. She was happy, she was high.

Later, in the loo queue, Sally nattered with Alex.

'What on earth is Catherine doing in there?' questioned Batman. And then it became clear just what she was doing. Catherine was being violently and vociferously sick. It did not take long for most of the queue to disperse, for most to decide that they did not need the toilet all that urgently after all. Alex and Sally stayed.

'Crikey, do you think she's all right? Cath? Catherine?' Alex implored. They heard her moan and then retch again.

'Should I get Bob? I think I will. Sally, would you, could you stay? I'll just find him.' Of course Sally would stay.

'Catherine,' she cooed gently, 'I'm here if you need me.'

100

Catherine chucked up her reply. It went on and on and on. She really was being desperately ill. Finally the toilet flushed and Catherine emerged, frighteningly pale, her eyes bloodshot. And an enormous grin on her face. Sally stared, puzzled. Catherine took her hand and squeezed it, giving her an odd, indecipherable smile. Bob had arrived.

'Sweetness, are you okay?'

'I'm fine, darling, just fine.' With that, she waltzed down the corridor and back into the midst of her party. Bob shrugged at Sally and jogged after Catherine, baubles and wooden figurines dancing out the Nativity on his head. Sally went into the bathroom but despite what Catherine's racket had suggested, there was absolutely no indication of it at all. She found some air freshener and gave a liberal spritz anyway. *Is she, isn't she?* she wondered as she looked at the plughole and envisaged a stack of redundant contraceptive pills beneath it. She washed her hands and looked up to see the Lone Ranger standing silent and strong behind her.

'Evening, Cowboy. Is that a gun in your pocket, or are you just happy to see me?' Sally chuckled at her clichéd corniness. The cowboy remained silent, locked the door, closed the toilet seat, sat on it and pulled her towards him.

It wasn't a gun.

FIFTEEN

'*C*ome on, everyone, fill up your glasses, it's almost time! Bob? Bob! Switch the telly on. Shit, where's my glass?' Catherine had made a remarkable recovery.

The music was turned off, the television on. People stood, excited and to attention. Big Ben was in close-up, the camera and all the eyes in the room fixed to the clock face, the minute hand just two notches away from New Year. Richard stood behind Sally and could see and feel her quivering with anticipation and delight. Andy Dalken's mask flashed and buzzed, Douglas cooled himself camply with a lacy fan. Almost there, almost. Any minute. Any second. *Doyng*! Cheer! One! *Doyng*! Hurray! Two! Richard squeezed Sally as she bounced on her tiptoes as she had at the penguins. *Doyng*! Eleven! And then the whole room shouted in unison: '*Doyng*! Twelve! Happy New Year!' Champagne corks hit the roof and spirits soared. Hugging was liberal and kisses were free. Douglas was quite keen to embrace Sally but Richard was hogging her to himself. 'Auld Lang Syne' was briefly launched but when tra-la-la-ing replaced unknown words, it was abandoned in favour of more hugging, kissing and champagne guzzling. Richard and Sally were still on last year's kiss, their celebratory drinks untouched and spilling.

The point of the party had come and gone but the festive air remained and the party rampaged along. Sally danced with Douglas. Lucky Douglas. And Richard helped Catherine to mop up a bottle's worth of spilt red wine. Bob had his goggles back on and danced a merry jig with Robert who suddenly had to throw off the gas mask, puce-faced and spluttering for breath. Margaret Thatcher and Marie Antoinette were in earnest conversation in one corner while Andy wrestled to release himself from his mask so he could taste the lips that Minnie Mouse was offering to him. Douglas had spun Sally off her feet. She was hot and ruffled and disappeared to reorganize her dress and mask and recompose her being.

In Catherine and Bob's bedroom, she sat on the bed and listened to her quickened breathing. She caught sight of herself in the mirror and smiled. She lay back on the bed in between the two piles of coats, listening to the thud and boom of the merry-making downstairs. She felt cosy on the soft bed with the silent mounds of other people's coats surrounding her.

I could quite happily either doze off right here and now, or I could party through the night and well into the morning.

She stared at a mark on the ceiling and soon lost the focus to gaze on at nothing in particular. Her body relaxed and her mind wandered. She made plans to service her car before she went to France. She mentally packed her suitcase and tried out a few sentences in French. She wondered just what that warm, cloudy herb was in the vinaigrette. Sage? Tarragon! She thought of the film *Jules et Jim* and was frustrated at being unable to remember the theme tune.

No, not like that, that's not it, that's the tune that Moreau sings. The theme is softer and sadder. Damn.

Now, what was Moreau's character called? Catherine!
How is Catherine? When will she know for sure? Will she
tell Bob? Tonight? I've got it! I've got the tune. Yes, yes!
Da da Da da Da da, mmm mmm mmm. Lovely.

Sally closed her eyes and let a head full of violins take
over the bare notes she'd remembered.

Richard found her, shoeless and maskless, half-asleep,
humming brokenly. He leant over and kissed her. Her
eyes opened slowly and looked at him with a sleepy
loveliness.

'I love you, Sally Lomax.'

The silence was startling. Richard waited for her smile
to break. But watched instead the shine in her eyes
evaporate and felt her whole body stiffen. Her eyes stuck
to him but he no longer knew them. She said nothing.

'I love you, Sal.'

It was a pleasure to hear his own voice, to hear himself
saying Those Words out loud. Slowly Sally pulled herself
up and sat. Still staring flatly. Still silent.

'Sally, I . . .'

'I heard, I heard,' she said in a horribly quiet voice.
Something else now laced her eyes. Richard brought his
face closer to hers for a better look. It was terror. He made
to kiss her. With her whole hand she pushed him away.
One finger caught and scratched the side of his nostril,
the other pressed into his left eye.

'Sally!'

'Don't you dare!'

'Sally!'

She leapt from the bed and fumbled into her shoes, her
ankles twisting. She was shaking, she was racking her
brains visibly, almost audibly. Richard, though, could not
tell what she was thinking. He grasped her tightly, to
steady them both.

'Sally!' She turned her face away. He brought it back in
his hands. He felt like a vet examining a reluctant pup as
he scanned her face and sought her eyes. Probing.

Needing a clue. Needing to know. He managed to bring her eyes into line and focus with his. The terror he had seen previously had subsided. Now there just seemed to be unbridled sadness.

'Sally,' he murmured. Good, she held his gaze. 'Sally, I have never felt before what I've felt with you. I have never felt for anyone what I feel for you. I love you and I want to share life with you. You mean more to me than anything. Sally.' He held her, silent and broken. He felt her tear, warm, fat and oily, splash on to the side of his finger and then course its way down his hand. He looked at her face. Her left eye was hazed and fuzzed by the tear that welled, impossibly large for the lower lid to contain. It fell, fast, smooth and horribly wet on to her neck and down through her cleavage. He kissed it away, tasting Sally's sad salt. He looked up and again into the face of the woman he loved and saw her eyes replenished with fresh, devastated, ready-to-fall tears.

'Sal?'

'No!' she said hoarsely, removing his hands from her face. She glanced distractedly around the room. 'Impossible,' she whimpered, refusing to meet his gaze. 'Absolutely not!' she said quite quietly as she found her mask and rummaged for her coat.

'Sally.'

She had found her coat and made for the door. Richard lunged forward and caught her. She wrestled back momentarily and then let her body go still. Still but rigid. Richard held her firmly and lovingly. He bent his head low and found unresisting lips which he kissed but which did not respond. He looked at her; she looked dejected, messy and small. Still he loved her.

'You can't love me,' she said. 'You mustn't. You've got it all wrong. It's all gone wrong.'

She looked lifeless and incredibly tired. Like a rag doll with all the stuffing beaten flat, Richard recalled later. He let her go.

I can't let her go.
Let me go.
He let her go and watched her head for the door.
'Sally?' he implored.
She shook a tear-stained face, caught his eye and held it deeply for a desperate, gorgeous, doomed moment. Then dropped her gaze and shook her head. She was gone.

Bob passed Sally in the corridor, he was searching for his elusive Catherine.
'Sally! What on earth . . .'
Her face was wet but set. She walked past him with as much dignity as she could muster, straight out of the house like Cinderella. Bob looked after her and then, on hearing the door slam, turned back and saw Richard standing motionless in the doorway to his bedroom. As Bob walked towards him, Richard leant the weight of his heavy and tired body against the door post. Bob led him into the room and shut the door. And waited, patiently and sensitively. Richard went over to the window and lifted the curtains to look distractedly down the street. He let the curtains go and they fell back into position, obediently, silently. Without turning around, he spoke, flatly, quietly and devastated.
'I told her I loved her.'
Without turning around, Richard could feel Bob's puzzled expression and hear his silent question.
'I told her I loved her and she's left me.' Richard turned to face his friend who was looking at him in shocked, disbelieving sympathy. Bob shook his head and raised his eyebrows and shoulders.
'I told her I love her more than anything, and as I've never loved before. And she left. She's gone. She cried, Bob. Cried and she said "No".'
Bob racked his brains for advice, anything constructive, comforting, both preferably.

'Richie, maybe she just needs time. God, women! You know, "been hurt before" and all that?' Richard turned away and looked through the curtains again. He shook his head and Bob watched his shoulders slump.

'But why say "No"? Why weep from the very soul? Why not say "I'm flattered, but I'm sorry"? Why not ask for time? Why the anger, the fear? It was as if she loathed me, Bob.'

Catherine burst in, sobbing hysterically. The men looked at her in wide-eyed disbelief. She looked at them wildly.

'Out! Get out! Leave me! Alone! Now!' They didn't need to be told twice. The men went next door into the spare room but Catherine's weeping was too disconcerting so they left for Bob's study at the end of the hallway. The men sat on different chairs, away from each other but very much with one another. The strength of their friendship and the deepness of their understanding saturated the room as supportive and nourishing silence. They were unaware of time passing. A feeble little patter at the door roused them from their sanctuary and Catherine popped a bedraggled face around the door.

'Bob?' she implored. Bob went to her. Richard remained motionless, statuesque, Rodin's Thinker once again. But try as he might, he could not think why his declaration of love had been met by anything other than the reciprocation he had anticipated. Could he be that wrong? Could he have read her all wrong? Could proclaiming his love for her be wrong? He thought not. So why?

Catherine pulled Bob into their bedroom and pointed to the waste-paper basket as explanation. In it he found her panties. Blood-stained.

'Poor darling, no wonder you were feeling ropy. Did you spoil your trousers?'

Catherine shook her head and gulped, holding out her arms for him. He came to her and held her.

The last of the die-hard guests were making a lethargic and drunken effort to leave.

''Bye, Andy. You're not driving, are you? Oh, Alex, you off too? Right then, 'bye. Happy New Year!'

'Bob, what time did Richard go?'

'Has he gone?'

'He has gone. Sally too, of course. Strange that they should just disappear like that.' Bob sighed and, taking his wife's hand, locked up, switched lights on or off and led her up to their room where he revealed the precious little that he knew. Not such a happy New Year after all.

SIXTEEN

*S*ally walked slowly to her car, a measured step to keep her bewilderment from running amok. Her hands, though, shook so much that the key missed its target again and again. Hardly surprising; she was using the ignition key. She fumbled with the key ring and was suddenly overwhelmed with hatred for the penguin dangling off the end. She pulled it and twisted it, she tugged at it, she even bit it. She grasped it and gave a determined yank. Off it came, the jag of metal tearing at the palm of her hand. Cutting deep, drawing blood. With venom, she hurled the penguin away from her and into the gutter. It stared back at her, an inane smile etched on its plastic face. Finally, she opened her car door and collapsed on to the seat. She pushed all the breath out of her in one long moan. She was involuntarily silent for a moment before a stuttering intake of air was released easily into racking sobs.

What have I done?

She beat her hands against the steering wheel. Her head dropped against her hands and she wept, tears of bitterness, wails of disappointment. *Bitch, bitch, bitch.*

Suddenly she stopped and sat bolt upright. She was alert, her head was clear.

Get out, get out, get away. Go.

She kicked her car into life and it roared at her indignantly. She turned it on a sixpence and vroomed off and away, seat-beltless and silent. Sally, you're doing sixty, slow down. Sally, that was a red light, watch out. Dodging the occasional pedestrian, she weaved in and out of what little traffic was there, like a pony in a gymkhana game.

Get me North, get me North. Get away from West London, away.

By the time she was at Hampstead, the roads were deserted and the pavements scattered sparsely with the odd reveller making a weary way homeward. Whitestone Pond shimmered in the new moon of a New Year but Sally gave it only a cursory glance. Hampstead Lane, and home was frustratingly near. With the Heath flanking her, dark and watchful, she belted along like a latterday Dick Turpin, fleeing to the safety of her stamping ground. Dick and Sally, fugitives in Highgate. Dick, Richard . . . no, no, not the same.

Come on, Mini, don't groan, carry Sally up the hill. She pulled her car around the corner into her road with a screech of tyres that was very Hollywood, most un-Highgate and very un-Sally.

Darling flat, I can see you. Oh, I'm home. I'm home.

Sally leapt from the car and left it unlocked, the steering wheel sticky with blood, headlights on. She didn't notice and even if she had, she was too desperate for the sure solitude and safety of her flat to care.

Sally is really quite beside herself. In fact, she is downright manic. She runs into the flat and greets everything that she sees. All is blissfully familiar.

110

Hello, flowers. Hello, comfy chair! Little teapot! Hello, my lovely, darling bed!

As she scampers from room to room, she sheds her clothes. She has ended up in the kitchen in her underwear, breathless, holding on to the ironing board, smiling at the crockery on the draining board, the dainty, matching teacup, saucer and plate from that afternoon which seemed a dream away and was indeed last year. Enough, Sally, go to bed, dissolve into sleep, empty your head, close your eyes and shut out your distress.

And Sally slept. She fell immediately into a fathomless and comatose world of soft dark numbness, a dreamless state in which Richard did not exist. And nor did Sally. Motionless and silent, sleep rescues her, she looks innocent and child-like. The weight on her shoulders, the burden she bears, now gone and forgotten until reverie will return it to the forefront of her being. Outside, her Mini stares down the street, its happy headlamps blaring away. Dejected, the battery withers and is completely flat by morning. On the seat inside, Sally's mask stares vacantly up at the rear-view mirror. Unseeing.

The first thing Sally noticed on waking was that the curtains were not drawn. Sunlight streamed in and momentarily she felt peaceful before memories assaulted her sleepy head and turned her stomach. She closed her eyes in a futile attempt to block them out. But she could neither do that nor fall back to sleep. Heart pounding, she lay staring out of the window at the linear patterns of the winter bare branches. She rewound the tape in her mind and played back Richard's every word again and again. And again. And still she hated them. And hated him. And really rather hated herself too. Sighing a hopeless sigh of failure, she rose and looked about her. One shoe, a crumpled mound of black crêpe, a little clump of streamers – where had they been? In her hair?

Bath. Let's have a bath. That's what they do in the

*films, in books. Wounded heroines soak long and con-
templatively in hot tubs, soothed by billows of bubbles.*

Sally is shocked. Her stomach is swiped with blood,
dried now and therefore brownish, but blood, definitely
blood. And it's on her left thigh. She ventures over to the
mirror and finds it smudged on her left cheek. She looks
at her left hand and sees that her nails are dirty with it,
the cracks of her fingers are trailed with it. She turns her
palm uppermost and sees the gash, quite nasty, scabbed
over with a very dark brown, crusty, shiny slug of it.
What would a palmist say, the lines and troughs picked
out in blood? Sally bravely holds her hand steady under a
hot tap. The water stings, the scab is but temporary and is
washed away. She looks deep into the cut, intrigued.

*This is what God must see, looking down and into an
earthquake*, she reasons.

The phone rings. Sally is frightened and sits awkwardly in the bath willing it to stop. It does. She cries.
Her face is sweaty. Her nose runs. The bath concept isn't
working at all. *Car?*

'Diana?'

'Ho, Sally! Don't *you* sound fragile today!'

'Diana?'

'Sally? Sal?' (*Don't call me that.*) Diana heard a faint,
strangled yelp. 'I'll be right there, Sally. Just hold on a
short mo'.'

0181 348 6523.

*Sally, Sally, I'm sure you're there. Answer it, answer
the bloody phone, talk to me. Sal, talk to me.*

Sally stared at the phone. It rang pleadingly. She did
not answer it. Richard hung up, his head hung low. He
went for a run. His head ached, but he went for a run.
Five miles, fifty minutes, shit time, *shit* time. What a shit
time.

112

Diana caught a cab to Sally's. The walk would have taken only twenty minutes but she felt a strong pull to be there as soon as possible. She walked the short path to Sally's door and noted that the curtains in the front room were ominously closed.

But it's one in the afternoon.

She pressed the bell. And pressed it again.

I'm here, Sally, it's me.

Sally heard the bell and backed into her bedroom. It sounded again. She had forgotten that Diana was coming. She heard the letter box flip up. She stood stock still.

'Sally? It's *me*! It's Diana.' Sally was released. It's Diana. She bolted to the front door, checked the peephole just to make sure and flung open the door and threw herself at her black and red confidante. And there she clung, Diana having to steady herself.

'Hey hey, Sally, let's go inside.' Diana sat Sally down in the Comfy Chair, the Lloyd-Loom with the tear and the faded, lumpy, patchwork cushion. She drew up a low stool and took Sally's hand, looking into her face, a wide-eyed and sorrowful world. Diana waited. She held Sally's hand and she waited. Suddenly Sally looked her straight in the eye, directly and unflinchingly. It was disconcerting. And so was her voice. Flat, toneless but strong.

'Richard,' she paused, 'is in love. With me.'

Diana broke into a spontaneous and genuine smile. She squeezed Sally's hand. Sally glowered.

'Richard is in love with me. The man has gone and fallen in love with me!' she cried indignantly. Diana was baffled. Sally leapt up and marched, irritated, over to the mantelpiece.

'Don't you see? It's all gone wrong. This wasn't meant to happen. He was *not* to fall in love with me. But he has. It's spoiled everything. It's all ruined.' Diana was amazed.

'But Sally, it's, it's *lovely*. Surely. Isn't it?'

The women looked at each other. Sally suddenly felt let down in some sort of way. Defensive. Confused.

'No, I don't think it's lovely at all.'

'But why not?'

Sally had to think. Suddenly she didn't feel like talking, she had neither the energy nor inclination to explain.

'Just *because*, Diana. Because actually I did not want him to. He wasn't meant to. But he's gone and done so.' Diana bit the bullet and shot her the fundamental question.

'Do you mean to say that you are *not* in love with Richard?' Sally stared at her blankly and then shook her head vigorously. 'Really?' said Diana, cocking her head, 'Are you sure? Not just the tiniest bit? A little hint of it somewhere in the deepest recesses of your heart?'

'My heart,' Sally declared, avoiding Diana's eyes, 'is not in this.'

Liar, thought Diana.

SEVENTEEN

O 181 348 6523

Come on, come on, come on!

January the second, the second time that day that Richard has called for Sally. January the first he spent listless and low. Today he feels determined and motivated, like someone with a big project to get under way. He lets the phone ring until an electronic voice suggests that he try later. Actually, Sally *isn't* in, she's walking on the Heath, trying to soul-search but failing. The space and the trees and the chill wind and the sharp bursts of sunlight are too distracting. She just walks and gazes and, in her aloneness, she feels safe and in control. Thank God. At last. Richard? Richard who?

That evening Mozart failed to soothe Richard. It was quiet and dark outside. *Enough* he thought, *enough*. He left his flat with music and lights still on and marched to his car in shirt sleeves not noticing the cold.

Highgate, I'm going to Highgate.

And off he went.

Blissfully unaware, Sally sat curled and comfortable in a chair, transferring her itinerary for Paris from mind to notepad. Antiseptic cream, plasters, underwear, two

115

jumpers, one thick, one lightweight, alarm clock; she was engrossed in mundanity when she heard the car pull up. The engine was unmistakable, the Alfa Romeo purred and then whispered to a standstill.

Hide. Hide.

She ran into the darkness of her bedroom and waited. Not with dread actually, but with excitement. Footsteps; Richard's. A pattern of knocks; Richard's. A gentle voice; Richard's.

'Sally? It's me. Can we at least talk?'

Silence; Sally's.

Richard tried again. He rang the bell too. Still no response but he knew she was there. And she knew that he knew. And he knew that she knew that he knew. Game playing, with a winner and a loser; Sally was both. He knocked, he called for her. And then all was silent. *He's gone, he's gone.* But she was perturbed and not relieved. She found herself walking to the door. Why? To run after him? Why?

I don't know.

She was halfway to the door when Richard knocked again and called her name; his name for her: 'Sal, Sal, let me in. Please?' She stood frozen to the spot. She saw the letter box flip open. As it shut she darted back to her room. A watched mouse scurrying back into its hole. The cheese can wait.

I don't want it anyway.

You do, Sally. Oh, but you do.

Richard stood outside. Now he was cold. But he guarded the door. He stood patiently, occasionally looking through the letter box, trying to detect signs of life through the drawn curtains, attempting to knock and call as imploringly and attractively as possible. Lure her out, lure her back. But how? It wasn't going to work. Not tonight at any rate. Like a cat whose dignity had been compromised by a cocksure mouse, Richard quickly composed himself. He raised his hand and hovered over the bell. Then thought better of it. He sauntered away.

I don't really want the mouse. I only wanted to play. I'll come back another time. She will be mine. She has my name written all over her.

From her bedroom, Sally knew that he was going. She rushed to the window and pinched the curtains just enough to admit one eye. She watched him go. Excited. Disappointed. She watched the headlamps blaze into life, temporarily obscuring the car from sight. She heard the engine. She watched the swift, effortless three-point turn, and she watched the car slink away, rejected but graceful. Turning to the silent brightness of her room, she felt lonely.

Why didn't you knock some more?

Richard absent-mindedly took a left, a right, he crossed some lights and took another left. He had no idea where he was going or where he was.

Come on, mate. Stop a minute. Get a grip. Let's think this one through.

He thought it through and decided that Diana might have an answer of some sort. A bit late, past midnight, but then she was a night owl. He noted with a smile the gangly holly bush outside her house, its leaves inked black by the night, its berries still defiantly red. How very Diana. She was in and she was delighted and relieved to see him. They hugged and held on to each other like people mourning a lost friend.

'What is she playing at? Is she playing? Has the whole thing been some long, perverted game?'

Diana looked at Richard. He sat stiff and forward on the sagging couch and looked decidedly wrong there without Sally. He clasped his hands, his arms on his knees, his hair tousled, his eyes tired. She felt enormous tenderness for him, but she felt singularly ill-equipped to offer him any truly worthwhile advice.

117

'I honestly don't know. I've tried to talk. She's incredibly distressed.'

'But,' panicked Richard, 'but what *has* she said? Now? In the past? Think, Diana, help me here.' Diana thought and could offer only a sympathetic shrug.

'Richard,' she shook her head and Richard watched her homemade holly berry earrings (were they real?) swing haphazardly in support, 'Sally kept saying that you shouldn't have fallen in love with her. That it had spoiled things. Not that I know what "things" mean. She didn't tell me. I asked, I tried. But actually, I don't think that even *she* knows what "things" mean.'

Richard sat silent and pensive for a while. And then started with another needy 'but'.

'But, in the past, Diana. In the past?'

'In the past, she's spoken of you, of you and her, with – well, with passion. With relish. I don't know, with a sort of *greed*. To tell you the truth, Richard, I've never seen her like this. She's so, well, *sassy*! But . . .'

'But?'

'I don't know. There was also an element of naïveté . . .'

'Explain? Please?'

'That would be impossible, Richard. It's just, well, just so *Sally*, I suppose.'

'But I'm in love with her, with her sassiness *and* her naiveté. What on earth is so terrible about that?' Diana shrugged again, feeling hopeless. What indeed *was* so terrible about someone like Richard falling in love with someone like Sally?

'Richard, Richard, give her time. I'm *sure* she'll come round, come to her senses and realize just what she has. What she is jeopardizing.'

'Diana, has she ever told you that she loves me?'

'No.'

'Implied it?'

'Richard, Sally has never used the "L" word. About anyone.'

'Nor had I.'

We'll leave Richard with Diana. He finds in her a tangible if indirect link with Sally, he finds her bohemian boudoir comforting and suddenly preferable to his comparably stark flat and his own, bad company. Diana will talk, she'll tell him the precious little she knows about the florid proclamations of love and the horrid tales of violence that Sally endured with the Jims and Jamies of her past. Richard will confide in Diana, he will use the 'L' word with such conviction and sincerity that she will feel moved to the verge of tears. Richard will compare Sally with the women he has known, and will declare her incomparable. But though Diana will comfort him, and will bolster him with her own belief that he could be the best thing to happen to Sally only Sally doesn't yet see it, she will also rightly tell Richard that it is Sally who has to come back to him. He must discipline himself to steer clear until then. Because if, or when, she returns, it will be off her own bat. And if she comes back it will be for good and for real. But for now, leave her be. Disappear. It will be difficult, Richard, but it can be done, it must be done. Listen to Diana, heed her advice – she has both your and Sally's best interests at heart. Do as you're told. Sally is off to Paris. No, you can't follow her there.

So we'll leave Richard, floundering in his anxiety, desperate in his longing, sorrowful in his thwarted love. We'll go instead to Sally, we'll cross a lurching English Channel with her and accompany her through Paris. We'll watch what she does and we'll see where she goes; unseen witnesses to her most private world.

EIGHTEEN

*I*t could have been England. The weather was so English, rain and a lot of it; the countryside looked like England – a lush landscape divided and organized into patchwork fields. But it wasn't England. England was over the sea and far away. This was France and you knew it every time the train hurtled past a station or through a village. It was France because the rural architecture said so. It was France because the men and women that the train passed were so, well, rustic. Where does British Rail pass through that affords the passenger a glimpse of a farm-worker in partisan clothes and a battered cloth cap, astride an ancient tractor held together with twine and with time? How many rural stations in Britain are bedecked with ceramic tiles and festooned with flowers?

The children were quiet; the ferry crossing had been rough, quite a few had been sick and no one escaped feeling peaky. This, combined with the early start and the soothing movement of the train churring along, lulled the class into a dozy, hushed state. Sally sat with two seats to herself. She bagged the window seat while her bags sat grandly next to her. Across the aisle, Madame Pelisou

(Head of French, Cleo to the staff) read *Paris Match*. Every now and then she pushed her glasses back on to her short nose. Everything about her was short: her stature, her hair, her fingers and their neat, square nails, her vowels, and of course her temper. She disliked children who did not try almost as much as she detested English bread. She was old but did not seem elderly, her true age being anywhere from mid-fifties to early seventies. Sally liked her. All the staff liked her. The children dreaded her. Madame Pelisou was one of a dying breed of French teachers who commanded respect and achieved consistent top grades through a style of teaching that was unashamedly dictatorial, tyrannical and tough. She was most generous at handing out humiliation and punishment. Many a child had left her lessons covered in chalk dust or doused with water (how else would they learn what *un seau d'eau* was?). Many a child had been reduced to tears. Many a child had a week of break-times confiscated. Many a child had been on the receiving end of a menacing, icy stare and a venomously spat 'Fool!' And yet not one child ever failed French and, deep into adulthood, the memory of Madame Pelisou remained vivid. With hindsight she was remembered fondly as a colourful and brilliant teacher. Sally watched her reading, saw her nod and frown and smile and tut. She looked up and caught Sally's eye and offered her a barley sugar. *Merci*.

By the time they reached Paris the rain had stopped and the city welcomed them, glistening grey and marvellously grand. It looked beautiful, enhanced by the postdownpour sunlight filtering between the buildings. A minibus awaited them and they travelled up the Champs Elysée and over the Pont Neuf heading for the Sorbonne where, down a snaking, overcrowded side street they found the pension that was to provide beds and breakfasts for the duration of their stay. For the children, this compared most favourably to their previous school trip under canvas in a waterlogged Welsh field. Now they were in France, in Gay (snigger snigger) Paris. Oh, la la!

Madame Pelisou suggested that she took the room on the floor where the children were, so Sally had a little room without a view but pretty anyway on the floor below. Diana had been considered for the trip but had requested Florence the following year. Sally thought about this as she unpacked. Uncharitably, she felt relieved that Diana was not in Paris.

I'm not having anyone telling me I ought to reciprocate Richard's love, that Richard's love is good and desirable. I don't want it and I do not want him either.

The bed invited one to snuggle down deep and Sally fell asleep, cosy and exhausted, staring distractedly at a corner of the room where the wallpaper was coming away in a perfect furl.

'Marcus, come here *now! Venez ici*! Rajiv, stop it. Class Five, settle down. Thank you. This is Notre Dame. This is a Gothic cathedral and we're standing in front of the west portal that dates to the 1220s. Marcus, you are really pushing it. Thank you. This is the main entrance so the sculpture is *didactic* – there are lessons to be learned by reading the stories depicted by the sculpture. Also, way back then, everything would have been painted in vivid colours. So, before people came to pray they would be confronted by all these tales in the sculpture. Now, why do you think that was so important? Alice?'

'Because most people couldn't read?'

'Absolutely! Marsha?'

'Also because they might learn from the scenes and then go inside and pray extra hard and properly.'

'Absolutely. Look up there, that's the Gallery of Kings. If you look above that, the sculpture depicts the Last Judgment and the Resurrection. Now those are the archivolts and if you look hard, you can see that the scenes up there are of the Damned and the Blessed. Look,

122

there are the blind riders of the Apocalypse, and here are the Damned being shovelled into the mouth of Hell. It's so fantastic! Now, these are called the socles and in the socles are carved *per-son-if-i-cations* of the Virtues and Vices. These were to show the people the ways of life of which God either approved or disapproved. Look (Marcus!), see over here, this man is hitting a Bishop so this is a warning against sins against the Church. But this vice was the worst – it's a monk running away and deserting the Church altogether. And here are the goodies: Faith over here, and then Hope and over there Charity. So in the olden days, you'd come along to church and you'd see all these terrible sins and above them, sinners being thrown to Hell – as Marsha says, you'd go into the Cathedral and pray pretty hard!'

The children stood, necks craning, heads back, mesmerized (apart from Marcus who was more interested in the donkey with the straw hat and sun-glasses). Madame Pelisou winked at Miss Lomax.

Bien, let's go inside.

The class stood stock still in hushed reverence. From the impossibly large nave windows, light hung silent in dusty, gossamer walls. From the east end, the rose window burst forth glorious colours and ethereal light. Wide-eyed and open-mouthed, children and teachers alike were cast under the Cathedral's enduring spell. Marcus was held motionless by the stare of the stone-weary face of a saint; Marsha closed her eyes as light from the stained glass blessed her face in a mosaic of colour and warmth; Rajiv looked up and up and up and still did not reach the vaulting; Alice stood against a column and hugged it tight, her outstretched arms covering a mere fraction of its circumference. Sally was thrilled, thrilled to be back in Paris and charmed by the response of the children. It was a job persuading them to leave after a good hour.

Just wait until they see Sainte Chapelle tomorrow!

123

In stark contrast, the Pompidou Centre that afternoon provided endless and irreverent fun for Class Five. They stared and they frowned and they sniggered their way through. Shrieks of 'Call that Art?' and 'I could do that' and 'That's crap!' assaulted Sally's ears. She was now genuinely relieved that Diana was not with them.

She'd have wept.

'I know it's just one colour blue, Alice, but don't you feel a sense of space? That the colour describes the space around it? That shape and colour represent movement and space?' Miss Lomax tried to reason.

'No,' came a defiant answer.

'But,' Miss Lomax pressed, 'why does painting need to represent *something*? These modern painters believe that painting need represent nothing but itself. The very act of putting colour on canvas justifies its existence.'

'Still think it's crap,' fidgeted Alice, who was actually starting to see Miss Lomax's point, but was too galled to admit it.

'Language!' warned Miss Lomax.

'Sorry,' murmured Alice.

'Is there anything here you like?'

'I like Pick Arso.'

Sally sighed in dismay and went off to buy postcards. She had a headache threatening and expounding the merits of Modernism had not helped. Could Madame Pelisou possibly manage without her for a few hours? Could she cope with all thirty on the *bateau mouche*?

Cope? Manage?

Bien sûr!

So Sally left them and wandered back to the Left Bank.

Meandering through the Latin Quarter, charmed by its quaintness, energized by its off-beat vitality, the headache never materialized. Sally felt fine and Sally felt happy. Up the Boulevard St Michel, window-shopping, she turned left on to the Boulevard St Germain. Opposite

124

sat the Musée Cluny; it was tempting but Sally decided not to be victim to Gallery Guilt and boldly strolled past with Catherine's song from *Jules et Jim* matching her footfalls as she went.

Wait! That's the Café de Flore, that's where Picasso et al whiled away their hours. And there's a free table! I'm there, I'm there.

'*Café au lait, s'il vous plaît!*'

Sally sits and sips and watches Parisian life bustle by. The day is beautiful, crisp and bright. Her eyes are slightly watery, her nose a little numb. She feels someone staring. She glances to her left and catches the eye of an impeccably suave, quintessentially French and devilishly good-looking man. Feeling reckless, she stares back. He leans with his arm on the bar, a very small, thick glass of Pernod nearby, an unfiltered cigarette resting idly between his fingers. Sally holds his gaze, intensely and unrelenting, until the man gives in and beams a salacious smile of perfect teeth. They talk with their eyebrows. May he join her? He may.

His name is Jean-Claude and he is a designer. This is his favourite café and usually he likes to sit alone. But he saw an English Rose and his own company was suddenly not enough. Another *café*? Please? *Garçon!*

As he ordered, Sally stared into her empty cup and took stock.

No one knows where I am! At this very moment, no one knows what I'm doing, that I am here, right here. This is all mine! I can be who I want and I can do as I please!

Sally felt a stream of warmth and satisfaction trace through her body at this realization.

He doesn't know who I am, and nobody I know knows that I am here. I am totally free; to be.

It felt illicit, it felt wonderful. And now his attention is back with Sally, she must talk and not think.

Talk? Flirt!

'Your English is excellent!' Thank you, he studied at Oxford and what is she doing in Paris?

'I'm a teacher, I have a class of thirty children. We are here for another two days.' Thirty children? But where are they? With much Gallic shrugging, Jean-Claude searches for them under the table and behind Sally's jacket. She shrieks with laughter, perhaps a little too enthusiastically, but what the hell? She will never see him again and no one will know anyway. They make small talk for a long time and Sally is won over by the way that simple English words and phrases ('Good Lord, you don't say?' *par example*) are transformed by a throaty French accent which oozes sensuality and Gauloises. Would she like to meet him later, right here, for a decent drink? Ooh, she would, that would be lovely. Only she can't promise; she may have teacherly duties to attend to. No matter, no matter, he is here most nights. If it is not tonight, maybe it is tomorrow night? Maybe. But Sally must go now, images of Cleo and Marcus have filtered across her mind's eye. She gathers her things about her and feels Jean-Claude looking openly at her breasts as they jut while she twists her body into her jacket. Again they stare. This time it is Sally who smiles first. See you. Yes, I hope so.

When Sally reaches the corner she looks back. He is still looking.

Longing, I do believe.

He raises his glass, she smiles widely and then sets off with a jaunty little stride and a discernible wiggle.

Sally has an idea.

She feels exhilarated, it is such fun mooting it.

Richard's loss with be J-C's gain; Richard's mistake will be J-C's triumph.

Wishing to define it further and in privacy, she walks straight past the turning for the pension and jigs along, head down, smiling distractedly, meandering in her walk and in her mind.

He won't fall in love with me. There simply isn't the time! I'll strip bare the trimmings and trappings of Jackie Collins.

Sally is scheming, Sally's spunk has returned. Sally has an idea, a plan, another project.

This time it'll be Erica Jong who's proud of me. I am going to pursue the Zipless Fuck.

NINETEEN

*S*ally did not make it back to the café that night. Cleo had suggested they take their entourage to Montmartre. Sally was temporarily disappointed, but reasoned that there was always tomorrow.

Mustn't appear too keen, remember, and he's there most nights.

An evening of potential lust was exchanged for a few hours of fun with the class but to her delight, Sally found that she could quite easily mind her charges while summoning up assorted images of wild love-making. Although she could not remember J-C's face his voice remained vivid and enabled her expertly to conjure up a body that could very well be his. While she walked, while she talked to the children or organized with Cleo, she was confronted by images of a firm and muscle-bound torso, of her own body being fondled dexterously. As she listened to Marcus's theory on French footballers, she dreamt up various positions for the next night; most of them were decidedly off-side. When Alice wanted to hear more about Modernism, Sally could say 'Art pour l'art' while undressing Jean-Claude very slowly with her mind's eye. It was like being in two places at once. It was fabulous.

But Montmartre was fun too. They were rewarded, after a steep climb, by a floodlit Sacré-Coeur soaring transparent-gold and beautiful. Montmartre was buzzing and Sally's tales of Toulouse Lautrec and Dance Hall Days put a spring in the step and a sparkle in the eyes of Class Five. Marcus and Rajiv performed a boisterous can-can which won applause all around. Crêpes were scoffed and caricatures sat for. Madame Pelisou was on hand to barter down the exorbitant prices so that the children could purchase the masterpieces.

'Miss Lomax, have yours done. Go on! And you too, Madame Pelisou.' So they sat for a double portrait. Watching Miss Lomax and Madame Pelisou being fashioned into bulbous-nosed, bug-eyed, buck-toothed caricatures provided the class with much hilarity. The likeness was tenuous but that was hardly the point.

'Look! The Eiffel Tower. Tomorrow we're going up, up, up! Can't we go there *before* the Loo?'

'Blaspheme like that, Marcus, and I'll have you in the Louvre until closing time and beyond. The plan for tomorrow, Class Five, is to visit Sainte Chapelle and then spend two hours at the Louvre – and not in the café; I want a page of writing or a drawing of something you see there. After that we'll go up the Eiffel Tower and then on to Forum Les Halles in the afternoon where you can spend your pennies – francs rather. Everybody happy? Good!' Madame Pelisou regaled the group with an embellished biography of Toulouse Lautrec, complete with dialogue and songs. They were back at the pension before they knew it. Tired but happy, Class Five were unanimously obedient and went straight to bed and to sleep.

It is the evening of the next day. Fun was had by all. Marcus loved the Louvre and was late to meet the group.

Géricault and Delacroix had become his new heroes. Climbing the Eiffel Tower seemed dull in comparison to entering a painting and becoming a fighter for *Liberté*, *Egalité* and *Fraternité*. He spent most of his money on a book on nineteenth-century French art. It was in French but the pictures were fabulous, and anyway, Madame Pelisou promised she would help him translate.

Now it is the evening. The children are packing. Cleo and Sally are chatting. Sally asks Cleo if she would like to go for a stroll, for a drink? She knows that she will decline. Cleo declines. She will keep watch on the third floor, should the young proletariat build barricades or find imaginary Bastilles to storm.

'Well, I think I'll go for a walk. I don't know when next I'll be in Paris.'

'Have a good time, Sally. When the children are asleep, I shall tuck down for an early night. I'll see you at breakfast, eight-thirty.'

'*À demain!*'

Sally strolled to the Boulevard St Germain. There was the Café de Flore and it was heaving. Will he be there? Is this a good idea? She weaved to the bar and ordered a Kir. She looked about, trying hard not to look like she was looking for someone.

He's there.

Sally spied J-C talking animatedly with two friends.

Catch my eye, catch it! I'm over here. Over here, J-C.

Jean-Claude looked up and saw Sally. She smiled, he looked momentarily blank, then registered and swiftly tilted his head up. Sally jumped at the response and made her way over. The jostle of people knocked her sideways, her wine spilled over the sleeve of her shirt but she recovered her poise by the time she reached her target. Her smile flashed sheepish for a second.

'Hello, Jean-Claude.'

'Hello, Susan.'

'Sally!'

'Sally. Hello, Sally.' If it is possible for an embarrassing silence to pervade in a noisy and frantic bar, then the café reverberated with it.

'These are my friends, Michel and Luigi.'

'Hello, hello! Luigi, are you Italian?'

'They speak no English. Luigi is French also.'

'Oh.'

Sally felt awkward and Sally felt shy. Suddenly she wished she had never come. She wanted to go.

Go, Sal. Just up and leave. You'll never see him again. No one knows you are here.

She was tempted but two words crept through her brain, across her eyes and down her body.

Zipless Fuck.

So Sally stays and is heartened when J-C replenishes her drink. She tells him what she's been doing. She asks him about his job, about living in Paris. Has he been to London? Yes. Did he like it? Yes. Will he come again? Maybe. In between one-word answers, Jean-Claude natters to his friends. They laugh a lot, raucous and guttural. Sally cannot join in. She shifts uncomfortably from foot to foot and runs her finger over the rim of her glass again and again, trying to keep a sassy smile in place. Once more she feels she ought to go. Yet again, Jean-Claude buys her another Kir so she stays. She is not having fun. It is trying and it is tiring.

But I must pursue the Z.F. I have to. And anyway, I'll never see him again. No one who knows me knows that I am here.

Sally feels a pearl of sweat trickle down her back. She knows her cheeks are flushed and she feels slightly self-conscious. How long has she been here? She takes a furtive look at her watch. Two hours. They're talking in French and they're talking fast. Sally takes a good look at J-C. Dishy is the most appropriate adjective. He is tall. Taller than Richard? Yes, a little. His hair is dark, glossy

131

and straight, cut into a classic bob. He has broad shoulders and slender hands. Beautiful fingers, long and elegant with well-shaped nails. There is hair on the sides of his hands and just above each knuckle. Richard's hands are smooth. He is wearing a pink shirt unbuttoned at the neck, dark blue jeans, penny loafer slip-on shoes and a navy jacket fashionably crumpled. She glances at his face and notes deep-set and dark brown eyes, a longish but aristocratic nose, a strong jaw line and an attractive smattering of stubble.

I like what I see. He'll do. He'll do nicely, thank you very much. 'Sally and the Zipless Fuck'; where are Ms Collins, Ms Jong? A book depends on this. Follow me!

And what does Jean-Claude see? A pretty enough English girl. Not really his type, not quite chic enough. Her dress sense could be greatly improved, the skirt is terrible, the length is all wrong. If she wants it short, then it must be knickers-skimming; just above the knee is so *passé*. But she's keen. She'll do. Beatrice is away in Lyons and Michel and Luigi have been goading him on. She'll do. For the night. Anyway, he'll never see her again. And it's been ages since he slept with an English girl. And Luigi says rumour has it that English Roses are tigers in bed. We'll see. She'll do.

Sally feels more relaxed. Luigi and Michel have gone. They said something to Jean-Claude and she understood it to be along the lines of 'give her one from me', 'and me'.

Bloody cheek! It's me that's calling the shots tonight.

Jean-Claude has switched on the charm that he gushed the day before and Sally has allowed herself to be swept along with it. He claims that he was talking business with the other two. Would Sally like a Gauloise? And another drink? Sally sucks the cigarette and is overcome by its strength, she lurches for her wine and gulps twice before she has exhaled. Yuk! And a head-rush too. Suddenly, everything seems terribly loud and she feels slightly dizzy.

Fool! Don't you remember, smoking doesn't suit you?
Just make the cigarette last two more drags. And easy on
the wine, that's the fourth. No, fifth. Damn.

Unaware, Jean-Claude saves her.

'Let's take a walk.'

Outside it has been raining and the pavement is
dressed in glistening pools cast gold under the street
lights. They don't walk, they saunter. The pavement cafés
are emptier now, just the die-hard bar-proppers sipping
Pernod and philosophizing. Jean-Claude suggests they
head for the Luxembourg Gardens but when they arrive
all the benches are wet; it has started to drizzle and Sally
feels chilled. Her head has cleared and she has sobered
up. She and Jean-Claude do not really have that much to
talk about. They both know what they want to happen.
And they both know that it *will* happen. And they both
know that the other is willing and waiting.

Sally cannot really be bothered to play out a whole
seduction scene. Just a means to an end. An abbreviation
will suffice. She wants her Z.F., and she just wants her
Z.F., that's all. She and J-C are walking heads down
against the rain, hands in pocket to keep warm; silent.
Sally's footfalls provide her with thinking time. She
remembers back to the party where she met Richard. She
recalls with a smile the flirting and the eye contact and
the euphoric energy she felt. She remembers the teasing
mini-kiss she planted on his lips before spinning on her
heels to mix and mingle. And she sees again the erotic
kissing that they launched into uncontrollably once the
front door of the party had closed behind them. 'Come to
Highgate,' she had suggested. Progress had been slow,
with every red light an excuse to grope and kiss each
other greedily. 'Pull over! Pull over!' Sally had cried
when they were but a mile from base. Richard had
swerved recklessly to the side of the road; Hampstead
Heath, silent and conspiring, flanking them. Sally had
dived for him. Richard, in ecstatic disbelief, remained

defenceless while she sucked and licked her way down to his groin into which she buried her head for a tantalizing and all too short moment. For both, it was a taste of what was to come. And come.

Sally remembers the desperation to shed clothes as soon as her front door shut. Initially, they had tried to undress each other but it had proven cumbersome and too time-consuming. So, while they kissed, they wriggled and ripped their way out of their clothes. Burning naked, they made it to Sally's bed, the kiss which had started on the doorstep never stopped and Richard was forced to walk backwards, eyes shut, body raw, as Sally grappled and guided him into her bedroom. There, they melted into the bed and fell fast and deep into the pleasures and needs of scorching flesh.

Sally has no inclination to seduce Jean-Claude. There's no thrill to this chase. She doesn't care if he is bowled over by what a sassy vamp she is. She just wants to see what pure sex is like, no emotions attached. After all, she will never see him again. They walk and make small talk. The drizzle has stopped and a brisk wind taken its place.

'I live quite close to where we are now. Would you like to come up? For coffee?'

Coffee, etchings! Here we go!

'Yes, I'll come.'

TWENTY

*S*ally was sorely disap-
pointed by Jean-Claude's apartment. As soon as she set
foot inside, warning bells rang out but she chose to
remain deaf to them. In her fantasy on the way to
Montmartre the day before, he had taken her to an old
tenement building where the high-ceilinged rooms
breathed faded grandeur. She had envisaged tall windows with billowing muslin, mismatched colour-washed
cupboards in a tiny kichenette, and a balcony with a
seen-in-a-dream view. And, of course, a bidet in the
bathroom. She had imagined his bed as old and high,
enclosed by sinuous brass bedsteads and banked with
white linen; crumpled and voluminous. She had imagined herself sinking into it while he deftly undressed her.
No fumbling. No zips.

But reality usually lets a day-dream down and the
details of Sally's were deflated in an instant. J-C's flat
turned out to be on the fourth floor of a modern block.
The lift was out of order so they had traipsed up the stairs
and wandered down a faceless corridor. On entering the
apartment, the first thing that Sally thought was: *The*

man has no taste. He is a designer and yet he has no taste.

Each item of furniture was obviously expensive but nothing went with anything. Each piece was merely and clearly some status symbol. Sally's prime dismay, however, occurred in the bathroom.

Yuk, look at the state of that bath! And where's the bidet? There is no bidet. Woe.

Toothpaste oozed, solid and dry, from a topless tube; razor clippings scummed the sink. Sally recalled Jean-Claude's attractive stubble and calculated that he could not have shaved for at least two days.

Sally, if he has a grungy bathroom and no bidet for you, why are you staying? Why not go? It is not too late. You need never see him again. Think of Richard's bathroom; tasteful majolica, spick and span.

Sally refuses to think of Richard. But he's there, oh, he's there all right. Unwittingly, he's the very reason for Sally being in this sorry bathroom. She glances at herself in the mirror and is taken aback by the puzzled expression that meets her gaze. Defiantly, she smiles back. Obstinately, she won't let go of the Z.F. concept. She *has* to try it. No one will know but she. Looking at and not into the mirror, she absent-mindedly cups her hands over her breasts.

'Sally, you are okay?' the husky French voice enquires.

How very considerate.

'Yes, I'm fine. Give me a minute.' A minute later she emerges and Jean-Claude is hovering outside the door. He approaches and she allows herself to be kissed.

Mmm, he's a good kisser. Yes, this is fine. A good idea. I'm going to have fun.

No you're not.

Jean-Claude pulls Sally closer towards him. He grabs her arm with one hand and grabs her breast with the other. He *is* taller than Richard, her aching neck confirms it.

136

Ow, my arm.

Sally tries to free herself but it serves only to excite him and he grips tighter and kisses harder. He pulls away and, with a chuck of his head, he motions to a room Sally has not yet seen but presumes to be his bedroom.

The bed is unmade, the linen is striped brown and beige. J-C is undressing himself. Sally's hands are behind her back, finding the zip of her skirt which snags and catches as she pulls it down. It affords an ogling J-C a good look at her breasts doing their famous jut and he lunges for them.

He is naked while she is merely skirtless and he lounges on the bed, his erection arrogantly leering at her. Sally doesn't take her eyes off Jean-Claude; he keeps his eyes on her body, soaking up what every shed piece of clothing reveals. Sally lies down next to him and rests her arms on his chest, her leg folded around his. They kiss and she looks at him; his eyes are closed and she hears him give a throaty murmur under his breath. She smiles.

It's working.

Now his hands are everywhere, at least they're everywhere he wants them to be but they're not quite where Sally would like. She tries to guide his hand to her secret erogenous zones but he takes them away too soon. Sally wouldn't say that her breasts were being fondled; mauled rather. He's found her clitoris but is hardly sensitive to its sensitivity. He has no idea. She flinches but he reads it as pleasure and increases the pressure. Firmly, she pulls his hand. He looks up, puzzled.

'Not like that, *comme ci*,' she guides. He looks sulky but obeys. Sally is enjoying the sensation, she is close, she is very close. But though her breathing quickens and her body writhes, he stops.

'Don't stop.'

'I just find Mister Condom.'

Already?

Jean-Claude seems to think so.

She strokes his back while he rolls and snaps the condom into place and as he turns towards her, she reaches to kiss him. Jean-Claude can't be bothered with that just now, there's work to be done. He spreads her legs very wide and then puts his arms under the base of her back and hauls her up high. He barges into her. Sally moans. It feels good though. They hump and grind and Sally feels her neck being bitten. It hurts, but it feels exciting. He is thrusting harder and faster and Sally uses both hands to pull his head up and into line with hers. It's heavy, but she has his eyes. They kiss.

He's devouring me.

Sally wants to go on top. She tries to shift him but he's a leaden lump of pumping flesh.

'Jean-Claude, wait. Stop for a minute.'

'Why, what's wrong?'

'Nothing's wrong! Just stop so I can go on top.'

'Okay, okay.' That's better, Sally feels she has more control. She sets a slower pace and rotates her pelvis in the way she enjoys, the way that drove Richard wild. But Jean-Claude has stopped moving. She looks at him, he is looking at the ceiling. She stops too.

'Enough?' he delicately enquires.

'No!' Sally retorts.

'Later,' he suggests as he flips her on to her stomach.

As he takes her from behind she feels a surge of excitement in her abdomen. But it disappears once he's settled himself into his own pattern of bumps. It does nothing for Sally but she reasons that it is his 'go' so that's okay. He lifts her on to her knees and after a moment's thrill for Sally, he finds his favoured pace again. He grabs her breasts and just keeps them grabbed. Sally decides it is time for a change but she cannot shift him. He is hurling himself into her, her arms are aching, her knees are getting chafed and her breasts hurt under his grip. She arches her back in an effort to free herself but his arms clasp her around her stomach and he squeezes her as he thrusts into her. Her breathing is distorted, it is not comfortable, it is not sexy at all. She imagines they must look like dogs mating.

This is not my mate.

She feels sore. She gives up. Faster he goes.

Come on, J-C, you must be close. Come on. Come.

She is bashed and she is bumped against. His pace is frenetic and he starts to moan.

Bébé, bébé. Mon Dieu, mon Dieu. Monde.

She can feel every spurt and every surge.

Mon Dieu.

He's finished.

Thank God.

Staring at the hideous linen, Sally bemoans that *hors d'oeuvres* was fundamentally *ordinaire*, that she had been deprived main course and there had been no suggestion of pudding. Now he flops down on top of her and her sore knees grate against the sheets. Her face is smothered by pillow and sweaty brute of a man. She wants to go.

'You want to stay?'

'No.'

So, Sally Lomax, you've had your Zipless Fuck. And how do you feel? You're walking back, through deserted Paris streets, it is almost two in the morning. How do you feel! Was it worth it? Was it as you expected? Did you like it? Do you want more? Has it made you feel good – in your body, your self? Are you now happy?

Was that it? What have I done? And why have I done it? So that was a Zipless Fuck. Erica J., you've got it all wrong. It can't have been. No, no, but it was. It wasn't like in the books, it was not like in the films. It's me – I've let Ms Jong down. I've let myself down. I feel down. I'm alone in Paris. And I feel lonely, full stop. I'm sore. Where am I? Oh, yes, first left then right.

What did I do that for? It wasn't like Ms Jong made out. I'm obviously not heroine material for her books. Richar. . . no, no, no, what am I saying? I don't want him. Jean-Claude, J-C, vous êtes un grand cochon. But if he's a pig, then I can only be a dog. I don't know what I'll think of myself in the morning, in the clear light of day. Well, I'll never see him again. I'll never do this again. But where do I go from here? Put it down to experience? It's an experience I wish I'd never had. There's the pension. I'm home and dry.

But it's not home and I'm soaking wet.

Sally crept up the stairs and into her room. She had a scorching shower and did not finish off with a blast of cold. Hot water felt more cleansing and she felt filthy. She scrubbed and rubbed and soaped her fingers, cleaning as far up as she could reach. Condom or no condom, she could feel and smell him still. He did not smell like Richard yet she was neither comforted nor pleased by this. She dried herself, pulling the towel over her body harshly. She looked at her knees, they were red. She looked at her neck and was reviled by the dark raspberry blotch she saw. A love bite was a contradiction in terms, this was a selfish lust suck and she wished it was not there.

Sally fell into bed. Her heart was pounding and her mind was rattling with a jumble of hazed thoughts.

No, no. Sleep.

She shut off and slept, dreamless but safe again.

TWENTY-ONE

*S*ally could not quite manage breakfast even though she knew that the croissants and hot chocolate would be as delicious as they had been throughout their stay. She retired, still tired, to her room to pack. The suitcase ready and by the door, she lay on the crumpled bed hoping she could find comfort in closed eyes. But her eyes were held open and fixed on the furl of wallpaper which, today, looked yellowing and sorry. A very hot, oily tear eased its way from her tear-duct, over her eyeball, to dribble lethargically from the corner of her eye down her cheek. Sally wondered what it was there for. She did not think she felt like crying. It evaporated, leaving a slight tightness to the cheek. She splashed her face with water from the tap and called 'I'm coming!' to Cleo's knock.

* * *

'Come in!' called Richard, over the sea and far away.

'It's *Mzzz* Filey, from Marlborough Ward *Ink*,' Sandra announced with a wide-eyed smile.

'Of course. Do show her in,' Richard motioned whilst sorting through the mock-Georgian folly plans.

A long pair of legs walked in, the longest that Richard had seen or thought could exist. He followed them upwards, travelling yards of sheer Lycra before arriving at a bright blue and very short skirt, teamed with matching and flatteringly cut jacket. Crowning the ensemble was a chiselled face with manicured eyebrows, perfect lips and a glossy, jet black head of hair organized into a sharp, clean, hundred-dollar crop. Sophistication personified. And in his office.

'Carlotta Filey.'

'Richard Stonehill.'

They grasped hands; hers were cool and strong, garnished with perfectly shaped and polished nails.

Stop gawping, Richard.

Rich-ard, *get a hold of yourself, man! What on earth!*

As she concentrated on the drawings before her, Richard absorbed the picture in front of him.

Quite frankly, I've never seen anything like her – like this!

Though hidden, he was aware and ashamed of his sudden erection.

Think Sally, think Sally.

But Sally is in Paris and she hates you and it's over.

Richard heard himself making small talk, asking after her flight, the hotel.

'How long are you staying?'

'I leave late Saturday.' Tomorrow.

Carlotta liked what she saw. She was delighted with the plans and was pleased with their creator.

A flying visit. A flying fuck? Perhaps. Gee, why the heck not?

'Listen, Richard, could I take these with me? I don't want to take up too much of your time right now.'

'No, no! But you're not. Please!'

She held his eyes and saw what an easy catch he was going to be.

'Really, I'd like to spend the afternoon going over them. Say, why not continue this over dinner?' His eyes lit up.

Richard, you're so transparent.

'Yes, let's!'

'You know some place nice?'

'Oh, yes!'

'You want to pick me up from the hotel? I've gotten so lost in London before. Eight, eight-thirty?'

'Yes! Fine, fine. I'll be at the Savoy at eightish.' He watched the legs slink away and saw his tube of drawings encircled by exquisitely manicured hands. His penis, enthusiastic and with a mind of its own, imagined vividly where those hands could be much better clasped. Richard's eyes admired the rear view as she breezed out of his room. His mouth was dry, his ears full of her slow, deep drawl, and her suggestion of dinner, eight, eight-thirty, replayed itself like a scratched record.

Well, Richard, we have seen what your eyes saw, we heard what she said, we know how your body has reacted but what, exactly, is going on in your mind?

Wow! he thought, while Sandra, dowdy and depressed, brought him a cheese sandwich.

Wow! he thought as he fingered the bread and tipped the food, untouched, into the bin.

What on earth! he thought as he swivelled in his chair and fixed his hands behind his head watching the cranes and the river being busy beneath him.

That was some woman, he mused as he dropped a hand to loll over his subsiding erection.

Some woman! he concluded as he twirled back to his desk to answer the phone.

'Richard? Bob! Squash?'

'No!'

'No? Why?'

'Busy.'

'Where?'

'Business.'

Odd, thought Bob as he hung up.

* * *

Sally brought up the rear of the crocodile as it trooped to the Orangerie. Today Paris was noisy and threatening to her. Suddenly it seemed to be a place she neither liked nor knew. Highgate seemed rosy and very far away. The children were impatient to run amok in the Tuileries gardens so they raced around the gallery, bought postcards under Madame Pelisou's approving supervision and then followed her outside until she reached her chosen bench near the fountains and released them. They scampered away on their final burst of holiday energy. Sally remained inside. She wandered down the stairs and found Monet's *Water Lilies*, silent and serene, just as she had left them three years previously. She had them all to herself. She was alone with them and they enveloped and soothed her like a grandfather. She sat herself down, shoulders drooping, her neck and head poking lazily upwards. She looked like a shabby zoo vulture but she felt like a mouse. She gave little attention to the paintings which surrounded her, she knew them well and they required little effort for their spell to be woven. The vast, encircling canvasses of muted hazed colours granted Sally the hush and peace she desperately needed, that her own company for once could not provide. She became lost in the privacy and calm of Giverny. Her head drooped and dropped lower than her shoulders. Noiselessly, she wept.

Unseen, Marcus, who had returned to search for his clipboard, watched Miss Lomax's hunched back heave with wracking silent sobs.

Miss Lomax is crying. Why is Miss Lomax crying?

Marcus realized in an instant that this was not the stuff

of playground gossip. He saw her take her hands to her face and heard her sniff and gasp, strangled and private. He wanted to sit on her lap and cuddle her as he had his mother when his grandfather had died. But he knew he couldn't and shouldn't and mustn't. He felt compelled to watch over her; he felt he should, just until she stopped. The water lilies seemed to smile benevolently over her but it was not enough. Marcus felt he should remain there, out of sight, just until she stopped crying. Eventually she did. Marcus saw her body slump exhausted and crumple a little bit more now that the sobbing had subsided. Silently he backed away and out of sight to the stairwell. A Rodin bust met him eye to eye. The bronze and battered face, alternately shiny and dull, black and silver under the spotlight, carried the sorrow and pain that Marcus recognized as Miss Lomax's. He left her there, being looked after by her water lilies, watched over and understood by Rodin.

When she emerged twenty minutes later, Marcus nonchalantly took time out from a game of tag and ventured over to the bench where she and Madame Pelisou sat. He offered her a piece of apricot-flavoured chewing gum, Madame Pelisou too. Miss Lomax took it gratefully and smiled weakly at him. The tears were gone and no redness around the eyes suggested they had ever been there. But behind the smile and behind the eyes, Marcus could see that her sorrow had not abated. He took it upon himself to sit by her on the train and to stand near her on the deck of the ferry, offering her a crisp, a sip of Ribena, another piece of chewing gum; peach melba-flavoured this time.

The party arrived back at the school at 7 that evening. The children stampeded to their parents with garbled tales of the time of their lives they had just had. Most hurried away to the family Volvos without a backward glance. Marcus, who had already re-enacted David's *Death of Marat* and had told his father about the donkey

145

with the hat and the sun-glasses, was just beginning a discourse on Delacroix when he stopped and caught Madame Pelisou's eyes. Beaming at her, he then looked for Miss Lomax and waved expansively. She raised her hand and held it there. Suddenly a wave was not enough. He charged back into the playground, shouting: '*Merci! Merci!*' to Madame Pelisou as he ran to Miss Lomax and told her that she was the best teacher in the whole wide world and that he'd see her in class on Monday morning.

'Home! Hello, little flat. Hello, chairs. Hello, dead flowers. I'm home.'

Leaving her suitcase by the door, Sally went through to the kitchen, thumbing through the mail as she filled the kettle and found her favourite mug. Disappointed that there were no handwritten letters, she set aside the bills and bank statement for the next day and dumped the circulars in the bin. It was nearly 8 o'clock and she dialled for Diana though she wondered if she really felt like talking. The line rang and rang, and rang redundant; Diana obviously was not in. What did Sally want to say anyway? Would she confide? Did part of her want to run to Diana, let go and reveal how ghastly it had been and how wretched she felt? Would she just say she was feeling low and hide the reason? But who is the reason, Sally? Richard or Jean-Claude?

Well, Diana was not in so Sally was saved the decision. She sipped her tea in the bath and considered the noise she made; a whistling intake of breath, the slurp of liquid travelling past her lips into her mouth, the hollow echo of the gulp as she swallowed. She acknowledged how the flavour and warmth of this humble beverage brought comfort to her tastebuds, her stomach and her mind. She acknowledged too that she was absorbed in such menial thoughts because she did not want to think about that which she knew she should.

At 8.30, Sally was in bed, her teeth brushed, a clean

pair of pyjamas on, and a cassette of *Woman's Hour* short stories filling the room and providing a welcome diversion from the knot of thoughts and emotions pressing on her mind.

When Sally fell asleep half an hour later with the tape still running, Richard wiped his mouth with a linen napkin and stared at Carlotta's lips, awaiting the main course.

TWENTY-TWO

'**A**re you married?'

'Good Lord, no!' Richard exclaimed. He scanned her left hand, saw no band of gold and decided against asking her the same. The remains of the main course, delicious and rich, had been cleared away. They were eating at the Savoy: 'So we can spread your plans out on the floor afterwards,' Carlotta had told him. *And I can spread my legs after that*, she had mused. Richard was dumbstruck by her beauty and elegance, but not so mesmerized that he could not assess, with slight dismay, that she was fashionably abstemious with her food. He remembered Sally gorging herself and swooning with pleasure at the meals they had enjoyed together.

Forget Sally.

The pudding trolley was wheeled before them for their delectation. *Don't*, prayed Richard, *please don't choose tiramisù*. Carlotta chose fresh strawberries and Richard was relieved, and silently bewildered that he was indeed relieved. But the chocolate-Cointreau parfait distracted him from the naggings of his subconscious.

This woman is a thoroughbred racehorse to Sally's half-breed filly.

'Let's have coffee over the plans in my room,' suggested Carlotta.

In the lift, Richard and Carlotta held each other's gazes unrelenting. Her eyes were an astonishing deep emerald accentuated by careful, precise make-up. Her lips were full and constantly pouting and Richard marvelled how they could keep their glossy red coating throughout an entire meal, many glasses of wine, and frequent dainty dabs on a napkin. She was wearing a startling dress; red, sleeveless, tight and short. In her high black patent heels, she was almost as tall as Richard who had changed into casual shirt and blazer. He followed two steps behind as she sashayed to her door and he watched, excited, as she calmly slid the key into the lock and flicked her wrist to open it. She used the side of her body to press the door open and Richard observed her calf muscle flex temptingly as she did so.

The suite was palatial if anonymous and they went through to the lounge area where, true to her word, the plans lay unravelled on the floor. Richard had no plans, he was happy to be led. Stepping out of her shoes, Carlotta laid a hand on Richard's shoulder to steady herself and left it there a suggestive moment longer once she was shoeless and a few inches shorter than him.

'Screw the coffee, let's have port!' Carlotta broke the silence uncompromisingly. Richard was dying for coffee, but if Carlotta said port, then so be it. He and his penis watched in awe and anticipation as she grasped the neck of the bottle and slid her thumb up to the mushroom cork and eased it off. She snaked over to him, two glasses in her hands, and came up close, very close, before handing him the fuller glass and coiling herself to the ground. Richard closed his mouth and sat down opposite her, the plans in between them.

'I like this,' Carlotta said as she leant across, affording Richard a front seat view of her fabulous cleavage. 'And this is cool,' she cooed, gesturing to the elegant portico.

149

'But couldn't we have bay windows with that neat leaded glass effect?' she asked, sitting back on her knees and placing her impossibly long hands on her beautifully dipped waist.

'No,' Richard murmured, and then cleared his throat, delivering the first few words of his reason in an unnaturally loud voice. 'No, I really don't think so. This is mock-*Georgian*, not mock-*Tudor*. It would be a travesty and the overall elegance would be compromised – decimated, actually. Awfully sorry. No can do.' *God, can I kiss you?*

'Okay,' Carlotta conceded. Richard looked at her, waiting for her next query. Architecture, architecture. A stunning woman across from him; think architecture. Richard dropped his gaze to his plans, beautifully orchestrated even if he did think so himself. He was pleased with his work and Carlotta Filey, on behalf of Marlborough Ward Inc., gave it their seal of approval.

'It's great. I just love it. We'll have it,' Carlotta concluded. 'Let's fuck,' she said.

Richard's head jerked up.

What did she just say? I beg your pardon?

Come on, Richard, why so startled? You knew from the moment she suggested dinner earlier this morning that you would have some kind of sex.

Indeed, he had known, from the way they caught each other's eyes and held them, smouldering, over dinner, that they would end up in bed. He knew, by the way they had stood so close and brushed against each other intentionally and unnecessarily in the lift, that desire was mutual and strong. He could tell by her body language, obvious and seductive, here in the room, that she wanted him. And he knew, by the messages relayed from his brain to his groin and back again, that he wanted her. And yet he was taken aback. It seemed so sudden, so aloof, so unsexual. Hands still on her waist, she looked at him, stonily, lips parted.

'You *do* wanna, doncha?' she asked him, a patronizing edge lacing her question.

Do I want to go to bed with this woman? Just look at her, man. Just look at what you can have. Sod Sally. Screw her. Screw Carlotta.

'Yup,' Richard declared, rising to his feet to follow her into the bedroom.

Carlotta breezed over to him and spun around so that he might unzip her dress. It caught halfway down and snatched at the material. She pushed his hands away and eased the dress off. She was trussed up in black lace lingerie, the whole works; half-cup boned bra, suspenders, minuscule knickers, lacy-topped stockings. *Like a billboard ad for Triumph or Playtex or whatever*, Richard thought later. He wanted to touch her but was not sure where. His palms were clammy too.

'Wait,' he said, 'I'm just popping to the bathroom.' Locking himself in as quietly as he could (*Don't want her to think I'm a prude or something*), he ran the tap on full until it gushed soothingly cold water. He held his wrists still, shifting his body so that the water no longer splashed back at him. He lessened the flow and cupped water to his face, keeping his eyes open all the time. He shook his head and looked at himself straight, in the mirror. He felt rather bewildered.

Richard, what are you going to do? Are you sure you want to? Is it to spite Sally? Is it to persuade yourself that you're over her, that she never meant that much anyway? Is it to reinstate your macho pride which she inadvertently damaged? What do you see as you look at your wet face? As you watch the drops fall from your nose and from your chin?

Richard Stonehill, do you want it? Is she worth it? Was Sally worth it? I thought so, didn't I? Sal, who were you? Were you trying to be a Carlotta, all vampish and sophisticated and alluring? Carlotta is a vamp but I can see her for what she is. That is all she is. I do want her. I

151

want to screw and be screwed. Illicit. No deep, meaning-
ful looks. Just sex, raw and uninhibited. Yes, I want it and
I'll go and get it. Sorry, Sally, but you lost your chance, so
play your games with someone else. Come on, Richie, dry
your face and let's get laid.

Richard lunged for the door to take him to the
pleasures of the body and, noisily, found it locked. He
fumbled with the bolt and, with a final clatter, burst into
the room where Carlotta stood pretty much where he had
left her. She began to unbutton his shirt and he slid his
hands to her waist.

Is it slimmer than Sally's?

Carlotta eased the shirt away from his chest and traced
a long, pointed and polished nail down his neck and
around and over his nipples. Down she went in a straight
line, dipping into and out of his navel until she arrived at
his trousers. She undid the button with an assertive pop
and then tugged the zip down. Richard pushed his
trousers away as Charlotta pulled at his boxer shorts. He
caught sight of himself in the mirror on the wall in front
of him yet, somehow, the image of a stunning woman
giving head was more of a turn-on than the sensation
itself. As blow jobs went, it was good. But it was familiar.
Richard shut his eyes from the mirror and saw Sally and
felt again the astonishing newness of their couplings.

Don't think Sally.

Richard opened his eyes and there again, in the mirror,
was the man, him, being sucked and licked by this
gorgeous woman. And once again, the physical pleasure
of the here and now subsided a little.

Don't look at the mirror!

Why, Richard? Afraid of what you see there? What
does the mirror reflect? Only the truth.

Shut up.

Richard pulls Carlotta to her feet and pushes his tongue
into her mouth. He can taste himself on her. He finds her

breasts and fondles them but there's too much itchy lace.
Get it off. He fiddles with the clasp but Carlotta rescues
him and now she is naked. That's better.

They're big, more than a handful. They're different.
They're not as firm or smooth as – stop it! These nipples
are much longer, sort of rubbery. Nice, though.

Carlotta pushes Richard's head down to them and he
decides they taste pretty much the same. He also decides
to concentrate more on the job in hand and to concentrate
on not thinking or comparing size, look and texture to
Sally.

Sally's in France. And Sally hates me.

They fall to the bed and Richard feels Carlotta up and
down. There is plenty of bare flesh *up*, but only a lot of
interfering material *down*. Get it off, get it off. It seems to
be desperately complicated. As Richard fumbles and
follows ribbons and cords to cul de sacs, Carlotta lies
still, bored; eyes looking at the plaster flourishes on the
cornice. She smiles sweetly at Richard as she pushes him
away and sits up to unsnap her suspenders and wriggle
free from her panties.

Perhaps he can manage to roll down a pair of stock-
ings?

He can, and expertly runs his soft, warm hands over
the cool, firm flesh of her legs and follows his touch with
kisses that she finds touching.

Get to it, baby, get to it, cut the crap and lick me!

Carlotta pulls Richard's head from her thighs, spreads
her legs and pushes his face to where she wants him.

Am I doing something wrong? Richard wonders. *Why*
won't she writhe? It occurs to Carlotta that the concept of
oral sex is far sexier than the reality itself so she is quite
content when Richard leaves off to travel his tongue up
and over her body.

He's got a great body, she assesses. *Good, broad*
shoulders, a strong, muscular back tapering to a tight,
firm butt. Let me look at your chest. You could be hairier

for my liking but I like to see your stomach. I just love those little boxes of muscles on either side. Oh, so you like it when I run my fingers feather-light over them? You do, do you? Well, I fancy feeling your dick, which I know you'll like too. About average, I'd say, neat little balls. Uncircumcized! Shit, cut the crap, I want you in me sooner rather than later.

Richard flips her off and under him, which excites her. He pins her arms above her head and lowers his face to hers, eyes closed. His flop of hair tickles her nose but ceases to do so once the kiss has been planted.

She doesn't do much work in the kissing department.

He lifts himself away and looks at what is beneath him. Glorious and picture perfect. Every curve and dip just where supermodels dictate they should be. Her skin is taut and smooth and evenly bronzed. Long legs, neat knees, pancake flat stomach. Almost too perfect to be real.

Let's do it.

Richard spreads her legs and lowers himself slowly, slowly, over her; masterful control thanks to his extremely strong arms.

'Hold on, Mister!' Carlotta interjects. With one hand on Richard's chest, he is held in mid press-up position while her other arm slides over to the bedside table, from the top drawer of which she brings back her hand, condom between her first and second fingers. Richard looks at her face as she unrolls it and fits it adeptly. She's categorically beautiful.

Very.

But?

Bland.

Carlotta lies on her back and lets Richard take control. He pushes into her and she moans which turns him on. He holds himself up on his arms and she grasps his straining biceps.

'Hard, hard,' she cries, so he grinds into her and she

arches her back and asks for it harder and faster. To accommodate her request, Richard lets himself down and lies on her, scooping her up slightly and folding his arms under her, around her waist, thus finding good leverage to hump her hard and fast. She moans and gasps and calls out, 'Yes, baby!' Richard smiles and then decides a little variety might be nice. He rolls Carlotta on top and tries to push her up so that she might sit and straddle him. No, no. She flops on to his chest and humps against him, hard and fast.

'Harder! Faster! Jesus, what's up with you?'

'I can't go any faster and I'm as hard as I'll ever be!' Carlotta does not see the joke and stops still to look at him, exasperated. Richard smiles at her, she scowls back.

Oh, so you want to play it mean, do you?

He rolls back on top and gives a most almighty plunge as hard and deep as is anatomically possible. She groans and says *yes, yes*. He plunges again. *Yes, yes*. And again. *Oh, baby*. And again. He looks at the clock – half-past midnight. *Faster, faster!* Okay, okay. The small of his back begins to ache as Richard plunges and surges as fast as he can. He looks at her face, flushed and strewn with wisps of jet black hair. Her eyes are closed, her lips mouth *faster, harder, baby, yes*. He tries to grant her request, consequently neglecting his own physical preferences. Suddenly her eyes are open and they both cry out; Carlotta as the orgasm assaults her at last, Richard as her pointed nails dig deep into his flesh, one set lynched on to his left buttock, the other ripping into his right shoulder. She's finished, she's still, her hold has dropped away. Richard finds his pace and moves into her. She remains motionless.

'Carlotta?'

'I'm pooped, hon. You take it how you wish. That's fine by me.'

Richard looks at the slumbering American beauty in disbelief and anger. He moves into her and still she just lies there. He stops looking at her face and drops his gaze to her breasts, jutting sky-high and still unbelievably pert.

Must be silicone.

They are.

He looks up at her, checking if she's asleep; alive even. He finds her analyzing the plaster work on the ceiling rose. Richard withdraws.

'What's wrong?'

'No, no, nothing.'

'I don't mind, carry on!'

'No, no, it's okay, I'm tired anyway.'

'Maybe in the morning, babe.'

'Maybe.'

Richard went across to the bathroom with the ulterior motive of masturbation. But once he had pulled off the condom and put a towel on the too-cold toilet seat, he lost the inclination, the desire and the erection itself. He crept back to the bed from where the audible sound of Carlotta sleeping rose. Sliding silently in between the sheets, he sidled over to the very edge of the bed, turning away from the foreign body next to him.

What on earth was all that? he wondered as he fixed tired eyes on the gap in the curtains.

Go to sleep, Richard.

TWENTY-THREE

*W*ell, Sally and Richard have both pursued what they thought they wanted. And both have been left dry and dismayed by their discoveries. What do they want now? They wonder. I think we know. I think we know that somewhere they must know too. How will they get there, though? Will they fight? Resist? Will pride prevent a happy ever after?

'Di!'

'Sal-*lee*! Whenjoogeback? How was it? How are you? When are you coming round?' Diana gabbled away and Sally surprised herself by doing something she thought impossible: she laughed out loud. Diana had the gift, given by God or genetics, of cheering up the saddest of souls quite inadvertently. She had no idea that Sally was caught in a chasm of gloom, that she had woken helpless and alone. Diana's happy self, coupled with her devotion to her friend, dribbled forth uncontrollably, travelling supersonic through the telephone wire, out of the receiver and slap into the very heart of Sally's being.

'Oh, Diana, it's good to be home. Please, come over to mine? I'll cook.'

'Yum. When?'

'How about a late lunch?'

'Sounds heavenly. Tell me, Sally, tell me everything! At once! No, no, no! Not now! Can't wait to see you, Sugar Pop. I'll come at one-ish?'

'Two-ish, please?'

'Oh. Shame. Okay. 'Bye-bye, 'bye-bye!' Sally was exhausted but her head felt lighter and a smile surreptitiously crept across her lips.

I'd better pop out and buy some food then. What shall I do? What does Diana like? I know, something nice with pasta. I'll zip over to Hampstead and go to that fresh pasta shop. Damn! What am I going to wear? I've been slacking, just look at that mound of washing, and that pile of ironing. Sally Lomax, you should be ashamed of yourself!

Scramble into anything, Sally, it's only ten o'clock on a Saturday morning. And anyway, who is going to see you? There must be something at the back of your cupboard. Come on, get your skates on.

Wearing an old floral frock whose hem hung low at the back, a shabby Aran-knit cardigan for warmth, trainers with ankle socks for comfort and her hat for good measure, Sally set out for Hampstead, greeting her car like a long-lost friend. She was temporarily set back by the gaze of her mask lying on the passenger seat but, after a moment's rueful contemplation, tossed it into the back where it nestled next to the de-icer on a tartan rug. The Mini groaned and wheezed. Sally cooed and coaxed, took the key out and blew on it; she urged, she goaded, she bit her tongue. Her car was lifeless, she was bemused. Sitting still and wondering what to do, she focused on a piece of paper held by the wind-screen wiper. Winding down the window she retrieved it, a handwritten note. She read it out loud: ' "*Dear owner, it is New Year's Day and I notice that your headlights are on. I do hope you make it to your car before the battery runs flat! Best wishes for a happy year, Bill."* ' Who's Bill? Sally moaned. She moaned for her poor car and blamed herself for its current death. She moaned for herself as she remembered New Year's Eve. She moaned as she gathered her bag, her list and her wits about her and decided what to do.

Walk; that was the solution and not a bad one either. It was a precious sunny January day, cold but invigorating. Sally's route took her via Kenwood and over the Heath to Whitestone pond and the reaches of Hampstead. Once she had traded pavement for path, her mien was restored. The ground felt good underfoot, it was soft but not muddy so she could put a spring in her step without collecting clods on her shoes. The sun, trying hard to break through the thick haze created by the chill air, hung as a luminous and distant pinky puff. Sally thought it most poetic and proclaimed, ' "Glory be to God for Dappled Things" ' to a robin who cocked his head in agreement as she passed by.

I feel really okay, she thought as she patted the bark of a particularly gnarled oak.

I think it won't be too bad a year, she decided as she stooped to pocket a perfect pine cone.

I have my health, I have my Self, I don't need another; I am full, she thought as she sat on a bench near the magnolia tree at Kenwood and regarded the great swathe of lawn to the mirror-flat lake.

Quite happy to stop awhile with her contemplations, Sally turned her gaze about her and felt cheered by the day. Energy and sound surrounded her; the shrieks of children, the hearty laughter of adults and the merry yapping of dogs. The residue of Christmas, its mood and paraphernalia, clothed the park. Small children rode shiny tricycles, not-so-small children tottered on spar-kling bicycles with stabilizers and thoroughly big chil-dren terrorized all asunder on already muddy mountain bikes. Christmas was in the beautiful micro-fibre macs worn with pride and aplomb, in the small puppies trotting skittishly on leads, the stunt-kites and dolls' prams, the Timberland accessories and the excited voices which passed by Sally. The happy atmosphere was infectious and Sally smiled broadly to all who caught her eye. More often than not, a nod and a 'morning' were returned. Feeling buoyant, she continued her trek to Hampstead, chatting to the flora and fauna on the way.

* * *

In his reverie, Richard wondered, quite calmly, where on earth he was. His eyes were half-closed, his left eye focused only on a bloom of whiteness which he discerned to be a pillow. His right eye made out a gap in heavily tasselled curtains. He was comfortable in the bed, warm and safe. But where was he?

'Morning, Dick.'

Who?

Richard raised his head in a relaxed movement and scanned for the owner of the voice. He found her, sitting statuesque at the other side of the room.

Of course, Carlotta. Damn!

Richard let his head drop back to the pillow and tried to lull himself back into that just-woken state of blankness. But could not. He heard her padding towards him and she sat herself down on the edge of the bed next to him. A long, strong nail traced patterns on his bare shoulder. It felt nice.

'Say, get yourself up. My plane goes this evening and I fancy taking breakfast some place nice.' Her voice, so deep and sensual the previous day, now grated on his ears as he detected a slight whine behind the transatlantic drawl. He looked at her and only half-recognized her. Something was different. What?

'Morning, Carlotta.'

'Why are you looking at me like that?' Richard looked perplexed and furrowed his brow in contemplation.

160

'Something's different. What?' She laughed and batted her eyelids at him. 'This London water made my eyes change colour!'

He looked at them. They were the most incredible violet, more violet than Elizabeth Taylor's. It came back to him. The woman he had slept with had lured him with strong emerald eyes. Beautiful eyes. Now they were violet. More violent than violet. Suddenly they didn't seem quite so beautiful. In fact, Richard thought the concept decidedly suspect.

'What colour are they naturally?'

'Heck, any colour I want them to be!'

Baffled, Richard made his naked way to the bathroom. On the side of the basin was a container, inside which two green contact lenses were held in suspension. Richard held them to the light.

How very bizarre.

He furtively peeped into the glitzy world of her vast wash-bag. Potions, lotions, brushes, slabs of colour, tubes of lipstick, cream for Thrush.

God! Please, no.

He rummaged as silently as he could and came across another container with 'Sultry Mahogany' written on the side. Two deep brown contact lenses glared back at him. He had a quick look at his own eyes and found he was quite content with the colour they naturally were. He glanced at his hands and thought his well-cared-for nails vastly preferable to the plastic talons in umpteen shades of red which Carlotta kept in little boxes.

Richard gave his reflection a chastising shake of the head. He drew his fingers across his eyes, dragging the skin down and around in a bid to shed their bleariness and reactivate. His hands may be elegant but his fingers smelt of sex. He was keen to have a thorough shower and did so, freezing cold of course. He felt depleted and sullen, his stomach felt hollow but not with hunger. The

161

shower helped physically, but emotionally he felt drained and desperate for solitary peace and quiet.

But the lady must be breakfasted. And not at my place, no siree!

He emerged, wrapped up in a luxurious towelling robe, his hair still damp and delectably tousled. Naturally.

Carlotta came over to him and slid her hands through his hair. He let himself be kissed and was surprised that his only reaction was wondering if any of her lipstick had transferred itself to his mouth or cheeks. He glanced at the mirror and was relieved to see that it had not. Still she held him. He didn't really want to be held, not just now, not this morning. Not by her. He took her wrists and smiled genially.

'I'll take you to Hampstead. We'll have breakfast there and you'll find it rather, um, *quaint*.'

Can you guess?

Ill-fated lovers who cross paths in the most ghastly and cruel of circumstances cannot be restricted to the novels of Hardy and Dickens. I apologize but there is little I can do. Sally is already in Hampstead and Richard's Alfa Romeo is now nearing Swiss Cottage. Must they bump into each other? Can it not be that we alone know that they're both there? Alas, such a meeting, unfair as it may seem, is now sadly inevitable.

Unbeknown to Richard, he chose Sally's Tea Pot Shoppe, which she had left twenty minutes before, having been revived by an incomparable cappuccino and Carlos's reverent compliments. 'My Engel Eesh Rosa, I know zat 'at anywhere. Please, please. Sit!' he had crooned, trying hard to disregard the rest of her appearance.

En route to the pasta shop, Sally was diverted by the antiques corridor and was caressing an old engraved pewter tankard that would make a fabulous vase but was expensive at thirty pounds while, a few yards away,

Richard tucked into a decadent cooked breakfast and Carlotta sipped orange juice.

'I like those green waxy coats,' she enthused.

'Barbour. Very popular. Very practical. Quintessentially English. Rather expensive,' ventured Richard.

'Well, I'd like a take-home present before I go, so I think I'll treat myself to one.'

'We could stop off at Austin Reed on the way back to your hotel,' suggested Richard, sorting through his wallet to pay the bill. Carlos scurried off for change; lots of small change to encourage a generous tip. But Richard did not know who Carlos was.

'I tell you what else I love, not my style though, and that's those pretty little flowery dresses that your English girls like to wear. They're so sweet, so countrified and old fashioned. So *Tess of the D'Urbervilles*. So oldy worldy. Look, like that one there,' she motioned.

Richard looked.

My God, it's Sally.

There she was, over the road and up a bit, window shopping. Richard watched as she scratched the back of one leg with the foot of her other, her arms out to either side steadying herself. His heart soared and raced and plummeted.

She can't see me here. Not with this woman. My God, but look at her! That dress? Those shoes! That cardie? Carlotta's right; so sweet, so pretty, so domestic and cosy. Well, this is a revelation. But a welcome one. She's lovely. So lovely. But she can't see me here. Not now. Shit, Sal, what have I done? And what have you done to me? It's no good, I've got to get out of here. Now. Quickly.

'Come on, let's go and get your Barbour.' Richard urged Carlotta to her feet and left without waiting for his change. Lucky Carlos, a tip twice the cost of the breakfast. Richard looked again but Sally was gone. He felt simultaneously greatly relieved and yet terribly disappointed.

Was it her? Just an apparition? It was her, of course it

was. I want her and I don't want her. I want her like that –
gorgeous in rags and colour clashes – but not yet. Not
now. Not today. Not 'till I've rid myself of this American
affliction; not until she wants me. God, where is she? Just
another peep to tide me along. Let me see her unseen.

Simultaneously desperate for another glimpse but
dreading being seen, Richard tried to set the pace, brisk
and assertive. Carlotta resisted, drawn compulsively to
the tempting shop windows. Richard's heart was heaving
and his breakfast sat defiantly at the base of his throat; his
stomach too tight to allow access. His palms were
clammy, his feet were cold and his knee joints stiff,
though he needed them now more than ever to carry him
away.

His car was around the next corner at the top of
Fitzjohn's Avenue; close, frustratingly close, and yet
horribly far away. He grasped Carlotta around the waist
and pleaded that they really should get going if she
wanted to shop for a Barbour. As he pulled her away and
made her walk, he saw Sally.

And she saw him.

And they were just a few feet apart, hopelessly headed
for each other.

Sally stood stock still. Richard was so overcome with
horror that he could neither prevent his legs from moving
nor remove his arm from Carlotta's waist. Fortunately
Carlotta, unaware of the tragedy of the situation, freed
herself to scrutinize a pair of boots and was soon inside
the shop, leaving Sally and Richard less than a yard away
from each other. Richard felt sick but not half as sick as
Sally. They stood there, defying Newtonian time; their
mouths open, their minds whirring, their eyes disbelieving and searching, their hearts in overdrive. He wanted to
push the lock of hair away from her mouth. He wanted to
fall on his knees at her feet. He wanted to swoop her up,
into his arms and take her a million miles away from this
place and this moment. He just wanted to touch her. But

164

all he could do was remain frozen and desperately remorseful.

Sally wanted to dissolve. She wanted to be back in childhood, away from all this. She wanted to cry, to be sick, to fall asleep and wake up yesterday. She wanted to be anywhere but here. She wanted Richard to cradle her in his arms and kiss her forehead.

No, I don't.

Yes, you do.

'Hon, I'm through, let's go.'

Carlotta, oblivious and brash, broke through their tragic barrier and destroyed the frozen moment. Richard heard Sally give a sharp and involuntary intake of breath and watched, helpless, as she fled across the road, the back of her dress dragging in a puddle as she went. He wanted to go after her; to catch her, to shake her, to explain to her, to kiss her. But he was rendered immobile. He had no strength to move, his body felt heavy, his eyes were fixed to the loaded space Sally had left, his heart was grinding to a halt. Carlotta, bored and still brash, hauled him to his car.

'C'mon, hon. Take me to Dustin Reeves or wherever it is I can buy an oily Barburry.'

Austin Reed, you stupid cow, Richard thought witheringly as he crunched his gears and sped recklessly away.

TWENTY-FOUR

*O*ur poor heroine, sad old Sal. Poor Sally of the shabby dress, she of the comfy cardie, of the tatty trainers; Sal of the dirge and frills.

How do you feel, scurrying to nowhere in particular just to get away? You can feel the gritty wet of your dress slap against the back of your calves. You can feel the chill in the air whistle its way through the holes in your cardigan, through the buttons in your frock. You're chilled, aren't you, chilled to the bone? Numb too. Poor old girl, what a nasty shock, what a beastly thing to have happened. What are you thinking, Sally Lomax? And how do you feel?

How do I feel? What do I think? I think I feel sick. I feel like I've swallowed a lump of lead. There is something in my head, a noise, it's thudding around. Every time I move my head it crashes against a side of my skull.

But what are you thinking?

What am I thinking? I'm thinking that I'm frightened, she frightened me. I can't get her out of my mind's eye. Did you see her?

Yes, we saw her, Sally, we've seen quite a lot of her, not that you'd know. But yes, we saw her.

Who is she? Who is she? Has he slept with her? Why were they in Hampstead? Does she live near me? When did it start between them? But did you see her? All high heels and couture clothes, cheek bones to die for and lips to pray for. Did you see her? I did. And I saw Richard's hand around her waist and he didn't even drop it when he saw me. He couldn't keep his hands off her. He had his hand glued to her gorgeous horrid tiny waist. It seems bizarre but I feel rather like Hamlet. Remember his distress and disgust with his mother for exchanging the love for a husband not two months dead, for the bed of another?

A *husband*, Sal? Oh, girl! If only you knew. Think not of Hamlet, but only of yourself. What do you make of it all?

He said he loved me.

And you hated him for it.

I never hated him. I just didn't like the idea of it. In retrospect, I loathed myself more, I think. Richard, Richie, who is she? Was she good? In bed? Did you think of me? Did you compare us? Well, I compared J-Bloody-C to you. And he was lacking. I bet I was far from your mind, from your soul, from the desires of your body. Get me away from all this. Get me to a nunnery!

Sally!

Where is Richard right now? What is he thinking just this very second?

If you want to know, he has dumped *that woman* at Austin Reed with a cursory farewell to her, and 'good riddance' racketing through his mind. He has just zoomed over a zebra crossing forcing innocent and indignant pedestrians to stand motionless and precarious in the middle of a road. He is on his way home. He does not feel very well. Like you, he's wondering about you.

'But you don't understand. He was with a *woman*,' Sally pleaded as Diana helped herself to the untouched pasta on Sally's plate. Diana chewed thoughtfully, gazing at the swirled irises patterning Sally's laminated Liberty table-cloth.

What does she want me to say? What can I say? I'm not likely to say: 'Well, it's all your fault, Sal.' Until she says it, says the 'L' word that she abhors so much, then I really can't say much, can I? After all, if the love-factor didn't exist, then I doubt whether she'd be this devastated.

Diana looked across at Sally, sitting shabby and collapsed in her funny old clothes that actually only seemed funny in the wake of her recent sassy wardrobe. Sally sat still, her lower lip jutting out; in a sulk, in anger, in sadness? It was difficult to decipher its provenance. But her eyes told her tale, downcast but constantly on the move, an eyebrow furrowing, pupils darting, eyelids beating fast to prevent ready tears. Diana had finished Sally's plate and was full. She'd had enough and she had had enough.

'Sally?' she ventured. Sally remained slumped but looked up with her eyes and scanned Diana's face desperately. 'What is it that you want?'

Sally's eyes dropped under the weight of such a question. She sat silent and let it go unanswered. Suddenly she spurted forth a torrent of uncontrolled woe.

'Diana! He saw me like that, like *this*!' She brushed violently at the bodice of her dress, pulled at her cardie and kicked her legs out to the side of the table to emphasize the socks and trainers. 'And Diana! You should have seen *her*! She was, she was horrible, she was stunning and slick, and such a . . . such a . . . She was a *vamp*,' she spat, 'a *femme fatale*,' she wailed, 'a *vixen*,' she moaned. 'She wasn't like *me*, you see.'

Sally trailed off, her voice now a defeated whisper. Diana waited, breath baited like an expectant fisherman's fly. All was silent and still and loaded. Bite it! Then movement. Sally turned her head and Diana glanced at the tear which had fallen with a sonorous splash on to the stamen of a printed iris. More movement. Sally rose, arms folded, hugging the Aran knit about herself. Passing Diana, she crossed over to the window. Diana swivelled in her chair and saw her as a silhouette, pressed two-dimensional and opaque against the cold, white January light. Immediately, she had an idea for a painting but tactfully put the creative inspiration on hold and returned in spirit and sight to Sally. And she waited. Finally, she was rewarded. In a voice that was broken and frail, Sally at last uttered the truth.

'She wasn't like me, you see,' she started, 'she wasn't like me because I'm not like her. You see. But, I wanted to be a sort of "her". That's what I wanted to be. And that's what I tried hard to be, for Richie, for me. It was hard work, but I did it, I got there, and I enjoyed it. I believed in it and I really enjoyed it. But I know now that it's just not me. I don't have the guts, I don't have the strength. I don't even have the style. Nor the money, nor the easy sophistication. And I don't have the body. At the end of the day, I don't really have the personality. It's not in my nature, it's not natural, it's just not me.'

Slowly, Sally turned to Diana. She shrugged her shoulders and dropped her head. Her shoulders drooped and shook twice before she checked the sobs with all her might and braced her body upright. Diana was drawn to her, drawn to her plight and drawn to her damaged, battered state. She went to her and placed her hands on Sally's shoulders. She shook her gently. And then she shook her more forcefully and spoke in rhythm and in time with her shakes.

'But, Sally, you're *there*!' she proclaimed. 'You know who you are *not*. You know who you *are*! Look what you've learnt, look what you've found out!' It all seemed very clear-cut and simple to Diana. Diana was smiling. But she was soon perplexed that Sally remained so unhappy. She shook Sally again. And again, almost irritated by the limp and feeble body in her hands. In fake submission and an effort to free herself from being shaken, Sally nodded her head reluctantly and Diana eased her grip but let her hands rest gently on the weary shoulders.

'But don't you see, Di? *She* wasn't like *me*. I'm not like *her*.' Sally nodded her head energetically, a frown cutting deep into her brow. Diana did not understand. In fact, Sally hadn't understood either, not until just then. The effort and discipline of organizing her thoughts and woe into coherent, spoken form had rewarded her with clear insight. She could see now what it really was that she felt, why she felt it, and what she wanted. Sally cleared her throat.

'Diana.' Diana tipped her head to one side inviting Sally to continue, unhurried, unjudged.

'Diana. I'm not like *her*. But Richard is with her. She's not like *me*. But Richard was with her. Richard,' she declared, 'wants that kind of woman.' The room resounded with the noisy silence of the wracking of brains.

Go on, Sally.

'But,' she faltered, 'I want Richard.'

'You want Richard?'

'Yes.'

'But, Sally, Richard told *you* that he loved you!' Problem solved, solution easy, happy ending in sight, rejoiced Diana to herself. 'He loves you. Go get him, girl!'

'Yes, Diana. No, no, Di. Richard wasn't in love with *me*. He was in love with the *me-type*. I mean the her-type. The wrong me – I'm not her! I am not like that. So that makes a nonsense, somewhat, of his words.' Now it is Sally who can see the clarity of the unfortunate truth, or what she believes it to be, and Diana's mind is in a muddle as she tries to decipher Sally's theory, assess the facts and present a helpful solution to still-suffering Sal.

Think, Diana, think.

170

Ah, but of course! Go easy here, tread softly.
'But you want Richard?'
'Yes.'
'Why?'
'Why?'
'Why do you *want* him?'
Sally looked at Diana with incredulity, as if she was dim and dippy.
'You know!'
No. Diana does not know, or at least makes it seem that way. She does, of course, know. But, until Sally says it out loud, umprompted, Diana will remain supposedly in the dark. Sally must remain untouched and have no prompting. Take your hands away from her just now, let her stand tall. Say it, Sally, say it.
'Dian-arr!' Sally looks at her, encouraging her to say it for her. Diana merely shrugs though it is excruciating to have to do so. A whisper of bewilderment flickers across Sally's face. Diana sees it. No, Diana, don't help her! Not now! Not for this! As much as you love her, leave her alone, you know it must come from her, you said as much to Richard. Let her say it.
Come on, Sally, feel the solidarity urge you on.
Diana, bite it, bite your tongue, bide your time.
'Sally. Are you in love with him?'
Oh, hush, Diana. Damn! Bad move, big mistake; huge. See how the Lomax barrier has come down, the shield raised? See Sally lower her veil? It may be as thin as gossamer, as transparent as muslin but it is as strong as steel.
An infuriating shrug with a twitch of the lips is all Sally's giving out today. Time to go, Di.

'Am I in love with him?' Sally later asked the African Violet as she watered it and tweaked off two dead leaves.
'Do I love Richard?' she asked the kettle as she waited for it to boil.

171

'Is it *love* that I feel?' she enquired of the tea towel as she turned her back on the kettle in the hope that, if unwatched, it might come to the boil faster. Sally could not find the answer in the flora or domestic appliances in her flat, so she sipped her tea and looked at the mismatched laces holding her trainers together.

'*Is* it love?' she asked the rain as it drizzled its haphazard way down the window pane.

'Is he the *one*?' she quizzed the tea leaves which had gathered conspiringly in the base of her cup.

If the tea leaves don't hold the answer, who does?

Sally continued to search for the answer as she made an inroad into the ironing. Needless to say, shirts, skirts and hankies did not have it.

'Am I in love with Richard Stonehill?' she asked her knees as she sat on the toilet, her legs suspended and stretched out in front of her.

But Sally knew where she could find the answer, where hitherto she had avoided looking. Sally knew she'd find it once she pulled the chain. She had only to turn around and confront it. Turn, Sally. Ask.

And there was the answer, staring her straight in the face. The mirror, of course. There was Sally and there was the mirror, and there, in the mirror, was Sally. There was no need to ask out loud.

Do I love him?

Yes, I love him.

TWENTY-FIVE

*S*o Sally is in love. Are we surprised? No, not really. But how will she show it? How will she deal with the inherent responsibility of such knowledge? And is she happy? Would she have acknowledged how she felt had she not seen Richard with the Other Woman? Miss Tiny Waist, Madam Long Legs, Lady Luscious Lips. (*Damn them and their perfect Cupid's Bow shape!*) And if Sally puts down her shield and throws back her veil, will she be lost mercilessly to daydreams of babies, of scones baking in an Aga and all the other things she previously deemed reprehensible? Who might she be letting down if she lets her heart rule her head? Ms Collins? Ms Jong? Herself?

Sally had chased fun – fun that was not chaste – through playing and creating a whole new persona, a very different woman. She had wanted The Richard Thing to be a delicious secret that she could recall with enduring pleasure at her leisure. She had orchestrated The Richard Thing to be something she could carry with her through her life, a sort of magic rune that she could take out at times when things might not be going well.

Tedious dinner parties – *oh! remember how he would kiss me!*

Trying Christmases – *and there was that time when he hired a box at the Opera and we made love while Violetta sang.*

Tiring school functions – *remember his eyes travelling my body, glazed with desire that burned unheeded.*

The Richard Thing would enable her to take a mind-flight away from being boring wifey with brood and Aga, back to the time when she was an outrageous vamp, desired madly by a living Rodin. The Richard Thing was to be fun, it was to be slightly reckless, somewhat irresponsible, rather naughty, thoroughly liberating – all the things Sally presumed adulthood and marriage to forfeit. She had envisaged standing in front of her mirror in her forties, fifties, sixties, even seventies, smiling gleefully at the memory of a man totally ensnared in her seductive web, one she had spun all by herself, following no known pattern. Maybe Sally, sweet Sally, good girl Sally, wanted to know that she had the ability and independence to be as she wished and to be whom she probably knew all along she was not.

But what is wrong with the real you, Sal? After all, it did not take our Richard long to see what was behind the veil, to be lost in the spell of you! Maybe you wanted merely to have a good time and great sex without suffering the consequences and catches of a rampant fling dampening down into a relationship. But why the fear of a relationship, Sal? Why the trepidation of going through life conventionally – marriage, children, dinner parties, school events? Is fun confined merely to an illicit fling? Are men who are the stuff of rampant affairs a different species from those who have the substance for a relation-ship? More to the point, are women?

Sally had neither envisaged Fling Thing falling in love with her, nor had she foreseen Fling Thing assuming his true identity as Richard Stonehill so quickly. She had been thoroughly unprepared for her reaction and for the consequences; she desired the person under the muscle, she respected the brain beneath the brawn, she felt the heart behind the hands, she saw the soul through the (beautiful) eyes. Fling Thing was fabulous but Richard Stonehill was far better. Sally had naively presumed that utter lust and deep love were poles apart. Now she must reconcile the two.

When Richard phoned her almost a fortnight later in the staff-room, Sally was relieved, and just a little thrilled too. Twice since that fateful morning in Hampstead she had ventured out to see him. Once, dressed in heels and black Lycra, she had made it as far as pulling the choke on her Mini but slunk home to eat chocolate instead. Two days later she tried again, this time making it right to his flat. She drove appallingly and her wits were truly frazzled by the time she approached Notting Hill. On spying Richard's Spyder, the surge of adrenalin made her head so light and her hands so heavy that she nearly veered straight into it. She drove straight past, round the block and then back again, juddering to a halt outside the building she so wanted to enter but just could not quite. She counted up the floors and took note of the lights that were on. *He must be in.*

Obviously.

I'll just wait until it turns 9 on the dot.

The clock read 8.57. As it turned 9, fear and timidity subsumed her and, with shaking hand and defeated soul, she made a lurching and not terribly swift getaway.

Unbeknuon to her, Richard had seen her and had been dumbstruck. There was he, bored on a Tuesday night, thinking of Sally, fantasizing that she might come to him. In his mind he acted out the scenario in such vivid and believable detail that he had, in reality, gone to the window to see if maybe her car was indeed there and that perhaps she was on her way up.

My God, omigod, omigod. She is here!

The shock was so great that Richard whipped away out of sight of the window, pressing himself flat against the wall, like a movie-star dodging the bullets of the bad guy. With his heart in his mouth and no gun in his holster he remained paralysed, released only by the unwanted sound of a familiar engine starting up. Keeping his body still but craning his neck to its limit, he witnessed the sorry sight of the little Mini clumping and chugging its way away.

Away. She's gone. But she was here.

Richard was very blue. Feeling uncomfortably numb, he sought solace in Pink Floyd. Wishing with all his might that Sally was here, he was wailing: 'We're just two lost souls swimming in a fish bowl' somewhat histrionically when the doorbell sounded.

He jumped.

Sally. Sally?

A patter of knocks followed.

'Hello?' implored a muffled voice through the letter box. 'Is there anybody in there? Is there anyone at home?' Richard opened the door.

'Come on now, I hear you're feeling down.' Waters and Gilmour had become Bob and Catherine.

'It was all my wife's idea,' explained Bob. 'She thought you'd probably not be eating, not looking after yourself,' he justified as he unpacked carton after carton from the excellent Mandarin Duck Takeaway. In between grateful mouthfuls (Richard had *not* eaten all day) Richard told all.

'It's all turning into a veritable nightmare, I tell you. Sally: I'm sure you've guessed. Pass the seaweed, please. You know she wouldn't open the door to me on New Year's Day? Oh yes of course, you counselled me that

176

evening. Sweet and Sour, please. Well, on Saturday morning I was in Hampstead. I bumped into her. Into Sally. It was absolutely horrendous. Crispy Duck, anyone? Mind if I finish it?'

'Finish the story, Richard!' squealed Catherine as she licked her fingers but then plumped for another dumpling. 'What happened?' she said, noticing with some horror that Jimi Hendrix rubbed shoulders with Bach (*'B' should be before 'H', and surely Jimi should be on the shelf below?*)

'She ran away.'

Do I really want to relive this? To share it? No amount of halving this problem is going to solve it.

'Did you talk to her?'

'No.'

'Whyever not?'

Richard raised his eyebrows.

'Are you *sure* it was her?' Bob quizzed, making neat piles with shrivelled tulip petals which lay forlornly on the floor.

Richard raised his eyebrows further and grabbed the dumplings off Catherine. 'Of course it was her.'

'Couldn't you've?'

'No.'

'*Shouldn't* you've?'

'Not possible.'

'Why?'

'I wasn't alone. I was with someone else. A woman. It's all a complete nightmare.'

Bob and Catherine sat gawping; Catherine had a trail of seaweed hanging on to the corner of her mouth, Bob's chin was smeared with Sweet and Sour sauce. Suddenly, Richard felt like bursting out laughing but, reading their true concern and bewilderment, resisted and continued unprompted.

'This woman is a client. Nothing happened. Well, I mean it did, but it is of absolutely no importance to me.

You know, just a dose of good old sex – only it wasn't very good. It wasn't a casting couch job – the contract was already in the bag. I just wined and dined her.'

'And sixty-nined her?' Catherine couldn't resist it, as if she needed to make light of it to contain the deep dismay she felt.

Richard, Richard – maybe you haven't changed all that much.

'*She* seduced *me*,' spelled out Richard, determined that the Woodses would not think him the perpetrator. 'Okay, I let myself be seduced. Only it wasn't very seductive. I'd given up on Sally. Well, what I mean is, I'd given up on her ever coming back to me. God, I want her back! Anyway, I'm in Hampstead, reluctantly breakfasting this *fling thing* when she points over the road to a "quaint li'le English gal" which just happens to be Sally. My, she did look quaint! In fact, she looked absolutely gorgeous. She was wearing this extraordinary amalgam of flowery frock, Aran knit, floppy hat – and trainers would you believe! It was a revelation to me and yet so very Sally too. Well, I was horrified and thought a hasty retreat should be beat – I knew it would be too awful if we saw each other. But it happened. We just stood and stared and then Sally was gone.'

'Did she see the other woman?' Catherine felt quite sick.

'That's the cruellest part. Desperate to get away, I was trying to drag her physically. That's when I caught Sally's eye. I was turned to stone. I couldn't do a thing. My hand was stuck to this woman's awful skinny waist.'

'Nightmare,' Catherine groaned.

'Nightmare,' agreed Bob.

'Nightmare,' confirmed Richard. 'Only something strange happened this evening. She was here!' Again the Woodses' mouths fell and again Richard swiftly diverted his gaze from the debris still adorning them. 'Well, she was and she wasn't. It was so spooky – I had been thinking about her, about her doing a real "Sally" and just suddenly turning up in a tutu or something. Anyway, I was so engrossed in the fantasy that I went over to the window just to check. Chrise-Orlmighty if her car wasn't double-parked right outside! It gave me one hell of a shock – I quickly hid! What a berk!'

'What a *berk*!' confirmed Catherine, racking her mind for a solution – or a good idea at the least.

'*What* a berk!' chastized Bob.

'And then it was all too late. I heard the car start up and I just watched her drive away.' Richard shook his head and the Woodses' heads' shook in sympathy. 'What am I going to do, guys?'

Catherine looked from Richard to his CD collection. With its former thematic, alphabetic splendour gone, it served to accentuate Richard's malady.

All really is not well. Schubert is as out of his depth next to Van Halen as Richard is without Sally. Think. We have to get through to him, raise and restore him.

'Well,' she said breezily, hoping she sounded reassuring, 'for a start, I think the very fact that she was here tonight should raise your hopes. You are obviously in her thoughts but I reckon Hampstead must have knocked her for six. I mean, you can't undo what happened – you did sleep with this woman and you did bump into Sally with her. That's a nightmare. You can't undo what happened but you could *reinvent* the past you know. And you *can* salvage Sally – I think that's probably what she wants but I think it's up to you.'

'Rein*vent* the past?' Richard probed. Catherine cocked her head and Bob finished her theory, utterly in tune with her drive.

'No sex. Business breakfast in Hampstead. Plane to catch. Contract won. White lie – smallish one. That's all.'

'Bloody brilliant!' exclaimed Richard. Though his problem was neither halved nor solved, it now seemed more manageable.

'Call her. You *must* call her,' insisted Catherine with very intense eye contact.

'You bet,' Richard nodded vigorously, 'bloody brilliant.'

'Tummies full. Problems solved. Time we were off,' announced Bob, handing Richard the tulip debris. 'We're trying for a baby, you know,' he beamed, 'every night! It's wonderful! Only if we don't wend our way home now, I'll be too shagged to . . .'

'Shag?' ventured Richard, absent-mindedly compacting the petals before dumping them in a take-away carton. Catherine gave Richard's arm a supportive stroke.

'Precisely!' she giggled. 'Only you'll have to wash all that goop off your face first, Bob.'

'And you, dear wife, must extricate that fine piece of seaweed too.'

So there was a phone call for Sally in the staff-room. Had she not seen Catherine the night before, quite possibly she would have refused the call.

'Sally? Catherine! I'm taking you out for dinner tonight. It's top secret. Bob's been told I'm cooking for my brother. I shall pick you up at eight sharp. Okay? 'Bye! Oh, Sally?'

'Yes?'

'Okay?'

'Yes.'

''Bye for now.'

They had gone to a particularly nice brasserie in West Hampstead, safe territory for both. They sat opposite each other, elbows defiantly on the table, heads together in enthusiastic conspiracy. Sally spoke first.

'Are you pregnant, Catherine?'

'No.'

'I'm sorry. Are you still trying?'

'But of course.'

'In secret?'

'No.'

'Oh! How's Bob then?'

'Frightened but happy – he's rather enjoying all the practice it requires! In fact, I'm six days late but trying not to think about it. You know, be nonchalant, cool and collected,' Catherine said, nibbling her lip and fidgeting with her hair, eyes bright and dancing.

Sally assessed this happy turn-about. So if pregnancy was no longer the problem, why the illicit dinner? Catherine's go.

'Sally?'

'Yes?'

'Are you in love?' The rocket and roast pepper salad had arrived.

'Yes.'

'With Richard?' Catherine ventured with her mouth full.

'Yes, with Richard,' Sally confirmed, licking her lips. 'Who else?' she grinned.

And so began a luxuriously long meal. Sally felt thoroughly safe with Catherine and was desperate for news of Richard. She was moved by what she learnt. Catherine told her about the end of the party. She thought hard for a moment and then decided to tell Sally all that Richard had said to Bob that night. And how he had said it. Sally felt wretched. She could have left the restaurant and gone straight to him, holding him in her arms and saying sorry. But she stayed because she wanted to listen and she wanted to talk.

'But I don't hate him, I never hated him. I just didn't want him to fall in love with me.'

'But whyever not?'

'Because I didn't want to fall in love with him.'

'Whyever not?'

'Because it would complicate things.'

'What things?'

'Life!'

'Oh, Sally, how pretentious and how silly. What do you mean, "life"?'

'Well, if you give yourself away, you leave yourself open to hurt.'

'True, but if you keep yourself to yourself, think how much life would lack. You can enjoy your own company, but if there are two of you, it is logical and it goes without saying that there is twice as much of everything – happiness, fun, sex, normality – they are all so much more *colourful*, they're all *bigger*, they are all so much more *worthwhile*.'

Sally smiled meekly at Catherine, timid at the thought of this colourful, big, worthwhile life lying tantalizingly close and potentially there for the taking. Catherine told her of their recent visit to Richard, to feed him and listen to him. Waiting for Sally to probe deeper, she spoke of the dead tulips and the fact that Jimi and Johann Sebastian now shared the same shelf. Unalphabetically.

'But, Catherine, what about Richard? That woman?'

'Woman? Who?' Catherine feigned ignorance so Sally told her of Saturday bloody Saturday. Catherine felt the tiny white lie was in order and Sally felt stronger for hearing that the vamp was merely one of the Americans for whom Richard had designed the Georgian folly. A client. Just business. Just a business breakfast. That's all.

'And Richard said what was so ghastly,' concluded Catherine, 'was that it was his own mercenary greed that led to his come-uppance in bumping into you like that. Now what did he call her? Something along the lines of an infuriating, attention-seeking transatlantic tramp. She was being evasive as to whether the company would take the work so he had to wine and dine and give her a breakfast-time tour of London before she caught her plane.'

'Did it work?'

'Yup!'

'Good for Richard. But you should have *seen* her.'

'She can't have been that great because we all know that Richard's *hobby* is to have and hold the most beautiful and perfect of things. He *loves* beauty – in anything, I mean look at his bloody hi-fi, his Sabatier knives, his Alfa flipping Romeo! (By the way, his Alfa's *filthy* at the mo'!) He loves beauty and appreciates it in a very objective way. Well, he didn't once mention this woman in terms of any of her physical attributes. But you! My, how he waxes Lomax lyrical! We could never shut him up. It was quite possibly the most boring Christmas I've ever had, listening him drone on about Sal-this and Sal-that, and Sal's eyes and Sal's smile. He even relates your tales of the classroom. I feel I know Rajiv and Marcus personally. What an old bore Richard has become. He's yours, Sally, just go to him with honesty – and a pretty please.'

Sally blushed and said nothing. Deep inside she was brimming with song and laughter. Catherine continued, unprompted.

'You know, in the past, Richard's women have all been rather, um, I don't know. He always had one, but I never warmed to them, and nor did Bob. Probably because Richard was so obviously not taken with them himself. He had a reputation, you know.' No, Sally did not know.

'I remember Bob pointing him out at a University Ball and calling him "Herr Heart-breaker". He didn't break hearts willingly,' she continued, 'it's just he never fell for any of the people who fell for him. And anyone who ever dated him fell hopelessly for him of course. So he became known as "Pump and Dump" and a whole host of other names.'

Sally hooted with laughter and Catherine thought how pretty she was. 'There was never anyone special, Sally, not till you. You wouldn't believe what being with you has done to him. Done *for* him. He's dropped that outer reserve, he's not so aloof, he's more open and he seems so much more at ease. He's happy – that's it. Really happy, true happiness. I mean,' corrected Catherine with dramatic emphasis, 'he *was*.'

Catherine trailed off and Sally felt sad. They sat still in silence awhile, Catherine gazing at the flickering candle and Sally looking at nothing in particular. Any awkwardness dissipated with the arrival of the dessert-trolley to which the women turned their attention with an expert eye and wicked delight. Sally felt simultaneously exhausted and high. Her head was zipping with the insights Catherine had so sweetly given her.

'Call him,' Catherine suggested, laying a warm and comforting hand on Sally's leg as she pulled up alongside her flat.

'Hey, Cathers, it's been the most wonderful evening. I really mean it, and I want to thank you for being so supportive and such a good listener.'

Catherine, who'd never been called Cathers and actually rather liked it, brushed away the effusive compliments and patted Sally again on the same leg.

'Call him.'

It wasn't a suggestion, it was an order. Sally always did what she was told.

Sally had summoned the courage and decided that it would indeed be this day, now, and not the infamous tomorrow, when she'd lift the receiver and make amends. Richard, however, beat her to it. He feared her driving away right out of his life as she had driven away, out of his street. Anyway, Bob and Catherine had urged him to call her, Diana too.

'Richardrichardrichard. You must *must* call her. I saw her and she's totally devastated. If you are with this other woman then call Sally so that she doesn't suffer much longer. If you're not, then call her and try and work things out.'

'Diana, is Sally suffering?'

'Yes.'

184

'Why?'

'I'm not spelling it out, dolt!'

'So why don't you tell her to call me?'

'I did. She won't.'

'Why not?'

'I'm not spelling it out! Please call her? Soon?'

As Richard contemplated the handset and smiled at Diana's kooky sincerity, he wondered how soon was 'soon'. It was too soon, just that day. Maybe tomorrow.

But when Catherine phoned him at work that Friday morning, he knew that 'soon' was now.

'I had supper with Sally while you and Bob played squash or whatever it is that you do!'

'Catherine!' cautioned Richard. 'I thought you were cooking for Alex?'

'I lied.'

'Catherine!' he reprimanded. 'How is she?' he asked. 'What did she say?' he implored.

'She's okay. All the better for hearing that the mystery woman was a client.'

Richard thanked her for her tact. Catherine continued, 'I think you should call her, right away. You really ought. I've realized something, Richard. You are both really quite similar. If you don't talk and get together soon, you'll both pull your "self-defence" blankets over your heads and that,' she declared, 'will be that.'

'Catherine, thank you. I appreciate it. But what did she *say*?'

'Call her.'

'That's what she said? Through you?'

'No. Just call her. You owe it to yourself. And to her. Call her – now. Here's the number for the staff-room at school. First Break is at 10.15. 'Bye-bye Richard.'

'Sal?'

Sally whizzed around, spiralling with phone cord around her body like a helter-skelter. No one could hear her and no one was particularly interested anyway. First Break was a very precious twenty minutes. There were cups of tea by which to be relaxed and weary eyes to rub. Had Diana been there, her eyes and ears would have been perked to straining point, but she was in the studio, making preparatory sketches for a screen-print of a solitary silhouette against a window.

'Hullo,' Sally replied in a hushed and gentle voice.

'Can I see you? Tonight at eight? Go for a walk. Talk?'

'Yes.'

'Somewhere different. Let's meet somewhere like Covent Garden. No, the river, let's meet on the South Bank, outside the Hayward Gallery. By that sculpture.'

'Yes.'

'Goodbye, Sally.'

''Bye-bye Richie.'

Richie, she called me Richie. Maybe all is not lost.

Hope tided Richard along for the rest of the day and the chairman's metaphorical pat on the back for the Georgian folly put a spring in his stride as he left the office for the weekend. Hope in his heart, his eyes longed for the sight of her.

'Good night Sandra, Mary.'

Sally felt quiet and timid, not nervous, not particularly excited. Just quiet and private. She looked hard in the mirror before she left for town. She scanned that familiar face, scouring for external proof of what she felt inwardly. She smiled benevolently at the furrowed brow and winked at the startled eyes.

'Hey hey, Sal,' she murmured comfortingly. She looked at her face so hard and for so long, staring relentlessly, until it assumed strange contortions and was her face no longer. She remembered doing the same as a child, staring and staring so her face would metamorphose into a completely strange visage: *the face of your husband*, the playground legend had said. But as she stared no man's face replaced her own, she was but a privileged fly on the bare wall of her mind's eye. She saw not merely into herself, but she saw herself. She liked her. She was standing on the threshold of something huge and daunting. But she had trust and she had faith. At that moment she loved Sally Lomax and she knew her very well.

No acting, she promised, *no acting*.

TWENTY-SIX

*O*ur girl from Highgate felt like a mole above ground, a timid creature thrust into the glare and not-quite-glamour of Friday Night In Town. Sally felt like a stranger in a very different and rather extraordinary country. Normal people sit safe at home, or celebrate the end of the week and welcome the weekend with a trip to their local locals, don't they? So who were these people littering the pavement and wearing down the concrete five yards either side of each and every aesthetically grimy pub? Men and women, and all in suits. Navy is the order of the day! Pints all round! I'll have a half. Mine's a double.

Ah-ha! It's the work-force that keeps the town ticking.

They seem like normal people, Sally thought, *but what are they all doing here? In the centre of town? They're not tourists. Maybe they don't have local locals. Maybe they even live in Zone 1 of the Underground network. Surely not?*

Sally thought them a happy race. As she weaved her way through Covent Garden, she observed how the scenarios she passed by were repeated with alarming regularity and subscribed religiously to unadventurous conventions. She witnessed the casting of wanton glances, she picked up on the licentious edge to the voices, she took note of the obvious-over-risqué *double-entendres*. Chit chat, chatter, chatter. Ah-ha! It's a chat-up! They're not talking shop; they've forgotten about the exchange rates, the press releases, and they've put the computers to bed until Monday morning. They are here to try and unravel the person behind the job, see if there's an inkling, a chance of post-work extra-curricular activities. Suggestions fly of 'this nice little restaurant I know'. It's Friday night! It's cliché time!

'I've had too much to drink.'

'Let me take you home.'

Travelcards open the gates to the tackily upholstered world of the tube train which will carry their loads weekendward and away from the safety of their weekday workaday personae.

'Want to come in for a coffee?' *What will they say at work?*

'I'm married, you know, but it's all over.' *Well, it is, isn't it?*

A hasty reinterpretation will always augur the faintest but sincerest hope that indeed 'it might be different this time'.

Who are they? Each and every one has a life, a home, a chest of drawers full of undies and shirts, a fridge with shopping and a front door that is opened and then shut tight and private for the night. I don't know any of them, not one! But they all clean their teeth, these people; they've all been ill at some point, cried, flown into a temper. They all fart! And all are naked beneath the navy. They have families, they're someone's little boys and little girls. They have secrets and sacred late-night last thoughts. And I'll never know! But they'll still be living! Every day they'll be waking up and doing things, saying things, thinking things – just like I do! I don't know them, nor they me. I'll go on with my life but they'll still Be. I'll never know them, these living people, and there are so many and they're all real! Do they see me? Might they wonder about me?

As she scurried her way through the throngs of these strange yet native folk, Sally occupied her racing mind with her usual intoxicating meanderings. It was far too scary to think of Richard. She was less than a mile, less than twenty minutes away from him. Her nerves coursed through her body with gay abandon, her mind raced faster than her legs and walking was further impeded by her quivering knees. Come on, Sally, do get a grip. It's only Richard. Nothing to be afraid of. Enjoy!

Funny, Sally thought, *how one can wander and wonder and be all absorbed in a world of funny old thoughts and yet still have your legs carry you to where you must be at 8 o'clock; negotiating traffic, dodging pedestrians and mastering all heights of curb, seemingly without the aid of eyes or ears or mind. From A to B as easy as ABC. And see, here is the Hayward sculpture, winking and humming its semi-broken neon welcome.*

It is 8, just gone; late, a little – a woman's prerogative indeed but still her tardiness, insubstantial as it is, irritates her. Is he there? Is he there?

Richard, where are you?

He is there. Here he is, coming towards the girl who has taken his whole being and turned it upside-down, thrown his machismo and reserve away and far, rid him of his vices and banished his negativity. Richard had watched Sally as she looked everywhere but at him. Now the two of them are tantalizingly close, within reach. Sally can see the legs of his trousers, even if she closes her eyes his smell tells her he is almost upon her, yet still she cannot look at him. So close now, almost there, almost together again. Sally's mouth seems full of something that is not anything at all, Richard has a lump of nothing stuck in his throat. Where are the cameras?

190

Where are the violins? A drum-roll at the very least. But there is nothing but silence thumping around the heads of these two people. Both wish they were a million miles away and alone, yet both would not be anywhere else than the here and now, together. They are reeling with relief. Their combined euphoria is tangible after so long, too silly long apart. See how Sally brushes past Richard and he catches her around the waist and draws her tight and close and quick. Watch him kiss her cheek. She kisses him back hurriedly, awkwardly, her teeth grazing the side of his chin. Happiness and hope are encapsulated in their silence, in the very fabric of their quaking bodies.

'Hullo, Sal!' Richard coos, but Sally doesn't reply. He looks at her face and sees her eyes shine and glisten in the chill and darkness of the night around them. He shakes her gently and she looks at him with such menacing intensity that it is Richard who darts his eyes away and rests them on the couple strolling huddled under an umbrella even though it is not raining. Sally takes stock of his profile; so clean and sculptured, his cheek-bones high, his cheeks hollowing slightly under them, his strong and defined jaw line. She is looking at him objectively and sees how quintessentially good-looking he is, yet she finds that she has the ability to see behind too, and there she finds his soul and his being and she likes what she sees, she loves what she sees.

'Hey, Richie,' she replies eventually. They look and they smile, sincere and open. Their eyes talk and say what they cannot utter with their mouths because those words are too clumsy and their voices are still too delicate. Very, very, intoxicatingly slowly, Richard cups Sally's face in his hands. Her cheeks feel so cold and soft and they look like porcelain under the romantic glow of the South Bank lights. Sally knows she is about to be kissed and she knows that this kiss will probably hold more import and be more loaded than any kiss she has had or will ever have. As Richard plants the gentle press of his mouth against hers, he sows into her heart and his a message that would seem inevitably trite if spoken with words.

They went and sat with Bailey's in plastic cups at one of the incongruously rustic picnic tables by the river outside the Royal Festival Hall. There was a chill in the air but they were snug in each other and glad to be gone from the brightness and the noise and the ladies-and-gentlemen-please-take-your-seats. As they fidgeted into relaxed positions, a young Waterloo boy jerked his cold and homeless way towards them. He only wanted 10p but Richard pressed a nugget of a pound coin into his twitching fingers. The smile on the boy's face was quite extraordinary as he graciously thanked him and bowed his way away from them and into the Festival Hall.

'Makes me sad,' Sally said gently. Richard raised his glass and they drank to him. Richard had planned what he wanted and needed to say, but the imminence with which he could instigate it was daunting and had rendered him verbally impotent. He was about to tell her that he had missed her, *a lot, you know*, when the young beggar emerged from the lights and warmth and made a bee-line for them. In his hand, he held on tight to a helium balloon, silver and blue. It had broadened his smile into a near-manic contortion.

'Look! Look what they gave me! It's a balloon!' His naiveté and happiness were at once charming and saddening. So much pleasure and thanks for merely a pound, for just a balloon. Who said that money could not buy love and joy?

'It's a fine balloon,' confirmed Sally.

'They gave it to me. There are plenty in there, maybe you could get one too. I think it's brill!' he concluded as he broke into a twitching trot away from them, looking back every other stride to check his balloon was there. It was his, his own, it had been given to him. It was his metaphorical friend, his substitute dog on the end of a piece of string. Pleasure had been brought into his life. Richard scanned Sally's face unseen. She was watching the boy and his balloon disappear into the labyrinthine concrete. She was watching after him, she was saying a prayer for him, futile she knew, but she had to. Richard saw the prayer and the care in her face and knew he was in love with what he saw. Her pretty face, her funny face, her familiar and Sally-face. She was transparent and he was warmed by what he could read there. The beauty of it.

'Sal?'

The boy was gone from sight. She turned to Richard and looked at him in anticipation with eyes that were large and soft and just a little timid.

'Talk?' she implored him tentatively. He held her eyes and though she wanted to look away from the enormity of what she prophesied was about to be said, his eyes and their deep and dark sincerity caught her in a magnetic hold.

'Sally, I love you. It's a word and not a very good one. But it's a word that we are brought up to understand, to trust and believe in. Believe me. I want you to know that falling in love with you has been an utter revelation. I realize that whatever I felt before for anyone else was not love at all. I'm desperate for you. I want you so much. You excite me, you calm me, you make me so frighteningly happy. I didn't think it could be like this, I wasn't expecting to find this in my life. I'd always sort of thought that I'd walk on through in my life, having fuck-flings, meaningless dalliances with women I could categorize as beautiful or fun – but never did I think that another person could so enhance the quality of my life. It's not as if I felt life was lacking before you came along, I never thought that something was missing, that life would be better *if only dot dot dot*. But now that I've had you, that I've felt you and loved you and discovered how you can make me feel, in my mind, in my body – now I know that I don't want not to have you here with me. Now I know that without you there will be a void, an emptiness which no one else can possibly fill. I want you to fill my life and I want to be there for you. Only you. There is no one else for me. I want *you*.'

There was silence, stunned silence. Sally mulled over Richard's words and replayed them to herself. She acknowledged the solemnity of the occasion, she was struck by his courage and volition. There was still a part of her that wanted to run, but there was a stronger impulse now to stay and for the first time it neither scared nor repulsed her.

But it did tie her tongue. She wanted to say to him, 'Yes, I feel it too.' She wanted to confirm that love was the last thing she had been looking for when she met him, that she had previously deemed love overrated, somewhat pointless and inherently dangerous. But Sally could not say a word, she certainly could not manage the 'L' word though it no longer terrified her so. All she could do was to reach out a cold and fragile hand and place it against Richard's cheek. She turned it over and stroked his face with the back of her hand, then she switched it back and laid her palm still, her thumb just resting on the corner of his mouth, her fingertips touching his ear-lobe, his neck, and the start of his hair.

'Quite frankly, Sal,' launched Richard in a business-like and decided way but let her hand stay as it was, 'I want to do something about it.' Sally took her hand away from him and waited, head cocked and eyes soft. Richard glanced at his cup and saw that it was empty though he could find no trace of Bailey's in his mouth or his memory. He asked Sally if she wanted another; her cup was practically full but she nodded anyway. Richard disappeared and left Sally wondering what his breath had been bated to say. She looked out across the river and thought how beautiful London looked for once. The lights from the Embankment fell into golden shards across the water and the buildings loomed elegant and proud behind. Staring at St Paul's, ghostly and emotive in the floodlit night, she was thinking about nothing in particular when Richard returned.

She greeted his approach with a soft little smile. But who is that walking beside him? Richard was accompanied by the crustiest, dirtiest person Sally had ever seen. 'Godforsaken' was the word she thought of later that night. He was Richard's height but half his build and wore the filthiest clothes, baggy and torn, shiny in parts with grease, dull in others with grime. His hair was hacked to an uneven, precarious mohican, tinged in green and peroxide. Little of his face was visible under the scraggly beard and tattoos which webbed over his cheeks and throat. The earrings, of which there were many, were not confined to his ears but were in both nostrils, on his right eyebrow and on his lower lip. As Sally recoiled she chanced upon his hands.

He had the most beautiful hands, she noticed, as he placed them flat on a table near her. Very much like Richard's; long, shapely and manicured. She was transfixed. Intrigued by her captivation, Richard curled her fingers around the cup for her and sat down astride the bench, cowboy style, just like Sally. Was *it*, that person, upsetting her? Would she rather they move? No, not at all. She was compelled by the man. The figure was immediately pathetic, even menacing, and yet he exuded a composure and elegance which were mesmerizing. Richard could see that she was neither frightened nor repulsed so they sat and sipped and looked at each other while casting frequent furtive glances to their neighbour.

With a slug of Bailey's to bolster him, Richard decided to bite his bullet and drew a deep breath accordingly.

'Sally,' he started, taking her hand and turning her face towards him. He cleared his throat but she kept her eyes trained on the other man. Richard took another deep breath but Sally pipped him to it with a whisper fringed with awe.

'Look, Richie, look!' she implored. Richard followed her eyes and they sat and watched in amazement and pity the man with Richard's hands. From every pocket in his old combat trousers and jacket, he retrieved a seemingly unending supply of the little free cartons of UHT milk and coffee whitener. Food; free.

Methodically he placed them to form a line. And another. And still they came. Another line, and another. He paused and looked steadily at the four even rows in front of him. Sally scanned them, ten in each, forty altogether – a glass-worth?

With concentrated and pedantic dedication, he systematically peeled the lids back from each pot. Again he stopped still and just regarded.

Like a teacher, thought Sally, *presiding over a class.*

Carefully he lifted each pot to his mouth and drank his way, daintily, scrupulously, up and down the rows. Sally saw his tongue dart to salvage every last smear. With maddening precision, each pot was conscientiously returned to its place in the row. Empty. Soon they were finished and the meal was over. He stood still a moment longer and then took his beautiful hands away from the table, out of Sally's sight, and buried them deep into his jacket. He rumbled off, oblivious to his audience. In silence, they hoped he had had enough, that he was satiated, that he might have a square meal tomorrow, though they doubted it.

Richard looked at Sally and saw how her eyes were smarting with tears. With his fingertips he gently eased her face away from the pregnant space left in front of the empty cartons. He felt no need to draw a brave breath.

'Sally.'

She looked at him. She was open and there, ready and committed to listen.

'I can't be bothered with game-playing and acting and waiting. I propose that we move in together. I want to live with you, I want to have you beside me every morning and night. Quite frankly, I can't be having the two or three times a week. I think we should move in together. Soon. Now. With a view to the Big "M". We have enormous potential. I've never wanted anything more and I don't want to settle for anything less.'

Like an eavesdropper, Richard clearly heard the words as they were uttered. Premeditated and planned for days and weeks, they had been proclaimed previously in the safety of his head, during the privacy of a run, in a lunch-time day-dream, in late-night, sleep-greeting sanctuary. And yet he took himself by surprise as the words tumbled away, out into the open unchecked by any better judgment. He recognized the sound of his own voice and heard the words he was saying; they were familiar, he knew them well, yet they induced a surge of adrenalin to course through his body and reach his stomach in a wave of nausea that was at once awful and pleasant. Though his head was high, his heart was full, his eyes were alight and his body trembled, Richard was racked with anxiety at the portent of his words. The very meaning of them engulfed him, the consequences they would have on his life, the effect they would have on Sally.

The very effect they will have on Sally is something Richard cannot foresee. Why should his words, spoken after all with honesty and great depth of emotion possibly bring her anything but great happiness and security? Why indeed? Because, poor man, they are the wrong words for someone who is only just feeling comfortable with the trimmings, trappings and whole idea of being in love.

The ensuing silence was unbearable. Richard was perturbed by the absence of the smile he was so desperate to see. Sally gulped, both with her eyes and her throat. Fear flickered across her face; it was manifest in the twitching and creasing of her brow, the purse and pucker of her lips.

'Talk to me,' Richard demanded, his voice breaking. Sally didn't trust her voice at all but the tears that she was desperate to vanquish threatened to choke her instead. Richard cradled her head in his hands, wove his fingers through her hair, pressed her face against his chest where she could feel his heart pounding and it frightened her.

'Talk to me, talk to me, talk to me,' he murmured over and over again, rocking her in rhythm to his words. Sally's mind raced and ran so fast that it was impossible to pin down her thoughts, to analyze her churning emotions, to organize them into sentences coherent enough to be said out loud. Richard was patient, his soliloquy had now a soothing effect on him, he felt light; a weight had been shifted.

Little did he realize how it had fallen twice as heavy on to Sally's half as broad shoulders.

'Sal?' he implored after what he considered to be a reasonable length of loaded time. She raised her face and slowly shook her head. Richard looked unbearably sad and Sally was surprised at how swiftly his pain restored her voice.

'Don't know, Richie, just don't know. Too soon, perhaps, I think.'

For some reason, she found it impossible to form a grammatically correct sentence. 'Can't think just right now. Can I think, go away and have time to think?' Her eyes were wide. 'Richard? Can I? Seems too big, scary and I don't know. Too much, don't know. Frightened. Need time and space. Can't answer you, it's too big. Richie?'

Richard looked at her and decided that he would grant her all the time in the world in the hope that she would find her answer quickly. As long as it was the answer he wanted to hear. He nodded at her and was rewarded with her smile. Sally's smile said 'thank you'. It said something else too, Richard could see it quite clearly but refused to believe it until she said it.

But Sally did not, she just could not quite say it to him that night.

In bed, warm and alone two hours later, she said 'I love you, Richard' out loud. She spoke the four words with conviction, a veritable proclamation. She heard her voice, she knew it was hers. She heard the words and knew they came from her head as much as from her heart.

As Richard and Sally had strolled across Waterloo bridge, they had passed the balloon boy. Minus his balloon.

'Where's your balloon gone?' Sally asked.

'It just flew away, I let it go – just to see – and it just flew up and away. It went over there somewhere.'

'That's a pity. But I think there are plenty more back inside, I'm sure they wouldn't mind you taking another.'

He smiled at Sally and she saw how young he was, his dirty face fresh and just pubescent. He looked a little like Marcus. 'There are plenty more,' she reiterated.

'No,' he said wisely, 'I don't want another one. I would just want to let that one go too.'

TWENTY-SEVEN

*I*t is a quiet, fresh Saturday morning. Sally has woken, thankfully alone, and is staring at nothing in particular through the gap in the curtains. Feeling small, tearful and sorry for herself, she is reluctant to rise and wants to start the day with a good old cry in the comfort of her little bed (a double bed, in fact, but so cosy and safe that Sally always thinks of it as her little bed). We'll leave her be awhile and travel south-westwards to Notting Hill where Catherine has just popped by, accidentally on purpose, to see how her husband's (soon to be father of her first child) best friend is faring today.

'Hey, Catherine!'

Richard, resplendent in grey marl jogging bottoms and a dark red sweatshirt, greeted her with a kiss on both cheeks. 'I was just off out for a run but it can wait. Come in, come in! Coffee? Tea? Juice? Juice coming up! Grapefruit? Orange? Both freshly squeezed in the groovy juicer-whatsit. What a great Christmas present. I did thank you, didn't I? Profusely, I seem to remember.'

Catherine was swept through into Richard's sitting-room, borne along on the stream of his cheerful bearing.

I have before me a happy boy. Thank goodness! she thought. *Come on Richie-ard, tell me do! Reveal to me the provenance of your smile, the reason for the spring in your step, the song in your voice!*

Richard, however, was whistling too sonorously to tune into Catherine's attempted telepathy.

She slid into his leather recliner and wriggled off her shoes. Daffodils caught her eye. Wherever she turned, their golden fanfare greeted her. The flowers were shoved into vases, crammed into jugs; haphazard and glorious.

Much much better than those de rigueur *hothouse tulips*, she thought, and smiled. With relief, she saw that Bach came before Bizet and, on the shelf below, Hendrix came after Genesis. Through the archway, she could see Richard slicing the grapefruit with fell swoops, nonchalantly tossing the halves into the juicer gadget. Watching him from behind, seeing his broad shoulders, tapered waist and neat bottom, she was happily transported back to memories of college days. Those evenings, what fun! Food and wine, on a budget but heavenly, lounging around, smoking joints and travelling to the dark side of the moon and back with Pink Floyd. Bob and Richard; fit as fiddles, keen chefs and devoted flatmates. Catherine had felt special to 'the boys', madly and deeply in love with Bob but treasuring too the platonic closeness and openness of her friendship with Richard. She had loved to watch dinner for four, a familiar occurrence, take shape. She enjoyed seeing Bob and Richard vie for space in their small, cramped but outrageously well-equipped kitchenette. She thrilled to their fondness for each other, manifest in every half-finished but intuitively understood silence, in their easy laughter, their incessant teasing, in their generous pats, slaps and nudges. She remembered how she would marvel at the flexing in Bob's forearms as he whizzed his knife through an innocent cucumber, how he would look up, hold her gaze and smile his dashing, winning smile, before setting to work on the carrots. Always Bob-and-Richard-and-Catherine. And X.

X was invariably long-legged and luscious but on the scene for so short a time that her name was a foregone forgotten inevitability.

Bob had proposed to Catherine a year or so later in a kitchen, a different kitchen but a kitchen all the same. He had cut his finger, she had laughed at his ever-so-injured face and had kissed the droplet of blood away. As she wrapped a wadge of paper towel tenderly around his finger (having caused him to squeal at the undiluted disinfectant) Bob had asked her to marry him nevertheless. Dumbstruck, she could only squeeze his wounded digit so hard in acceptance that he very nearly reneged his proposal. Here she was, a decade later, the very Mrs Woods, watching Richard, the self-same Richard, still King of the Kitchen.

Something's missing, something's changed.

Sally was most noticeable by her absence. Catherine was struck by how alone Richard looked tinkering in his kitchen. He looked wrong, awkward somehow, minus his shadow, his Sally; getting in his way, sticking her finger in this and that, sniffing and fiddling and tasting, her eyes never leaving him. Catherine had watched her well; she had recognized something, a vestige of herself in Sally. She had seen her gaze at Richard's forearms, she had seen the smile spread as Richard wielded his Sabatier with gay abandon along the length of an unsuspecting cucumber. Catherine had watched Richard too, observing how he gently guided Sally away from his path with a tender push at her waist, his hand, inevitably, lingering.

It won't be long, Catherine had thought, *before he's proposing to her.* Whether it would happen in the kitchen she could not know, but she hoped that it might. A good omen, a good beginning.

But of course. Sally's not here.

Catherine returned, somewhat reluctantly, to the day at hand and wondered instead just what it was about a man expertly slicing cucumber that solicits utter admiration from a woman, inspiring a flutter both to heart and groin. Here she was, Catherine Woods-née-Daniels, married and pregnant and blissfully happy, being handed juice in an elegant wine glass by Richard Stonehill who drew up a chair and sat astride, cowboy style, opposite her.

'How's the morning sickness?' he enquired, matter-of-factly.

'It's evening sickness and it's terrible and I love it!' she hooted, consequently snorting into her grapefuit juice and finding much mirth in the mess.

'Want a bib, Catherine?' Richard laughed, handing her a piece of patterned kitchen paper. 'I'm so chuffed for you both. I hope it goes without saying that I'll be godfather. I mean, who else could you trust to show your child *the way*? I'll teach him/her the Stonehill Statutes; I'll ensure that my morals are engraved at the very centre of their being. What better start in life, hey?'

'Lord help the little thing!'

'Seriously, Catherine, Bob's utterly thrilled. Thrilled to the extent that's he's becoming a domestic bore. *I'm going to be a dad! I'm going to be a dad!*' Richard mimicked, then took a contemplative sip and continued, nodding earnestly, 'Seriously, though, it's great news. What names have you decided? When is it due? Do godfathers have to be at the birth? Phew! Can you start thinking about names now? Or does one buy the pram and nappies and decide when the thing arrives?' Richard was manic and Catherine laughed. He carried on in two voices:

'*Mmm, looks red and wrinkly to me, must be a Roger.*'

'*Nonsense, his name's Bert, it's written all over his face!*'

'*Have you got a pram?*'

'No, but I have a baby in my womb called Janet-if-it's-a-girl and John-if-it's-a-boy.'

'Stop, stop!' Catherine pleaded. 'If you split my sides there won't *be* a baby! But to answer your question, we'll call *her* Sally, or we'll call *him* Richard.'

Richard jerked. His face was startled and the sparkle in Catherine's eyes eluded him. She reached forward and placed a hand on his arm. 'Joke, it was a joke,' she assured him, 'but I'm sitting here with curiosity enough to kill a pride of bloody lions let alone a humble cat, wondering when on earth you're going to tell me how it went!'

'It?'

'Rich-*ard*!' The silence was excruciating but Catherine held her ground as she held Richard's gaze. She felt well within her rights to expect a not-too-ambiguous response and she was rewarded as Richard began to smile and cast his eyes downwards, coyly even. Chuffed, to be sure.

'Sally?' she prompted.

'I think,' he faltered, 'that the definitive happy-ever-after is on the horizon.'

He raised his head and looked at Catherine directly; the light of the still relatively new year streamed through the elegant sash windows and struck his eyes with an aesthetic ferocity to add drama and impact to his words.

'She needs some Time with a capital "T". But the signs are there. In her eyes, in her confusion, in her willingness to listen, in her need and request to think. I never thought that I'd want someone, actually really *want* someone. I don't need her, I just want her, plain and simple. And I've told her what I want. You see, Cath, I can see through her veil and behind her outer reserve. I know they're there for her protection and self-preservation and I understand, I respect that.

'I don't know what it's been like for her in the past, the way she's felt, other men. It's always been nothingy for me, as you know only too well. There's something private and guarded with Sal, yet I have no desire to pry. I want her to realize that that's her past and it's passed. And that my only request is that she unwind herself and lay herself bare, that she accept me and my true desire to make her happy. She's a steel butterfly, my Sal, a steel butterfly. Beautiful and strong, fragile yet determined. Awesome! I think, Catherine, no, I *know* . . . I know she's going to come around. She just has to shake off her fears and greet herself with honesty and courage. Like I have. And I feel happy. I'm a happy man. I'm in love and it's the best thing in the world. Funny how I ridiculed Bob all those years ago when he talked about you, and him and you. He said to me once, "The time comes when you know, *you just know.*" And the funny thing is, you *do*, you just do!'

Richard knocked three and a half minutes off his best time on his run half an hour later.

Catherine returned to Bob, threw up the grapefruit juice, thought, *Shit, morning sickness*, and told him that she thought she could hear bells. Bob didn't understand, he thought perhaps it was a vagary of pregnancy and made her a cup of tea. But two days later, when he saw Richard who slaughtered him at squash, he understood. He could hear bells too. Faint. Distant. But there.

Diana heard bells, phone bells. *Sally!* she thought intuitively.
    'Of course I'll come over, of course it's not a problem. No, it's not inconvenient. Will you *hush*, dear girl, I don't have anything planned. And even if I did, you silly old thing, nothing takes precedence over my Sally! You'd be the same for me, wouldn't you? 'Xactly! 'Bye-bye, I'm there already.'
    Sally had been morose all morning. She had dithered and shilly-shallied and had been thoroughly incapable of

pulling herself together. In fact, subconsciously and somewhat perversely, she had made a concerted effort to keep herself entrenched in her low ebb. There was something rather cathartic about being maudlin; Samuel Barber's 'Adagio for Strings' filled the flat and she even read the closing pages of *Black Beauty*.

'*My troubles are all over, and I am at home,*' she wailed out loud with a good sniff.

Well, they've only just started and I wish I was far away.

Sally bumbled her way through Saturday morning half-doing only half the jobs she'd earmarked. She was continually, uncharacteristically, distracted. With half a shirt badly ironed she hurried to her bedroom to change the bed-linen but did not manage the pillowcases because the bath implored her to scrub it instead. She even heard herself calling 'Mummy, Mummy' out loud yet her mother was the last person but one that she wanted and she had never called for her before. So why now? Sally heard her voice. It was worryingly quiet and feeble.

Sal! Get a grip!

Phone Diana.

I'll phone Diana.

Lifted a little by the anticipation of her friend's imminent knock on the door, Sally charged about her flat collecting debris and retrieved a piece of crockery from every room. On each, the remains of some food or other lay forlornly: a piece of toast, a boiled egg, a portion of corn flakes. Spasmodically half-eaten, the egg was now cold, the toast bendy, the cereal soggy. No time to feel guilty chucking them all away, there was so much to do: the ironing, the cleaning, the thinking . . .

What thinking?

The Richard-Thing thinking. He wants you, remember – the whole shebang? Remember?

Gracious Good Lord, I can't even think straight, let alone have the time to think at all.

Of course you do. You may have relegated it to the furthest reaches of your mind, but it is still there.

Well, I'll take down the net curtains to wash instead. Yes. No, no! I must empty the Hoover and oil the wok. Diana will be here in a mo'.

Knowing she was soon to be saved by the bell, Sally continued her chores humming the theme to *Love Story.*

As Diana wriggled her arms through her red duffel coat and jostled with the mittens (black) attached playground-style to elastic, she thought how fragile Sally sounded. Not desperate as she had done on Other Woman Day, just frail and feeble. Half an hour later, Little Voice Lomax welcomed Diana in to the warmth of her relatively tidy Highgate home and the knots of her troubled soul. Initially, Sally was still falling over her grammar and sentence construction but Diana tried her best to sift and make sense of the bits and drabs offered. Soon Sally was pouring out the details of the previous evening, in a veritable torrent. Out came Richard's proclamation, the balloon boy, the milk man with the beautiful hands. Diana had an idea for a painting, no, maybe a lino cut, so much more emotive.

Hush now! Listen to Sally, help her through.

'So, have you thought about it?'

'Di-*anarr*! It's only the next day. But I have thought about it quickly, and quite frankly I don't know what I think. It's like I'm trying to think of so much but there isn't the space. I feel so *bewildered*, like I don't know what's going on. Like I have no control. What is happening to me? Why don't I feel overjoyed, over the moon, high as a kite? I don't know, Di, I just feel sort of low and overawed and overwhelmed and not very happy. I thought, if and when I fell in you-know-what, that I'd be singing from the roof-tops and floating and smiling and feeling invincible. Instead I feel rather vulnerable and utterly confused.'

'What about? That you're not sure of your feelings?'

'No!' Sally retorted. 'Yes?' she furthered. 'I don't bloody know!' she wailed.

'*Are* you in you-know-what?' Diana ventured.

'I am deeply and irrevocably very much in love,' proclaimed a sad Sally, 'with Richard,' she sighed, 'who is everything I thought no man could possibly be. I love him totally, with my body and with my Self. The point of no return is way back there somewhere,' she continued, gesticulating wildly at nowhere in particular. 'It's gone from the safety of my view,' she concluded, down, dejected, diminutive. There was silence, an initially awkward soundlessness which eerily metamorphosed into a graceful and welcome peace. Only Sally broke it. Giving Diana an almighty shock, she shrieked an urgent and most un-Sally-like: 'Fuck!' Slapping her hands flat, smack, against her soft cheeks, 'Shit!' she fulminated, her eyes wide and darting, her hands scratching and pulling her face. 'Bugger, bugger, what am I doing! Get me away. I don't want *this*! I'm not nearly ready. I can't, I won't!'

Everything fell; tears, her hands away from her red cheeks, her shoulders, her head, everything tumbled down.

'Cope,' she whimpered, 'I can't cope. I want to be like before, by myself. It's just too much.' Sally crumpled to the floor of her sitting-room and sobbed.

She was broken yet it was she who had broken herself, and though Diana rushed to her side and crouched beside her and laid a hand of comfort and support upon her shoulders, she knew and Sally knew that only one person could help. She lay broken and smashed about herself yet it was she who had wielded the metaphorical hammer. So she would have literally to pick herself up. Of all the King's horses and all the King's men, none would be able to help her; she was the only one who could put herself together again.

'What should I do, Diana?' But Diana couldn't find her own voice, let alone offer Sally constructive advice of any merit. Still Sally sobbed, on the floor in an embryonic hunch, her face contorted with the frustration of it all, the salt of her tears reddening her eyes and stinging her cheeks. Diana looked on and saw for the first time that Sally was noticeably thinner; her face had a new gauntness that threatened to overpower its former prettiness. Her shoulders looked a little bony, making her head seem a little too large. With a degree of horror, Diana conceded to herself that she looked quite pathetic.

'Why not go away for a little while?' she ventured. 'To your Mum's, to Lincoln?'

Sally gave her a don't-be-so-stupid look.

'Paris?' Diana suggested. But suddenly J-C, his bedroom, his bathroom, his smell, his taste, rushed uninvited into Sally's mind and she shuddered until she had quite shaken him away.

'I can't. School, silly,' Sally whimpered.

'But you seem awfully poorly to me,' Diana cooed, stroking her hair. The maternal connotations of the word 'poorly' coupled with the action of hair-stroking caused Sally to crumple down again. This time she let Diana soothe her, huddled in a muddle on the floor.

Sally made it through Saturday, Sunday too, on the steel of her butterfly wings. Just. She avoided thinking about that which she knew she had to; she just looked after herself and made sure all was neat and tidy, spick and span, safe and sound, comfy and cosy. Her voice remained silent. It was unwanted, untrusted. Her self-constructed mute world was a safe one. She mooched around in her snuggly socks and her tatty dress and her Aran-knit cardie, she darned four pairs of socks and

209

finished off the skirt she had been making. The clacketting of the sewing-machine lulled her into a settled state and she was pleased with the finished item.

Sally made soup. Two batches subdivided into eight Tupperware containers, six to freeze, two for the fridge. Leek and potato. Pea.

Nice and hearty. Thick slush.

Tupperware containers, six to freeze, two for the fridge. Leek and potato. Pea.

Nice and hearty. Thick slush.

TWENTY-EIGHT

*S*ally sprinted with the speed of a cheetah and the grace of a gazelle. The warm wind buffeted her ears as she ran with it. She sprung a gravity-defying *jeté* over the irrigation dykes which loomed, with east-coast regularity, every forty strides. She thought of Hopkins:

The hurl and the gliding rebuffed the big wind.

Whoosh! Sally was master of the wind, a part of the air; the ground beneath her feet spring-boarding her upwards so she could greet the sky. Boundless energy, freedom and delight. Sally felt exhilarated. On and on she pelted, lungs and legs going strong and keen for more. The land looked lovely and felt soft, welcoming her back after every leap. The ditches glinted shards of crystal as she flew over them.

Plotted and pieced . . . Hopkins again. All her senses were alight; she could hear the soft thuds of her footfalls, her fast breath, the wind; she could smell the grass, the earth; she could taste the very freshness of the day. The day was divine and she felt so alive.

She could make out something strangely vertical in the

distance silhouetted against the sun, defiantly upright against the uncompromising horizontality of the Lincolnshire landscape. On she ran. There was a lovely rousing tune in her head, what was it? Smetna. It was like being in a film. Oh, yes! Most certainly a film because as she neared the distant post, it assumed the irregularities that told her it was a figure. A man. And as her feet raced closer, her heart hurtled to her head that maybe, just maybe . . .

Yes, it was!

Two ditches separated her and Richard.

Joy of joys! Praise be!

'Richie!' she shrieked and the breeze swept her call to his ears. His outstretched arms carried his reply. Sally's smile was so wide it could have fallen off her face but the wind held it there, forcing rivulets to run from her eyes instead.

But I'm not crying!

She leapt the last dyke and was sure that she flew; oh, the ease of it! the softness, the power, the hush and rush of the abetting wind. A final graceful leap delivered Sally into the arms of Richard. His face was kissed by the sun so she kissed it too. His eyes swallowed her and, with his strong, lovely arms about her waist, she melted into him, her head cradled close to his heart. She was breathless with excitement, speechless with joy. She could feel herself slipping out of her body into his. Oh, RichardRichardRichard.

'Darling, darling Richard. I so love you. Oh, my Richardrichardrichard.'

You're not Richard. You are not Richard.

Sally opened her eyes and stared drunkenly at the blurred face in front of hers. The fuzziness slowly lifted and the features asserted themselves. Familiar yes, Richard no.

'Marcus!'

'It's okay, it's okay, Miss Lomax. Are you all right? Stay still, we've gone to fetch someone. Relax. Don't worry.'

Miss Lomax did as she was told and kept her arms fixed about Marcus's straining uncomplaining neck. She closed her eyes. Nothing. Richard was gone. Gone too was the landscape and the flying and the wind and the water and the big sky and the thrill and delight of it all. All that was there was a murky brown nothingness and an infuriating thrumming.

'It's all going to be fine, Miss Lomax,' comforted Marcus. 'You just sort of tumbled. You banged your head. But you'll be right as rain. Right as rain, Miss Lomax. Promise.'

Thank God. The grown-ups were here. Phew!

'God, Sally!'

'Good Lord! Miss Lomax!'

Miss Lewis and Mr Tomlin, Diana and Geoff, Art teacher and Headmaster, friend and employer.

'Marcus, what on earth happened?' Mr Tomlin crouched beside Marcus, voice gentle, his panic hidden well.

'We were doing Alfred the Great. She – I mean Miss Lomax – stopped talking. She just kept looking out of the window. Only there wasn't anything there. She sort of came to a halt – you know, like a car? We didn't know what to do. It seemed like ages. Then she made this horrible funny noise in her throat and she just crumpled. Didn't she?'

Young voices murmured confirmation. Marcus continued: 'She just went crash. Like a tree falling. It was like in slow motion. But she clonked her head on the corner of the desk.'

'How long has she been like this? After she crumpled? Since she clonked her head?'

'Well, that's my desk there, you see, so I could get to her immediately. I leapt up as soon as she started to fall, didn't I?' Class Five said 'Yes' in unison. 'I was with her practically straight away and told Rajiv to fetch someone. I shouted, actually – I didn't mean to. I was scared, we all were. Are. Anyway, then you came. Only about three or four minutes, I suppose. I – ' Marcus faltered ' – is . . . ?' He could not do it. There was a loaded pause while little Marcus, our brave boy and Sally's saviour, bit his lip and scrunched his eyes in a futile attempt to keep tears at bay. 'Is Miss Lomax dead?' he sobbed. 'Please don't let her be,' he begged his headmaster.

'Darling Marcus,' cooed Miss Lewis, 'no, she's not dead and she's not going to die either. It seems Miss Lomax fainted. Banging her head has probably made her unconscious. You did wonderfully, all of you. Brave, darling children.'

They managed to pry Miss Lomax's arms away from Marcus's now bowed-down neck and put her feet up on a bench, crossing her arms over her chest.

'Are you hurting anywhere?' Mr Tomlin asked quietly, bending down right next to Miss Lomax's ear. She could hear him asking, somewhere in the distance, but she had forgotten how to open her eyes.

'Sally, are you hurt?' trembled Miss Lewis.

Yes, in my heart.

With enormous effort she gave a slow small shake of her head. A trickle of blood coursing down her cheek said otherwise.

'Can you sit up?' Mr Tomlin implored. He turned away from Sally and spoke in hushed, urgent tones. 'Rajiv, run to my office – *run*. Ask Mrs Gates to call an *amb-ul-ance*.' He mouthed the word, not wanting Miss Lomax to hear, not wanting to alarm the children. Rajiv bolted. Mr Tomlin turned to Miss Lewis who sat stroking Miss Lomax's hair. The tips of her fingers were wet with blood; Sally's hair was dark with it.

'Sally sweetie, can you sit up?' Diana urged.

Sally blinked twice to say, *I'll try*, and with the help of Mr Tomlin and the gallant Marcus, up she sat, Diana's

214

hand-holding and neck-cradling supporting her all the way.

'I'm okay,' she croaked. 'Just fine,' she stammered. 'Dizzy,' she whispered. 'Want to lie down.' Marcus was out of his blazer in a flash and proffered it as a cushion. Where was Rajiv? Where was the ambulance? The class were silent. Golden children. A siren came and went, and with it their hopes. Rajiv arrived with an anxious, tearful Mrs Gates. Mr Tomlin suggested she wait by the main doors. They waited on. Another siren, louder, louder still. Here.

The stillness was gone, their job was done. Marcus, Miss Lewis and Mr Tomlin stood by, feeling sheepish even, as the paramedics swung into action. They eased Sally on to a stretcher and put orange blocks around her head and neck, placed a mask over her nose and mouth, and wrapped a blanket around her body. She no longer looked like Miss Lomax, nor did she look like Sally. Swiftly, she was stretchered away, out of their sight. Gone. Then sirens. Gone. Silent prayers, intense wishes of get-better-come-back, followed the ambulance right into Casualty.

Miss Lewis presided over shell-shocked Class Five for the rest of the afternoon. She was delighted with the way they had all pulled together, there was a great feeling of solidarity, hugs were liberal, chocolates were shared and patience was abundant. Mr Tomlin had been thoroughly impressed and was planning a special trip to the Planetarium as a reward – once Miss Lomax was back, of course. Class Five remained impeccably behaved and an air of utter concentration imbued the room as get-well-soon cards were lovingly designed. Crayons, pastels, charcoal, even pencils were set to task. No erasers, of course. Any mistakes – and there were few – were triumphantly incorporated into the overall design. Diana gathered a clutch of thirty cards, and took them, along

215

with thirty special messages and thirty kisses, to the Whittington hospital after school that afternoon.

'Sally?'

'Di?'

'You okay? Know where you are? How are you feeling? Don't talk if it hurts. Just wink or squeeze my hand or something.'

'Why are you talking like that?'

'Huh?'

'All nasal. Funny?'

'I hate hospitals, I hate the smell! That's why I'm talking through my nose. Don't laugh, shush! Are you ready to go home? Please say you are or else I'll expire then I'll land up here and that really isn't the point so why don't we get you to your feet and go homeward Highgate-bound!' Saying a sentence with no pause for breath took its toll on Diana who flopped into a plastic chair and breathed heavily, deep into the sleeve of her jumper. Sally stared at her and tried to make her brain work.

'I feel fine. I keep telling everyone here that I'm fine. Just had a funny turn. Funny. Never happened before. Yes, Di, yes. Take me home.'

Diana bustled. She marched Sally out of the hospital holding her in a most matronly manner. She bundled her into a taxi and kept her arms locked about her for the entire journey home. She insisted on Sally staying put while she paid the driver, and then insisted that he help her walk Sally to the front door.

'You earn your tip, my man!'

Once inside, she sat Sally on the edge of the bed and eased her out of her clothing, tutting sympathetically whenever she neared her head. She put Sally into her pyjamas and added bedsocks and an old cardigan for good measure.

'Warmth, my girl. Must keep you warm. You've had a shock. You mustn't catch cold.' She tucked her in tightly, bunching the duvet around her like a cocoon. Looking quite the sorry caterpillar, Sally muffled, 'Sorry to put you to all of this,' before welcoming the comfort of her familiar pillow and drifting effortlessly to sleep. Leaving the cards by her bed, Diana kissed her carefully on the forehead, tutting some more. She watched her awhile, sleepy and childlike, and then left.

'Richard, listen! No, calm down. Richard, shut it, I can't talk if you don't shut up a bit. It isn't serious, she's okay. She fainted in class and banged her head on the desk as she went down. No, you can't visit. Certainly not you and certainly not now. She really is very woozy. She needs a quiet, long night. It's what the doctor ordered. And I'm ordering you too, so listen up! Do not worry, young man. You have a good night. Promise me? Promise! Good! Night night, ducks.'

Richard felt sick.

My poor darling baby.

After ten minutes pacing up and down, hugging himself and murmuring 'Sal, Sal', he grabbed his car keys and left the flat, lights blaring and CD still on.

Grapes, I must stop to buy grapes. No, chocolates. No, no flowers. She may not feel like eating. Flowers it is. Damn, it's nearly eleven. Quick.

He hovered outside Sally's front door with a bunch of rather vulgar gladioli, not knowing quite what to do and dreading Diana suddenly appearing and giving him what for. He flipped the lid of the letter box and peered inside. A dim light edged its way out from the bathroom, casting soft shadows.

Night light. Good idea.

He peeled his ears and sought out any sound. He thought perhaps he heard a rustle from the bedroom and cooed, 'Sally! Sal?' He thought he heard something. He couldn't be sure so he gave himself the benefit of the doubt. 'Poor bunny, don't say a thing.'

Oh God, talk to me!

Richard eased himself up from the crouch he had almost frozen into. He chewed his thumb thoughtfully and studied the grain of the front door.

I want her to know that I'm here. But I don't want to disturb her.

The flowers, Richard.

The bunch would not fit through the letter box. He toyed with propping them against the front door but knew they would have the life and colour frozen out of them before morning. There was only one thing for it. One by one he posted the stems through the letter box. He blew a kiss through it and then left, hoping sincerely that Sally found the flowers before Diana.

She did. And she knew who they were from. She thought she'd heard him last night, but there again, she also thought she'd had a chat with Queen Victoria sitting on the edge of her bed.

We hate gladioli. She smiled as she trimmed the stems.

He likes tulips. I like cornflowers. We both like love-in-a-mist. But we hate gladioli!

She stroked the knobbled stems and placed the vase surreptitiously on the mantelpiece in the sitting-room so that she could see them from her bed but would be spared any explanation to Sister Lewis.

'Darling, darling girl! How are you! Have you eaten? Toast! Well *done!*' Sister Lewis had arrived in a bustle of good cheer and nurse-knows-best. 'Is it all awfully fuzzy? Do you remember anything?'

'I've tried and I've tried and I can't. I thought I was in Lincolnshire, near home, the place I've told you about. I was running and dancing and Richard was there. Then

218

all of a sudden I had this cracking headache and woke up in hospital.'

'Well, it appears you fainted in class and whacked your head on the desk. You were absolutely out of it when we arrived. You were hanging on to Marcus like he was your knight in shining armour.'

'I thought he was.'

'Huh?'

'Oh, nothing. Go on.'

'Well, an ambulance came and whisked you away. Luckily you didn't need stitches but they had to chop off a little of your hair to bathe the wound and put on that dinky butterfly plaster. Here.' Diana handed Sally a tiny round mirror from her bag. First Sally looked at the wound and was less distressed at the hair loss than she anticipated. She then angled the mirror downwards slightly and snuck a little look at her face. She looked rather grey and her lips were very pale.

Silly old Sal.

TWENTY-NINE

*D*iana tucked her tight in bed with a cup of tea, a gossipy magazine and the radio, and made it to school just after First Break. She gave a running bulletin to anyone who came into the art room and phoned Richard with an update.

'I took flowers last night. I was quiet as a mouse — promise. Does she know?'

'How very disobedient you are, Mr Stonehill. She didn't mention anything. But, come to think of it, she did keep shooting her gaze over to a vase of pretty vulgar gladdies lurking on the mantelpiece. And I thought you had taste!'

'It was late at night!' protested Richard, somewhat relieved. 'Next time I'll run along to Covent Garden.'

'*Next* time?'

'God forbid. Di, can I call her? Pop round tonight?'

Diana paused and pondered the merits of tact against truth. She plumped for a diplomatic blend of both.

'Richard, we don't even know *why* she passed out. But I would hazard a little guess that it had something to do with the state she's been in of late. Of course it's not your fault, you daft old bugger! I just think, for Sally's sake, that she'll probably recover and be back to her good old self if left to her own devices. *Compris?*'

'*Oui.*'

'*Bien.*'

Diana found Sally asleep with the radio on when she called in during lunch break. She noticed with fabricated disdain that the gladioli were now on Sally's dressing table. She warmed the pea soup and put a note by Sally's bed saying she had done so. Sally woke at three, ravenous, and sung Diana's praises as she sipped soup and listened to the afternoon play. It was riveting and she was held a happy captive by the incomparable voices of Judi Dench and Martin Jarvis. A short nap was broken by Diana calling in after school. Sitting on the edge of the bed, she chattered away while Sally tried to look fit and fine.

'First, how are you, my poppet blossom? Did you eat? Sleep? Good girl. Next, I come with strict instructions from the powers that be: no school for Sally – you're to take the rest of the week off. Hush it! I won't hear any of it, girl. You clonked your head and knocked yourself clean out, remember? Do you know how many brain cells you destroyed? Can you really *afford* not to replenish them, ho ho? You have to be one hundred per cent, Lomax. Doctor's note 'n' all. Understand?'

Sally felt tired and groggy and, though she did not want to admit it, Diana was exhausting her. A strange transformation had occurred in the face of crisis; daffy scattiness had been replaced by an unwonted bossiness – a conversion enhanced by a crisp white shirt (spattered though it was with red paint) and a pair of well-pressed trousers. Sally thought it best to remain a malleable patient. Diana thought it wise not to mention Richard. Sally did not dare. She was quietly relieved when Diana bade her farewell with kisses to the cheek and strict instructions not to move from her bed until the next morning.

She lay in stillness and in silence for a little while and, when she was quite sure all was safe, clambered out of bed for a shaky walk around. She settled in the sitting-room, curled cosily in her old Lloyd-Loom with the thirty handmade cards on her lap. Most of the children had chosen to draw a down-mouthed Miss Lomax in hospital, swathed in bandages like a mummy. Rajiv, however, had created a comic strip featuring Miss Lomax as a lump lying in the lower left corner of each frame while another figure (Rajiv, who else?) saved the day with sword, with shield, with astonishing ambulance-driving skills and with superhero powers too.

Marcus's card brought tears to her eyes.

He's my real superhero.

With glitter, crêpe paper and lusciously thick paint, Marcus had made her the most exquisite bunch of flowers, the blooms themselves filling the entire page. The intensity of the colour and the overall richness of the surface seemed to symbolize Marcus's devotion and twanged the strings of Sally's heart. Inside he had written:

> *Dear Miss Lomax, you're the best*
> *Please get better, have a good rest!*
> *We hope your head doesn't hurt or ache*
> *Come back to school soon, for Goodness Sake!*
> *I'm sure you'll soon be as right as rain*
> *So you can be our fave teacher again!*
>
> *Marcus (x)*

Sally kissed the card back and decided she would keep it for ever. She remembered Marcus on the last day in Paris, looking after her with Ribena and apricot-flavoured chewing gum; she could see him again racing back across the playground to tell her she was the best. Had he somehow known? Had he had caught drift of her sorry soul? How discreet he had been.

Children are the most intuitive of creatures. He'll go far, Sally thought. *Somewhere out there is a very lucky ten-year-old girl! I'll be an old bag when they're ready to court. There'll just be me and my bloody memories. Just me, rocking away in the Lloyd-Loom, wizened and grey, reliving my antics over and over. Might I cringe? Might I shudder if J-C pops into mind? And Richard . . . how will I feel? Remorse? Guilt? Joy?*

Dread swept over Sally and engulfed her.

But I don't want him to be just a memory.

She sat, silent and horrified. Turning to the hat stand, she furrowed her brow and declared in a small voice: 'I don't want merely to *remember* him; I want him to be there. I want to reminisce *with* him. Gracious Good Lord, what does that imply?'

She cocked her head and contemplated the carriage clock on the mantelpiece. She had found it in a jumble sale at the Students' Union in Bristol and, despite her dwindling grant and the fact that the clock was irreparably broken, had bought it all the same. A walnut case enclosed a very pretty face with beautifully scrolled numbers, the filigree arms outstretched at ten to three for ever more. There was something vaguely comforting about it; the caught moment, time standing still, no tick-tocking the days away. There was a sense of stability about a timeless clock; the years might pass and a whole host of events befall but it would always be ten to three between Sally and the clock.

She fell asleep, waking in the small hours of the new day – perhaps it was indeed ten to three – and was distressed to see she had crushed Marcus's card. She felt hot and bothered and realized she was wringing wet; the back of her neck was clammy and her hair stuck to it in rat's tails, her forehead bristled with sweat, her eyes felt puffy and hot. Feeling very unstable, she made a slow passage to bed aided along the way by furniture, door frames and determination. She was freezing by the time she made it there but had neither the wits nor the energy to fetch a jumper. Shivering, she cocooned herself as best she could and was compliant when dreamless sleep fetched her away.

The next morning, Sally saw spots before her eyes.

There was a large one slap bang in the middle of her forehead and, on further exploration, two on her chest and one on her right wrist. She stood stock still in front of the mirror and wondered what on earth to do. She noticed that her whole body was tingling; she was hot, feverish and bemused. Resigned to the fact that something was most certainly amiss, she called for the doctor.

The cold stethoscope felt blissful against her raging skin and the doctor's umming and poke-out-your-tongue-please comforted her. Two more spots had sprung up on the top of her left thigh and a rather large one was forming below her ribs before their very eyes. Dutifully, she told him about the fainting, and he did not seem in the least surprised.

'Well, Miss Lomax,' he announced after he had taken her blood pressure, explored her ears and beamed light into her eyes, 'it's not the Lurgy, it's chicken pox!' Sally was stunned.

Chicken pox! It can't possibly be, I'm a grown up! I don't know anyone with chicken pox! Do you mean to say it's not the Richard Thing that's making me poorly? That I am no damsel in distress? Just plain old chicken pox? Damn!

A very quiet part of her felt disappointed. A greater part of her felt embarrassed and irritated. The greatest part of her was just plain hot and tingly.

'What does that mean?' she asked at length.

'Well,' came the bedside manner reply, 'expect the spots to continue for another day or so. And then be

224

prepared for the itching. DO NOT SCRATCH or YOU WILL SCAR. Calamine should soothe but DO NOT SCRATCH or YOU WILL SCAR. What do you do?'

'Do not scratch or I will scar,' Sally said miserably.

'No, no,' tutted the doctor. 'What do you *do*, for a living?'

'I'm a teacher,' Sally replied, somewhat indignantly.

'That probably explains how you caught it. You are highly contagious,' he warned. 'Bed rest for at least three days,' he ordered, 'and no school for at least two weeks.'

'Two *weeks*?' Sally exclaimed.

'You are highly con-ta-gious,' he reiterated. 'You don't want to inflict this on your pupils, now do you?'

Sally felt thoroughly ostracized. Snapping shut his Gladstone, the doctor smiled at her, propped up by pillows and pouting.

'The spots'll go in a couple of weeks and should have faded by the end of the month,' he assured her. 'That is, if you don't scratch. You will scar otherwise,' he concluded sternly. Laying a caring-profession hand on her shoulder, he said, 'Don't worry yourself. Get some rest. I'll see myself out. Cheerio!'

Just like on the bloody television, Sally later thought, feeling utterly sorry for herself.

'Sally? Sally! Open the door. Are you all right? Heavens, girl, where are you?' Diana rang the bell again and snapped the letter box open and shut, open and shut.

'I'm coming,' came a muffled reply.

Sally opened the front door a fraction of an inch and saw Diana standing there, all but obscured by a large brown bag of groceries.

'I thought I'd made spag bol!' she announced triumphantly, brandishing a packet of spaghetti and poking herself in the eye in the process.

'You can't!' cried Sally through the crack.

''Course I can! It'll have to be veggie of course – I've bought that dried soya stuff. Open up, old thing!'

'No, you *can't*,' stressed Sally. Diana was flummoxed and pulled an appropriate expression.

'I've got bloody chicken pox,' wailed Sally, 'I'm in isolation. In quarantine. I'm VERY CON-TA-GIOUS. I can't come out for two weeks.'

After a moment's silence, Diana laughed and laughed and kept asking: 'Really?' Sally was bemused.

'Let me see! Let me see!' hooted Diana so Sally poked out her pocked wrist. 'Heavens above! It's true.' Nurse Lewis vanished at once and Diana stood there, quite horrified and starting to itch. 'Poor duck – I'm off! Look, I'll leave this bag right here on the doorstep. You watch through the spy-hole and when you're quite sure that I am a safe distance away, you can open the door and retrieve them. DON'T SCRATCH or YOU WILL HAVE FRIGHTFUL SCARS!' With that, Diana ceremoniously dumped the groceries and made off. Sally, who did not have the energy to point out that Diana would have caught it by now, waited before opening the door to take in the bag. Suddenly Diana reappeared from behind the hedge, waving and jumping up and down.

'Let's see some more!' she squealed.

Smiling now, Sally took a surreptitious look around and then lifted up her pyjama top, the cold air providing instant relief and giving Diana a good eyeful.

'Blimey! You're *covered*! I'm out of here! I'll give you a ring as soon as I'm home – you can't catch it down the phone, can you?'

When Diana phoned her an hour later, Sally did not want to talk. She had discovered a spot inside her mouth and could feel that they were in her throat too. Silent and unfed, she shuffled to bed hoping it was all an unfortunate dream.

THIRTY

'Oh, hi, Bob, hi.' Finding it impossible to hide the disappointment in his voice, Richard decided not to beat about the bush. 'Sorry, mate, not a good time. I need to keep the line free – I'm waiting for a call. About Sally. She's been in hospital. Concussed.'

Inevitably, Bob's concern (and by now Catherine was glued to the other phone too) impeded Richard's speedy getaway so he divulged all and said, 'Yes, flowers would be nice.' He was desperate to go for a run but incapacitated by the lack of news. He had rung Diana twice but there had been no answer. He was dying to ring Sally but knew he should not. The phone rang.

Pleasepleaseplease.

'Diana. Thank God. Talk to me!' Richard gasped. 'She's got *what*?' His hand shot up to his brow. 'Chicken pox?' It dropped down to his hips. '*Chicken* pox! Good Lord!' He threw his hand up to the heavens. 'Does that account for the fainting? Chicken pox. Is she covered? Is she in pain? Discomfort? Poor lamb. Has she any calamine? What can I take her?' He was out of breath. 'What!' he exclaimed. 'Two *weeks*?' he cried. 'Can I phone her? Can't catch it down the phone. What?' he whispered. 'In her *mouth*? Her *throat*? Poor darling girl.'

Richard felt hoarse and strangely excited. He ran very fast over to the Woods's and panted out Sally's ailment.

'Two weeks,' gasped a horrified Catherine. 'Whatever'll she do?'

Sally wondered the same thing on waking the next day. With trepidation, she went to greet herself in the mirror. She was rooted to the spot (sorry, Sally, bad pun) and could not manage even a groan of displeasure. Wriggling out of her pyjamas, she stood and stared. Poor Sal.

There are too many to count. They are everywhere. They are even on my scalp and in my ears. My trunk is the worst, they are so blotchy and puffed up there. They are neat and small on my arms, larger on my legs, and I can't even see my face for them. I look sort of roasted. I look awful. Christ, they're even between my toes. And on my buttocks. And – Gracious Good Lord – not there too?

She still felt feverish and could bear no more clothing next to her skin than a pure cotton vest, knickers and Aunt Celia's hand-knitted cashmere shawl. She teetered around the flat chanting 'Feed a cold and starve a fever' but thought perhaps it was 'Starve a cold and feed a fever' and was at once in a dither, convinced that if she put into practice the wrong permutation, the spots would surely wreak vengeance. What was she to do? The solution lay in the cashmere shawl.

'Hello?'

'Aunty Celia? Guess who!'

'Sally? Gracious, what a treat, how are you, my wee one? Everything okey-dokey?'

'Yes, yes. No, actually. I have *chicken* pox.'

'Poor bairn. You must be feeling rotten. Have you a fever?'

'Yes.'

'Starve it!'

It seemed trite to delineate the coincidence so Sally received the advice graciously and said, yes, she was strong enough for a little chat.

'I'm wearing your lovely shawl.'

'Ach, it must be threadbare! I made it moons ago, for your sixteenth birthday, no? I shall start a new one for you, if you like. It will be finished by May the nineteenth. How old this year? Twenty-four, is it?'

'Sorry, Aunty, twenty-six actually.'

'Eeh, tish! You're a well and truly grown-up lassie. Maybe another shawl won't suit your fashion taste?'

'I'd love another shawl, but this one's just fine.'

'A woman can never have too many hand-knitted shawls, she should have one draped on the back of every chair in her house!' Celia declared with aplomb. 'I have some lovely yarn, there was a craft fair at the Town Hall in Tobermory. It's a linen-silk mix, so soft. A lovely sort of mauve. Does that sound nice? Does that tickle your fancy?'

'Yes, Aunt Celia, I think I should love it. I love mauve,' Sally lied kindly.

They bade each other farewell with a promise to lessen the gap between calls. Feeling hungry but keen to starve her fever, Sally took a nap instead. She dreamt that Celia came to see her in her lunch-break at school. She had bustled into the staff-room and called over to her, 'Sal, my lassie,' for Aunt Celia was the only other person from whom Sally welcomed the abbreviation. She had brought the shawl, it was vast and very mauve. She wrapped it around Sally's shoulders and then went to teach Class Five rounders. Sally watched from the window, breathing in deeply (in the dream and out) the unmistakable aroma of an Aunt Celia hand-knit.

It is now tea-time. Reluctantly, Sally has gone to the mirror to check the spot situation. The pox has shown no

229

mercy and has rooted out the last patches of clear skin to inhabit; behind her left ear, above her right eyelid and under her armpits where they are particularly painful. Feeling ravenous, fed up and not so feverish, Sally has retrieved a bumper block of milk chocolate from the fridge, taken the phone off the hook, put a Genesis tape on low and clambered into bed armed with a clutch of old diaries and photo albums. She is soon lost in adventures of old; painted in retrospect with a tint of rose and a hint of sepia.

Where's the chocolate?

It is under your pillow.

Ah, Scotland. Mull. Heather and dampness, the light, the water, the clarity. Tobermory: those pretty, brave little harbour-side houses, candy colours yet not at all twee. Look, you and Aunt Celia throwing the frisbee on the sweep of soft sand at Calgary Bay. Whose is that shadow, who is taking the picture? Must be Uncle Angus, the late Uncle Angus, gruff with whisky but always on for a reel.

Does she miss Angus, whom one only ever heard her call 'LoveLove'? It was so lovely to speak to her today. It's been so long. It must be a good two years since I last saw her.

Sally feels like having a day-dream, she wants to transport herself to Mull. Trying hard to look at nothing in particular, she finds her eyes continually stray to her mottled limbs. Mull remains far away. Take another album, Sally, another piece of chocolate. Let Phil Collins's night-time voice be a certain calamine.

Oh, look! Sally aged nine and in a tutu. And here! Sally aged thirteen, in a tutu and on points. And here is Sally aged sixteen, tutu, pointes and taking a graceful curtsey. Look at the make-up, the impeccable bun, those sinewy arms! Remember how elated you felt? Do you really miss the bleeding toes, the straining tendons, the pulled muscles, the damaged joints?

No, but I miss the poise and energy.

Don't dwell, Sal. Turn the page. Giggle at your brown and beige childhood wardrobe from the seventies, cringe at the ra-ra skirts and stretch jeans you wore with pride during your teenage years. Lose yourself again in University days. Here, a batch of photographs of friends and cohorts at Bristol: living it up at faculty balls, looking tired but cool in shabby student houses, looking dapper in mortar-boards and fur-trimmed gowns at graduation.

Where's my diary? Where's the corresponding text? Oh, this is fun! I'm right back there – chicken pox? What chicken pox! The present is unpleasant, the future is a burden, but the past is safe so back I go!

Oh, yes! Remember that first week at University? How timid I was! Every one seemed so worldly and bright, they all seemed to play so hard and work so hard too! Look here!

15 October: I bet I don't make any friends. I went to the Freshers' Fair and joined nearly all the clubs, even the Winnie the Pooh Club, whatever that might be. No one seems quite my type but I'm willing to talk to anyone really, at this stage. We were given our timetable. Not very full, really, lots of free time in which we are to read, because we are 'reading' for our degrees, as Professor Wratchett said, rolling his 'r's. I've got three years ahead of me and Bristol seems pleasant enough. Haven't spied any talent yet but I'm not looking for love of course. The Rambling Society are going on a weekend to North Devon, I wonder if I should go? I'm a paid-up member after all.

You did go, remember? And twisted your ankle but were too embarrassed to mention it so you grimaced your way through the rambles and tried to blot it out with a good sup of ale, which tasted foul but was the thing to do in the evenings.

231

Flipping in and out of the years, Sally dips in and out of the events in her life, as if she is chattering with someone she knows well and has not seen for years. She reminisces about drunken weekends in Devon, she rereads about hectic holidays on Greek islands, she remembers flatmates she would rather forget, she ponders on the whereabouts of friends not seen for years. The memories are fond and fun. Fun until one word assaults her eyes: Jamie.

Shuddering involuntarily, Sally has snapped shut the book and sits very still, eating chocolate distractedly. Come, come, Sally, the past is safe, the past has passed. Open the book, face the pages, face the past. Read out loud if it helps. A small voice filters through the room, reading flatly from pages written three years previously.

' "I have to get out of this relationship, if you can call it that. Jamie frightens me but what frightens me more is my inability to say: 'Stop. Go away.' He hit me again and I apologized. *I* actually apologized. Why on earth did I do that? He accepted my apology – ungraciously of course – and sulked all evening. Predictably, we had sex later. Or at least he did. I didn't want to but I didn't dare say so. And my arm hurt throughout; it's still bruised today. When he climaxes he's like an animal, really base and vulgar. I can't wait to get to the loo; we use condoms but I have to pee him away.

' "He broke my little teapot, the one James bought for me before my finals. I said to him, 'Be careful.' He said, 'Why?' I said, 'Because it's precious to me.' He said, 'Why?' I told him and he slowly lifted it above his head and let it topple. It fell at my feet. The spout scuttled across the floor, a chip of china from the lid fell through the side of my shoe. I felt sure I was about to cry but I bit it back. Jamie laughed at me. I hated him for it. I hate him. Then he went all soft and said that it shouldn't mean anything to me now, I am with him now. I wish I wasn't. How do I get out of it? Where's my strength?" '

I got out of it when he broke my nose. I covered him with blood. I was unconscious and woke and was sick and he thought I was seriously damaged so he called an ambulance and told them I'd fallen down the stairs even though I was living in a ground-floor flat.

It was that lovely nurse . . . what was her name?

'Sister Watts. I'll never forget.

She sat on your bed. He had visited with flowers and charm: there had not been a peep from you.

Sister Watts sat with me and just said, 'You owe him nothing. You don't have to stay. You're far too precious. You owe it to yourself. Leave him.'

So you left! Brave girl!'

I severed all contact. I moved to Highgate. I have no idea where he is. It's been a good three years. I don't live in fear. It's as if it happened to someone else. I rarely think of him.

Time has softened his blows, healed the wounds and faded the scars.

They are still there, you know.

We know.

I want Richard

Call him.

'Richie?'

'My dotty spotty angel! My darling dalmatian! How *are* you?'

'Don't ask. I'm very contagious. I can't go to school for two weeks. Oh, and I fainted too and wound up in hospital. But I think you know that.'

'Do you have any calamine?'

'No. But I'm not itchy.'

'Yet – that is. You will be. And you MUSTN'T SCRATCH.'

'I know, I know, or I WILL SCAR.'

'What say you that I pop to an all-night chemist and buy you some calamine?'

233

'But I'm CON-TA-GIOUS.'

'You are certainly that! I caught the Sally bug long ago and I just can't shake it off.'

The definitive pregnant pause filled the room and broke the flow.

'Sal?' Richard enquired quietly.

'I'm sorry I called,' she faltered. 'I shouldn't've – called, that is. I . . . er. You see, I haven't really thought about, you know, *It*,' she mumbled.

'Hush! Of course you haven't,' Richard chided gently. 'You've hardly been *compos mentis*! Listen to me, Sal, I'm offering calamine. No strings attached – promise. I'll just slip it through the letter box. You can even pay me, if it makes you feel easier.'

Half an hour later Sally hovers by the letter box. She is starting to itch. Itchy feet, itchy everything. She hears the purr of the Alfa Romeo, Richard's assertive footsteps. Should she hide, open the door, peep through the curtain – what? The adrenalin is churning and her heart is heavy. She watches as the lid of the letter box flips up. She can hear Richard clearing his throat.

'Richie?' she whispers quickly. Crouching down, they can look eye to eye. They are shadows and the encounter has a dreamlike quality. They are latter-day Pyramus and Thisbe and the letter box serves as the chink in the wall. However, this is no midwinter night's dream, this is the here and now. Sally has chicken pox and Richard is sitting on his heels outside her front door, trying to keep his balance.

'You don't look too bad at all!' His voice is as lovely as the cool night air whispering through to her. 'Not too bad at all.'

So Sally puts the light on and crouches down again. Richard now has spots before his eyes. Desperate to think of something diplomatic to say, he decides on, 'Oh.'

Sally hastily switches the light off, buttons her spots

away and slips back into the safe shadows. A bulky paper bag is jostled through the letter box. Richard's knees ache like mad, cramp threatens in his calves but he daren't tell her. Spots and all, he just wants to be near for as long as he can.

'Thank you,' she whispers.

'Don't worry about anything, Sal. Just get yourself better.'

In the ease of his voice, the kindness of his words, she can see his smile and it fills her head with a delicious lightness.

'Thank you,' she says again.

There is silence among the shadows. Neither he nor she wants to go, yet they do not know how best to stay. Richard pokes his index finger through the letter box as far as he can, grazing his knuckles though he neither feels it nor cares. Tentatively, Sally meets his finger with the very tip of one of hers.

For a sweet but all too short moment, they touch.

THIRTY-ONE

*T*he itching set in and took hold with such force as to render Sally utterly at its mercy. She had never known anything like it. It was infuriating, it was excruciating, it frequently took her to the verge of tears. It was unbearable. In her exasperation, expletives spewed forth and she spat with venom words she had spent her adult life trying to avoid. Calamine soothed but only in the cool cloud of the initial application. Once dry, and it dried all too quickly, its flakiness merely added to the overall itchiness. Sally's bed-linen and clothes were peppered with salmon pink blotches, and great clods of the dried lotion were welded to her hair. During the day, only enormous self-discipline and sheer determination, coupled with viciously clenched teeth and unbridled execration, prevented her scratching for England. Night, however, was different; even going to bed wearing mittens was little guard against the dreaded sleep-scratching. Though she detested the itching and hated the spots, she loathed herself more for having scratched – albeit in her sleep. Her chest and arms suffered the most, the tops of the pocks scratched off and a stinging pus released which dried a hundred times more itchy.

I'm going to scar, I'm going to scar, Sally thought wearily. Short of tying her hands behind her back on going to bed, there seemed to be no solution.

Sally was in a foul mood. Well-wishers would phone throughout the day to say *there, there* and to warn DON'T SCRATCH or YOU WILL SCAR. Lacking the humour to accept such advice graciously, she decided to leave the phone off the hook. Even a batch of another thirty cards from Class Five failed to lift her spirits. The children had found prodigious artistic outlet in Miss Lomax's predicament and by the end of the week, red crayons were a rare commodity in the art room. The figure of Miss Lomax was treated to a liberal and energetic dousing of red dots. The noise of thirty crayons rapping down to create them caused Mr Bernard, who was trying to teach Maths next door, to pull Miss Lewis to one side, begging her to change to collage instead. Ultimately, the cards were of little comfort; even Marcus's card, with another classic rhyme and signed *Marcus (xx)*, could not coax a smile from Miss Lomax.

Poor Miss Lomax is not well
Itchy spots are making life hell.
Get well soon, for our fave teacher you are –
But DO NOT SCRATCH or YOU WILL SCAR.

By the end of the week, the itching had abated but those spots Sally had unwittingly scratched were sore and scabby. Her mood was made even more foul after a phone call to Mr Tomlin. Sally used her brightest voice and breezed on about feeling 'one hundred per cent' even if she did not look it. She begged, she pleaded, she even flirted to be allowed to return on Monday morning. Mr Tomlin, however, who liked to do things by the book – as is the wont of a headmaster – would hear none of it.

'I believe the doctor suggested two weeks?'

'Well . . .' started Sally.

'Well then!' he declared in his most headmasterful voice. 'And, Miss Lomax,' he warned, 'considering that the chicken pox did not take hold first thing on Monday morning, we won't be counting this as a full week. We shall look forward to seeing you bright and early a fortnight on Monday – not a moment before.'

'But that'll be nigh on three weeks!' Sally squealed.

With his most qualified stern-but-fair voice, Mr Tomlin delivered his *coup de grâce:* 'Miss Lomax,' he said, 'I've had calls from anxious parents. *Anxious parents,*' he reiterated gravely. 'We simply cannot afford to have you back a minute too soon. I know you understand. Bright and early, a fortnight on Monday. Take care.'

In the face of such autocracy, Sally was as helpless as any pupil. Fearing that further begging would result in a metaphorical Detention and arguing would warrant something far worse, she let it be and sulked all afternoon, occasionally sucking in her pouting lower lip to swear at nothing in particular. There was no more 'Gracious Good Lord' in Sally's pock-marked vocabulary; her atypical effing and blinding now rhymed Him with banker.

For perhaps the first time in her life, Sally felt thoroughly anti-social and was quite content to do nothing about it. She did not even feel like chatting to her plants, the kettle or to anything in particular – let alone to Diana or Richard who were both keeping a wise and generous distance. Sally found comfort and relief only in chocolate and soap operas (preferably those of Antipodean origin, made in the mid-seventies and screened in the early afternoon). She had neither the manners nor the goodwill to respond even to the Woodses' sumptuous flower arrangement.

Yet this is the girl who took such pride in her little cards of effusive thanks for even the humblest cup of tea; this is the girl for whom *Ps* and *Qs* had hitherto been the prerequisite for honourable living. This is the girl with manners and grace constituting the very essence of her being. But see her now, stomping and slouching and swearing indiscriminately. Look in the waste-paper basket and find a batch of 'get well soon' cards barely out of their envelopes tossed nonchalantly away. See how the Woodses' bouquet could do with some water. Sally is feeling sorry for herself – and why shouldn't she? She is wallowing in a formidable sulk, seething at the cruel irony that the doctor has said she is probably contagious no longer. Even the mirror holds little solace, reflecting back a glowering, bespotted creature with a clump of spiky hair above her left temple.

There must be a solution. Someone must hold the key to unlock Sally from this unbecoming petulance. Indeed there *is* a key. It is nearly five hundred miles north and it is lying invisible in the lap of the treasured Aunt Celia.

As Sally flounces down into her Lloyd-Loom with a mug of cocoa and a sullen sigh, Aunt Celia has just come in from her small garden, ruddy-cheeked and eyes glistening. It is a glorious day on the Isle of Mull; crisp, clear and sunny with a fortifying breeze. If truth be known, it is also a lovely day in Highgate – but sulky Sal remains defiantly unconcerned.

THIRTY-TWO

*A*rranging a fat bunch of daffodils from her lush crop in an old earthenware jug, Celia thinks of Sally. Admiring their sunny, joyous faces, she decides if Sally were to be a flower, she would most certainly be a daffodil.

And if I were to be a flower, I would be heather. Tough, not much to look at, but clinging on, year after year after year!

Celia Lomax, sister-in-law to Sally's late father, is now seventy but looks a good decade younger, a blessing she accredits to Mull's vitalizing air. She loves her western isle passionately. It has been her home for almost fifty years and every day she is thankful that she has the good fortune to live in such a wonderful place. The first twenty years of her life were spent, anaemic and entrenched, in Glasgow. Now every morning Celia still races to her doorstep to take greedy gulps of the clean, incomparable air, and she sleeps with the window open throughout the year.

Mull cannot cease to enthrall her. She finds she still stops in her tracks to listen and look about her in awe. She never tires of the sounds of the island – it might be an uncomfortable silence to a city-dweller, but for Celia there is a veritable din and her head is filled and thankful for it. Beneath it all, she tunes into the eternal sound of the ocean. Whistling in from the sea, she can listen to the dance of the thin wind slipping its way between the hills and shaking the Scots pine with regular rattles. Under the wind, she can pick out the shimmy of the heather and the rustle of the bracken; above it, the plaintive mew of buzzards, the caw-cawing of hooded crows, the calling of the gulls. Every day, for half a century, Celia Lomax has taken grateful stock of all that is on her doorstep. She can look about her panoramically, for no tenement buildings and no grimy haze deny her a horizon. There is so much sky for the gazing! Under it, the majestic hills are swathed in hues of blue and brown from the tracts of heather and cloaks of bracken. The single-track road winds out of sight, linking the humble white cottages that pepper its way. Pattern and colour, shape and light – the beauty of Mull is a revelation to Celia each day of her life.

Angus Lomax had brought his young Glaswegian wife to Mull soon after their honeymoon in the Cairngorms. Having worked for ten years as doctor in his childhood town of Oban, he leapt at the chance to take over the General Practice for North Mull. He had never wondered or worried whether his city-bred wife would adapt and be happy out on the isle. From the moment he met her, he knew at once that her eyes were those of Mull; they were the colour of heather and as glassy, private and deep as Loch na Keal. His intuition was proved right and Celia adapted to rural life with passion and with pleasure.

While Angus busied himself with the practice and the patients, Celia made home. She limewashed the exterior of the old cottage and painted the interior. She treated the wood, she cleared the chimney, she smoothed down and buffed up the old stone floors. She made curtains for the deep windows and cushions for every chair; the kitchen she filled with local pottery. Handmade shawls adorned the furniture and a painstakingly pieced quilt bedecked their great iron bed.

If her house was her castle, her small garden was her kingdom. She furrowed and she dug and she turned the land. The native peat was a godsend, the Gulf Stream a blessing. Tomatoes, marrow, potatoes, cabbage, beans, thyme, rosemary, alpine strawberries and fat blackberries – they all grew sweet and plentiful. Bulbs and shrubs vied for space amongst the liberally strewn wild flowers, and small alpines grew bravely in the picturesque rockery. Through every season, Celia's garden sang with colour.

At the moment, it is carpeted in yellow and blue as daffodils and crocuses run amok. The daffodils have called Sally, her favourite niece, to mind. A treasured rapport exists between them. Their bond is certainly stronger than that enforced between Sally and her mother and, secretly, they both glean a somewhat perverse satisfaction from it.

Mildred Lomax never liked Celia. ('Your strange aunt up North.') Mildred Lomax was not in tune with the sky, the wind or the sea; she found little to wax lyrical about in heather, and growing your own vegetables seemed a downright tedious pastime. ('Rather unnecessary and *affected* in this day and age, don't you think?') Mildred Lomax was a Home Counties, Women's Institute, Bridge Club and afternoon tea sort of woman. Her 1930s semi had been delectably interior designed and she had a cleaner ('my daily') to administer its upkeep. A gardener tended a very neat garden where the lawn did not look real and hybrid roses were pruned to perfection. She had never had the inclination to bake bread nor to lift a needle and thread – after all, there was a most useful little lady down the road for all of that.

What really set Mildred against Celia was her late husband's fondness for the woman and her daughter's devotion to her. Family holidays on Mull, an annual occurrence until Sally was fifteen and her father dead, had been the bane of Mildred's life. She found Mull a forsaken and bleak place, invariably swamped by mist and midges. She did not like trudging across hillocky heather wearing wellington boots, and found all that sea air rather tiring. There was nothing for her to *do* on Mull, and Mildred Lomax was not very good at doing nothing. Of course, there were walks to go on, wild flowers to seek out and wildlife to watch, but such pursuits left her cold in every sense of the word.

Her disaffection for Mull, however, stretched far beyond its terrain and was deeper seated than a mere antipathy towards outdoor pursuits. It was seeing her husband so relaxed and rustic, her daughter so free and so *muddy*, that struck a dissonant chord within. It shamed her that their unbridled laughter, an integral and unforced part of such holidays, never rang out in Lincoln. Celia irritated her; she was so wholesome with her naturally tanned, attractively weathered skin, her lithe frame, her meals (*delicious, damn them*) thrown together effortlessly from fat, flavoursome, homegrown ingredients. Celia was unswervingly generous and accommodating towards Mildred; which of course made matters far worse. There really was nothing to dislike about Celia, yet Mildred's thoughts were wholly uncharitable. She did not envy Celia her life-style nor her skills, but she bitterly envied the adoration and respect she commanded from all who knew her.

As Sally finishes her cocoa and sighs again, Celia settles down with a nice cup of tea. Mildred meanwhile has just come in from arranging the flowers at the church. Sally's ears are burning but she puts it down to a vagary of her affliction; after all, she is not to know that both aunt and mother are dialling her number simultaneously. Anyway, the phone is still off the hook. Sally regards the telephone and replaces the handset with a despondent clatter. Almost immediately, it rings and Sally finds she is pleased.

'Hullo?' she croaks in her finest 'I'm-so-poorly' voice.

'Hullo, my poppet,' soothes the familiar lilting accent. Celia has pipped Mildred to the post. Mildred has just slammed the receiver down on finding Sally's number still engaged. ('*On her death-bed, I don't think!*')

Sally is delighted that it is Aunt Celia and she talks at length about the state of each spot. Forty years married to a General Practioner has left Celia a legacy of surprisingly detailed medical knowledge.

'You'll not be contagious any more, you know.'

'Well, that's the daft thing, Aunt C. I've been literally quarantined,' Sally proclaims. 'Banished,' she declares, 'from school. I'm not allowed back until a fortnight on Monday!'

'Tush tush!' sympathizes Aunt Celia.

'I'm beside myself with boredom and ashamed of it. I feel so cooped up! I daren't go out because I look such a freak and if people stare and point, I'm sure to feel like one too!'

'What you need is to convalesce,' says Aunt Celia.

'I know, I know,' sighs a dejected Sally.

'You need rest,' her wise aunt stresses. 'You need rest, fresh air and good food.'

Sally agrees with her.

'Well!' exclaims Aunt Celia. 'When shall I expect you?'

Sally is stunned. The penny drops and a smile creeps across her face. She is at once galvanized and speechless; better already, to be sure.

'You *mean* it?' Sally squeals. 'Are you *sure*? Are you sure you've *had* chicken pox, that I'm not con-*ta*-gious? Can I really come up and stay? It won't be too much trouble for you?'

'My wee bairn,' laughs Aunt Celia, 'it's what the doctor ordered!' she declares, winking at a photograph of Angus.

*

'Darling?'

'Oh, hello, Mother.'

'I've been trying you for ages. You've been perpetually engaged. Per-*pet*-ually.'

'Sorry. The phone's been off the hook. I needed to rest.'

'Well, darling, I've been speaking to Dr Peabody. He doubts very much whether you are still con-ta-gious. I thought it would be a good idea for you to recuperate here; you know, let me look after you. Nothing that a bit of TLC and your old bedroom can't cure!'

'Oh, Mum! That's very kind – truly. And I'm not contagious any more. And I do need to recuperate . . .'

'Well then!'

'. . . so I'm going up to Mull. To stay with Aunt Celia. All that lovely air. I'm leaving tomorrow.'

'But it's *Feb*ruary! You'll catch your *death*! I'm not sure that your strange aunt up North has the *nous* to nurse you back to health. Darling, reconsider!'

'Mother,' Sally took her time, 'firstly, Aunt Celia is *not* strange. Secondly, I'll wrap up warm. Thirdly, I can't think of anywhere else where convalescence is a foregone conclusion. And fourthly,' she faltered, 'fourthly, I can't think of any place I'd rather be. I can't *wait* to go.'

My heart is in the Highlands, my heart is not here.

THIRTY-THREE

Whatever possessed Sally Lomax to pack her bag and take the high road to Scotland without telling a soul?

As the M1 unfurled ahead of her, she felt no pang of guilt, not even the slightest twinge. She was too busy singing 'Bridge Over Troubled Water', the choice of that week's castaway on Radio 4's *Desert Island Discs*. As she neared Milton Keynes, Sally was revising her eight discs for the second time but just could not choose less than nine. By the time she joined the M6, she decided that, along with Shakespeare and the Bible, her book would be a Robert Burns anthology and, as she passed Birmingham, she chose ballet shoes as her luxury. As Lancashire slipped into Cumbria, Sally decided she would have rather a good time on her desert island, dancing away to Beethoven, Stravinsky and Genesis, and would not feel a 'wee sleekit, cowrin, tim'rous beastie' in the slightest. Switching the radio off, she motored at a steady seventy and smiled at the hills as they loomed. It was a fine day, the sky seemed very high and the early-spring sun hung large and low, like a luminous pink sweet; Sally could have licked it. She felt an exhilaration she had not felt for a long while, an intoxicating mix of solitude and freedom. Glasgow lay three hours away, Oban an hour or so after that, then there was just the Firth of Lorn to cross to Aunt Celia. She was at last taking a journey whose destination was known and desired. She could not wait to arrive.

Diana was livid, Richard was not amused, Catherine was nonplussed.

'Richard?'

'Hullo, Diana.'

'I think something's wrong.'

'Whajoomean?'

'Have you spoken to Sally?'

'Well, er, no. I'm er, letting her call the tune – you know, at her own pace. I took some calamine round a few days ago but I haven't heard from her since. What is it, for heaven's sake?'

'I think she's gone. I've been ringing her, on and off, for the last two days – nothing. So I popped round half an hour ago and looked through the letter box.'

Our letter box, thought Richard. 'And?' he enquired.

'Well, it was all eerily silent. I couldn't really see anthing at all because the curtains are drawn. Thing is, I have her spare keys but I'm a bit nervy about going in by myself.'

'I'll be right there.'

With a quick call to Catherine and Bob to say he'd be late for dinner, Richard drove to Diana's with a strangely empty head. Parking at the end of Sally's street, they walked slowly to her flat, noting as they walked that her Mini was nowhere to be seen. Diana unlocked the door and Richard went in first and rushed back the curtains. All was predictably spick and span and a faint smell of polish hung in the air. The bed was without linen, its mattress turned on to one side; there was nothing perishable in the fridge; all the plants were well-watered and the bathroom and kitchen smelled of bleach.

Well, these were the clues, but where was the proof? 'Bingo!' muttered Richard. Diana swung from the window where she had been looking at nothing in particular in the hope of infiltrating Sally's psyche. From Richard's fingers a small piece of paper dangled. She took it from him and read in a voice soon tinged with tears and threaded with anger: *'Gone to Scotland. Back soon. S.L.'*

Unable to speak, she looked at Richard but saw his face blank and stony. She tossed the note aside and Richard retrieved it, carefully placing it back on the mantelpiece where he had found it.

'S*cot*land?' Diana's exasperation, though barely audible, filled the room.

'That's what it says,' replied Richard flatly. There was a loaded silence as they wondered how best to react. Diana went for spontaneity.

'Stupid, ungrateful, insensitive cow!' she spat.

Richard chose silent contemplation.

Bitch, he thought. *Why? When? Stupid cow indeed.* There was silence again as each wondered what to say to the other.

'Diana,' Richard soothed at last, 'there must be an explanation. Maybe something cropped up.'

Diana was aghast.

'Cropped up? Like what? The only person she knows in Scotland is her old aunt who lives on Skye or Shetland or somewhere.'

'Mull,' mulled Richard.

'That's *not* the point,' Diana growled, 'she can go to Timbuk-bloody-tu for all I care.' The force of her anger quite took Richard aback. Her mood was as black as her jumper, her face the same furious red as her leggings. 'But the fact is I *do* care,' she yelled. 'Am I worth so little to her that she can just up and leave without a backward glance?' Without even the tiniest phone call? Without even a scribbled note posted with a second-class stamp?' Diana stood scowling with her hands clenched to her hips. She stamped her foot and grabbed her hair. 'Who does she think she is? She's needed me and I've been there – unswervingly,' she fulminated. 'Even a "piss off" to my face wouldn't be as hurtful as this couldn't-care-less disappearance.'

Fearing that Diana was on the verge of tears, Richard eased towards her and put his arm around her shoulders. She looked up at him, wide-eyed and wounded.

'But, Richard, what about you? How on earth can this make *you* feel? Can you bear it? Will you tolerate it?'

He shrugged in a non-committal way.

'It can't possibly *not* have crossed her tiny mind that we would worry, that we would be hurt,' Diana concluded. Richard remained silent and pensive – it seemed safer that way. The hurt he felt was so deep it was nauseating. How *could* she indeed? Why Scotland? Why the secrecy?

There was no need for it – it's not as if I would have been in the position to say 'Hold on, Sal, I'm coming too'. What can have filled her head? What did she think as she locked the door? As she hit the M1?

The horrible thing is, I'm almost certain she did not think at all, let alone twice. Thoughtless. Ungrateful. Tedious. This is the last straw, the short one, and Sally has just pulled it.

Not knowing what to do with his thoughts, much less how to express them, he gave Diana a squeeze and then ushered her out, taking a last look around before he closed the door on Sally's silence. Though the flat was clean and fresh, its cosiness had disappeared with her and he now felt an intruder, a stranger. Knowing that its inhabitant did not want him there – or anywhere – cut straight to his heart. He closed the door and double-locked it dejectedly. Driving Diana home, they said of course they would keep in touch, with or without the slightest news. Yet as they parted, it dawned on both with some displeasure that Sally, the very cause of their suffering, was holding them captive, that they were at her mercy, at her beck and call. Their worlds, at which she had seemingly stuck two fingers, were still revolving around her.

Was that it?

Did she want the world to turn because of her?

Sally? Manipulative?

Surely not!

Both Richard and Diana felt beholden, and the very realization was thoroughly repugnant. At last, they hated her for it and felt fine about it.

But ask Sally why she did it.

Did what?

Ask her what went through her head as she shut the door on all around her and headed carefree for Scotland.

This time tomorrow I'll be with Aunt Cee!

Do you believe her? Mention Richard and Diana to her. Why did she not call either? Ask her if it really did not occur to her that they would be hurt, worried, confused.

See. She cannot answer.

She may falter: *I'm a burden. They've done so much. I don't want to bother them, to trouble them.*

She may limp: *I've been so unbearable, spotty and sorry for myself, I just want to creep away and return restored.*

But you will not hear her say: *I'm sure they won't mind. I know they'll understand. I would too, you know.*

Nor will you hear: *I know it'll probably land me in trouble, but I've got to do it; there's something fun about it, jetting off in secret! I wonder what they'll think when they find me gone! Will they worry? Might they be angry? What'll go through their minds? Will they care?*

You will not hear this from Sally because she cannot

250

yet hear it herself. Banished to the back of her subconscious is the nub of the matter: *God, I shouldn't be doing this. I should at least call, leave a note. But I want to do it – just to see.*

We certainly will not hear Sally say it out aloud for a while longer. Not until she has played this, her last hand in the game. It is a game to her, and though no one else is playing, she does not seem to realize that just yet.

So, Sally must lose if she is to have a chance to win.

To Catherine, Sally was an open book. A mere glance at the pages was enough; she had read it before and it was all very familiar. She knew well the form, the semantics, the beginning and the middle. Did she know the end? She thought so. Should she divulge it?

What – and spoil it for everyone? Tell them the punchline before the joke?

Only this is not very amusing.

Read them the last line when they're but half-way through? Tell them what'll happen in the end? I have no right to do such a thing!

Catherine's dilemma was threefold. She was torn between her concern for and loyalty to Richard, her solidarity and understanding for Sally, and her soreness that she too had been rejected. However, she did feel equipped to shed light on the syndrome and believed it was her responsibility to all concerned to do so.

Bob had alleviated a portion of Richard's melancholy with a particularly frenzied game of squash. Catherine, who had spied a bumper but half-empty bottle of HP Sauce next to a jumble of takeaway cartons in Richard's kitchen, was now trying to reason the remainder away.

'Richie – er, sorry, Richard. Please believe me, please trust me – I know women.'

'Catherine, how pretentious,' Richard retorted. '*You know women*,' he mocked. 'What on earth does that mean?' Catherine took her time.

'What I mean is, I've *been* there' she declared with gentle confidence. 'You know the saying – seen it, done it, bought the T-shirt?' Richard grimaced at her. She took no offence and clarified, 'But Sally, I think, is right *in* there, She's *seeing* it, *doing* it, she's *wearing* the T-shirt. She's just got to throw it away.'

'I do *not* understand,' Richard said tersely, his voice brittle and pinched, 'what on *earth* you are talking about.'

'I know you don't,' eased Catherine, 'that's why *you're* hurting so much, while *I'm* merely nonplussd. I *know* what's happening to Sally, it happened to me too. I've done it before – most women have, or will. I *know* the book she's reading, I *know* the game she's playing.'

'That,' declared Richard, 'is precisely it. I am thirty-five years old. I have grown out of playing games.'

'Richard,' pleaded Catherine, 'if you can just hear me. It's not malicious, it's not vindictive. It's like she's testing the water before she leaps on in.'

Still his face was pale, his brow furrowed, his eyes hollow.

'Richard,' she cooed, 'Sally is doing this to reassure herself. You know: "will he love me if": "could he love me if".'

She could see she had made no inroad into Richard's melancholy, so she pulled out her trump card.

'Look, don't you remember how I was with Bob? How I'd sometimes flirt at parties? That I'd often be late? Sometimes I'd be aloof, sometimes downright moody? Remember when I jetted off to Corfu with two girlfriends giving Bob just a day's notice *and* expecting him to drive us to the airport to boot?'

A glimmer of a smile crept into Richard's face. 'You were a prime cow, Catherine. I remember saying to Bob, "bin her".'

'And?'

'I remember how he'd just shrug it off and smile. I couldn't work him out. I thought he'd gone soft.'

252

'See!'

'But *why*, Catherine? I don't feel soft at all. I feel livid, absolutely livid.'

Catherine could now wrap it up.

'Look,' she said kindly, taking Richard's hand, 'Sally is teetering on that diving board. *Teetering*! I bet every time she motions to leap something leers up at her: be it that awful bloke, the one who hit her; be it wedding dresses and *"I do"s*'; be it saying sorry to you, to Diana – to me! After all, what is it that she'll dive into?'

Catherine's question hung in the air as the light began to break for Richard. She answered methodically: 'She must forsake all for a responsible, grown-up, death-do-us-part existence.'

Richard nodded. 'Normality!' Catherine exclaimed. 'Mundanity!' she declared. 'Gone will be her little flat, her total privacy, talking to herself, eating a tub of ice-cream in bed – she'll have to trade all that in.' Richard's face was softening and he continued to nod.

'Richard, the girl's got to find herself by losing herself,' Catherine announced with conviction, 'and what better place than Scotland – all those lochs, all that heather! I'm not belittling the situation and you might not like what she might find. This is the make or break. Whatever the outcome, it will be for the better; for both of your futures. Sally may be playing a game of sorts, Richard. But the prize she's pursuing is Truth.'

THIRTY-FOUR

'*I*t's at times like this,' said Sally out loud, drumming her thumbs on the steering wheel, 'that I wish you were a Jaguar and not a Mini.'

Though she had completed well over half the journey, it was already afternoon and she knew she would miss the last ferry from Oban. Moreover, she wanted to enjoy the journey; she wanted to stand on the shores of Loch Lomond with bagpipes playing in her head and have a browse around Oban.

Having long thought the Lakes to be a mediocre imitation of the Highlands, Sally decided to turn right, and not left, off the motorway at Penrith, and chose a farm bed-and-breakfast near Lazonby Fell. The room was just as she hoped, with very little floor space due to a profusion of family heirlooms. The mahogany bed was high in itself but had been further banked up with feather mattresses. It reminded Sally of her favourite childhood tale, 'The Princess and the Pea', and she could hardly wait for bedtime. (Later, though she felt daft, she did check under the mattresses for an errant pea, and though she felt dafter, she was disappointed at finding none.) There was a Lloyd-Loom chair, very similar to her own, in which she sat and smiled. She admired a beautiful walnut chest of drawers and a very pretty dressing-table with filigree sconces for candles at the mirror. She creaked open the cavernous wardrobe which took up almost an entire wall and thought of C. S. Lewis; it was big enough for her to walk into so she did, but Narnia did not open up for her.

Not this time, not here.

Looking out, the Pennines rolled away, cut and crossed by dry-stone walls and thickets, and blessed by the late-afternoon sun. Venturing downstairs, Sally talked silently to the grandfather clock before pulling on her walking boots and greeting the fresh air – the first she'd had in days.

'Would you like to see the lambs?' She presumed him to be Mr Barker. ('I do Been Bee, he do farm, see,' Mrs Barker had trilled.)

'I've had chicken pox,' Sally offered by way of an explanation. Mr Baker sucked on his pipe, and cocked his head.

'The lambs'll not catch it!' he mused after awhile.

'No! I know!' stammered Sally. 'I just wanted you to know. I'm not con-ta-gious any more. But I know these spots are a fright.'

'To tell the truth, Missy, I thought it just a bad case of adilessent acme.'

Sally bit her tongue until the pain drove away any inkling of laughter.

'I'd love to see the lambs.'

Having had a very good night and a hearty breakfast of duck eggs and home-cured bacon, Sally said a last goodbye to the lambs and continued on her way. Carlisle was soon upon her and she picked up the A74 to take her into the Borders. She switched off the radio, wanting no distractions.

Here it is! Scotland!

She could have wept but motored on, shaking her head and marvelling at how distinct from England the landscape was already; laughing as she passed Gretna Green; moved to reverential silence as she saw the signs for Lockerbie. Glasgow loomed and, with some dexterity, Sally made sense of the proliferation of roads and was, at last, on the road to Oban. As always, she was struck by the vicinity of Loch Lomond to Glasgow though the hubbub of the city seemed a million miles from these lovely shores. Though she was now itching to be on the ferry, she had promised herself a few moments at the great loch and no journey to Aunt Celia's would be complete without it. Sally clambered her way through a thatch of Scots pine and crouched by the edge of the water. She thought of all the times she had done so. She thought of her father. She touched upon all the times she and he had made their pilgrimage to the shores of the loch while Mildred sat in the car eating boiled sweets. She dipped her whole hand into the water until her joints froze, then she swiped her fingers through her hair and felt anointed. *Now* she could continue to Oban.

There was one small hurdle – was she to take the magnificent road via Crianlarich, or the slightly longer route around Loch Fyne to the coast road? Showing enormous restraint, she opted for the latter. It suited her mood. It was important that this journey to Mull should be as symbolic and as Romantic as possible.

Anyway, I'll take the high road home.

Sally wound her way down into Oban. The town was bustling and she made slow progress to the dock. She bought a ferry ticket for herself and her car and then went in search of scones. Sitting over a cup of tea, she dabbed at the last crumbs and tuned into snippets of the conversation that surrounded her. She loved the accents and tried hers out in the mountaineering shop where she bought a small rucksack. No one batted an eyelid, either at her spots or at her Scottish lilt.

Och aye! I can be who I like, they'll have me for me!

Time to set sail, Sal. Caledonian MacBrayne will take you across Lorn to Craignure. All aboard the CalMac!

Herring gulls swoop and call and hover at eye-level with Sally, effortlessly defying the sharp gusts of sea breeze which take the breath away from her. Her eyes are smarting but she knows they would be so, even if there was no breeze. With a lump in her throat and a quivering smile on her lips, she hangs as far over the railings as she can, tasting the oily salt spray on her lips. The sea is wearing diamonds. Oban looks like toy town. Duart Castle is looming, standing dark and proud at its commanding position on the first point of the island. Sally can hear her father's voice. He is whispering in hushed, excited tones as he always does at this point on the journey.

'Sal, my bird. Look! Duart! "Dark Headland". Walls *fourteen feet thick, my girl!'* Sally sings softly with him:

> *'The Isle of Mull is of isles the fairest*
> *Of Ocean's gems 'tis the first and rarest*
> *Green grassy island of sparkling fountains*
> *Of waving woods and high tow'ring mountains.'*

They sing together again. Sally is home.

THIRTY-FIVE

So, Sally is now on the last leg of her journey. We have a feeling it is the last leg of her other journey too. She is but half an hour from Aunt Celia. Mull spreads its beauty before her and she marvels at its mystery. I could tell you of the colours put out by the heather, I could describe the incomparable beauty of the hills and of the light that the lochs contain and reveal, the sound of the sea; but Sally is now bursting to arrive and we are keen that she should reach her destination without further ado. Suffice it to say, the day is perfect, the scenery is spectacular, the colours could make you cry: Mull, in all its splendour, welcomes Sally back.

Though it has been at least two years since Sally's last visit, all seems comfortingly familiar. Tobermory looks radiant but she does not stop. She comes across the village of Dervaig, as picturesque as when she last left it, and pays a brief visit to the eccentric little shop selling just coffee and books. She buys a packet of freshly ground Costa Rican, and a small book on local walks. The proprietor cocks his head to one side in semi-recollection but Sally flinches away from his eyes, her pock marks and the vicinity of Aunt Celia preventing a 'hello' just now.

Celia stands at the end of her pathway and can see the Mini from far off. As the distance between the two diminishes, the driver can be seen bouncing up and down at the wheel, the car's horn ringing out, parp parp! Celia waves expansively, Sally parps some more before screeching to a halt and pelting to her, the engine still running, door open.

There are squeals, liberal hugs, wide smiles and much hair-stroking, but we shall let them enjoy their reunion in private.

Sally went from room to room, routinely closing her eyes to soak up remembered smells then opening them wide to take stock of all the familiar furniture, the bits and pieces, the nooks and crannies. A lick of paint had changed nothing, all was intact and her memory had served her well. She stood awhile in the kitchen, Celia quiet behind her, a hand on Sally's shoulder. The smell of baking led her eye to the scrubbed table on which a batch of perfectly risen scones cooled on racks. The smell of flowers led her eye to the deep window sills where a bowl of hyacinths took pride of place. Pretty china greeted her when she looked upon the dresser; the glint and sheen of polished copper rang out from the hanging rack above her head. Slung over the back of an old Windsor chair, a shawl felt soft to her touch; under foot the stone floor was smooth and satisfyingly uneven, all the dints and chips at once familiar.

'Want a cuppa?'

'Mmm! I'll just take my stuff up to my room.'

My room! It is my room, and it is just as I left it! Darling bed, how are you! Hello, little etching of Iona! Curtains! Oh, such lovely flowers, bet they're from the garden.

Mmm, wardrobe smells just as it should – polish with a distant whiff of mothballs. Pink padded hangers, just for me! I'll hang everything up, I'll put everything away, I'll brush my hair and have a quick wash, but first I just want to sit here on the bed and look out of the window.

For once, Sally did not gaze at nothing in particular, but ranged her eyes as far as she could to the horizon and then slowly travelled them back over the hills, through the forest, over the shaggy flanks of the cattle, across the road and back into the garden. No detail was left unobserved and, though she knew the view off by heart, she gazed out with virgin eyes and hailed all she saw.

With hair brushed, face washed and revived with ice-cold peaty water, she made a slow passage downstairs, peeking into Aunt Celia's bedroom and the sewing room as she went. Silently, Sally stood in the sitting-room, smiling at the sound of the table being laid next door. In the range, embers of the morning fire glowed and crackled, the surrounding bricks sooty, the grate spilling with ash and charred wood. The mantelpiece heaved with photographs and Sally worked her way from left to right, pleased that she was in most, her father too, her sisters in few, her mother in but one. She dwelled upon a lovely sepia photograph of her Uncle Angus, so handsome, hair waxed and waved. She looked into Angus's eyes and wondered how well she really remembered him. With a certain dismay, she supposed true memory counted for only a part, assisted recollection for most.

After all, Sally had only been ten years old when he died. His voice was unforgettable and memories of dancing merrily with him on the sand were still clear, but she wondered if she really knew the man he was, the man her aunt adored, the man her father so mourned? She did remember one night vividly, a late summer evening, the Highland dusk just drawing in, an eerie light pervading. She had dozed off into a troubled dream and had woken in a panic. Going downstairs in search of reassurance and a cuddle she had seen, unseen, Aunt Celia and Uncle Angus whiling away the evening; Aunt Cee knitting and looking over to him, Uncle Ang drawing on a pipe and gazing at her through half-closed eyes. The knitting needles provided the only sound in the room, the smell of sweet tobacco whispering through. A sense of peace pervaded and, no longer needing to go right in, Sally crept back to bed, safe and warm. She had fallen asleep hoping that, when she was all grown up, she too could be like Aunt Cee and have an Uncle Ang.

How old can I have been?

You were seven.

By the telephone was a photograph of Angus and his brother Robbie, Sally's father. She considered how similar they had looked, Angus six years older and slightly greyer, her father more portly. Their smiles were so similar, somewhat lopsided, their identical eyes crowned with neat, long eyebrows. She recalled how both shared the same gait, and remembered Aunt Celia finding much hilarity in walking behind them, trying to impersonate their loping, swinging stride. The photograph, in technicolour, showed the brothers standing on the sands at Calgary, Angus bare-chested, hands on hips, Robbie with shirt sleeves and trouser legs rolled up, his hand on Angus's shoulder, a football at their feet. Both squint at the sun with out-of-breath smiles etched wide and skewiff. Sally grinned back at them and traced her little finger around their faces.

She had loved to see them together, so comfortable in each other's company; talking earnestly, laughing privately, standing side by side thigh-deep in the sea, casting their fishing rods in unison in pursuit of elusive salmon. She recalled vividly how they would sit together in silence, always absorbed and at ease in each other's company. Scanning the bookshelves, Sally smiled at memories of bedtime fireside stories being read to her while she snuggled deep into her uncle's or her father's laps on alternate nights throughout her holiday. Their voices were almost indistinguishable and once again they filled her head as she touched the spines of the books and took down *The Just-So Stories* and buried her nose, Best Beloved, within.

'Yoo hoo! Lunchie!'

Celia's call brought Sally back to the day in hand. The Camel got his Hump, the Rhinoceros his Skin and the Leopard his Spots. Angus and Robbie finished the Sing-Song of Old Man Kangaroo and returned once more to the frozen time of the photograph, happy and strong. Much missed.

I wish they were here.

The women feasted on barley soup and cracked rolls plastered with chunks of hard, cold butter which oozed into the soup as they dunked. Dunking was an institution for the Lomaxes and Sally smiled at Celia as they plunged their bread into the soup and then swiped away the predictable dribbles from their chins. Sally remembered the annual look of disdain on her mother's face at such meal-times; she remembered too her father's furtive winks as he plopped his bread in and out of the soup – a pastime absolutely forbidden in Lincolnshire. There was nothing slovenly about such table manners, the soup tasted fundamentally the better for it. Dunking went without saying at every meal; at breakfast it was toast in and out of egg yolk (fried or boiled), at lunch it was bread into soup, at tea-time it was home-made digestive biscuits into mugs of tea, at supper it was bread into anything that could be mopped up, lastly it was short-bread into bedtime cocoa.

Today, Sally dunks with aplomb and Celia dunks as she always does.

'Well, my duck, I must say you are spotty! Do they itch still? Did you manage not to scratch? Do you feel terribly self-conscious? And that poor patch of hair – it'll grow! Well, no need to worry – you'll hardly pass by two people while you're here! I thought you might like a blow-through on the beach this afternoon.'

'Absolutely!'

'You brought muddy clothes with you, I hope?'

'Wellies, walking boots, windcheater, thermal undies, woolly hat – I'm a dab hand, remember!'

'Oh I do remember! Ach, this is fun, is it not? I have missed you, my lass. I say, "Hurray for the chicken pox"!'

'It's not just the chicken pox,' Sally said quietly.

Celia decided not to pry.

Calgary Bay was deserted and the sweep of white sand implored Sally to run as fast as she could to the sea. Celia's laughter was carried on the wind to and from Sally's ears as she ran; it was eerie. Jumping back from the waves, Sally flung her arms above her head, singing, 'It's so beautiful, so beautiful!' A grey seal bobbed his head above the swell as if to see what the commotion was about. They looked eye to eye for a caught moment and then, as if to say, 'Oh, it's you again,' he disappeared leaving Sally motionless and open-mouthed, arms still suspended, until Celia arrived by her side. The women stood and gulped the invigorating air, occasionally turning their heads to follow the swoop of a gull. They scoured the water but the seal had gone.

'You were blessed,' said Celia.

'Oh, I do believe so,' agreed Sally and, linking her arm through Celia's they strolled along the water's edge and chatted awhile about wildlife. Stooping to pick a smooth pebble, Sally skimmed it across the water – four, five, six, seven – a skill painstakingly learnt from her father. Celia clapped.

'Ach, Sal, it's so nice to have you here. You remind me so much of Robbie, and thereby of my own LoveLove too.'

'Am I like Daddy? How?'

'Well, it's not just your stone-skimming! Let me see – it's your zest for life, my duck. And that expression of wonder your face often wears – pure Robbie. Also, the way you talk to inanimate objects. He would talk at length to anything made of wood! Most of all, I see him when I see you gaze and gaze at I do not know what!'

'At nothing in particular,' confided Sally.

'Ah,' nodded Aunt Celia.

'Aunt Cee,' Sally ventured because it seemed timely to do so, 'Uncle Angus . . .' She paused. 'Do you miss him still?' Celia looked at Sally and a momentary wave of angst swept across her face.

'Every day!' she said aghast.

'No, no!' cried Sally. 'Of course you do! I mean, the *missing* him – how *is* it?' Celia looked into her niece's eyes and saw a comforting naiveté, a white page waiting to be filled with the advice, the experiences – perhaps the reassurance – of one who knew. She looked at her open face and saw an ingenuous young woman with the desire to know, to be informed, to learn, to listen. She felt touched and heartened.

'Well, girl, I miss my man. During my waking hours and in my sleep too, do I miss him! Something will happen each day that makes me turn for him – and each time I find him gone.'

Sally watched her looking out to sea as if searching for her lost husband amongst the waves. Celia saw the grey seal but was too far into her thoughts to point it out to Sally.

I think her face is so beautiful, thought Sally. *I love all those lines – they're not wrinkles, see how tight and firm the skin is, no baggy neck like Mother. These lines trace the paths of her life. She's walked with conviction through it and her lovely, brown healthy face is both her story and her reward.*

With the grey seal gone again, Angus too, Celia turned

back to Sally and took her face in her gloved hands. 'Your uncle died fifteen years too soon,' she told her, 'and next year, it was be sixteen years too soon.' Sally took Celia's hands from her face and held them in hers.

'But isn't it just too painful?' she asked, a furrow of worry knotting her brow. 'How can you bear it?'

'It is painful,' explained Celia, 'but that very pain tells me I'm alive. I can bear it because I would rather have had just six months with him than never to have had him at all. And I had thirty-five wonderful years with him. He was my light, you see, but my life is my own.'

Sally looked puzzled. Celia chortled. 'It's a bit daft when people say someone was their whole life, don't you think? Angus died but I still live. He was the light in my life and that light shines on, my duck, shines away.'

They continued in silence for a few strides. Sally stopped, closed her eyes and held her head.

'But Aunt Cee, would you have had it any other way? Fifteen years of unhappiness, loneliness – doesn't the pain you feel vanquish the pleasure of the love you had?'

'Sal, my funny thing.' She hugged Sally very close and when she spoke again, Sally heard her voice through her ribcage; magnified, unhindered. 'I am not lonely,' Celia said, 'I am just alone now. It hasn't been fifteen years just of unhappiness. Yes, I have grieved and I wish with all that I am that he was with me now. But had I not loved him so, I should not miss him, hey? And I rather *like* that feeling. It is a comfort for it can but remind me of what we had together. The pain can only be as great as the love we had, my girl. The love we had was limitless, the pain is indescribable, but the strength that love gave me allows me to sail on. *Amor vincit omnia,* my girl, *vincit omnia.*'

They looked at each other and Sally wondered how Aunt Celia could smile so benignly when she felt like crying at the injustice.

'Do you see?' Celia continued. 'Had I not loved so, had I not been so loved, then sure enough, I may not hurt. But then what would my life be like? It would be black and white. Silent. I like colour and song. Our life was full of both.'

'But he's not *here*,' stressed Sally. Celia nodded but smiled on.

'Would I that he is not here now, but was then, than he never was here at all.' Sally regarded her aunt. Her eyes shone back at her and the confusion on Sally's face slowly lifted. Now she understood and her gratitude rendered her temporarily mute. However, her smile, as it unfurled, spoke volumes to Celia.

They continued their walk, both serene now, and were blessed by the magnificent aeronautics of two golden eagles who seemed to be flying just for the sheer sake of it.

'Would I that he is not here now, but was then, than he never was here at all.' Celia's sentence had been so perfect, so full; the domain of a true poet, of one who knew. It had stuck in Sally's mind instantly.

It is 9.30 and Sally is tucked into bed; the crisp sheets, heavy blankets and a beautiful, hand-quilted eiderdown. Celia's words reverberate around her head and images from the walk assault her mind's eye. She is held a happy captive and falls asleep blanketed by the hills and accompanied by the seal. The rhythmic sound of the waves lulls her deeper and the eagles soar to keep watch overhead.

She wakes in the small hours and lies in velvet darkness for a pleasant moment. Drawing back the curtains and throwing open the window, she marvels at the true blackness of the night, no street lights invading, only a tiny patch of orange glinting from a distant cottage. If she listens well enough, she can hear the sea.

'Would I that he is not here now, but was then, than he never was here at all.'

Well, would I? Would it have been better never to have

met Richard? Would my life have been black and white and without song?
  Well?

THIRTY-SIX

*A*s the days passed, Celia watched the colour bloom back to Sally's cheeks – the spots were no less prominent, but the sparkle in her eyes and the glow of her face detracted attention away from them. Though Sally slept until lunchtime the first morning, she was soon down in the kitchen with the break of day, making porridge with a pinch of salt the Lomax way. She was very happy tinkering about with Celia and their days had a loose but welcome routine.

After breakfast, they took a tour of the garden to check that frost had been kept at bay, and to admire new faces amongst the flowers.

'Wood anemones,' Celia cooed as she and Sally crouched in awe over the low little mauve flowers.

'Wood anemones,' Sally repeated to herself, trying to commit leaf shape and petal formation to memory.

Celia's garden was a font of nostalgia for Sally. Despite the brisk air, she could travel with ease back to those heady summers of her childhood. Though it was midwinter, if she closed her eyes she could even fill her nostrils with the scent of fragile dog rose and wild honeysuckle. Gazing at the rockery for long enough turned it back into

268

the harsh mountain her dolls had struggled to climb. Feeling the springy, peaty land beneath her feet, she remembered well the secrets of the garden that not even Aunt Celia knew. Here was the place, the space, in which she had been absorbed in play, absorbed in herself.

The garden seemed so much smaller now, but though Sally's years had altered its scale, its charm had not been compromised.

'Wild violets?' she enquired.

'Next month.' Celia informed.

And I'll miss them, rued Sally.

Having ensured that all was well in the garden for another twenty-four hours, Aunt Celia's timetable read elevenses time, and chocolate brownies were dunked into cups of coffee. After that, the infinite bits and pieces to do around the cottage took them to lunch-time. Sally implored her aunt to load her with chores. Somewhat begrudgingly, Celia obliged and Sally set about waxing the tables, scrubbing out the hearth, polishing the copper, dusting the books and giving all the window-sills a fresh lick of gloss paint. Seeing Sally beavering about her work, so thorough and attentive to her task, struck Celia.

She's me!

Where's her Angus then, Celia?

Has she an Angus?

Why not ask.

Och, no! That's for her to tell – not for me to pry.

Lunch-time was invariably followed by an excursion.

'The beauty of being retired, so to speak,' Celia had told Sally, 'is that you can turn a trip of necessity into a little outing for the afternoon! I may need a loaf of bread, but why go to Dervaig to buy it when I could have a jaunt to Salen, to Bunessan even!' Therefore, each day Celia made sure there was something to buy and whether it was a couple of apples or a fresh salmon, a pint of milk or a pound of potatoes, she ensured the route took them to far-flung corners of the island and passed outstanding viewpoints. They even took the ferry to Iona to buy soap, because Celia justified that the soap in the Abbey gift shop was not tested on animals and smelt heavenly too. Similarly, the journey back from Tobermory took them around two sides of a triangle so that they could enjoy a stroll to Loch Frisa. Invariably, they were home for tea-time dunking. One afternoon, they forsook a jaunt alto-gether – the film of *Greyfriars Bobby* was on the television and, armed with handkerchiefs and a bowl of home-made fudge, they munched and wept the afternoon away.

In the mellow hours between tea and dinner, a fire would be lit and the two women snuggled deep into armchairs to read, sharing their space and often snippets from their books too. Celia sang old Gaelic songs while Sally shut her eyes and let the warmth of the fire and the sweetness of her aunt's voice course through her body. Sally read passages of Scott and verses of Burns out aloud, Celia assisting her accent.

'Make it rounder, my duck, rounder. Smile while you speak. Use all the muscles of your lips. Hear the words *sing* in your mind first.'

> Ye banks and braes o' bonnie Doon
> How can ye bloom sae fresh and fair?
> How can ye chant, ye little birds,
> And I sae weary fu' o' care?

'Magical, Sal. You've got it! Robbie would be proud – both of them, Burns *and* Lomax!'

Sally drifted along, content that each day should come and go like the tide. Mull enchanted her so much that she exclusively devoted her sight and her soul to its gifts. Richard and Diana and Highgate and School were way down South, metaphorical miles from her mind too. After nearly a week, she had slipped easily into Celia's way of life, and Mull and its ways became the norm. This then freed Sally's thoughts and they began to wander. As

270

she dug in the garden, or worked a hard-bristled brush over the flagstones, her mind travelled. Sometimes to nowhere in particular, often to her recent past, rarely to the present and never to the future.

The future will of course become apparent when the past is analyzed and the present confronted. For the time being, however, it was enough for Sally to think back over her time with Richard. Mostly she called upon specific events, blissful evenings, thrilling love-making; allowing herself a private smile, a guarded giggle, a stifled sigh. She realized with some surprise that the last time she had had sex was nearly two months ago. And in Paris. And with J-bloody-C.

I haven't made love with Richard since last year.

Occasionally, she contemplated just what it was that she had with him. She understood what had been intended as a dalliance had drifted into the Richard Thing which had in turn established itself, unasked, as a relationship.

What is it now? Is it anything? Does it exist at all?

She could not quite ask herself if she missed it.

As Sally started to mull and consider, cogs of recognition and springs of curiosity began to turn in Celia's mind.

She had been silent witness to Sally standing stock still, duster redundant in her limp hand, staring intently with a peculiar smile at the tall standard lamp.

Gazing so deep, Celia considered, *as if caught by the eyes of someone. So who?*

Moreover, at breakfast one morning, she saw Sally's shoulders give a little shake as she washed up at the sink and a mute reflection from the window pane revealed that same quirky smile. Furthermore, browsing around a bric-à-brac afternoon at Tobermory Town Hall, she was choosing notelets when she caught sight of Sally at another stall. Oblivious to the vendor's expression – oblivious to all around – she was holding a jar of honey aloft while staring distractedly, mouth half-open, at nothing in particular.

Or is it at something very particular? Celia had wondered.

'Can't I stay here? For ever?'

'Sally Lomax, Scotland may be in your blood but you've never felt your blood chill, your kidneys ache in the full grasp of a Mull winter! How would you fare then?'

'I'd wear lots of layers!'

'When the generator grinds to a halt weekly?'

'I'd fix it!'

'I think not. And the rain and the mist?'

'But it's so wonderfully sombre! Romantic! To just make out the shrouded hills, but the distinction between land, sea and air all blurred!'

'It's sombre all right!' Celia said, looking Sally straight in the eye. 'And after week upon week it's no longer wonderful. You cease to look at the mountains as ethereal, romantic. You just want to be able to see them clearly. You long to see where the land meets the sea. You crave to see the sky again. It can pull a man down, Sal. Folk this way often *hibernate* – as a precaution against depression.'

'I still think it's preferable to Highgate and all that stuff,' Sally said grudgingly.

'Well, *I* think you'd miss it,' said Celia quite sternly over the top of Sally's pout. 'I don't think you're giving enough credit to the freedom, to the very predictability it affords you.'

Sally looked hurt.

'Things seem easier here,' she said quietly, raising doleful eyes.

'It is not an easy life,' said Celia calmly. 'It suits me because I am old and set in my ways. I have few expectations. You, my lass, should be bombarding yourself with expectations, standing as you are on the threshold of your adult life.' Sally made a half-nod. Celia continued gently, 'If Things seem easier here, maybe you're saying Things are not easy in England. In Highgate? To forsake Highgate for Mull is hardly the answer. Merely geography.'

Sally remained silent and stared fixedly at the embers.

'Though Mull won't solve your problems for you,' said Celia gazing at the photograph of the two brothers, 'it might very well help *you* to do so.'

Sally let it lie. After a subtle silence she changed the subject and they chatted the afternoon away. Easier that way.

Sally has lived on Mull for a week. Last night they had fish and chips at Tobermory, eschewing a table and crockery for a harbourside bench and vinegary newpaper.

'The only way to eat fishy chips!' praised Celia.

'I'll say "aye" to that!' hailed Sally.

To Celia's delight, Sally has offered to cook tonight. Earlier, they had driven twenty miles in one direction for a bottle of Chardonnay, and fifteen miles in another for a head of garlic, the trek home readily interrupted by tea and scones (dunkable) at a small café near the shores of Loch Ba.

Celia is now helping Sally prepare – she is chopping what she is told, slicing as she is instructed, dicing as she is asked. Mendelssohn's Hebridrean Overture has been chosen to accompany their labour and the women sway and *la la* in harmony as they work.

'OK, Aunt Cee!' chirps Sally, 'off you go now. Away! Put your feet up, have a Scotch – ooh, pour me one too! I'll cast my top secret magic over this lot and a feast for two will be on the table in precisely half an hour's time!'

They dined on cheese soufflés, followed by grilled trout lashed with butter and smothered with toasted almonds, and finally a breathtaking bread and butter pudding. For the most part they were silent, occasionally catching each other's eyes to hum with appreciation.

'Mmm, can you *cook*, my lassie!'

'Mmm, thank you! More potatoes?'

Because the trout had been small and so light, seconds and thirds of pudding were justified. As one of the penultimate spoonfuls from Celia's bowl neared her lips, she bit the bullet instead and let the spoon hover as she spoke:

'Well, Sal! Seems a shame not to lavish such culinary expertise on someone more special!'

'Aunt Cee! Who could be more special than you?'

'Who indeed?' smiled Celia, letting her question hang in the air for a moment or two before she leant towards Sally and probed further.

'Who indeed? You know they say the way to a man's heart is through his stomach?' Sally cocked her head. Celia continued, 'Is there a man, Sal, whose stomach you seduce, hey?'

'Gracious, Aunt Cee!' said Sally, trying to look taken aback rather than downright taken off guard.

'Tish!' announced Celia, scraping the last of the pudding from the bowl. 'What am I saying? I shouldn't be prying, Sal. Apologies, apologies. I just remember how terrible it was for you with that insufferable chap – you know, the one who . . . I was just hoping that perhaps there was someone making you happy?'

Still Sally looked non-committal and Celia tried to look nonchalantly everywhere but at her face. She heard a stifled sniffle and glanced round to see that it had its roots in a smile. Sally tipped her head and ran her finger around her bowl. Sucking it clean, she then wrapped her napkin around it and decided to welcome her aunt into her private world.

'Well, there is *someone*, Aunt Cee.'

Silence hung like dark velvet curtains, heavy and

274

containing. Celia wondered whether that was all from Sally and was just about to change the conversation to the merits of trout over salmon, when Sally spoke again.

'His name is Richard Stonehill. He is thirty-five years old and drop-dead handsome!'

Celia decided there were plenty of fish in the sea so she let the trout and salmon go and turned, all ears, to her niece. With a smile that she hoped was persuasive, she put her elbows on the table and cupped her chin in her hands.

'Ooh, do tell me more, Sal!' she cooed, eyes sparkling in what she hoped was a conducive way.

'Richard is an architect. A very brilliant one, I think. He believes buildings are the backbone of our environment and must be sympathetic to, and reflective of, our lifestyle and our needs.'

Celia nodded approvingly, believing it was what Sally wished to see. It worked; Sally continued.

'He's very manly and has a lovely flat in Notting Hill – always clean; fresh flowers; good food. He's fit and healthy – and a wonderful cook!'

Celia continued to nod and felt a little prompt or two would not go amiss. 'And how long have you two known each other?'

'Since the autumn,' said Sally.

'Going steady, then?' Celia asked rhetorically. Almost instantly, she sensed Sally pull back.

'Well, I don't know if you could call it *that*,' she said somewhat flippantly. Celia mouthed 'Oh' in reply. They sat awhile contemplating their empty bowls. Sally refilled their glasses with the last of the wine.

'I call him Richie and he calls me Sal – you and he alone, an honour indeed!'

'I'll say!' said Celia, raising her glass. Taking a thoughtful sip, she steered the conversation back. 'Well, if you've been with him since the autumn but are not going steady, what is it that you have? Please, dear God, not one of those "open" relationships?'

Sally giggled. 'No, not very open at all,' she mused under her breath.

'Go on,' encouraged Celia.

'It's difficult to explain. It started as a bit of a rampant fling – you know, Jackie Collins bodice-ripping and all that?'

Celia had never read Jackie Collins.

'Erica Jong?' ventured Sally.

Celia shook her head.

'Xaviera Hollander?' she suggested.

Still Celia drew a blank.

'Anyway, Sal, I'm sure my reading matter isn't relevant. After all, we're not *talking* fiction or fantasy, are we? Just life – yours.' Celia's swift overview of the reality of the situation made Sally feel vulnerable and somewhat belittled. She felt defensive.

'Aunt Cee,' she corrected sternly, 'you'd be surprised what I can get up to in my little life in Highgate. It may not be Los Angeles or Paris or wherever, but my small flat can be a hot-bed of passion, a boudoir of sins of the flesh! What goes on in there can compete with the best of them – the very stuff that books are made of!'

Sally's eyes glinted, Celia's soul winced.

'I – I'm not sure I quite follow, duck.'

Sally was on a roll. 'I set myself up as a true *femme fatale* to trap a man,' she explained triumphantly. 'And did I ensnare a prime catch! It was fabulous and all so naughty!'

'But what about Richard?'

'I'm *talking* about Richard!' Sally laughed. '*He's* the man.'

'But *he's* the architect,' reasoned Celia, 'sensitive, mature – upright. The one who calls you Sal?'

Sally nodded vigorously, missing the point utterly. 'I thought it would be fun to be a bit of a vamp. And it was certainly the most liberating thing I've done. Only it all went horribly wrong.'

'How?'

'Love.'

Sally uttered the word in much the same tone she used for 'chicken pox'. It quite shocked Celia.

'And that was *wrong*?' she gasped, aghast.

'Oh, yes.'

'Why?'

'I suppose it made it all seem too dangerous.'

'I don't understand, Sally. How can *love* be dangerous? I'd have thought playing the tart would be much more so.'

'I wasn't a tart,' faltered Sally. Celia raised her eyebrows almost imperceptibly but enough to hit Sally in the chest. 'I just wanted to have fun,' she chirped, somewhat unconvincingly.

'And was it fun for Richard?'

'Oh, yes,' Sally answered rather too swiftly, and paused for a moment, trying not to fidget. 'At first,' she clarifed, 'then he fell in love with me so the fun stopped.'

'Why?' probed Aunt Celia sternly. 'Surely, with more substance to it, the fun would have increased, the pleasure deepened?'

'Theoretically,' stumbled Sally.

'I'm lost again, Sal,' Celia said, her voice quiet, almost flat.

'Aunt Cee, it's all such a headache. I'm sure it's part of the reason I've been run down. You see, it was wonderful when it started. I felt so strong, so high, when it was carefree and just pure passion.

'When love came into the equation, it complicated the purity.' Celia raised her eyebrows high. 'I know purity is a funny word to use,' Sally conceded, 'but when Richard told me he was in love with me, I felt absolutely swamped and smothered. Let down.'

'But, Sal, how could that be? He fell in love with you

because he finds you lov*able*, surely nothing could make one feel stronger?' As hard as she was trying, Celia could see little merit in Sally's theory. 'Is he not lovable?'

'Oh!' Sally assurd her. 'On the contrary.'

'Do you love him?' Celia suggested, watching pain scurry across Sally's brow.

'Yes,' she sighed, shaking her head forlornly, 'I do.'

Sally could see that Celia looked even more confused than she herself was feeling.

'Aunt Cee, I needed time,' she explained as gently as she could, 'time to recuperate – and not just from the chicken pox. Time to think, to consider. To make up my mind, if truth be told.'

Celia's frown slowly lifted. 'So you came to Mull? What better place! I think I see now, Sal my duck. What started as a bit of fun became serious and you wanted some space to take it all on board? Might this be *it*, then – the Big One? Might Richard be your Angus?'

Sally cast her eyes downward and smiled coyly but remained silent.

'Well, I think that's very sensible of you both and I'm sure Richard is behind you one hundred per cent, am I right?'

Suddenly the enormity of what Sally had done hit her with such force that, though she wanted to push Celia aside and run, she sat stock still and silent; winded.

'Sal?'

Slowly Sally raised her head, darting her eyes to and from Celia's face. Still she could not find her voice but a small whisper filled the room.

'He doesn't know.'

'What?' Celia's gasp was edged with horror and suffused with disbelief.

'I didn't tell him. Or anyone. Just Mother.'

Celia was flabbergasted. 'Whyever, *ever*, not?'

'I thought it would be a test?' ventured Sally feebly,

flinching away from Celia's expression. 'You know, just to see?'

'See *what*?' Celia barked, standing up. She looked down on Sally, a remoteness tinged with disgust etched on her face. 'No, Sally Lomax, I do *not* know. What on earth do you mean "a test"? Don't you think you've played with the poor man's emotions enough? Using him as some unsuspecting pawn in your stupid little game?'

'But – ' Sally pleaded.

'Hush it!' chided Celia sternly. 'I cannot believe that you, your father's daughter, just *left* without having the courtesy, let alone the conscience, to inform him. You'll be a lucky girl if he still wants you after all this. I wouldn't be in the least surprised if he passes you off. I think it's preposterous, really I do.'

'Aunt Cee!' protested Sally.

'No!' Celia scolded back. 'Here is a man who loves you. Do you know how difficult that is to come by? It takes courage and maturity to recognize and proclaim it. He loves you and you string him along – I can't believe it's you, Sal. Not you!'

Sally fiddled with her napkin, twisting it this way, then that. There was so much she wanted to say, to explain, to apologize for, yet she was struck dumb with shame and could give no voice to her tumbling thoughts.

It isn't me. It wasn't me, was it? It was the idea of who I could be.

Ultimately, someone not preferable to who I really am. But how was I to know, without this hindsight?

You are right, Aunt Celia, I've been a callous bitch and I must make amends, if it's not too late. But do I have the courage and maturity you speak of?

Regarding her downcast expression, Celia shook her head sadly.

'Sal, my lass, God only knows what got into you. I suggest a long, solitary walk tomorrow, a good ten-miler.

Do some thorough soul-searching. And then you make a phone call. I'm going to bed now, thank you for supper.'

Sally sat alone in the kitchen for a while longer. She then washed up as quietly as she could.

I will *walk tomorrow. I will walk and walk and look to the sea, to the sky, to the heather for my answers. I'll strip myself bare and I'll find the answers. I'll call Richard. I'll restore Aunt Celia's faith in me. Courage and maturity: I'll find them. They are there – somewhere.*

THIRTY-SEVEN

Sally went to bed. Her sleep was troubled, deep in parts but broken. She was impatient for the next day to arrive so that she could find the answers she sought. She kept the curtains open and scoured the sky for the first hint of morning and dressed before dawn had broken. She breakfasted in careful silence, not wanting to wake Celia. In fact, she did not want to see her at all – not until she had found the answers. To help in her quest, she prepared sandwiches and took a compass, a thermos flask and the book of walks she had bought. She wrapped up warm and put plasters on her heels as a precaution. Before she left, she propped a small note against the kettle for her aunt:

'Gone walking. Love, Sal, x'.

As she closed the door silently on the cottage and stepped out into the early morning, the mystical low silvery light that suffused the island quite took her breath away. It was beautiful and sombre and matched her mood, for it seemed to veil and distort all she'd previously thought she had known. Watched approvingly by two impossibly shaggy Highland cattle, she eased her car into life and headed for the coast.

Her destination was the Treshnish headland. She remembered her father and Angus setting off for day-long walks there but, at nine years old, she had not been allowed to join them.

'But I want to see the Magic Beach,' she had protested.

'It'll still be here when you're big enough to find it,' her father had soothed. Now Sally was going to find the beach and felt sure it would proffer answers for her.

She parked at a small quarry and although it was a beautiful morning, leaving the car was oddly difficult. She stood contemplating it awhile with her hand on the bonnet, wondering whether to go for a long drive instead. As she locked it and then double-checked all the doors, she felt tearful and nervous, but of what she was unsure. Adrenalin was coursing through her veins and a host of other emotions ranging from fear to sadness flowed through her body and wrapped themselves around her mind.

Come on, Sally, it's only a walk and you half-know the answers you are walking to find. The waves and the heather and the sky and the cliffs do not really hold them and you know that. However, being alone with the land might help you unlock them from your private core. So, on your way.

'Bye-bye little Mini, I won't be long. My, the island seems so big today. Look at all that sky. Come, come, read the guide. See, it's a logical circular route and I needn't do the whole lot if I don't feel like it. It will be lovely, just what I need. There's the old Whisky Cave to find – remember all those daft stories of Uncle Angus's? Oh, and I'll see the Treshnish Isles. Maybe I'll be lucky enough to see the grey seals too. Best of all, I'll find the magic beach at long last. I'll be all on my own and it will be good for me. And, most importantly, for the others too.

She set off with a purposeful stride, interrupted every

now and then by a few haphazard steps when certain thoughts or emotions swept over her. The walk from the quarry to the cliffs was longer than she'd expected but it helped her pace herself into a comfortable stride. To assist, she conjured up a good walking chant. Her father had impressed upon her their importance: 'They focus your mind away from your feet. You can walk for hours and miles with a good 'un in your head.'

A childhood favourite had been: *'Left! Left! I had-a-good-job-and-I-left, left'*. Sally tried it for a while and lulled herself into believing her father was right there by her side. They were striding along in harmony muttering 'Left! Left!' when a squabble between two crows overhead brought her back with a jolt to the day in hand; she was twenty-five and her father was ten years dead. Though perplexed and tearful, on she went.

Walking in silence, however, seemed too noisy so she decided to create her own chant in honour of her father. It came to her quite quickly, and she winked at the sky as *'Courage! Maturity! The-answers-I-will-find! Courage! Maturity! The-answers-I-will-find'* gave purpose once again to her step. She passed through a farm to pick up the ancient track to the cliffs. The objective of the walk was already working, for her rhyme had changed. Under her breath and in her mind *'Strength! Truth! The-questions-I-must-ask! Strength! Truth! The-questions-I-must-ask'* now rang out with her footfalls.

Sally reached the cliffs. The still-distant sea stretched before her, marvellously flat and metallic; it looked like a surface one could walk on, even run on. Occasionally, patches shimmered grey, even black, before the wind restored the silver. She was smiling out loud.

I'm here!

The cliff path, though narrow, was not precarious and she felt some resentment that she had been deemed unable to tackle it at nine years of age. Down she walked, liking the way the earth was crumbly underfoot, making

her steps into a dance of sorts, *The-questions-I-must-ask!*
The-questions-I-must-ask!

She wound her way downwards, allowing her eye to
stray out to sea once her feet had found their ground. At
the base of the cliff, there was no sand, no sea, just a
broad, smooth flat swathe of land. And then nothing.

The Magic Beach! I'm here!

Sally contemplated the geography, or was it the geol-
ogy? She was not sure.

Having just walked down the cliff, she was standing on
the hundred-foot ancient raised beach, covered not by
sand but by a downy, very fine grass. The edge of this
beach formed the top of further cliffs, dropping this time
to the true beach below which finally met the sea. She
looked behind her and in front of her.

It's like a giant pair of steps!

Delighted with the find, she stood still with arms
outstretched and welcomed the sea breeze which came in
whispers and gusts but with no clue as to which would
be next. The crisp air forced out oily tears which dried
almost immediately on her cheeks. Her face felt tight but
rosy, and despite the chill in the air, she felt warm and
supple.

Sally spent a happy hour on the raised beach, going
right to the edge to gaze way down, and then back to the
base of the first cliffs to ogle upwards

It was as if she were caught between the two.

The sky was in layers; above the first cliff a buzzard
circled and climbed, beneath the second cliff gulls
swooped and skittered. Sally stood buffeted amidst it all.
She imagined the air falling from the first cliffs, rising
from the second and fusing just where she stood.

Feeling that she was invested with the very power of
the wind itself, she spontaneously sprang a loop of
cartwheels, four, five, six. Could she pirouette in her
walking boots? Yes, she could. She wanted to travel

284

through the air again so, after springing three pliant *jetés*, she returned to cartwheeling. Four, five, six to the left; three, four, five to the right; three, four, five towards the sea; four, five six, back to the base of the first cliffs. She then ran as fast as she could across the entire length of the beach, stumbling slightly as she went; a smile plastering itself, along with her hair, to her face. She cartwheeled back to her rucksack (eight, nine, ten, eleven) and sank to the soft earth, breathless and elated.

Curling up embryonically, she discovered that it was warm and windless lying so close to the earth. She could hear the wind but could not feel it and decided to tune into her heartbeat instead. It was easy to believe the land itself had a heart. The earth had a warmth of its own and, coupled with that of the hazy sun, Sally was extremely snug. Feeling suddenly sleepy, she struggled to keep her eyes alert and contemplated the merits of her thermos, hidden away as it was in her rucksack. But she had no need for tea and soon dozed off and dreamt of nothing at all.

Sally slept only a short while but was revived sufficiently to continue cartwheeling. This way she went, then that; nine, ten, eleven, twelve. Soon her hands were tingling and itchy and striated with the pattern of grass. Time to stop and walk on.

Strength! Truth! The-questions-I-must-ask. Strength! Truth! The-questions-I-must-ask!

Go on then! Ask away!

In a minute.

She really could not bear to leave the raised beach and would have been quite happy to cartwheel the hours away in between a nap or two. But the decision to walk on was made for her; to her horror there were other people approaching the Magic Beach.

What are they doing here? At this time!

It is 10.30.

So? What are they doing here? Gracious Good Lord, they're wearing skirts! This is my beach. Damn. Better find somewhere else unpolluted, *as it were.*

Sally continued on the trail and covered the land as swiftly as she could, catching her breath now and then as she went over her ankle or felt her knee give way. The views were so compelling that her eyes were often seduced away from the path she was tracing until a stumble restored her concentration. Descending to the true beach, she gazed in wonder at the rock stacks and natural arches carved by the sea into the strangest of shapes. She was constantly aware of the changing formation of the Treshnish Isles, six small islands of intriguing silhouette. Now they formed a perfect line astern and she thought of them as a flotilla, sailing and sailing, yet never sailing away. She scrambled about for the Whisky Cave and found it, cleverly hidden behind a large grassy mound.

Grass on the real beach – and a grass beach that's not the real beach? Wonderful!

Although she poked her head into the cave, she ventured no further – caves were not her thing and she had no desire to vanquish such fears now. Instead, she dawdled along the water's edge and picked a selection of pebbles that begged her to do so. All the while she kept her eyes and ears peeled for wildlife. Apart from the gulls and cormorants, she was alone.

Sally decided that she would make a detour back up the cliff to a deserted village described in the book. Angus's tales of the Highland clearances had long struck a chord in her conscience and she wanted to pay homage to such a village, to Angus. After all, it would also afford her another visit to the Magic Beach.

*

Fate accompanied Sally on her upward grapple and dealt her a harsh blow.

The fall happened so quickly and yet in slow motion too. Her rucksack snagged, her foothold crumbled, her pockets full of pebbles unbalanced her, her ballet-weakened right knee gave way and she tumbled. She had not been on a very steep part of the cliff and she did not fall far, but she fell awkwardly and as she landed she heard a snap that she knew was not her thermos cracking. She needed no doctor to tell her she had broken her leg.

She sat very still while she tried to make sense of the situation. Her heart was racing too fast for her to grab any of the thoughts that were scurrying through her mind. She felt sick but she felt high and she did not feel any pain. She heard voices and wondered if they were in her head. No, they were too Scottish.

'Och, 'tis a very beautiful day, hey?'

Of course! The beskirted walkers who dared interrupt her solitude on the Magic Beach.

'Aye, I'll say. Just look there at the islands! See the Dutchman's Cap? The High One? The Flat One?'

'And that's the Little Lump!'

There's a little lump down here who needs your help.

Shout, Sally.

I can't.

Try.

She can't.

Feeling sicker and not so high, Sally was resigned to the walkers passing her by. She had no voice with which to alert them and a hang of rock obscured her from their view. Snippets of their conversation were carried to her on the wind. One was called Mary. They were talking about shags but Sally could not even manage a smile at her Freudian reinterpretation. The voices were becoming softer and she caught only drifts. They were walking away.

Please let them come back. Even if it's not for a few hours.

But, Sally, is it not a circular walk?

Fate will extend a gentle hand but Sally does not know that yet. Straining her ears and closing her eyes to assist, now only the faintest of voices reach her.

'I say we walk just over the next brow, Isla, and then have a nice cuppa.'

Sally thought perhaps she should have a cuppa too. Trying to locate her rucksack, she caught sight of her leg. It was all wrong; twisted anticlockwise with her foot pointing to her body. Whether it was the sight of her leg, or the effort of turning her head to find her rucksack Sally was unsure; whichever it was, she felt very unwell and was slowly and painfully sick.

God, where am I? How long have I been asleep? The walkers, the skirts, have they come and gone? Oh God, I've been sick. I want to move. Can I move? Let me try. Christ, my leg! I can't move. I can, I can. I'll pull myself away; away from the mess. I'll drag myself over to that clearing. Come on, Sal, come on, girl. You can do it. I can do it. I have to.

The pain was almost overwhelming but the need to be found, to be rescued, was stronger. It took forty minutes to haul her broken body less than twenty yards to a low, bunker-like clearing; the scar of a small land slip.

Sally was a good girl, a sensible girl, and though she did not really feel like it, she sipped at the tea which tasted nostalgically plasticky.

When was the last time I used a thermos? Was it the trip to the Zoo? I think it was. Richard and the penguins, how could I ever forget? That darling key-ring he bought me – that I threw away when he told me he loved me. What I'd do for it now. What I'd do for it now.

Every time she moved, be it a fraction of an inch, a sharp stab of pain ran through her body. It seemed that breaking a bone of one limb had taken its toll on her whole body. The leg itself felt simultaneously heavy yet not there at all. The base of her neck and the small of her back seemed to ache the most, though thankfully the sickness had gone. She was perspiring yet she was cold. Tears threatened as she took stock of her recent run of medical dramas. It really did seem most unfair.

In a mess. Focus your mind. Focus it.

On what? One, two, three, four, five, six Treshnish Isles. The Dutchman's Cap? I suppose it does look like one. But I want to be on the walk. The guide says I can view the islands in a line abreast later on.

The realization hit Sally: she would be going nowhere and, unless she was found, she would be staying put for goodness knows how long.

'If that is the case,' she reasoned out loud, partly to keep the tears at bay, 'I'd better keep calm, concentrate on being warm, concentrate the pain away. Just concentrate.'

Time to start, Sal.

I know.

See the young woman, propped up awkwardly on her elbow, her head resting on her shoulder, one leg stretched out, the other twisted as it should not be. See how she is looking out, way over the cliffs, seawards. She is looking far beyond the sea, beyond the horizon even. Nothing in particular meets her gaze and yet she sees everything. The panorama is exclusively hers for it does not really exist. It is not the Isle of Mull which captures her gaze for, though her eyes are directed ahead, they see only within.

The breeze and the purity of the sea air clear the tangle of her thoughts.

If she were not here, she would not be able to see, and yet it is not 'here' that she sees at all.

Mull itself does not hold the key to unlock her door nor

does she hold the key herself. The key is in her lap –
dropped there by the situation.

Sally is truly alone and for the first time in her life,
lonely too.

She is in pain, she is frightened. She is sitting, disabled
and vulnerable, in a landscape that is at once beautiful
and mean, majestic and cruel, seemingly hospitable yet
wholly unforgiving.

She sits askew, asking questions and answering them
too.

*Why did I come to Mull? Was it really to recuperate from
the chicken pox? Was it really to have some 'thinking'
time?*

*No, it was neither. I came to Mull to continue my
adventure. I came here so that I could leave with no
explanation; I left with no explanation to see the effect it
would have. On Richard, of course.*

*And yet how could I monitor that effect if I am here
and have made no contact?*

How do I really think he would have reacted?

*I wanted him to contemplate my actions and think,
'Wow, the woman is certainly an enigma and has me
bound by her spell. Oh, Sally, Sal, come back to me.'*

*In truth, I think he was probably immensely hurt and
subsequently very angry too. Justifiably so. I must remedy
that. I must abate his anger with an apology and I must
soothe his hurt with honesty.*

*And yet if I restore him, his feelings for me to how they
were, then what? And why? Do I want him to regard me
as he did? Do I want to undo the knot I have pulled tight?*

*I was, as Aunt Celia said, a stupid, immature girl
playing a heartless game with the goodness of my man's
soul.*

There's my answer.

He is my man.

Will he still want to be? If I can help it, yes. I hope that I will not live to regret my appalling actions of late. I am here in Scotland, lost and yet found, but Richard – so far away and for so long – does not yet know. All may be in vain indeed.

So, am I ready? To share? To compromise? What will I gain and what will I lose? I will lose my name. But I don't have to.

I will lose my flat – but I will gain a new home.

I will forsake my independence – yet Richard has made me feel stronger and more liberated than ever I felt when alone.

My late-night last thoughts – who says they have to be given up?

Talking to my plants, my things? But Richard loves me for that. Who says a Mrs Stonehill can't gaze at nothing in particular like a Miss Lomax can? Really, there is little that I will lose, much that will change, and so much more to be gained.

Why did it take me so long to see? Did I have to break my leg to break my block? Who set this block anyway?

Jackie bloody Collins, that's who, J Bloody C indeed. Erica Jong – it's her fault too. Xaviera Hollander, she has to answer for this.

No.

You ladies are in the clear. My apologies to you all.

The person at fault was the Sally Lomax who never was.

'Mary, what's that?'

'Gracious! It's the cartwheel girl.'

Through a haze of semi-consciousness, Sally saw disembodied tartan skirts run into and out of her view. Then she saw nothing.

It was time to open her eyes again and, as she did so, two pairs of tan leather, sensible lace-up shoes with hefty crêpe soles came into focus. She forced her glance upwards, over two pairs of sturdy ankles, up two sets of well-stockinged calves to the tartan skirts. One she recognized as McKenzie, the other she knew to be classic Black Watch. Her eyes travelled on and arrived at two good, weather-beating anoraks. Both were zipped against the wind, one enclosing a wiry figure, the other a more portly frame. Sally completed her tour, alighting on the faces that belonged to the skirts which had been at the back of her mind since she fell. Glinting eyes, kindly smiles and worried brows met her gaze benevolently.

'My dear lassie, look at you! Hush, hush, fear not, all is well. My name is Mary McKenzie,' spoke the wiry one in the predictable kilt.

'Poor duck, what happened?' cooed the portly one in Black Watch who Sally deduced to be Isla. 'We were admiring your cartwheels earlier and now you're all fall doon. How did it happen? Can you talk?'

With all her might, Sally spoke, choosing the most salient information, knowing she could not manage much. The two ladies crouched down beside her; Isla took her hand, Mary stroked her forehead.

'My name is Sally Lomax. I am twenty-five. I think I have broken my leg. I have had chicken pox but I am not contagious. Celia Lomax is my aunt. I'm sorry to spoil your walk.'

'Celia! Well, *we* know Celia very well and have heard her speak of you often – you are the one she says all her hopes are invested in! Isla, I'll nip back, you stay here with Sal and keep her comfy.'

Without further ado, Mary was off, heading for Sally's beloved Magic Beach, heading for help.

'We'd better prepare ourselves for an hour or so,' said Isla kindly, plumping herself down on the grass next to Sally. 'Would you care for some tea? I have some in my thermos.' Sally shook her head and murmured, 'I had some too, in my thermos. I've been sick.'

'Well!' announced Isla, and it sounded like 'wheel' in her tender, jovial voice, 'I have just the medicine for you, my lass!' From her anorak pocket, she pulled a small, pewter flask. 'Ten-year malt!' she confided triumphantly.

'No, thanks,' said Sally meekly.

'Come, come. 'Tis not an offer, 'tis an order! It'll do ye good. Just try – for Celia.' Sally did as she was told and, after a dicey moment when she felt the liquor burning its way to her stomach, it worked wonders and she felt stronger.

'There!' declared Isla. 'More?'

'Please!'

'Have as much as you like. In fact, finish it off.'

'I'm not contagious.'

'That's not the point at all.' Isla laughed. 'Mary and I have had a fair few swigs – we don't want folk to think we're drunk!'

Sally sipped the whisky slowly, gazing at the Treshnish Isles which seemed darker and more distant. She asked what was the time and was surprised to hear that it was nearing four o'clock.

'I thought perhaps you had done the circular walk and would not find me. You see, I saw you this morning – while I was cartwheeling. I wanted the Magic Beach to myself. Later, when I fell, I could hear you and Mary talking about shags and the brow of the hill and having a cuppa. But I couldn't call for you, my voice broke down with my leg. I was over there,' Sally pointed precisely, 'on a ledge. I hauled myself here because I thought I'd be safer, more visible. I prayed that you'd come back. And I assessed my life while I waited.'

'Gracious!' exclaimed Isla. 'Thank heavens we came back, hey! Mind you, we always walk A,B,A, here. Never A,A.' Sally looked puzzled. Isla clarified: 'No point doing a circular walk at Treshnish – who cares for miles of bracken and the silly old road when you can have all this twice!' She waved expansively. 'Did you call it the Magic Beach?' she asked. Sally nodded. 'May I ask why?' Sally nodded again and answered.

'Because my Uncle Angus and my dad said it was so. I wasn't allowed to come as a kid. I had to wait till now to find it. It is so magical, isn't it?'

'I'll say "aye" to that. Is that why you were cartwheeling?'

'Yes, I think it must have been.'

They sat quietly, Sally trying hard to be polite and cheery and to keep her mind from straying to the pain now focused in her leg. She looked at Isla and thought her plump, glowing face very pretty indeed. Isla returned her gaze and smiled.

'Cartwheeling and assessing life, hey! Well, you could find no better place to do either.'

The whisky had lubricated Sally well and she replied with gusto.

'The cartwheeling came first. Although I had come to walk by myself, to think a few things over. I had questions to ask and answers to find.'

Isla nodded and cocked her head. Sally continued.

'I've never broken anything before although I had my nose broken for me. And, if truth be told, I've gone and broken someone's heart.'

Isla tutted sympathetically and Sally was compelled to elaborate – for her own sake as much as for her companion's.

'While I was waiting here, I suddenly saw my mistakes so clearly. Yet I didn't flinch from them; I believe I really confronted them. You see, there is a man whom I love as I have never loved another and yet I have never told him so. In fact, I have spurned him.'

'And now you want to set things right, to ensure the happy ending?' interjected Isla. Sally nodded.

'I'm so impatient to do just that – but I'm stuck here with a broken leg. Do you think it might be too late?' she asked timidly.

'Och, no! If he is a good man, and if he is worth loving,

with all that you are, he will understand, I'm sure. Mine did.'

Sally laid her head in Isla's lap and closed her eyes, listening intently to Isla's story and hoping that history might repeat itself.

THIRTY-EIGHT

'**M**orning, Mr Stonehill.'

'Morning, Sandra. Please call me Richard. You make me feel so old, "Mistering" me!'

Mary winked at Sandra who blushed vigorously.

'What time are Ben Shaw's lot coming in?'

'Ten o'clock, Richard.'

'Right ho! Hold all calls until then, could you?'

'Course I can, Richard.'

'I'm sorry, Mr Stonehill is in a meeting. Could I take a message? Celia Lomax, 016884 156. Lovely, I'll ask him to call you as soon as he's free. 'Bye-bye.

'Who's Celia Lomax, Mary?'

'Never heard her.'

'Richard did say hold all his calls, didn't he?'

'Richard did, Sandra. Oh, it looks like his ten o'clock has arrived. Hello, gentlemen, Mr Stonehill is expecting you. This way, please.'

'I'm telling you Sandra, that assistant of Ben Shaw's couldn't take his eyes off you!'

'Leave it out!'

'I'm *telling* you!'

'Nah!'

'Yeah!'

'Really?'

'Sure!'

'He *was* pretty gorgeous! Do you know his name? It just says "et al" here!'

'Just one moment, I'll see if he's available, please hold the line ... Damn! It's that Cecily Lomax – from this morning. I forgot to pass her message to Richard.'

'You did have a lot on your mind!'

'Can you believe he asked me out? I think Mr Shaw even gave me an approving wink. Martin Blakely ... I've never been out with a Martin. Oh, Mary, what do you think? Sandra Blakely, Mrs S. Blakely – has a ring to it!'

'Sand*ra*! The phone! Buzz Richard, for heaven's sake.'

'Richard, there's a call for you on line one. A Cynthia Lomax.'

'Hello?'

'Richard Stonehill?'

'Aunt Celia?'

Celia filled Richard in on the bare bones of Sally's fall; she knew he was a busy man and did not want to swamp him with the minutiae. Richard, however, wanted to be deluged so Celia told him all she had gleaned from the doctor, from Isla and Mary, and from Sally herself.

'Could I speak to her?'

'I've put her to bed. In fact, I've had to rummage through her address book to find your phone number. I presumed that the "R" contained within the heart was you!' Richard laughed and wanted to weep.

'What can I do for you, Mrs Lomax?'

'Celia, please. Well, Sally was going to head home at the weekend but of course she cannot now drive. I wondered perhaps if you would fetch her? Maybe you would like to make a weekend of it?'

Richard thought for a moment.

'Does she know?'

Celia thought for a moment.

'No.'

Richard was silent. She spoke again.

'I do know that she has done a fair bit of thinking, and that she is not very proud of the way she has behaved. But I can see the impact you have had on my girl, and if at my old age I can assist in a bit of enforced match-making, then I'll jolly well do so!' Richard swallowed hard as a sudden burst of sunlight streamed through and struck his face.

'What's tomorrow? Friday, Friday . . .' He thought aloud. 'I may as well take the sleeper tonight. So, Aunt Celia, we'll meet at long last tomorrow morning. No, no, please . . . I'll take a cab from the ferry. Thank you so much for calling. For understanding.'

'Richard,' Celia faltered, anxious to hold him a moment longer, 'you sound – well – as lovely as you sounded.'

Richard regarded the replaced handset and then asked Sandra to book a one-way ticket to Oban. For once, Sandra did not mind that he gave no explanation. In fact, she was not remotely interested.

'Hi, Di!'

'Hullo, Stonehill!'

'I'm off to bonny Scotland.'

'Sally! When did she call? What did she have to say for herself?'

'Actually, it was the venerable Aunt Celia who called. The girl's gone and broken her leg in two places while soul-searching in the heather.'

'Serves her bloody well right!'

'She doesn't know that Celia called me. She doesn't know that I'm going up.'

'Ha! Serves her even more bloody well right!'

'Any messages?'

'Tell her she's a stupid old cow and I hate her. Tell her I'll break her other leg when I see her.'

'Right ho.'

'Oh, and Richard?'

'Yes?'

'Send her my love. All of it.'

Richard packed a small bag with a host of emotions crammed into his head. He had been so relieved to have had the contact, albeit indirect, with Sally. Yet he felt somewhat peeved that once again he was at her beck and call. And yet Celia's lovely voice, her words, had created a hope he had not felt for a long while. Though he was concerned to hear of Sally's new plight, a part of him was really rather satisfied.

'After all,' he mused to his toothbrush as he packed it, 'there is no come-uppance more severe than that dished out by oneself.'

Catherine had clapped for joy on hearing the news. 'See, Richard,' she had said, 'the time is coming. One way or the other; for better, for worse. It's what you need. Whatever happens, it will be for the best. And we love you lots.'

Richard was simultaneously excited and yet filled with dread; he brimmed with sympathy yet boiled with anger. Only the one emotion lay intact, and that was his love for Sally. It was unconditional and that irritated him supremely.

The journey passed without mishap. He had a surprisingly good sleep and an even more surprisingly good British Rail breakfast. Catching the Oban train at Glasgow, he felt relaxed and fresh and sat back to enjoy the immense scenery of the West Coast. With time to kill in Oban, he browsed through the town and visited the porcelain factory, buying a small seal for Celia, and a penguin for Sally.

If she's lucky.

As the CalMac took him across the water, he hummed 'Speed Bonny Boat' and made up his own verses replacing *'Skye'* with *'Mull'* and *'carry the Lad who's born to be King'* with *'give me the girl who's born to be mine'.*

Richard, who had never had sea legs, silently thanked the boat as he left it at Craignure. Filling his lungs with the salt-tinged air, he was swept with a sense of well-being and a feeling that his trip was indeed positive. As he turned to find a taxi, a figure amongst the busying throng caught his eye. Instinctively, he knew she was Aunt Celia and by the smile on her face, she'd recognized him too. She lifted her hand and he responded, sauntering over to her. They contemplated each other quietly for a moment or two before he tipped his head and kissed her cheek, saying it was his true pleasure. Celia said she was delighted.

As they strolled to her car they scanned each other's faces, for here in the flesh, at long last, was the other about whom so much was known already. Both felt immediately at ease in each other's company and both felt a certain sense of relief that their expectations had been met.

This is Sally's aunt.

This is Sally's man.

Waves of approval accompanied their conversation about vernacular architecture, whisky without an 'e', and Sally.

'She hadn't even woken when I set off. And her morning bath now takes her a long time. Of course, she won't have me help. But hearing her thumping and thudding, wincing and cursing – I tell you, it is all I can do to stop myself from rushing in to bathe the bairn myself!'

Privately, Richard thought how long it had been since he had bathed her.

Not since last year.

From the corner of her eye, Celia observed him looking far out of the window, scanning the landscape and smiling widely at the lochs and hills. She sensed he was itching for news of Sally but could see he was too well-mannered to pry. Feeling it was her duty and debt to Angus and Robbie, she broke the proverbial ice for him.

'I'll think you'll find that breaking her leg is a blessing of sorts.'

Richard looked puzzled but his eyes implored her to elaborate so she did. 'We had words the night before, you see. When I discovered she was here *illicitly*, so to speak, I gave her my mind. I suggested a good, long walk and a long look within. She set off at dawn the next day. Well, she didn't make the long walk but sitting alone in the open with a broken leg afforded her plenty of time for reflection – and plenty of space, in every sense of the word!' Celia laughed.

'Has she come to any conclusions?' Richard broached delicately. Celia felt that a kindly wink would suffice. Feeling bolstered, he decided to leave it there and judge for himself on seeing her.

'She's a funny old thing,' he mused, 'never known anyone quite like her.'

'I'll say "aye" to that,' agreed Celia. 'She says you've been together since the autumn?'

'Mmm. It was quite fortuitous that we met – it was a party that I decided to go to only at the last minute. And there she was.'

'There she was,' echoed Celia with a distant look in her eyes.

'She had this magnetism – I couldn't quite put my finger on what it was specifically. Still can't! I mean, our Sal's a pretty girl and has a nice figure but not really, well, eye-catching. I think it's the whole package. There's so much to her, like a huge box of treats – each time you dip in, you find something new.'

Celia laughed. 'Well, the lass certainly has a treat in store today. Are you ready?'

Richard clapped his hands together and whispered, 'I've been ready for quite some time.'

When they arrived at the cottage, the kitchen was empty with Sally's breakfast things still laid. Celia motioned Richard to sit down and mouthed, 'Tea?' Feeling quite nervous now, he shook his head and flicked through a copy of *Rob Roy* distractedly. From upstairs drifted Sally's dulcet tones singing Simon and Garfunkel most melodiously, totally unaware of the surprise awaiting her. Relaxed now, Celia and Richard giggled together and settled in at the kitchen table, nibbling digestive biscuits with half an ear on the staircase.

Sally began her clumping descent, singing 'Bridge Over Troubled Water' to steady herself.

'Aunty Cee? Crikey, I'm pooped!' she called from halfway down the stairs. 'Is the kettle on? I'll certainly need reviving, it seems to be getting harder and more tiring each day!'

'Just boiled!' Celia encouraged. Richard forced his eyes away from the door and fixed them to the spine of *Rob Roy* instead. His stomach churned with adrenalin, his palms were clammy and his mouth was dry.

Clonk, clump, here she comes.

'Mor – ' she cried, shunting open the door with a crutch, '– ning!' she croaked, flabbergasted and rooted to the spot, eyes enormous, mouth gaping.

'Morning, Sally,' Richard replied, in a voice that gave nothing away.

Sally was speechless, Celia was silent, Richard was defiant. Eventually, Sally remembered to close her mouth. She shut her eyes and opened them again,

302

shaking her head to ensure she was not dreaming. He was still there.

'Richard?' she mouthed, aghast.

He nodded his reply, still holding on to *Rob Roy* for moral support.

'I, er, better check on the, um, daffs!' stumbled Celia as she backed away, tactfully if noisily, into the garden.

Richard took in all he saw. There she was, that wretched girl who'd played havoc with his heart, hair still spiky in the one patch, face still spotty but neater now. She was standing before him, a vision on crutches, swamped in a dirndl skirt of Celia's for she had brought only trousers, not having expected a plaster cast to hinder their wear during her stay.

He noticed how her eyes glinted and her face had a fresh bloom. He observed her wrists and saw how the tendons and veins were visible from the strain of the crutches. Her good leg was coddled in a thick sock, the broken one was obliterated by a very large, very white plaster cast – only the tips of her toes were visible and they were slightly blue.

Their eyes were fixed to one another. Quietly, he walked over to her and took away her left crutch, propping it against the door frame. Holding her left hand firmly, he took the right crutch away too and, holding that hand, steadied her. He cocked his head and looked at her; she gazed back, open and ready.

'Hey, Richie,' she said meekly.

Their embrace, after so long, too long apart, contained neither passion nor desire. It was infused wholly with tenderness, and they stood still, locked and close in each other's arms. Richard rested his face against the top of her head, Sally buried hers deep into his chest, lost in his heartbeat.

Celia found them thus when she ventured back from the garden, her arms laden with daffodils. These she promptly thrust between them while hastily brushing a tear from her eye as if it was not there at all.

THIRTY-NINE

*R*ichard eased a sock over Sally's plaster cast.

'Richard,' she said softly, 'I cannot believe you're here.'

'I can,' he replied.

Taking her arm over his shoulder, he helped her hobble out to the Mini. Celia waved expansively from the doorstep. 'Have fun, my lovelies. Looks like the day will be fine.'

True, thought Sally.

I hope so, thought Richard.

Fine indeed, thought Celia. Watching them drive away, she turned back to her cottage and chatted to the photograph of Robbie and Angus.

I'm sure all will be fine. When two inherently good people come together, there is so much room for happiness and unity. Our Sal may have been a silly girl but she's worked very hard to redeem herself and though I feel she is restored to me, all that's left for her is to do the same to Richard. Now, there's a man who breathes courage and maturity. It can't have been easy for him, this journey into unknown territory of every kind, but he is here and I love him. I see you in him, my Angus. And

305

Robbie, you're living on in your daughter – she is so very full a person. I do believe a happy ending may be in sight.

'So, which way now, Sal?' Richard asks, looking as settled behind the wheel of her Mini as he does behind that of his Alfa Romeo.

'Which way now, Richie?' smiles Sally, ridiculously pleased that she's Sal once again. 'Why, forward, forward, forward!'

They take the coast road and tootle along at a relaxed pace to take full advantage of the magnificent views. At Loch na Keal, they stop but the rain starts, soon to swallow the view. Sally tries not to take this to heart. As the engine dies away, she takes a deep breath and holds it.

I've got to do it. I must tell him now. Say 'sorry'. Tell him 'yes'.

Do it, Sal.

In a minute, but I can't hold my breath any longer.

'My, that's a big sigh,' teases Richard. Sally looks shyly at her hands.

Why is he here? Did he want to come? Did Aunt Celia ask him to, to taxi me back to Highgate?

'Richard,' she asks, making a tangential start, 'did you ever read Rudyard Kipling?'

'Avidly,' he replies, batting not an eyelid at her incongruous enquiry.

'*The Just-So-Stories*?' she furthers.

'Cover to cover,' he declares. They sit in silence which is neither awkward nor heavy. Frowning a little, Sally ventures her hand to his.

'Do you remember the Leopard?' she says softly, her eyes downcast.

''Course I do,' he replies.

What is the girl getting at? Is this some big build-up to a let-down? Is she still toying with my emotions?

'It was one of my favourite stories, as a child. My dad

and Uncle Angus used to read it to me over and over. We'd chat about it afterwards, reasoning away – I can only have been eight or nine.'

Richard nods as she curls her fingers around his. He tips his head and his eyes say, Go on, Sal, go on.

Come on, Sal, come on. It's time.

Yes, it's time.

'Remember how the story starts, how the leopard has no spots and how the stripy zebra and patchy giraffe have one up on him?' Richard's nod encourages her to continue. 'Well, I suppose I felt a little like the naked leopard. You know, somewhat powerless in the face of Mother, of Jamie.' She looks at Richard with large open eyes. 'When you came along, I decided I'd create my *own* spots – moreover, that I'd be a spotless vixen rather than a leopard!' She laughs sadly. 'But I should've known.' Her voice trails away. 'We all have our spots, it's just that sometimes we can't see them.' They sit quietly and watch the light rain drizzle disjointed snakes down the windscreen.

'What I am saying is, spots have been my downfall and my salvation.'

She sees that Richard looks just a fraction confused and can feel him working hard to keep abreast of her drift.

Quick, quick! Restore him.

She looks him boldly in the eye. 'You see Richie, I thought I had none, so I painted some myself and I wore them with aplomb. Or so I thought. And then, of course, I woke to find myself covered by others uninvited.' Richard's eyebrows twitch and cross.

'Chicken?' hints Sally, gesturing at her face.

'Ah ha!' Richard says triumphantly. She nods and beams at him.

'You see, these awful itchy spots proved to me how superficial my painted ones were. I have realized that beneath them both – the chicken and the painted – are

307

my true spots; those I was born with, those I had spurned, those that define me as, well, Me.'

Clasping Richard's hand with both of hers, she summons her will and confides: 'A leopard can't change her spots, we all know that, yet I tried to change mine. I wanted to obscure them from view beneath a veil of contrived subterfuge. But now, I should like to show you them. If you would like? If I may?'

They gaze out over the loch. The rain has caused an eerie vapour to whisper along its surface and the hills are shrouded by the mist. Richard turns slowly towards her and summons her eyes away from the water. She raises them to meet his. She is crystal clear.

'Sal,' he starts with an affectionate tap to her nose, 'at first, I was utterly blinded by your so-called painted spots. But, if truth be told, it didn't take long before I was utterly blind *to* them and could see way beneath them – that veil was pretty transparent and what was beneath was infinitely more beautiful.' He pauses. Her gaze has been unflinching and he is heartened.

'Remember how, once the leopard was accustomed to his spots, his life was good?'

Sally nods, a little forlornly. Richard takes his time, treading carefully, rather enjoying it.

'Well then!' he declares.

'Well *what*?' she worries, scouring his face.

Richard lets it lie for a moment.

And why not, Richard? The girl's led you a merry dance.

'Well then,' he says with a big grin, 'spots and all, you'll do for me!'

If Sally could have said 'sorry' in all the languages of the world, she would have done so, again and again.

Richard settled for just the one which was delivered with conviction and honesty before she kissed him.

'I'll never do it again, Best Beloved. I am quite content as I am.'

Richard returned Sally to Celia a different woman. Only her leg was broken, her spirit was whole again. While Sally slept in the next room by the fire, he declared Celia had restored his girl to him and thanked her. Celia was quite taken aback.

'It wasn't me, but you!' she gasped.

Richard shook his head gravely. 'If she hadn't come here, if you hadn't scolded her, if she hadn't walked and broken her leg, we would still be at an impasse.'

Celia refused to agree and they stood deadlocked, both too well-mannered to take any personal credit for Sally's salvation. Both felt indebted to the impact the other had on Sally. And yet both had been integral to her redemption: Celia with her directness, Richard his tact; both for their strength, support and patience.

'Let us put it down to this old isle, hey? Mull has treated Sally well – in breaking her leg, it has repaired her soul,' Celia concluded.

'I raise my glass to the Isle of Mull!' proclaimed Richard.

Celia turned to the Aga, hiding a private smile from him.

Taking a glass of whisky to the living-room, they padded around Sally. Swathed in dirndl and enveloped in an old Aran knit of Angus's, she was snuggled deep into the sofa. Her lips were slightly parted and her cheeks were rosy; one hand rested under her chin, the other was pressed between her knees. She was fast asleep, as much a part of the fabric of the sofa as the woollen shawls and hillocks of cushions. Richard and Celia sat down in the armchairs either side of the fire and sipped contemplatively. Every now and then they looked to the sleeping almost-beauty, but before long, the warmth and glow of the embers seduced them away and held them captive. Indeed, only a particularly loud crackle from a spliced branch roused them some time later and they saw it was now quite dark outside.

Still Sally slept.

On the occasional table at Richard's side teetered a pile of books. He browsed over their spines, smiled at *The Just-So Stories* but forsook Kipling, Hardy and Scott, for Burns. Celia beamed at his choice.

Closing his eyes, he caressed its worn leather cover and traced his finger over the embossed lettering. Taking the volume to his nose he breathed deeply, savouring the evocative aroma of well-thumbed pages. He laid the book in his lap, closed. Looking first at Sally, he then regarded Celia and grinned:

> *To see her is to love her,*
> *And love but her forever;*
> *For nature made her what she is,*
> *And never made anither!*

Celia clapped her hands and clasped them to her heart, exclaiming, 'A Burns boy! What joy!'

Sally woke, bleary-eyed and blotched, mumbling, 'Huh? Hey? What?'

Richard merely shrugged his shoulders at her while directing a conniving wink at Celia.

It is time for Richard and Sally to head home. Into the proverbial sunset? Would you really have wanted it any other way?

Celia will miss them both enormously but sends them on their way with a tin of home-made shortbread and a silent wish.

Sally and Richard receive it unconsciously and bid her farewell with a firm promise to return in the summer. Sally feels quite tearful to be going but both Richard and

Celia remind her that it is Sunday and there is school tomorrow. She senses she is leaving Mull to embark on the rest of her life and feels a little timid. But Mull will stay as it is, hugging the coastline of western Scotland, its treasures guaranteed. It is time for Sally to take home all she has discovered there. She knows now that mundanity and romance can happily co-exist but to put it into practice she must return home, to Highgate and school and the patch of rising damp in the bathroom.

With a chorus of parps and their hands reaching high out of the windows, Richard and Sal tootle away from the cottage and Celia soon becomes just another vague shape in the rear-view mirror.

Part of the heather, part of the cottage. Part of the land, thinks Sally.

They take a worthwhile detour to Glencoe and then follow the road to the Grampian mountains.

'It's going too quickly!' Sally rues when the shores of Loch Lomond arrive so soon after Crianlarich.

'Want to stop?' asks Richard.

'Would you mind?'

Richard parks as near to the shore as he can and helps Sally hobble to the water's edge. In she dips her hand and waits until her joints ache. She holds her fingers aloft and sees how the hazy sun is caught in the droplets the moment before they fall. Richard allows her the ritual, the space, but she gives him her wet hand and touches his lips so that they glisten.

They are now but a mile or two further down the road because the promise of a warming Scotch at a pretty pub was too hard to resist. The room is quite empty, wonderfully cosy but bright. They sip away beside the fire.

'Anything else I can get you people?' asks the landlord.

Richard and Sally shake their heads with a smile. The landlord excuses himself. Richard and Sally chat away happily. He asks her if she feels ready for school. Yes, she says, she does. She asks him if they will make it home in time for an early night. Oh, yes, he assures her, they will. Briefly excusing her actions, Sally reaches over to a neighbouring table for a clean knife. She pokes it down the side of her plaster cast and her eyes close in bliss at the sudden coolness of the steel.

'Gracious, Sal,' says Richard, 'it's quite bare!'

They regard the pristine plaster of Paris, mostly smooth but dented a little, here and there. 'We can't have that!' he cries as he searches his jacket pockets for a pen. 'Damn!' he says.

'Hold on, I may have one,' says Sally as she rummages through her bag. 'Damm,' she says.

Richard goes over to the bar, but despite his strong 'Hello?' there is no sign of the landlord. Undeterred, he leans right over in his quest until his feet are quite off the ground. Sally giggles behind her hand. With a glance to his left and to his right, he nips under the counter and searches furtively among the pint pots and peanuts.

'Aha!' he exclaims, holding his trophy aloft. 'It won't be an oil painting,' he explains, brandishing a very thick marker pen, 'but it'll do.'

Here is Richard, sitting on a stool opposite Sally. He lifts her leg on to his lap and looks at her face which glows and glints. He thinks her quite perfect. Pen poised, he ponders awhile.

Sally waits.

Richard is ready.

He writes.

Two words. Thick black. Permanent marker. Permanent.

WILL YOU?

As she looks at the shape of the letters which she read

in an instant but has now forgotten, she sees a cine film of her life flash across the white screen of her plaster cast. Childhood, youth, adolescence, young womanhood, now. Here she is and the present tells her all about her future. Here she is and she twists her head this way and that, reading it from every angle though it was quite legible, as it was, upside down.

¿ΠΟ⅄ ꓕꓶꓲM

She looks at Richard gravely and eases her leg off his lap, unwittingly clonking his shin but he neither winces nor does she even notice. Leaning forward, she puts her hand on his face. Her fingers lie on his cheek, her thumb rests over the dimple in his chin. His day-old stubble feels rather nice under his skin, like a coarse velvet. There is no need to clear her throat for it is as clear as her mind and as strong as her soul.

'Oh, yes,' she says, 'I will.'

FORTY

‘*S*he's back! She's back.'

‘Have you seen her?'
‘She's broken her *leg*!'
‘Wow! Is it in plaster?'
‘Of course, stupid.'
‘Has she got crutches?'
‘Yup.'
‘Poor old Miss Lomax.'
‘Yeah, but at least she's back.'
‘Too right! No more killer lessons with that Mrs Westford.'
‘Dragon!'
‘Broomstick rider!'
‘Hurray for Miss Lomax!'
‘Shush! She's coming!'
‘Hullo, Class Five. It's lovely to see you all, at long last.'
‘Not half as nice as it is for us to see you!'
‘Oh, Marcus, what are you after? Late with your homework?'
Snigger, chuckle. She's back.

Miss Lomax launched into her lessons with gusto and

ease. The children were delighted to have her back again. She instigated a post-mortem of sorts and Marcus and Rajiv filled her in on the missing details of her fall.

'We were so worried,' frowned Marcus.

'Some of us even cried,' confided Alice.

'I had to summon the ambulance,' Rajiv informed her.

Miss Lomax thanked each member of her class and answered their probing questions about chicken pox and breaking a leg.

'I mean, did you actually hear it go *snap*?' gawped Marsha who had chicken pox last summer but had never broken a bone.

'Oh, yes!'

Thirty gasps of approval filled the room. 'Well,' Miss Lomax clarified, 'it wasn't so much a snap as a hollow crack. Very loud.'

The children went: 'Ooh!'

Miss Lomax told them how she waited and waited and was careful not to panic, to keep warm and to sip tea.

'Why the tea?' asked Marcus.

'I'm not really sure, because I wasn't thirsty. It just seemed a sensible thing to do – and I knew I had to keep my wits about me. Anyway, how often have you heard your mummies or grandmas say "have a nice cuppa tea" when you're upset?'

'How did they get the ambulance to you?' asked Rajiv with a head full of helicopters, mountain rescue teams and St Bernard dogs with brandy barrels on their collars.

'Two wonderful women happened to come across me, Mary and Isla – I'd seen them earlier in the day – walking in the wilds wearing skirts, I ask you! Well, Isla sat with me and Mary went for help. There was a farm nearby and a big, burly chap – rather like you Sam! – called Fraser drove a tractor and trailer as near as he could. He then gave me a fireman's lift over to it and they trundled me back to the farm on the back of the trailer. An ambulance picked me up from there and I was plastered up and back at my aunt's two hours later. Here, would you like to see my X-rays?'

What a question! The children could not leave their desks fast enough.

X-rays! A broken leg! Wow!

'Cor!' said Marcus.

'Blimey!' said Rajiv.

Miss Lomax held the X-rays up to the light and thirty pairs of eager eyes admired the spliced bone. Some were secretly quite envious and made sure that they fell as dramatically as they dared when playing football at break-time.

'Now, children, back to your seats. We really should do some work, for heaven's sake!'

They groaned and moaned and slouched back to their places.

Miss Lomax felt even less like doing any work than her class, so, with a furtive smile, she told them to close their books and take out their atlases instead.

'See, here's Mull.'

'But it looks tiny!'

'Well, it is, comparatively. But turn to page ninety-four.'

'It looks huge!'

'My aunt lives right – here! And this is where I broke my leg.'

'Why is everything called "nish"?' enquired Marcus, and the children pored over the map, finding as many as possible. Quinish. Fishnish. Mornish. Mishnish. Treshnish. Miss Lomax told them of the Magic Beach, only she called it the raised beach and the children were utterly rapt. They talked about the sea, the tides and time. Only the entrance of Miss Lewis crying, 'Sal! You're back!' brought them back down to Highgate again. Blimey! Break-time already! Twenty-nine children scampered out. Marcus hung back. Miss Lomax and Miss Lewis questioned him with their eyebrows.

'Miss Lomax,' ventured Marcus. Miss Lomax raised her eyebrows and cocked her head. 'It's just that – well do you think I could sign your plaster?'

Miss Lewis and Miss Lomax smiled.

''Course you can!' said his favourite teacher as she heaved herself on to her desk, stretching out her leg and raising her skirt to her knee. With his red felt pen held aloft, Marcus sucked his lower lip contemplatively.

Miss Lewis's mouth had dropped open.

'What's "*Will you?*" ' Marcus asked.

Miss Lomax smiled at him fondly and avoided catching Miss Lewis's bulging eyes.

'Why, Marcus,' she said, 'it means will-you-sign-my-plaster?'

* * *

'What's "*Will you?*" ' whispers Diana, desperate not to squeal.

'Why, Di,' Sally says, 'it means, will you forgive me for being such a thoughtless and ungrateful old trout!'

'What's "*Will you?*" ' threatens Diana, hands on hips.

Sally catches Diana's face in her hands and kisses her firmly on the lips.

'And I said yes!' she laughs.

FORTY-ONE

*O*181 348 6523.

Richard stretched out his wrist to check Cartier time.

She must be home by now, it's Blue Peter.

He rang off and played Solitaire on the computer. Sandra popped her head around the door to enquire whether 'taking an early' would be all right.

'Of course. Away with you! Somewhere nice?'

Sandra really did not have the time – nor now the inclination – for a chat with Mr Stonehill so she said, 'Theatre. Yes. Really should go,' and offered a quick wave in farewell.

Good for Sandra. I think she had eyes for me once. Wasted!

0181 348 6523.

Richard mimicked the ringing tone and, with the receiver hooked under his chin, started another hand of Solitaire.

Come on! Where are you, girl! Oh, Christ. Diana – quick!

'Di?'

'Stonehill!'

318

'Where's Sally? Did you take her home? I can't seem to get a reply – I tried during *Newsround* and before and after *Blue Peter*. Dear God let things be fine? Di?' Diana cleared her throat.

'I dropped that Lomax woman back at her flat just in time for *Jackanory*.'

Richard's sigh of relief whistled down the phone line into Diana's room.

'You're right – I'm an old hen. I just worry, you know? After everything – after all.' He laughed. 'See you soon, Di. And thanks.'

'Don't you dare hang up, young man!' Her bellow hit Richard in the solar plexus and rendered him incapable of speech, let alone manoeuvres with telephone receivers. 'Richard? You there?'

'Here,' he answered in a small voice.

'Would you please,' said Diana, 'per-*lease*, explain the precise meaning of *"Will you*?"' '

Richard's face broke out into a smile so infectious that Diana caught it at once. They sat in silence, grinning inanely for a moment or two.

'Whaddayathink!' Richard laughed.

0181 348 6523.

Last chance before I call the police.

Let it ring, Richard. Ring right through.

'Hello?'

'Sal?'

'Hey!'

'I've been ringing for ages – you had me worried.'

'So it *was* you, was it? Have you forgotton a small matter of an enormous, unwieldy plaster cast preventing swift access to phone – or anywhere else for that matter?'

'Oh, Sal, say "unwieldy" again.'

'Unwieldy.'

'God, I love it when you say "unwieldy".'

'Richie Stonehill, you've rung three times in half an

319

hour, haven't you? And I'm bashed and bruised because of it. I've knocked over a lamp, dropped a dictionary on my good leg, whacked my arm on the door and bashed my good ankle with my bloody plaster cast.'

'Bashed and bruised?'

'*All* over.'

'Kiss it better?'

'That,' said Sally, covering her joy with a douse of teacher's sternness, 'is the very least you can do, Stonehill.'

Sally hobbles across to her Lloyd-Loom and eases her leg on to the upturned wastepaper bin which she has taken to carrying around with her.

Let's see, I reckon about an hour. And then he'll be here. It seems so long since he was here, in my little flat, with me. When was the last time? Was it calamine night? Was it really then? I think it was.

It was indeed.

Seems a world away. My spots have practically gone now, apart from these faint ones on my arms. Shame about my hair, I know it'll grow but it's taking an age.

It's been less than a month, Sal. Since the faint, the pox and the fall.

Tell me Jean-Claude wasn't the last person I slept with?

Sorry.

But never again. Just Richie now.

If you say.

I say so because I now know so. Because it's all that I want. I think, actually, it's all that I've ever wanted. Gracious Good Lord, there! Out in the open. At last.

At last.

Richard thought of very little as he negotiated an infuriating belated rush hour. He listened to *The Archers* for the first time in his life and made a mental note to catch the omnibus on Sunday.

It's not bad!

Richard Stonehill!

Sally listens to it avidly.

Oh, well then!

He hummed the theme tune with gusto as he sat in traffic on Hampstead High Street.

Nearly there. At last. Nearly there. Poor Sal, bashed and bruised and all my fault. My God I feel horny. I wonder if we could?

She's no longer contagious.

But logistically – with that unwieldy plaster cast. Oh, God, just five more minutes and she can whisper 'unwieldy' to me!

Red light, Richard. You've gone through a red light.

The doorbell rings. Sally positioned herself nearby five minutes ago so that she can answer it as elegantly as possible without causing herself further injury.

I'll let it ring, though. Woman's prerogative and all that!

Richard dutifully rings it again. He flips up the letterbox lid. He can see one leg bare to the knee, the other incarcerated by the now much-grafittied plaster cast. He watches their careful procession towards him.

Sally opens the door and finds Richard crouched, looking up at her with those impossibly alluring eyes.

'That's what I like to see!' she coos. 'On your knees, boy!'

With a slight creak, he pulls himself upright and plants a kiss passionately, deep into her mouth.

'I think you'd better come in,' says Sally whose neck has reddened and whose voice is hoarse.

Richard's lust is momentarily subsumed by intense relief that he is at last back in her flat and that, finally, she is by his side. She is holding his hand, she is pulling him right into the room. Welcoming him back.

Stay. Stay.

I'm not going anywhere.
Neither am I.
'Tea?'
'Please!'

He gazes after her, his head faintly bobbing in sync with her hobble. A quick recce tells him that everything is in its place. Nothing has changed though everything has changed. He hears her singing softly, tra-la-la-ing as she coaxes the kettle to come to the boil. He cannot see her for she is tucked out of sight around the corner but he knows exactly what she is doing. She is singing the theme from *The Archers*, tweaking leaves off the poinsettia, her back turned away from the kettle so that it will come to the boil.

Tea for two. Sally hands Richard cup and saucer and perches herself on the edge of the settee in which he is so comfortably ensconced.

He looks so right.
This feels so comfortable.

Tea for two but not a drop passes their lips. Sally has hovered out her leg and rotates it slowly through 180 degrees. Simple physiotherapy really, but its effect is quite astounding.

'Do you like my plaster?'
'Most artistic!'
'But somewhat *unwieldy* . . .'
'Oh, Sal!'

Tea for two can wait. Richard lunges for Sally and pulls her on to his lap. A look of hunger etches its way across his face; slightly, ever so slightly, demented. She wants to giggle and to say something witty but the urgency of Richard's kissing distracts her at once. She lets her body melt and sinks herself deep into the crook of his arm. Her eyes are closed but she is wide open.

He can have me all. Every little bit of me. There's nothing to hide. It's all for him.

She kisses him hard and bites him squarely on the

322

lower lip. He drops his mouth to her chin and sucks it. And bites her sharply. She winces in delight and cradles his whole head between her outstretched hands. His breathing is fast and her heart is racing. His eyes are on line with her breasts so she gives a little heave or two which drive him wild. As he fondles and kisses them, he appears to be unaware of the Aran-knit jumper which hides them from view.

'Off,' Sally whispers. 'Take it off!'

They wriggle her free and pull at his shirt. It's toasty in the flat and the curtains are drawn. Sally looks in awe at his chest. She deems it spectacular and gazes on as if she is seeing it for the first time. And yet she knows it so well: she knows that if she places her hand just here, and strokes just there, his pulse will go into overdrive. She does both and Richard moans. He is wearing button-fly jeans but the strength of his erection makes unpopping them an easy task. In fact, the one in the middle has popped all by itself already. Sally looks triumphant, Richard looks glazed. He feasts his eyes on her pretty breasts and realizes he had forgotten just how alluring her nut-brown nipples are.

They have to be kissed. Eaten.

'Skirt,' says Sally huskily. 'Take it off!'

They pull it over her head not wishing to disturb their lower limbs, now so comfortably entwined. They press against each other, rub and twist into each other. They are getting hot and are now quite wet around their faces.

I want to taste her eyelashes again.

I want to lick his sideburns.

Give me your nose.

I'm going to chew your earlobe.

Richard is wriggling out of his jeans but Sally is keeping her thighs clamped around him.

Ten years of ballet had its uses, you know.

He forgot that he still had his shoes on. Laced neatly, of course. Socks from Dunhill. Of course. He has kicked his jeans down to his shins which is far enough for his purpose. Sally grabs at his legs and wriggles herself ecstatically over their muscular form.

My Rodin.

Hands travel everywhere, all over each other's bodies as well as over their own. Richard finds her hand inside her knickers and covers her fingers to discover what they're up to.

Let me try.

'Off,' gasps Sally, 'take them off.'

They discover that, in the height of passion, removing a pair of knickers is not as easy as it should be. Especially when a plaster cast is involved. The elastic wraps itself taut around Richard's hand and threatens to cut off the blood to his little finger.

'Off!' shrieks Sally. 'Rip 'em off. Like in the films! Quick!'

How do they do it? In the films? It doesn't work. In real life.

Sally's knickers are now at her knees but Richard is loath to stop kissing her and yet his right arm will not stretch to her ankles and beyond. Sally crooks her good knee up and between them they manage to wrestle the fabric free. It has, however, caught over the top edge of the plaster cast and pull as he does, Richard cannot budge it. Sally has arms clamped about his neck and refuses to let go.

Never, never again.

She is chanting: Off! Off! Off!' With an almighty tug, the fabric tears free and Sally's plaster cast springs across and thwacks Richard on the funny bone.

'It's not funny!' he hollers.

'Yes it is!' laughs Sally, tears streaming and breasts wobbling.

Richard concedes that it is exceptionally funny and they collapse into each other, shaking and giggling. Sharing the mirth and the moment.

324

'May I say,' Richard starts, most politely, 'that this settee is giving me backache, that these cushions will make me sneeze very loudly very soon, and that cramp now threatens in my right buttock?'

Sally looks at him adoringly. 'You may.'

'Come then.' He beckons with his head in the vague direction of her bedroom. Sally nods and kisses him twice with the gentlest of kisses; one for the tip of his nose, one for the innermost corner of his eye.

Tea for two remains untouched. Tea for two has spilt all over the carpet and the settee. To the bedroom they shuffle, Richard with his jeans around his ankles, Sally limping along at his side. Hand in hand. Still laughing. Richard sneezes.

There we shall leave them. They go to greet the climax of something started long ago. Last year in fact, Gracious Good Lord.

EPILOGUE

19 June
Highgate,

Dear Ms Collins,

After careful consideration, I am afraid I really cannot take up the post as heroine in one of your stories.

Being the vampish vixen was such fun, but though I found the whole deportment so enjoyable, I must decline the role.

I did love the clothes, and I wear them still – with or without knickers, depending on my mood and the weather.

Seducing and being seduced is still, you might say, my chief leisure pursuit. Indeed, I find that I am now even more imaginative and abandoned. Please find enclosed a page of scenarios that I have enacted and can vouch for. You may use them if you wish but I would appreciate anonymity.

I have thought about this long and hard, I do assure you. (You may use 'long and hard' if you like.) The opportunity was so tempting for a while, but I have decided to pass it up.

Please do remember me to Ms Jong and Ms Hollander.

Though I am still a leopard of sorts, I must concede that Rudyard Kipling is much more my thing.

With best wishes,

    Sally Lomax . . .